FRIENDS OF THE
SACRAMENTO
PUBLIC LIBRARY

THIS BOOK WAS DONATED BY
FRIENDS OF THE
NORTH SACRAMENTO LIBRARY

The Sacramento Public Library gratefully acknowledges this
contribution to support and improve Library services in the community.

SACRAMENTO PUBLIC LIBRARY

BY EVELYN SKYE

FOR ADULTS

The Hundred Loves of Juliet

FOR YOUNG ADULTS

The Crown's Game
The Crown's Fate

Circle of Shadows
Cloak of Night

Three Kisses, One Midnight

FOR CHILDREN

Princess Private Eye

THE HUNDRED LOVES OF JULIET

THE HUNDRED LOVES OF JULIET

Evelyn Skye

NEW YORK

Copyright © 2023 by Evelyn Skye

Published in the United States by Del Rey, an imprint of Random House, a division of Penguin Random House LLC, New York.

DEL REY and the CIRCLE colophon are registered trademarks of Penguin Random House LLC.

Hardback ISBN 978-0-593-49924-5
Ebook ISBN 978-0-593-49925-2
International ISBN 978-0-593-72417-0

Printed in the United States of America on acid-free paper

randomhousebooks.com

2 4 6 8 9 7 5 3 1

First Edition

Book design by Alexis Capitini

For Tom—
This book is my love letter to you.
To us.

THE HUNDRED LOVES OF JULIET

There are more things in heaven and earth, Horatio,
Than are dreamt of in your philosophy.
—Shakespeare, *Hamlet,* act 1, scene 5

HELENE

ALASKA IN JANUARY IS A FAIRY TALE, WITH FROST-RIMED BRANCHES glittering in the pale moonlight, like lace woven by a snow maiden. Icicles on rooftops twinkle like Christmas frozen in time, and I swear the spiraling snowflakes beckon to me as they fall. Fairy tale indeed. Or at least it's a great first impression for my first evening here.

At thirty years old and after too many uninspiring years as an assignment reporter in the Los Angeles bureau of *The Wall Street Journal*, I'm finally chasing my dream of writing a novel. An actual book of my own! Not just telling other people's stories. I've been jotting down short stories ever since I was a teenager—bits and pieces of a novel—and now I finally have time to figure out how it all comes together.

Truth be told, I *need* this. My recent past—hell, the last ten years—are best swept into a fire pit and doused with gasoline. The death of my two golden retrievers, one right after the other. My Pied Piper of a soon-to-be-ex-husband, who attracted interns and affairs like rats at cheese orgies. And my so-called best friend, who stole the promotion that was supposed to be mine.

However, she unwittingly did me a favor. If I'd been promoted to columnist, I wouldn't have left. If she'd been a true friend, I'd still be stuck in a nowhere life, married to a no-good husband.

Instead, she betrayed me, and by doing so, she handed me the match I needed. I lit it and burned the past down, metaphorically speaking.

Goodbye, old Helene Janssen.

Hello, new and better me.

My mom always says that everything happens for a reason, and I obstinately hold fast to that belief. So when I saw super cheap plane tickets to Alaska (tourists don't usually visit here in early January) plus an "artist's cottage" for rent in a quaint fishing town, I saw it as a sign that this was where I was supposed to go to begin work on my novel, and my future. And I think I was right. Being here in this winter wonderland is already helping me feel better about my odds going forward.

I hum to myself as I lock the door on the cottage and head down the street in search of dinner. It's only half past six, but it's been dark for hours now, which will take some getting used to. So will walking through the snow in these clunky boots, although it's better than driving. I've got a car stashed in the garage, but the trip this afternoon from the airport to the cottage was harrowing enough for one day. I'm used to driving down sunny, palm-tree-lined boulevards, and I don't want to use up the rest of my daily allotment of luck on the icy streets of Ryba Harbor.

Luckily, my rental is only a few blocks from the picturesque downtown. On the corner, a cute, nautical-themed bookstore cozies up to a little souvenir shop for the few tourists who venture away (in summer) from Anchorage and Ketchikan. Wood smoke billows out of a barbecue place, scenting the air with brisket and ribs. There's also a record store (I didn't know they still existed, and the fact that they have one here delights me), several bakeries, and a coffee shop.

When I see a bar called The Frosty Otter, though, I know *that* is where I want to be on my first night in Ryba Harbor. It reminds me of a saloon from the Wild West, but with an Alaskan flair, the blue paint weathered by snow and salt from the roads. A wooden statue of a bearded fur trapper stands outside the door, rifle in one arm and beer stein in another, and ragtime piano music jangles from speakers inside.

Three flannel-clad lumberjack types charge amiably through the front door ahead of me, laughing at jokes in that deep-throated, belly-shaking way of people who've known one another for years. I slip in through the door behind them.

Inside, The Frosty Otter is everything I hoped it would be. Two-thirds of the tables are full, and the patrons are as eclectic as the decor. The lumberjacks go straight for the far corner to sit beneath a large mural of a grumpy-looking otter. Along the back wall, a cluster of older women who look like kindly grandmothers knit beneath faded twentieth-century advertisements boasting Wild Alaskan Salmon! The Klondike! and a cartoon of a giant king crab wearing a gilded crown (I think that might be my favorite). Most of the others here are men—probably those who work at the nearby seafood processing plant—but there are also a few families, the kids eating chicken fingers while Mom and Dad have a beer.

"Welcome to The Frosty Otter," a spunky, white-haired waitress says. "You new around here?"

I laugh. "Is it that obvious?"

"Well, it's a small town and I know everybody. Plus your hair is that pretty deep gold that happens when brown meets the sun. Unlike the rest of us pasty and vitamin D–deprived folk." She winks. "I'm Betsy, owner of this joint. Sit anywhere you like, and I'll bring ya your first drink on the house. What'll you have?"

"A local beer, maybe a pale ale?"

"Comin' right up."

I find a smaller booth along the wall where I can see everyone in the room, and I slide onto its cracked pleather seat. A giant moose head trophy hangs above me, and it's both impressive and a bit gruesome at the same time. Still, it fits into the over-the-top decor of The Frosty Otter just right, and I can see why this place is so busy.

Betsy brings me an ale from an Alaskan brewery.

"Your watch is way off, hon," she says, gesturing at my wrist. "You need to reset it, and to local time."

I smile and shake my head. "Can't. It's broken."

It's not even a particularly impressive watch, just a standard blue and silver dive watch. It used to belong to my dad, and it stopped working after a deep-sea scuba expedition. But he never bothered to fix it, just kept wearing it broken. "Time doesn't matter," Dad liked to tell me and my sister, "because if you live with one eye fixed on the end, you've already lost."

It's a lesson I haven't always been good about following, but I plan to now. Which is why I wear his watch like this. It was broken when Dad used to wear it, and it was broken when I inherited it. The watch might not keep time, but it's a good reminder for how I *want* to live: both eyes on the present.

Another group of boisterous men pours into the restaurant. The room breaks out into cheers as the seven of them enter, and people lift their glasses to toast their arrival.

"Who are they?" I ask.

"King crab fishermen from the *Alacrity*," Betsy says. "Every time they're back in port, they come here to celebrate their haul."

"Fun for them, but why is everyone else cheering?"

Betsy smirks. "Self-interest. The *Alacrity*'s captain, Sebastien, is legendarily generous. He buys a round of drinks for the whole restaurant whenever he's here. Speaking of, I better get back to the bar, 'cuz orders are about to flood in."

I thank her for the beer and settle in to people watch. I take a sip—it has a lovely hint of honey in the finish—at the same time the tallest of the crab fishermen takes off his coat and turns toward the bar, his silhouette framed by the light cast from the gold glow of the bulbs overhead.

Déjà vu whispers against the back of my neck like winter's breath, prickling my skin and tingling down my spine. I freeze.

I know him.

"A round for everyone, on me," Sebastien says, and The Frosty Otter erupts in another cheer.

Only I am quiet. Because I'm staring at his profile—one I've known for too long in my own head. When I was being bullied in middle school, I made up an imaginary best friend to help me through it. And then I kept him around and he grew up with me, even though I should have given up a juvenile idea like that forever ago.

He's also been the star of every short story I've ever written.

Now he's standing right here. In the flesh. It's hard to tell how old he is, because he has one of those faces that's impossible to pinpoint. But if the inconceivable is true—that this man is the same as the one I conjured in my mind—he's about thirty, like me.

And his features are all so familiar. That mess of dark hair and those quiet blue eyes that seem to hold a locked icebox of secrets. That J-shaped knife scar along his jawline, which matches a vignette I wrote about a bar fight in Portugal. Those shoulders, proud yet heavy, as if the man to whom they belong has seen a little too much of the world, yet survived.

In my stories over the years, he's shown me adventure and laughter, the sweetness of first love, and the devotion of true commitment. I know what he looks like with wind whipping through his hair as he dives off a cliff into the ocean. I know his skin tastes of salt afterward. I know the sound of his voice when he sings his soulmate softly to sleep, and the rhythm of his breath when she wakes before he does.

But I've never met him—never even knew his real name—until today.

Sebastien.

My palms sweat against the pleather seat, despite the cold. How is it possible that someone I made up is actually *real*?

I watch as Sebastien goes over to the bar to help Betsy carry all the beers. He certainly doesn't have to do that; after all, he's the one paying. And yet, I'm not surprised. It fits with what I know of his personality.

What I *think* I know.

What I made up.

Still, I can't stop following his every move. He walks across The Frosty Otter, handing out beers to everyone he passes. He doesn't say much but he smiles broadly, and as hands reach for the drinks he's paid for, they also pat him on the back, press a hand to his arm in thanks, beam a smile back at him. Clearly, Sebastien is well loved here.

I want to know him, too.

The old version of me would slide lower into my seat, cowed by disbelief and anxiety into doing nothing at all. I wouldn't consider talking to him, for fear of rejection. I'd stay here in the booth instead, where I already understand the lay of the land, preferring a known torment to an unpredictable risk.

But that's Old Helene, I remind myself. New Me is determined to do things differently.

Get up. You can do this.

When Sebastien's done distributing the beers on his tray, he returns to his table. The fishermen are in high spirits, clinking glasses with one another, but Sebastien retreats to a dim booth, like he's glad to let his crew have all the glory.

Heart pounding, I rise slowly, weaving through the crowd that's gathered to congratulate the crew on another great crab catch.

At first, Sebastien doesn't see me approach, so I catch him spinning his beer glass absentmindedly on the table—clockwise twice, counterclockwise once, then the pattern repeats. I pause midstep, because that's one of the little character details I've given him over the years in my stories. Doesn't matter if the vignette is set in a mountaintop cabin or a tent in the middle of the Sahara—if there's a table with a cup on it, he spins it exactly this way each time.

I don't understand how any of this is happening.

But now that I've decided to approach him, I can't stop. I'm a snowflake caught up in a current of wind, and there's no stopping me on this careening path I've chosen. Plus there's something else, too, something between him and me that draws me closer, that won't let go.

It's only when I'm right at his table's edge that he glances up.

A flutter of a heartbeat wings between us.

Sebastien blinks. And then his mouth drops open and he stares at me like a sailor who's been lost at sea but suddenly sees the North Star in front of him.

I'm no better. As soon as our eyes lock, I'm lost in his. Not because they're perfect—there's actually an angry white scar that runs across his left brow and eyelid and continues below—but because I can't believe these eyes are here, right in front of me. Real.

"Hi," I breathe.

"Hi." His voice is a rumble low in my belly. I can already tell by the way he holds his silences that *this* Sebastien—like my imagined one—is a man of few words. But if those words can make me feel this way, I want as many as he'll spare.

"It's you," I murmur, nearly nonsensical from the impossibility of this moment. "I know you."

Sebastien's expression shifts in an instant, defensive walls going up behind those glacier-blue eyes. "I beg your pardon?"

Our connection snaps. I feel it physically, like a gust of wind ripping through a kite string drawn too tight. I've said too much.

But I'm still unable to approach this conversation rationally, so I plow on. "I know you," I say again, as if this will somehow make him believe.

Sebastien purses his lips, brow furrowed—not confused, like I'd expect. But something else.

Upset.

"You're confusing me for someone else," he says.

I shake my head. I'm convinced now that it wasn't just an airfare sale that brought me to Alaska.

"I'm Helene." I want to reach out and touch Sebastien, to feel him solid beneath my fingers.

I offer my hand to shake instead.

But the muscles in his neck tighten, and he doesn't offer his name, doesn't take my hand. He gives me a tight, impersonal smile, the kind that anyone who's ever been in a bar knows means *I'm not interested,* and says, "If you'll excuse me, I just remembered I have to take care of something at home. Forgot to put out food for my dog."

One of his crew is within earshot and frowns at us.

Sebastien slides out of the booth past me and mumbles something inaudible to the frowning guy. The man protests, but Sebastien passes him a credit card and bumps fists with him. Without looking back at me, without acknowledging that I'm still standing here, Sebastien walks out of The Frosty Otter and then . . .

He's gone.

SEBASTIEN

I FLEE TO THE PARKING LOT AND CLIMB INTO MY TRUCK, WHERE I press my head against the steering wheel. My entire body shakes.

I know you, she said.

You're confusing me for someone else, I replied.

I lied.

Of course I know her.

The moment I saw Helene, I tasted the faint sweetness of honeyed wine on my lips, a ghost of a kiss. It happens every time she comes back into my life, a memory lingering from the first night we met, centuries ago.

She has no idea who she is, of course. That her presence—or absence—in my life has defined my entire existence.

I may go by Sebastien now, but my name was originally Romeo.

And hers was Juliet.

"WE SHOULDN'T BE here, Romeo," Benvolio says as we step into the masquerade. The gilded ballroom brims with masked guests— unicorns dancing with lions, knights clinking goblets with dragons, a sun strolling the edges of the party arm in arm with a moon. "May I remind you that we're Montagues, and our families are engaged in a blood feud? If Lord Capulet discovers us in his manor, he'll have our heads on pikes by sunrise."

"Ah, but that's the brilliance of a masquerade, dear cousin." I gesture at the bronze mask upon my face, at my elegantly draped toga, and at the wings on my back. "No one knows a Montague from a Capulet behind the mask of a Roman god. Besides, Rosaline will be at this ball."

"Forget Rosaline. She's forsworn love to devote herself to the church; you have no future with her. And your father is eager to arrange a far better marriage, one where your wife will be required to listen to and respect you."

"And that's supposed to be tempting? A woman forced to love me?"

Benvolio laughs. "You are too much a romantic, Romeo. In fact, pray tell—which god are you dressed as? Might it be . . . Cupid?"

"Tease me again, and I'll shoot you straight through with an arrow," I say.

He only laughs harder. "You're a hot-blooded fool, but that only makes you a true Montague. I'm going to fetch myself a drink. Can I trust you not to fall in love with yet another girl while I'm gone?"

I shove him lightly. "Go. I'll be glad for a moment of peace without you."

With Benvolio gone, I scan the ballroom for Rosaline, but she's nowhere to be found. I sigh. Benvolio's right. Rosaline is probably at home, chastely saying her prayers. Suddenly, I'm quite ready to leave. There's no longer a reason to be at this ball.

But then Juliet appears at the top of the staircase.

A hush falls over the room. Violins and clarinets stop playing. Unicorns and lions freeze in the middle of their dance. All eyes turn upon Juliet, like daffodils to the rising sun.

I forget to breathe.

She's dressed in a white toga, with a tiara nestled in the brown braids of her hair and a delicate butterfly mask over her face.

"Psyche," I whisper.

The mortal princess who falls in love with Cupid.

Juliet glides down the staircase, giving out smiles as if they cost her nothing. She smiles not only at the nobility attending her father's ball, but also at the footman who helps her down the final steps. She smiles at each and every musician in the band, and at the servants shuttling food and drink around the room. She smiles at her arrogant cousin Tybalt, and at the elderly aunt everybody has forgotten in the corner. And no one can look away from Juliet, because her smiles are a golden light in our world that is usually shadowed by bloodshed and spite.

She is beautiful, yes. But it is her radiant kindness that tugs on me. I've only ever been infatuated with the superficial before, but in this moment, I know what it's like to bask in the glow of the sun.

Benvolio returns with goblets of hot honeyed wine. I take only a sip before I set mine down on a table beside us. He follows my gaze to Juliet, then back to my wineglass, which I spin around and around.

"Nooo," he groans. "All I asked was that you not fall in love while I was gone. It was but a handful of minutes!"

In my defense, everyone in this ballroom is in love with Juliet tonight.

Perhaps I should better heed the mythology of Cupid and Psyche, of all the trials and tribulations they battled through for their love. But I'm spellbound by Juliet as if shot by my own arrow, and I abandon Benvolio, leaving him with his protests and our wine.

A crowd has surrounded Juliet, complimenting the butterfly mask and wishing her a felicitous birthday, which is in a little more than two weeks, on Lammas Eve. I thread my way through the throng, until I am face-to-face with her.

Juliet's eyes light up as she recognizes my costume. "It's you," she says. "I know you."

"Not yet," I say. "It's only the beginning of our story."

She laughs. "Fair enough, Cupid. Then how shall we become acquainted?"

"Dance with me."

"Bold."

"Very." If only she knew I was a Montague.

But then her fingers touch mine, and lightning crackles across my skin, family feuds forgotten. Never have I felt this way before, as if the world were a stage built just for us.

The musicians strike up a *ballonchio,* and as Juliet and I dance, our heartbeats pound so loudly in our ears we can't hear the beat of the drums. I haven't seen her face behind her mask yet, but I don't need to, because from her costume alone, I already feel fate's hand upon us.

We are young, yes, but not as young as future bards would tell it. Juliet is nearly seventeen, and I but a few years more. We are old enough to steal each other's breath away, to know that what we hold in our hands this night is singular. The spark that will begin an extraordinary life.

THE STORY IS not quite as Shakespeare told it. He was brilliant and prolific, but like many artists, he borrowed stories from real life and wove them through his imagination to make them his own. Julius Caesar, Hamlet, Macbeth . . . and most of all, Romeo and Juliet.

What Shakespeare didn't realize was that the tragic tale of star-crossed lovers was about more than one boy and one girl. He envisioned only a small sliver of history, and not the span of all time.

Unfortunately, I know the true story all too well. I age at a glacier's pace—roughly a year for every fifty—but I am still Romeo. A more weathered, battered version of the hero of Shakespeare's play.

Juliet, however, changes, reincarnated again and again. Sometimes she's blond and Rubenesque; other times she's raven-haired and thin as a feather. Tonight she is soft curves and hair as rich as butterscotch. But she always has the same soul, twinkling with curiosity and wit. No matter how her appearance changes, she is the same woman I first kissed all those lifetimes ago. I've loved her over and over across centuries.

And lost her, every time—in one way or another.

Helene doesn't know she's the Juliet I've loved my entire, accursed life, though. Juliet, whom I miss when she isn't here, whom I long for during the in-between years after she's died but before her reincarnation finds her way back to me.

"But you weren't supposed to find me *this* time," I mumble as I bang a fist into my truck's steering wheel. For more than ten years, I've been hiding. Because I actually saw Helene once before, when she was a student at Pomona College. I'd been considering going back to grad school and was touring the nearby campus when

I heard the music of her laughter across a grassy square and tasted the telltale honeyed wine on my tongue.

I observed her from a distance. She was beautiful in an amber-colored sundress, lounging on a picnic blanket with a group of friends. A young man had his arm around her as he recounted a story, his charm evident in the way he held everyone in rapt attention, Helene most of all. She watched him with a glow in her eyes, as if he were a prince who'd slain a dragon and come back to tell his kingdom the tale.

At that moment, she looked up, and our eyes met briefly across the lawn. But then I tore myself away and fled. Helene—my Juliet—was happy, and I didn't want to take that from her. If I left her alone, perhaps my curse would leave her alone, too.

I had walked away from the last version of Juliet in order to let her live, and she did. From that experience, I learned that the curse doesn't trigger simply because our paths cross. Something more is needed. Perhaps Juliet and I have to actually fall in love.

Which is how I was able to force myself to leave that grassy lawn at Pomona College, to walk away from Helene, even though it had, by that point, been more than seven decades since I'd held Juliet's hand in mine, felt her hair brush against my cheek, fallen asleep with my love beside me. I missed her as much as the stars would miss the sky if they ever fell to earth. But still, I left.

Because I knew with certainty what would happen if I stayed, if I became part of Helene's life. The story was always the same:

Romeo and Juliet fall in love.

They believe they finally found happiness.

And for a small fragment of time, they get to be heedless, euphoric, pure.

But then Juliet dies, and Romeo mourns, eaten away by grief and guilt.

I feel it now, like acid, nipping at my soul. I don't understand how the cycle repeats, again and again. Every Montague I am, no matter what name I bear. Every version of Juliet, who never remembers me, never remembers *us*.

All I know is I didn't die that first time, like Shakespeare claimed.

I never die, but Juliet always does.

And it's entirely my fault.

I hoped, however, that I could evade the curse again this time. Alaska was supposed to be a safe place for me to hide. The harsh landscape favors hermits and outcasts, and the ratio of men to women tilts more heavily male than most places. I buried myself in work, built a house in a frozen forest far away from the already remote town, blockaded myself from the rest of the world.

So what is Helene doing here, in Alaska, of all places? I tried to stay away from her. And how does she know me?

Does she . . . remember?

She never has before.

Now I'm breathless again—not in a good way—just thinking about her standing at my table tonight. It takes all of my strength not to leave this self-imposed prison in my truck, not to run back into The Frosty Otter and scoop Helene up in my arms and tell her, *You're right. You* do *know me, and our souls are intertwined, our story retold over and over for centuries. Romeo and Juliet. Cupid and Psyche.*

Me and you.

But I remain in the truck, crumpled against the steering wheel, because everything about this is wrong. Juliet and I only ever meet on the tenth of July, and it's now January. She's not supposed to know me, not even recognize me; every Juliet is a blank slate.

Unless the curse has changed. Perhaps I toyed too recklessly with fate when I walked away from Avery Drake, the version of Juliet before Helene, and now the curse is back with a vengeance in the form of a Juliet who thinks she remembers me. Punishment for my attempt to thwart fortune.

Yet I cannot succumb. I recall all too vividly each time I let Juliet love me, and how she suffered as a result of it. A spear impaled through flesh. Heat stroke and dehydration in the desert. A pyre of hungry flames leaving nothing but ash and bones. And more.

I won't let her die again.

Which means keeping Helene away. I can chase her out of town before she settles in. Or if I have to, I'll leave Alaska. No matter what it costs me, I'll try once again to save her. Because Helene deserves to live a life in full, not one cut short because I bring our crossed stars into it.

And all I deserve, after everything I've put Juliet through, is to keep letting her live, even if it means an eternity without her.

Someone knocks on my truck window. I startle, hitting my head on the ceiling.

It's Adam Merculief, co-owner of the *Alacrity* and my best friend. Of course he wouldn't just let me leave The Frosty Otter so suddenly.

He opens the door and climbs in uninvited. Adam is two hundred twenty pounds of pure muscle, but an accident with one of the eight-hundred-pound crab traps a couple of years ago left him with a limp; I'm sure he would've been at my truck window sooner if he could.

"You want to tell me why you ran out of the bar like that?" Adam asks. "'Cuz I know you don't suddenly need to rush home to feed a dog you don't own."

I dig the heels of my hands into my eyes. "It's complicated."

"Try me."

If there was anyone I could tell, it would be Adam. His family is Unangan, and they have their fair share of myths and superstitions. But growing up listening to old legends is still vastly different from truly believing that you're afflicted with a centuries-old curse.

Besides, how does a grown man tell another that the tale of Romeo and Juliet is his gospel? That "the one" is real, and if she falls for me, she'll die?

All my past loves—and losses—echo like horror stories in my head. If I get involved with Helene, she'll have two years to live, at best. At worst, two days. And every ending is full of torture. I can still see and feel each of Juliet's deaths as if they were my own.

I think I'm going to be sick.

"You okay, man?" Adam asks. "Seriously, you look green."

I exhale heavily, trying to shake off the grievous burden of history.

"I'm a little under the weather, that's all. Sorry to bail on the crew tonight."

"I don't buy it, Seabass." Adam has never called me Sebastien. He's the kind of guy who has a nickname for everyone, and because he's got a perpetual grin etched onto his face, no one minds it.

"Don't know what else to tell you," I say with a shrug.

Adam sighs, but he's used to me not saying much. He's a solid friend, which is why he came out into the parking lot to check on me, but he'll also respect my boundaries.

He punches me in the shoulder. "All right, man. But don't be pissed when we ring up a fortune on your credit card."

I manage a reluctant laugh. "Deal."

"Get some rest. I'll see you at port tomorrow."

Adam jogs back into The Frosty Otter. I give myself another minute to gather myself, to think about what it means that Helene is here.

Then I start the engine for the long drive home and shift my thoughts to what I'm going to have to do to get rid of her.

HELENE

WHEN I WAS IN EIGHTH GRADE, I WAS CAST IN THE SCHOOL PLAY AS Juliet. I was over the moon, because I share a birthday with Juliet—the thirty-first of July—so I'd always felt a connection to her. Plus, Chad Akins, the most popular boy in school, was Romeo, and I was thrilled to get to be onstage with him.

But after the first rehearsal, I accidentally overheard him and his friends in the theater when they thought everyone else had already gone home.

"I can't believe Helene Janssen's gonna be Juliet," Chad said. "She's so fugly."

"Seriously," one of his guy friends said. "Dumpy as a potato sack. And that headgear! And inch-thick glasses that give her fish eyes."

"And her *perm,*" a girl spat.

"Right?" Chad said. "Juliet should be someone super hot if Romeo's gonna instantly fall in love with her, you know?"

But I *didn't* know. (I was still naive enough then to believe the world was a meritocracy.) As I hid among the curtains in the wings, I wanted to shout at them: *It's not about looks! Romeo falls for Juliet because he sees something special in her—maybe the intelligence in her eyes or the confidence in the way she moves.*

That special something I wanted someone to see in me someday.

Mostly, though, I just wanted to cry. Which I did, all the way home as I rode my bike, nearly crashing into several trees and stop signs because I could barely see through my tears.

When I finally got inside my house, I locked my bedroom door and hurled myself onto the mattress, burying my face in my pillows. I cried for hours, ignoring my mom's and sister's attempts to soothe me through the door.

It was my dad who finally got through to me. Just a few months before, he'd received a diagnosis for an incurable, aggressive brain tumor, so when he knocked, I couldn't bring myself to push him away. I wanted space, but I wanted time with him more.

"Hey, kiddo," he said as he sat next to me on my bed. Dad was so thin by then and had to walk slowly with a cane, but no matter how thin or weak he got, his smile was still the same radiant one he always had for me and my sister, Katy. "What's upsetting my Broadway star?"

The whole incident with Chad and his awful friends spilled out in a rush. When I finished, I was a mess of snot and tears again. "Don't just say what dads have to say, that Chad's wrong and I'm actually beautiful. It won't help."

Dad stroked my back. "Okay, I won't say that, although I think it's true."

I buried my face deeper into my pillow.

"Do you know why I like *Romeo and Juliet*?" Dad asked. "It's not because of how reckless Romeo and Juliet are, because let's face it, those two could have slowed down and made better choices. But that's not really the point of the play. The point was the failure of the Capulets and Montagues to set aside pettiness, and that failure clouded over the most important aspect of life: love."

I mumbled in vague agreement.

"Well, I was thinking," Dad said. "What if you approach your situation with Chad differently?"

I peeked out from the pillow. "What do you mean?"

"Don't let his pettiness take you down. Focus on the love story."

"Ugh. With Chad?"

"No. If he can wish for a Juliet who suits his taste, then why don't you wish for a smarter, sweeter Romeo? When you're on-stage, envision someone else standing opposite you. Think of it like a silent form of revenge, erasing Chad and putting your own Romeo in his place."

The idea seemed, at first, immature, akin to creating an imaginary friend. But Dad was right—visualizing someone other than Chad onstage got me through rehearsals, and it even made my performance better. The more I developed Sebastien in my mind, the more I fell in love with him, and it showed when I received standing ovations every night during curtain call, because I was acting out the role of Juliet falling in love with the dashing Sebastien version of Romeo, not small-minded Chad Akins.

Dad came to every performance. By then, he was in a wheelchair. But every night, he managed to push himself up to standing with the rest of the audience, and he was always the last one to sit back down. I knew what a monumental effort that was for him, and it made every clap of his hands even more precious.

"It's like you're really Juliet," he said after the final performance.

I blushed. "If I were actually Juliet, I'd be reciting my lines in Italian."

"You should study Italian, then," Dad teased. "More authentic."

Two weeks after the play ended, he died.

Months of grief followed. Mom, Katy, and I hardly slept, hardly ate, hardly even spoke. Dad was the boisterous center of our universe, and with him gone, we floated around aimlessly. The house was too empty, too quiet, even with the three of us there.

Eventually, though, we managed to trudge on. And one of the things that helped me emerge from my sorrow was learning Italian. It probably hadn't been a serious suggestion, just a one-off comment Dad made, but still, it was one of his last to me, and I held tight to it.

Maybe that's also why I never relinquished the idea of Sebastien. I invented him, at first, because Dad suggested it. And then when Dad was gone, Sebastien remained.

Writing stories about Sebastien became an escape. I'd never been a big writer before, but after Dad died, story ideas started popping up in my head, almost fully formed. They were just small, romantic vignettes, but in my mind, I always cast Sebastien as the lead actor. It was probably a survival mechanism, allowing me to focus on something sunny in the face of sadness.

Whenever my real life got tough—a high school breakup, or losing all my money in my first job postcollege that turned out to be a pyramid scheme, or each instance of my husband Merrick's infidelity—writing stories about Sebastien would sweep me away from the dreariness of reality. I could live vicariously through those tales and understand what it was like to be loved unconditionally, for someone to listen, to care, to keep his soulmate safe.

He had different names in each vignette, of course, but in my mind, he always had the same face. I wrote romantic adventures where the heroine rides on the back of a camel through the desert while he walks through the sand on foot, holding the camel's lead and guiding the way. My characters have done grand things like sailing on Portuguese caravels and helping Gutenberg with his printing press, and smaller things like attending a Victorian-era horse race. (I love history as much as I love books, which means I have a penchant for writing historical vignettes. Plus, the period costumes! The heroine in the horse race story wore a very fancy hat decorated with a pile of blue feathers and lavender roses.)

Then yesterday at The Frosty Otter, he was there! In the flesh! After all this time of knowing him only in my head.

Had I written him to life?

But that was impossible. So how?

And poor Sebastien. I came at him like a wave of hungry locusts wanting to devour him while he had no idea who I was.

Now I stretch in bed and look at the clock on my nightstand.

It's eight-thirty in the morning, although still dark outside. Part of me wants to curl back beneath the covers, but the new, go-getter Helene pep talks my body into rolling out of bed.

This little cottage is drafty, though, and I immediately regret leaving the blankets. The wood floor is freezing, and I actually yelp; it's so cold that it almost hurts. My clothes are all still in the suitcases, which means I jump ridiculously from foot to foot while I dig around for socks (I put on two pairs) and an oversized hoodie. Thank god I live alone and there's no one to witness the new Alaskan Waking Ritual I've just invented.

When I'm acceptably bundled up, I wander into the kitchen. It's a cozy nook with flowers painted on the counter tiles, an old stove from the seventies, and a refrigerator that huffs and puffs as if it wants to make sure I'm aware how hard it's working. It reminds me of one of those animated trains my little nephew loves, Thomas the Tank Engine and his railroad friends, each with their own personality. I smile wryly at the fridge and say, "I dub thee Reginald the Refrigerator." It sounds like the name of a curmudgeonly old butler and fits my long-suffering fridge quite well.

There's a welcome basket on the counter with a starter pack of pods for the coffee machine and a package of English muffins. I'm grateful for the gift of breakfast already made, because there's no other food in the cottage. I'll have to run some errands today, like going to the grocery store to stock up Reginald the Refrigerator and the pantry.

I brew a mug of hazelnut coffee and inhale deeply as I sit on one of the two stools at the counter. There's something luxurious about flavored coffee. Maybe because my life before was so focused on making other people happy—namely my soon-to-be-ex—and small things like adding sugar and milk to coffee were forbidden, lest the extra calories show up on my hips and he find yet another thinner, cuter intern to suck his dick.

Stop thinking about him.

I squeeze my eyes shut, as if that will also wring away the infidelity, the feelings of helplessness, the despair of never being enough despite how hard I tried.

When I open my eyes again, I reach for one of the yellow note-books I have stacked on the kitchen counter. Immersing myself in a happily-ever-after story gives me a boost, a reminder that better possibilities exist. I flip to one of my favorite vignettes I've written, set in Versailles, when Marie Antoinette and pretty dresses and fancy petits fours still reigned. The protagonists in this story are Amélie Laurent and Matteo Bassegio, but of course Matteo looks, in my mind, just like Sebastien. And I'd much rather think about him than Merrick.

In the gardens of the palace at Versailles, Matteo admires Amélie from across their little rowboat, the bright light off the Grand Canal silhouetting the slight upturn on her button nose, her delicate chin, the blond ringlets pinned elegantly at the nape of her neck. Behind them, the golden palace sits like a king overlooking his botanical realm. There is politicking and backstabbing and gambling in those glittering, mirrored halls.

But out here in the gardens, a deceptive tranquility reigns. The royal demesne is vast, full of groves and hidden pavilions, parterres and paths, an orangery, statues carved by Europe's preeminent artists, and fountains that put on spectacular shows. In the middle of it all is the Grand Canal, a long stripe of water populated by swans and rowboats. A slight breeze skips across the water, and Amélie laughs as she holds her ribboned hat to her head.

She and Matteo have seen each other nearly every afternoon for the past two months, ever since he arrived here in France as an ambassador from the Republic of Venetia. Amélie's family is minor French nobility, high enough on the hierarchy to maintain residences on the outer perimeter of Versailles, but not so high that Amélie has to worry about spending a little time with Matteo. The courtiers around

King Louis XVI have more important political intrigues to attend to than harmless flirtations.

"Is the rowing a great deal of work, Monsieur Bassegio?" Amélie asks. "I hate to think I'm enjoying myself while you labor in the sun."

"Nothing is work when it comes to you, Mademoiselle Laurent. Although if you don't mind, I might take off this waistcoat. I know it isn't proper, but—"

"Oh, you poor thing, you're probably steaming in that. Of course you should take it off." Marie Antoinette's court is forgiving of these small slights to etiquette.

Nevertheless, Matteo catches the blush rising on Amélie's cheeks as he sheds his waistcoat. What he wouldn't give to cross this boat and kiss her right now! But that would only unbalance their boat and land them both in the Grand Canal, and seeing as they are surrounded on all sides by other courtiers strolling through the gardens, Matteo restrains himself and resumes the rhythmical rowing of the oars instead.

"Tell me about Venetia," Amélie says. "I've never been, but it sounds terribly romantic."

Matteo smiles but pauses for a moment, considering what to say. Venetia is a large republic, spanning from the Adriatic Sea all the way inland to the Duchy of Milan. Matteo lives in the capital city of Venice as a newly appointed doge, something akin to elected nobility.

He rows farther down Versailles's Grand Canal, away from the clutter of traffic near the boathouse. The shush of the waves reminds him of home.

"Venice is a poem built on water," Matteo says. "Gondolas glide silently through the canals like the carriages of angels. The sea daily courts the land, the tides kissing the steps of the brick buildings good morning and good eve. The noble campanile in Piazza San Marco keeps watch over us like a proud sentry. And the bridges grant wishes to lovers who dare to meet under the shy light of the moon."

Amélie sighs. "How divine. I hope to see it someday."

"I shall take you there, if you like," Matteo says boldly.

The blush blooms again on her cheeks. "Would you really?"

"Let us go today."

She laughs. "If only!"

Matteo pulls the oars out of the water and rests the handles in his lap. The boat slows to a gentle drift. "Why not?"

"A million reasons," Amélie says, still smiling. "First, even if I could go, I would need to pack, and that alone would take several days. Second, an unmarried woman cannot simply run abroad with a man. It is one thing to be here at court with you, but quite another to go gallivanting unchaperoned to a foreign land."

"Then marry me."

Her parasol nearly drops into the water. "What did you say?"

Matteo locks the oars in the riggers and inches closer to Amélie, carefully maintaining the balance of the boat. He takes her soft hands into his. "Marry me, and we'll move to Venice, and you shall live like a princess on the edge of the sea."

He can feel her pulse fluttering through her fingers. What he is asking is far more than an innocuous flirtation. His heartbeat matches the nervousness of hers.

Whatever her answer, though, Matteo will bear it. Because ever since that first afternoon when he joined her party for an impromptu game of pall-mall in the gardens, he cannot relax unless she is near. In the mornings, when the business of the Venetian state requires his attention, Matteo's restless pacing in his offices has worn a trough through the carpet. At night, his incessant tossing and turning in bed and frequent calls for yet a different pillow or a warmer blanket drive his attendants to drink. It is as if the fabric of Matteo's soul has frayed, and only Amélie's words and sweet smiles are capable of weaving the threads back together.

She slips one of her hands out of his and fans herself. But her other hand still rests in his clasp. She hasn't made a decision thus far.

He holds his breath.

"Your proposal is utter madness," Amélie says quietly. But then she looks up, and the shimmer of the sunlight on the Grand Canal reflects in her eyes. "And there is no one I would rather be mad with than you."

Matteo's heart pounds like a tiger about to be set free from its cage. "Is that a yes?"

"Against my better judgment, it is." She smiles, and he thinks that there has never been a more beautiful woman in all of history. Not Nefertiti, not Lady Godiva, not even the Mona Lisa.

Matteo shifts forward to kiss her, but the boat wobbles, and Amélie waves him back.

"Sit, sit, you'll capsize us!" She laughs. "We have forever and a day for kisses. Waiting until we're on land won't kill us."

Nevertheless, Matteo rows as quickly as he can back to the boathouse. As soon as their feet touch the dock, he pulls Amélie into his arms and presses his mouth to hers, etiquette be damned. Her hair smells like roses and summer storms, and she closes her eyes and kisses him back, and he knows for certain that her lips, her caress, her love, is what it feels like to be home.

I SIGH HAPPILY as I close the notebook, calmer now. The sun is beginning to show, just a little, a pinking of the sky at the horizon to herald the coming light. My thoughts come back to Alaska.

To *this* Sebastien.

There's no guarantee the real version of him is anything like my dreamed best friend, my soulmate. It could simply be that their faces match, that it's a trick of my mind. Maybe I saw someone who looked like him in the past—in one of those black-and-white

Calvin Klein magazine ads or a waiter-who's-really-an-actor-waiting-for-his-big-break (they are plentiful in Los Angeles)—and I merged that face into my daydreams.

Here is what I know as fact, though:

His name is Sebastien.

He is captain of the crab boat *Alacrity*.

And getting out and having new experiences is key in stoking a writer's creative juices.

"It's settled, then," I say aloud, and give myself permission to smile. I'll go down to the docks under the guise of researching a piece on Ryba Harbor and use that as a way to cross paths with Sebastien. It's plausible; I used to be a journalist. If he's there, I'll approach him more cautiously this time—more *normally*—and see if I can engage him that way. If he's not at the boat, I can still interview people at the port, because hell, king crab fishing is interesting and maybe it'll make it into my novel. Either way, the time won't be wasted.

However, that will have to wait until tomorrow. Today is my first full day in Alaska, and I need to run errands. I'd like to take care of them during the few hours the sun is out, since I don't know where everything is yet in this town, and I definitely don't have enough confidence in my driving-through-snow capabilities to do it in the dark.

I finish my coffee and send a quick text to my mom and sister to set up a video call for later today since they want to know how I'm settling in here. Then I shower and get dressed, making sure, as always, to put on my dad's broken watch.

All I have to do is get through today's humdrum errands, and then tomorrow, I really begin chasing my dreams.

SEBASTIEN

Snowcapped mountains cut through the purple of the late morning sky like a serrated knife, the lazy sun just peeking over the horizon, as if deciding whether or not to grace us with a few hours of light today. The chill in the briny air bites into my cheeks—the only exposed part of my skin—and I finish up checking the crab traps for rips or any weak spots in the lines.

The *Alacrity* isn't set to leave port until tomorrow, and the crew has already cleaned the ship from bow to stern. But while most of the other men have families to spend time with, this boat is my love. Here in the harbor, in my routine, I'm secure, and the weighty worries from The Frosty Otter feel lighter.

I can figure out what to do about Helene later, because soon I'll be on the sea again, wearing the cold like a mantle of icy armor. To some, Alaskan winters are bitter and unforgiving, but they've been a solace to me. King crab fishing is backbreaking work, but out on the ocean, there's no time to lament old curses.

When Adam and I bought the *Alacrity* five years ago, it was already a wizened veteran of the freezing Alaskan seas. The boat was iceberg-dented and bitten by rust, half its weight composed of barnacles and war stories of legendary crab hauls and once-in-a-lifetime storms.

The retiring captain had made a fortune; this profession pays exorbitantly well for the danger required to bring in king crabs worth their weight in gold. "If you're wise," he said as Adam and I signed the ship's bill of sale, "you'll make a pile of money and then you'll get out of this business. There are only so many years a crab fisherman can live before the ocean claims him. Greed never serves a man well."

"I'm not afraid of death," I said.

The captain studied me for a minute, and then said, "Yes, you are. Just not in the same way as most."

But I try not to think about that conversation and its underlying truth right now. Colin Merculief, Adam's eighteen-year-old nephew, has just arrived to stock the boat with fresh groceries. As the greenhorn—the newest member of my crew—Colin took care of the Costco run today. His truck bed is loaded with enough to feed our six-man crew for up to ten days. The length of our fishing trip will depend on both the weather and how well our traps do.

"You sure you got enough?" I ask, laughing. Colin has four coolers full of frozen pizzas, burritos, and hot pockets, and who knows how many pounds of bacon, chicken, beef, and cheese. I count two dozen boxes of cereal, ten loaves of bread, a flat of peanut butter and jelly, tubs of protein powder for shakes, and several twenty-pound sacks of potatoes. And that's only what's in the bed of the truck. There's more food inside the cab.

Colin's cheeks color, which is impressive since they were already pink from the cold. He fumbles in his coat and produces a dog-eared, palm-sized spiral notepad. He holds it out to show me the notes he's scribbled. "Uncle Adam said we burn ten thousand calories a day when we're out on the water, so he told me it's better to overbuy. And he gave me a list of things that are good sources of complex carbohydrates and protein. That's what I tried to get."

I laugh again. I'd forgotten what it was like to be so young and eager to learn. "I was just giving you a hard time. You did good, rookie."

That makes Colin flush even more.

It takes us five trips back and forth from the truck to the boat to get everything on board. I sing an old sea shanty under my breath; work puts me in a good mood.

"What about bait?" Colin asks when we're finally finished.

"We'll get that tomorrow morning right before we leave. That way it's as fresh as possible."

"Oh, right," he says, pulling the notepad out of his coat pocket and jotting down this new information.

Down on the dock, Adam appears, waving at us. "How'd our greenhorn do?" he hollers.

"I'm still alive, Uncle!" Colin shouts.

Adam chuckles at the joke, although there's an undercurrent of somberness to his laugh. This may be Colin's first season of king crabbing, but the Merculief family has been in this industry for generations, and they're well aware of the dangers that take place in the pitch-dark skies and freezing waters of January. On average, one crab fisherman in Alaska dies each week.

Thankfully, Adam's girlfriend, Dana Wong, appears from the parking lot with a picnic basket and changes the subject. "Lunch?" she asks.

"Depends," I say, although I'm already smiling as I climb down the ladder to the dock. "What do you have?" Dana owns the sole barbecue joint in town, and my stomach growls just thinking about what might be in that basket.

"Oh, nothing much," she says with faux solemnity. "Smoked brisket, barbecued chicken, baked beans, cornbread."

"And beer," Adam adds.

"Well, if you've got beer, then I'm in," I say. "Otherwise, I wasn't the least bit interested."

Dana shoves me, a little harder than playful, but that's just the way she is. "Come on, boys. Let's get out of the cold and I'll feed you."

The four of us head into the small trailer in the parking lot that serves as our operations office. The desk is neat but covered in stacks of invoices for the seafood plants that buy our king crabs. I'm damn grateful that Adam takes care of all this accounting and paperwork. He's a "people person," and the customers love him. I, on the other hand, tend toward taciturn, and that isn't the personality you need to land big accounts.

Colin unfolds a card table, and Adam and I rearrange the only chairs in the office around it. It's a tight fit when we sit down—my back is pressed up against the window, Colin's wedged in by the door, and Dana and Adam are flush against the desk—but once Dana unpacks the picnic basket, it doesn't matter. The office smells gloriously of charred wood and smoked meat.

"Babe, you outdid yourself again," Adam says, leaning over to give her a kiss. Unbeknownst to Dana, he's been saving his share of the profits from this season's catch so he can propose next month with "a ring so big it'll give her arthritis."

I look at them across the table, perhaps too wistfully, because Dana says, "You know, Seb, you could have what we have, if you let yourself."

I shudder. I know full well what'll happen if I give myself permission to be happy. Thoughts of Helene flit through my mind, and I have to bat them away like flies.

A cloud drifts over my mood. But I don't want to spoil the lunch, so I shrug at Dana in that insouciant way of dedicated bachelors, with only one shoulder, as if it's hardly worth the effort to explain how irredeemable I am. "I'm not the type to settle down."

"True," Adam says. "He's already married to the boat. Better if Seabass sticks to flings with tourists who stay in Ryba Harbor for a couple days, then never come back again."

Colin looks at me with teenage admiration.

"Ugh," Dana says. "You can do better than that, Seb. You *deserve* better."

Do I, though? I've tried relationships with women other than Juliet. But they've always failed, because I'm "too aloof" and my girlfriends "can't get close" to me. I made an effort, I truly did. But once you've been in love like I have with Juliet—once you've known what it's like to pour your entire being into another, to hold your soulmate in your arms, to feel that warm sense of safety and comfort and belonging—you're ruined for anything else. That's why I don't date. It's not fair to break hearts because I'm incapable of giving mine to any save Juliet, who already owns it.

Meanwhile, Dana gives Adam the stink eye. "I can't believe that's the kind of relationship advice you dole out to your best friend."

Adam crosses his index fingers in an X in front of him, laughing, and says, "Back, woman! Don't hex me with your glare."

She looks at me and sighs. "See what I have to deal with?"

Adam darts in and steals another kiss from her. "You know you love it. You can't resist trying to reform us."

I laugh, and Dana takes a bite of her brisket to hide her smile.

When we've all eaten as much as we can, Adam hands me a bottle of cheap chardonnay. Alaskan lore provides that pouring wine on deck will bring fortune to the fishermen. "For tomorrow," he says.

Dana clucks her tongue. "You're supposed to use *good* wine, not bargain barrel dregs."

"We drank all the good stuff from Napa, babe."

"Doesn't matter," I say with a smile. "I'm sure this is just as lucky. We'll break it open first thing in the morning."

HELENE

EVERYTHING IN ALASKA IS WAY MORE EXPENSIVE THAN I THOUGHT IT would be. And my nerves are completely fried from having to drive in the snow. I skidded in the Walmart parking lot and almost hit a family with young children. Then when I got back to my cottage, the driveway had iced over, and I nearly smashed the car through the garage wall.

After unloading my groceries (Reginald the Refrigerator is grateful to have a full belly), I decide that what I need is cake. Thank goodness I can just walk down the street to the coffee shop in the picturesque little downtown. Driving to Walmart had been a necessity, because it was in the next, bigger city. But I'm not getting in that car again unless I absolutely have to.

After The Frosty Otter, the interior of Moose Crossing, the

coffee shop, is a little disappointing. It's kind of a Starbucks knock-off, with the same layout and similar utilitarian furniture. The store's sign is even the same shade of Starbucks green, although it's not a mermaid but a moose on the logo.

Still, the café smells like fresh roasted coffee beans and the pastry case is well stocked, which is good enough for me.

I order a latte and a fat slice of lingonberry pecan fruitcake that boasts a Handmade Locally sign, along with a note that declares: "Try it. I promise it's nothing like the doorstop fruitcakes everyone makes fun of."

There's only one other patron in the shop, hammering away at a laptop, so I head toward one of the many empty tables. But as I get closer to him and catch a glimpse of his silhouette, I stop short, and my cake almost slides off its plate onto my boots.

Fuck fuck fuck. Is that Merrick?

I can barely see his profile under the waves of blond hair, but the sharp jawline and perfect posture look exactly like my ex-husband. *Soon-to-be* ex-husband, who refuses to sign the divorce papers. Who calls and texts several times a day, asking me to reconsider. *Demanding* me to.

Has Merrick tracked me down and followed me here?

My stomach crawls up my throat. And he must feel my presence, because he looks up.

But . . . he has brown eyes, not green. Not Merrick!

"Uh, hi," the man says, unsure what to do with me just staring at him. First Sebastien, now him. If I'm not careful, I'm going to start getting a reputation: California Tourist Who Gawks Awkwardly at Local Men.

"Sorry, thought you were someone else." I laugh stupidly and hurry to the farthest table in the room.

Real smooth, Helene, I chastise myself as I cram a huge chunk of fruitcake into my mouth.

But even though that wasn't Merrick, now I can't get him out of my head.

When I first met Merrick Sauer, we were undergrads at Pomona College, and later, we went to journalism grad school together at Northwestern. What he lacked in brawn, he made up for in whip-sharp intelligence, and his charisma and mild arrogance at twenty was raffish in a nerdy, devil-may-care way. Everyone loved him—his professors, our dormmates, and especially me. He had ambition and talent in spades, and his future as a superstar was plain for all to see.

I loved basking in the golden light that seemed to follow him everywhere. I was an excellent writer, too, winning accolades like the Dean's Award for Exceptional Journalism. Merrick and I were a young power couple back then, Northwestern's most promising grad students, who would go out and conquer the world together.

But even then, he was changing subtly, without me noticing. Maybe I couldn't see the warning flags because optimism is coded into my DNA—from both the way my mom looks at the world, and my dad's broken watch that serves as a constant reminder that life is too short to waste on wallowing. So when Merrick and his greasy friend Aaron Gonchar were kicked off the university newspaper for ethics violations, Merrick wove a believable tale about the editorial board's jealousy and incompetence. And I didn't question otherwise. He was so charming and persuasive, and I was blindly in love with our potential, so I couldn't see the alternate possibility: that maybe Merrick and Aaron had actually been in the wrong.

I didn't realize that, over time, too much success and praise would irretrievably warp Merrick. I followed him from promotion to promotion, always putting my own career on hold. I turned down plum job offers overseas—assignments in Europe, where I longed to live—because Merrick and I had agreed to take turns, and his turn kept coming first.

Meanwhile, his charismatic confidence evolved into a condescending disdain toward not only those who worked for him, but also me, his wife. As brilliant as he was, he was horribly insecure—terrified that someone would discover he wasn't all he was cracked up to be—and so he built armor around himself with insults and scorn.

Which was also why, as his professional reputation grew, he kept cheating with interns. They would look up to him with stars in their eyes despite his arrogance, awed by the fact that he was the youngest bureau chief in the history of *The Wall Street Journal*.

Their reverence buoyed his ego, and apparently other, more physical body parts, and inevitably he'd stay late for work or go on long business trips with that intern in tow, forgetting to call or even text me the entire week he was gone.

I tear off a piece of the fruitcake and realize how lucky I am to escape him.

For a long time, I was actually oblivious to Merrick's cheating, even though apparently everyone else at the *Journal* gossiped about him and his latest conquest whenever I was out of earshot. When you're deep inside a relationship, you don't see the stumbling blocks, the fatal flaws. Sometimes, you don't *want* to see them, so you willfully put on your blinders and continue telling yourself that everything is great.

Maybe that was a flaw I took on when I adopted my dad's interpretation of *Romeo and Juliet*, that the bumps in life don't matter as much as love does. I overlooked Merrick's glaring defects because I was too focused on the love story I wanted out of it.

But when I didn't get promoted to columnist, I was done. Especially since I deserved the promotion, and my husband was the bureau chief, for god's sake—he could have made it happen.

Or maybe the last straw was that I caught Merrick in the act of cheating and I couldn't *not* see the intern on her knees, his pants around his ankles.

Or maybe it was my two golden retrievers—Rex and Cookie—dying only days apart, Rex from kidney failure and Cookie from a broken heart.

That confluence of life disasters was the gut punch I needed. When I saw the flash sale on flights, I went on a shopping spree and bought plane tickets for Alaska, as well as Europe in the spring. (I was finally going to travel there! And my sister, Katy, wanted to come, too, which seemed like a perfect incentive to hunker down and write my novel: FINISH MANUSCRIPT = EAT ÉCLAIRS WITH KATY WHILE STROLLING THROUGH THE GARDENS AT VERSAILLES.)

Maybe my mom is right, and everything does happen for a reason.

Still, my therapist told me it'll take a while for the traumas of the past to stop haunting me. Months, years even.

But I'm impatient. I'm eager—desperate—for my new life to begin, for the old one to disappear.

Burn it away. All of it. Ashes.

Eventually, everything will smolder: the anger, the hurt, and the sadness. And then new trees will sprout from the ruins of the forest fire. My new life.

I pour two heaping spoonfuls of sugar into my coffee, because Merrick isn't here to judge me anymore. I rip off another fat hunk of fruitcake and eat it with my hands, licking every single crumb off my fingertips. Food isn't supposed to be comfort, the health experts all say. But the truth is, food is absolutely comfort. It is self-care, it is meditation, it is healing. When I have a pastry or cookie or other sweet, I know for certain that I'm not the timid, beaten-down Helene anymore. I am a woman who eats cake, whenever and however she pleases.

When the cake is gone, I consider buying another piece. I'm starting to feel better, although I'm not 100 percent there yet, and another slice might help.

But then I see Shipyard Books through the window, and I realize how I can feed two birds with one scone: I'll go buy myself a new novel to read—that always lifts my spirits—and I'll also pick up a book on how to write fiction, since the purpose of me being in Alaska is to work on my own novel.

As I leave the coffee shop, I pass by the man-who-isn't-Merrick and grin as I say, "Have a great day!"

He startles, again unsure what to do with me, but I don't care.

New Helene does not care.

SEBASTIEN

I LIVE AN HOUR OUTSIDE OF RYBA HARBOR—I LIKE THE SOLITUDE OF the forest when I'm not on the *Alacrity*—but before I drive home, I decide to stop by the bookstore on Main Street. I always carry a paperback in my coat pocket, so if I get stuck in a long line at Costco or elsewhere, I have something on hand to entertain myself. I'm too old-fashioned to see the appeal of filling downtime with a glowing screen; I don't even own a cellphone. Besides, reading reminds me of my publishing days, although that was a long, long time ago.

The bell rings as I step into Shipyard Books. It's a cozy shop, with a blazing fireplace near the entrance to thaw frozen fingers and toes. The front door is decorated with a porthole, and the interior walls are painted in nautical stripes. A thirty-foot papier-mâché Moby Dick hangs from the ceiling in the middle of the main room.

Angela Manning, the silver-haired owner, glances up from the novel she's reading behind the register. "Hello, Sebastien. Good to see you again. Can I help you find something today?"

"Yeah. I'm looking for a couple books—"

But I stop short because an elderly couple, Margaret and Andrew Ullulaq, emerges from the shelves and slowly strolls arm in arm toward the register. She's wearing a hand-knit purple sweater, and he has on suspenders that match. They're always a matching set. Even now, with arms linked, Margaret and Andrew each carry a novel in their free hand, bookish mirror images.

Beside me, Angela lets out a deep sigh full of admiration. "Can you believe it? Today is their sixty-fifth anniversary. They met in a bookstore, you know. Now, on every anniversary, they come in here and buy each other a book. Isn't that the sweetest tradition? I love that they've kept it up all this time."

I have to close my eyes as a sharpness slices through me, like a blade slashing through a canvas sail. Other people's wedding anniversaries remind me that Juliet and I didn't make it a week past our vows. And because of the curse, we will never have a chance at even five years, let alone *sixty*-five.

What I wouldn't give to be able to grow old with Juliet, to share such sweet anniversary traditions, to ultimately die peacefully in each other's arms.

What I wouldn't give to be able to die at all, to put an end to the curse.

I thought, perhaps, I had managed to break the cycle when I walked away from Avery Drake back in 1962. Our paths crossed in Kenya—she was a wildlife photographer about to set off on safari, and I a cartographer on assignment to update the rivers on maps of Africa—but as soon as our mutual friends introduced us in that palm-shaded café in Nairobi, I fled and abandoned my job.

Avery went on to great success. I purposely avoided news of her to avoid the temptation of seeking her out again, but every so often, I'd come across one of her photographs—on the cover of a *National Geographic* left on someone's coffee table, on a poster in the window of a home furnishings store, and, finally, on a set of commemorative stamps issued by the U.S. Postal Service after her death.

To my great relief, Avery Drake had lived into her fifties, twice as long as most Juliets. And even more important, more than thirty years after she met *me*.

I believed that meant I'd finally broken the curse. I believed it might mean that, I, too, could finally die.

But I didn't.

And now in front of me are Margaret and Andrew, this couple that'd spent contented decades together, and I can only yearn for a drop of what they've known, and for how they will eventually get to shuffle off this mortal coil while I remain ensnared in its neverending twists and turns.

Angela doesn't notice my pain, though, because she's still watching the happy couple. I force a smile back on my face as they approach, and I step aside to allow them to go ahead of me at the register.

"Happy anniversary," I say.

"Thank you." Margaret gazes at Andrew with the ardor of first love, and he returns the look with equal intensity. "I can't believe we made it this far."

"Oh, I knew we would, darling," Andrew said. "I always knew we'd grow old and crochety together."

She giggles. Actually giggles. "We're not crochety."

"No," Angela says. "You two are sublime. You're what we all dream of being."

Margaret blushes.

I need to look away, though, because it's becoming hard to breathe. I turn toward the fireplace, arms wrapped around myself as if trying to warm up, but really because I'm trying to hold myself together.

I'm truly happy for Margaret and Andrew, I am. It's just that I'm also awash in the wretched awareness of what they get to have, and I don't.

Not until the front door chimes with them leaving do I turn back around.

Angela returns her attention to me. "Now, what books did you want, Sebastien?"

It takes a moment to refocus on why I'm here. "Books. Right."

"You mentioned two of them?"

"Um . . . yes. *The First Fifteen Lives of Harry August*—the author's name escapes me—and *Death with Interruptions* by José Saramago."

"Saramago, huh?" Angela starts looking up the books on her computer. "Didn't he win the Nobel Prize for Literature at some point?"

"Indeed he did."

Her mouth curls into a grin. "A well-read, philosophical fisherman. Sebastien, you are the strangest crabber I've ever known."

I give her one of my half shrugs. I am what I am.

Angela scrolls through a list of titles on her screen. "Okay, looks like I'll have to order the *Harry August* book for you. But I have two Saramagos in stock right now. The one you want, as well as *Blindness*."

"*Blindness* is great. I read it years ago in the original Portuguese."

She squints at me. "You speak Portuguese?"

I laugh as if it's a joke. "I'm kidding. I read the book in translation in college."

But the truth is, yes, I speak Portuguese, among other languages, because you acquire them when you've lived in as many places as I have. It's just that nobody knows that about me.

"Anyway," I say with as much nonchalance as I can manage. "You said the Saramago book is on the shelf?"

"In the literature section, third row."

"Thanks."

Angela nods, already picking up her novel again.

I walk deeper into the store to grab my book. But as I approach the shelves I want, a chill blows through me like a warning, knocking over each hair on my arms as if they're dominos blown over by a ghost's exhale.

And the taste of honeyed wine brushes against my lips.

I go rigid.

Helene emerges from the row with her face buried in a book. She has two others tucked under her arm.

She crashes into me and drops them.

"Oh my god, I'm sorry, I—" Helene cuts herself off when she sees that it's me in front of her.

We stare at each other in silence, unmoving.

I don't know what she's thinking, but I know I should probably get as far away from here as possible. If I'm right—that falling in love with each other is what triggers the curse—then I still have a chance to save her.

Yet I stay, because I'm drawn to her like the tide to the moon's pull, all of our history surging through me at once. And because we're just standing here, I get to really look at Helene, better than when she caught me off guard at The Frosty Otter yesterday. Her butterscotch hair in messy waves around her shoulders. Eyes flecked with copper. The arc of her neck like the curve of a harp, yearning to be played. My fingers twitch.

And she likes to read . . . Not all Juliets are book lovers—they may be the same soul, but they're never the same person—yet this one, Helene, does. I store that fact away, a fact I shouldn't keep because I should be putting more space between us, not more yearning. But I can't help it, because I want to know everything about Helene. I want to keep every scrap of Juliet I can. It's a flaw that will hurt me later, but I can't resist.

I have to stop looking at her.

I dive down for the books she dropped.

The Craft of Novel Writing, by A. Shinoda and S. Lee.

Wolf Hall, by Hilary Mantel.

And the very same Saramago book I came looking for.

I inhale sharply. What are the odds?

But then again, what are the odds for star-crossed lovers to keep meeting each other over and over, across centuries?

We defy probability, for better or for worse.

"Thanks," Helene says, reaching for the books I've gathered as I rise from the floor.

But I don't give them back. Instead, I hold the books against my chest, because she'd touched them only a moment ago. It's a poor substitute to holding Helene herself, but it's all I can allow myself.

She tilts her head at me quizzically. A second later, though, she smiles. "You know, I was hoping to run into you again. I, um, wanted to apologize for yesterday. And I swear, this right here"— she gestures to herself and me in the bookstore—"is pure coincidence. I promise I'm not stalking you."

I swallow the dry patch in my throat. Her voice has the same cadence as all my past Juliets. And there's a spark in Helene's eyes, as if the entire sun has been captured inside them. It's the same brightness that's caught me so many times before.

Her soul tugs harder on mine.

Helene moves cautiously closer to me, like I'm a wild animal she doesn't want to alarm. "Can we forget my crazy declarations at The Frosty Otter and start over?" she asks.

I take a deep breath. Clutch the books tighter. "I wish we could." It comes out like a croak.

"Great!" She holds her hand out to shake mine. "Hi, I'm Helene, and I—"

"No." I say, too curtly. Every word, every sentence between us, is a connection, and I need to stop them before they form.

Confusion flashes in her eyes, and I'm immediately remorseful, but I have to push on. "I mean, I wish we could start over, but we can't. I don't want to know you."

"What? Why not?" Her entire body droops.

I hate that I'm causing her pain. I almost change my mind.

But I can't give in to what I want. It's better for Helene to live than to get involved with me and die. She's already had a decade since I saw her at Pomona College. If I can keep her away from me again, hopefully she'll be able to live for decades more.

So I just turn and walk away.

"Hey! Where are you going? Those are my books!"

I forgot I was clinging to them like a lifeline, but I can't back down now. I have to get away from Helene. I want so badly what Adam and Dana have, but that part of my life isn't mine to control. The curse has struck too many times. I won't let it hurt Juliet again.

I can't.

Instead I do the first thing I think of, driven solely by emotion. Benvolio always told me I was too rash.

But if I have to be a jerk to make Helene go away, I will.

"Actually, these books belong to whoever pays for them first. And I came in specifically for the Saramago novel." I reach into my wallet, grab four twenties, and toss them onto the counter as I stride past the register. "Keep the change," I tell Angela.

I flee Shipyard Books, not bothering with the handrail even though the front steps are icy. Halfway down the block, Helene's voice catches up to me.

"What the hell is wrong with you?"

Slowly, I turn around.

Even mad, she's beautiful. Snowflakes fall and catch in her hair like glittering garlands, and her cheeks and the tip of her nose grow rosy with the cold.

She shivers, and I want to offer her my coat. I want to give back her books. I want to . . .

Stop. I have to end this madness. I promised myself I'd let her go.

I force myself to send her the sharpest scowl in my arsenal. She staggers back at the force of it. The misery of hurting her blooms in my chest.

"Goodbye, Helene."

It's for the best. Because I've been fool enough before to believe we could turn out to be anything but a tragedy.

VERSAILLES, FRANCE – 1789

Despite Amélie's warning that she would need days to pack, she manages to be ready by nightfall. I promise she'll be able to buy everything she needs and wants in Venice. I don't flaunt my wealth, but the fact is, my treasury houses a considerable fortune.

Besides, it's best if we leave Versailles as expediently as possible. The longer we wait, the more likely our plans will be discovered. Even though the Laurent family is not close to the king, they do have social aspirations and will stop Amélie's elopement to avoid any whiff of scandal. A proper courtship and wedding would likely have been acceptable, given my title and rank. But the clock has been ticking on Amélie's life ever since our hearts tumbled hopelessly in love on the pall-mall court. I am determined that she will see Venice before she dies.

My horses and carriage are ready when Amélie and I arrive at the stables. The footman loads her sole trunk of belongings while I help Amélie onto the blue velvet cushions inside.

"Lord Montague, this is one of the grandest carriages I've ever seen," she says as she strokes the gold that trims the windows and the rich brocade that lines the walls. My family crest—a wolf and two swords—graces the backs of the seats. The ceiling is a painted mural of the Venetian canals.

"I promised to make you a princess by the sea, did I not?" I kiss her hand before settling on the cushion across from her.

"I thought perhaps you were exaggerating. Men do tend to do so, you know." Amélie smiles, and like always, I melt happily in her radiance.

The coachman pokes his head through the carriage door. "We are ready for departure, my lord," he says in Venetian.

"Very good," I say. "Let's be on our way."

I hold Amélie's hand on my knee, and we are silent as the carriage makes its way toward the gates. Each hoofbeat echoes like a thousand war drums to me, sounding the alarm to the sleeping residents of Versailles. I hold my breath.

But soon enough, the carriage passes through the gates, and not long after, we're away on the dark road. My shoulders release their tension, and Amélie lets out an exhale in relief.

"Will we pass through Paris on the way?" she asks.

"Do you wish to?"

"If it isn't too far out of our path. I should like to see the city once more before we go abroad. I don't know when we'll return."

"Anything within my power is yours." I open the window and lean out to give the coachman new directions.

When I return, Amélie is yawning. I sit on the seat beside her. "Rest your head on my shoulder and sleep," I say.

"What will you do?"

Memorize everything about this night, I think.

But aloud, I say, "Perhaps I shall doze as well. We'll be two birds nestled together in a pretty cage."

"That somehow sounds both picturesque and awful," Amélie teases.

I laugh. "It's late. My literary prowess wanes in the evening."

"Well, dreadful metaphor or not, I love you, my handsome Venetian bird." She nuzzles against me, fitting her head perfectly against my shoulder and the crook of my neck.

Within minutes, Amélie is asleep. I hold her and feel the gentle rise and fall of her body as I watch the dark landscape of the countryside fly by. At some point, I nod off as well, and when I wake, cobblestones and glowing streetlamps greet me.

"My love," I say softly. "We have arrived in Paris."

Amélie blinks the slumber from her eyes and presses herself to the window. "What a beauty the city is," she says as the river Seine comes into view. The streets beyond it glimmer as if lit from within. No wonder Paris is sometimes called La Ville Lumière.

Our carriage continues along the riverfront, past quiet bakeries and empty street corners. It seems for once that Paris is at peace, the recent calls for the king's head and the stirrings of revolutionary fervor swept clean from the cobblestones for tonight.

The quietude lowers my guard, and the coachman's as well, for we do not see the mob in the shadows until torches flare up in front of the horses, and bayonets and muskets surround the carriage.

Amélie jumps back from the windows.

"*Liberté, égalité, fraternité, ou la mort!*" the revolutionaries shout.

The last word—death—shakes me into action.

"Don't move, and don't say a word," I tell Amélie.

I scoot to the window. "*Scuxéme,*" I say in Venetian. "We are only passing through on our way home . . ."

For a moment, the mob outside is confused by the fact that I'm speaking another language. Then the leader—a square-jawed youth with a bayonet clutched in one hand—steps forward and spits. "We demand the heads of the nobility, who treat the people like garbage and spend their taxes on finery and cakes."

Amélie's grip on my hand is so tight her nails draw blood. Still, I do not ask her to let go.

I usually speak perfect French, but I purposefully inflect it now with a heavy Venetian accent as I again address our captors. "*S'il vous plaît,* we are foreigners. We have no quarrel with you and only wish to pass through to return to our country."

The leader considers this and consults with two others in the mob. Muskets aimed, they question the coachman and the footman, who both babble in fright in Venetian, confirming my claims of not being French.

Perhaps there is a chance we will be allowed to go on our way.

Tears quiver down Amélie's cheeks. There is so much she wants to say—I can see it in her eyes—but she presses her lips together and remains quiet as I instructed. Bless my sweet, dear Amélie.

The mob leader steps back up to the carriage window. "Tell your coachman to take the next street out of the city. If we see you again, we will not be so lenient."

"*Grasie*," I say in Venetian. Then, "*Merci beaucoup*."

The coachman yells at the horses to move. Amélie collapses in my arms and sobs. "I thought that was the end. I thought they would take us and we would never see each other again."

"No, my love," I say, clutching her shaking frame to mine. "I will never allow us to be parted."

The horses have gone only a few paces, though, when the mob roars and stops the carriage again. I look out the window in panic.

The leader has been shoved aside. His revolutionaries want the blood of the nobility, and they do not care whether it's French or Venetian.

A door is wrenched open. Angry, ravenous hands tear at Amélie's gown and grab her arms.

"Matteo!" she shrieks.

I wrap myself around her waist to keep her inside. But a musket clubs the side of my head and knocks me back.

Stars cloud my vision. The last thing I see before I fall unconscious is the terror in Amélie's face as the men drag her out into the night.

When I wake, the moonlight hurts my eyes. They've beaten me to a pulp and left my body—thinking me dead—on the streets of Paris for the ravens and raccoons to pick at my bones. I slowly stagger to my feet.

The carriage has been battered to splinters. The footman and the coachman hang by nooses from the streetlamps, examples to the working men of Paris that there are sides in the coming war, and they'd better know where they belong.

And then there is Amélie . . . Beautiful, precious Amélie.

She is bludgeoned on the bank of her beloved Seine, face smashed in. The word "*Liberté*" is scrawled on the cobblestones in her blood.

I crumple and vomit on the street.

When I finally have the strength again, I rise. I scoop Amélie up from the ground, my arms shaking uncontrollably.

I hug her to my chest.

"I love you," I whisper.

I'd promised that I would never allow us to be parted.

And then, with her body to mine, I lurch to the river and throw us in together.

I don't die. I never do.

But every time, I wish I could.

HELENE

IS IT POSSIBLE TO HATE SOMEONE YOU DON'T EVEN KNOW? I WATCH Sebastien leave. With *my* books.

I hate him I hate him I hate him.

Real Sebastien is nothing like Story Sebastien. There isn't a kind bone in that fisherman's body. All he shares with my imagined soulmate is a face. Otherwise, he's made of snips and snails and puppy dog tails. Or rotten king crab claws.

Ha!

It's a stupid joke and it doesn't rhyme, but somehow it makes me feel better. Sebastien belongs in the same category as Merrick (read: scum not worth even thinking about).

In a huff, I stomp back toward Shipyard Books. (Also, it's arctic out here, and my coat is on a hook inside the store.) I can try to forget about Sebastien's assholery, but that doesn't change the fact that I still need a book about novel writing. That's the reason I came to this remote town in Alaska in the first place—to finally figure out if there's a way to string together the vignettes I've written over the years into a coherent novel. They were jotted down piecemeal, but I feel like there's a common thread in there somewhere, a theme or something. I just need to figure out what the through line is that makes it all one story.

I swear at myself for not buying a novel-writing book before I left L.A. But I'd had to leave Merrick quickly, before I lost my nerve. Before I let him talk me out of the divorce, before he convinced me, like he always did, that *I* was the one whose head was mixed up, that it wasn't his fault. I didn't want to be his doormat anymore.

A frigid wind kicks up, and I hurry up the steps of Shipyard Books, careful to hold on to the railing so I don't slip on the ice. I practically hurl myself through the door.

Warmth from the fireplace embraces me, and I think I actually moan. The store owner laughs from behind the register.

"Sorry," Angela says. "It's just that your face went through the entire span of human emotions in about five seconds, from fear and pain to surprise, then relief, then gratefulness and adoration. I never knew someone could fall in love with a fireplace like that."

I let out a snort of a laugh because she's right. I am ridiculous, a Californian running after an imaginary man in the Alaskan winter, all without a coat.

Time to get my head on straight again.

"I was wondering if you happen to have another copy of *The Craft of Novel Writing*, maybe in the back?" This is a cute bookstore, but their selection on writing is slim. Meaning, there was literally only that one book on the shelf on the subject. (In contrast, there were plenty of books about woodworking and snowshoeing.)

Angela shakes her head. "I can order another copy for you. It'll be here in three to four weeks. Sometimes sooner, but usually not."

"Three to four *weeks*?" I didn't know anything took that long anymore.

She smiles apologetically. "It's harder to get things up here than in the Lower 48. Especially with the on-and-off blizzard conditions this time of year. But I have to ask—what happened between you and Sebastien to make him storm out like that? He's the most even-keeled person I know."

I wrinkle my nose. "*Him?* Even-keeled? I've been in Ryba Harbor for about twenty-four hours and already run into him twice, and both times, he treated me like I was a chamber pot he'd stepped into."

Angela raises a brow at "chamber pot."

"Sorry. Historical fiction nerd," I say, pointing at myself.

Angela smiles at me. "Well, all I know is that you've rattled a man who can't be shaken. Do you know what Sebastien once did?" she says, leaning forward on her counter like she's about to reveal the secrets of the universe. "The *Alacrity* was on its tenth day out at sea. The waters were more violent than usual—fifty-foot waves—and the storm was subfreezing wind and sleet. The crew was already exhausted from a rough trip; the boat iced relentlessly, and some of their traps had been lost. All they could hope for was surviving the night.

"And then, Sebastien saw a baby polar bear stranded on an iceberg. It was clearly injured, maybe a broken leg. The mother was nowhere in sight, and the cub couldn't swim to safety. So what did Sebastien do, in the middle of one of the most dangerous winter storms in recent Alaskan history? He jumped onto thin, fractured ice, rescued the baby bear, and brought it back on board."

I burst out laughing. "That guy? No way. I don't believe for a second that he could care about another human, let alone a baby bear. Besides, Sebastien would have fallen through the ice and frozen in the ocean. Or the bear would have mauled him to death. That's a tall tale if I ever heard one."

"Girls Scout's promise." Angela holds up three fingers like an oath. "I was there when the *Alacrity* docked at port—the whole town was, because the crew had radioed ahead to Adam in the office—and a vet from the Wilderness Conservatory came to take the cub. There was a TV report about it, and it was a big deal when the bear was recuperated and returned to the wild." Angela's eyes gleam the way the patrons at The Frosty Otter looked at Sebastien last night—a beloved citizen of Ryba Harbor who buys beer for everyone and saves baby bears in his free time. A hero of mythic (small town) proportions.

I barely restrain myself from rolling my eyes. (If I didn't, they would have rolled so hard they'd fall out of my head and across the bookstore floor.) Instead, I smile sterilely, just like I did whenever I was passed over for a promotion at the newspaper, or whenever Merrick made another excuse for working late with the interns. It's my "this is mildly uncomfortable, let's pretend I believe you and move on" smile.

Angela gets the hint and turns back to her computer. "Anyway, I digress, and I apologize—I shouldn't have pried about you and Sebastien. So, should I place that order for *The Craft of Novel Writing* for you?"

I drum my fingers on the counter. Three to four weeks. That's half the time I've got on my cottage rental. I *have* to make progress on my novel before that. Plus, my sister, Katy, and I leave for Europe two months from now. I can't celebrate in the streets of Amsterdam and Cannes if I haven't even started the thing I'm supposed to be celebrating.

Argh. The faster solution is an unpalatable one: track down Sebastien and demand the writing book back. He doesn't need it. He just took it because it was mine.

I am so, so tired of people like Sebastien and Merrick, who think they can push me around.

But screw them. Tomorrow I'm going to the harbor. Unlike my original plan of swooning over Story Sebastien, though, maybe I'll punch Real Sebastien in the face. (But *after* I get my book back.)

"You don't need to order it," I tell Angela. "Thanks, though."

I grab my coat from its hook and start to leave. But the musical laughter of small children stops me before I get to the exit, and my heart turns to mush at the sound. Three toddlers huddle around a little table in the children's section, giggling at a board book. Their parents sit in armchairs close enough to keep an eye on them but far enough to be able to chat among themselves. There's an empty armchair next to them, and for a second, I imagine myself sitting there, a fellow mom on a playdate at the bookstore.

I've always wanted kids, but Merrick didn't want the responsibility. It was a point of tension between us. Not the thing that broke us, of course, but still, my biological clock started ticking around twenty-five and it never stopped. But at thirty years old, soon to be divorced, and disillusioned about men, I might have to give up on the idea of having my own babies. Instead, I soothe that maternal instinct by spoiling my nephew and watching other people's kids from afar.

"Aren't they adorable?" Angela says. "Kids are the main reason I opened this store. I have such fond memories of browsing picture books when I was a girl, in what seemed like miles and miles of shelves."

"They *are* super cute," I say, maybe with a little too much longing.

But Angela doesn't seem to notice, because she's looking at the giggling toddlers in almost the same way I am.

"Do you have kids?" I ask.

She nods. "A son. He lives in Arizona, and he and his wife just had a baby girl. I want to visit them, but I haven't been able to get away from the store."

"No one can cover for you?"

"I only have one employee. Ryba Harbor isn't a big reading town, other than the kids."

"That's too bad."

She shrugs and turns back to the register.

But then a thought occurs to me. I worked in the college bookstore during my undergrad years, and I still know books because I'm a voracious reader. And to be honest, I could also use a bit of income. Today's grocery shopping cost more than I'd expected—apparently, food and everything else is more expensive in Alaska, because it all has to be shipped up here. If I took on even a short gig at Shipyard Books, it'd give me a cushion and spending money when I go to Europe.

I didn't used to be the type of person who would ask for what wasn't obviously available. At restaurants, I never request substitutions or order off-menu. I certainly don't inquire about jobs without a Help Wanted sign in the window. But the new me is trying to be bolder, braver in both the big and little things. Besides, what's the harm in asking a question? The worst is a no, and I've survived much worse than that.

"Hey," I say to Angela while smiling at the kids at the little table. "What if I covered for you while you go see your granddaughter? I used to work in a bookstore, and—"

Angela claps her hands together with glee. "Really? Can you start tomorrow afternoon?"

HELENE

MY PHONE RINGS AS I PULL UP INTO THE HARBOR LOT THE NEXT morning. The sun hasn't even risen yet, but I have a feeling I know who's calling this early; I glance quickly at the screen as I put the car into park.

Incoming call from Pees Sitting Down.

I snicker. After I told Merrick I was leaving him and wanted a divorce, I changed his name on my phone. He might fashion himself as the paragon of virility—what with all the cheating—but those interns don't know what a little boy Merrick really is inside. He still calls his mom Mommy. He sleeps with a nightlight on. And he pees sitting down like a toddler.

Am I mean for changing his caller ID? Maybe. But it's also not a lie. Plus, walking out of a relationship of ten years (eight married) isn't painless, and being able to give Merrick an innocuous nickname that nobody else will see makes it a tiny bit easier for me to assure myself that I did the right thing by leaving him.

Of course, it would also be great if he would stop calling me twenty times a day. Then I wouldn't have to see his name—or nickname—at all. (I can't block him, in case he actually has something important to tell me about signing the divorce papers, which he has so far failed to do.)

I decline the call and send him directly to voicemail. I already know what he's going to say anyway, because every text and voicemail has been the same since I left L.A., a classic Merrick mixture of charisma and insolence. He's charming enough that, if you're not careful, you'll fall for the wrong part of that cocktail. Most things Merrick says seem logical on their surface; it's just the small twist of self-righteousness at the end that gets you.

"Helene, we have a relationship too good to walk out on, and you're such a wonderful, reasonable person, I know we can work this out. What happened with Chrissy wasn't what it looked like, but I'm sorry anyway that it hurt you. Come home so we can talk this through."

"Helene, I know that not getting that columnist job must've upset you. It was my fault that I didn't talk to you about your feelings, and things spiraled out of control. That's probably why you thought you saw Chrissy in my office and misinterpreted it; you were hurting, and your eyes deceived you. But that's okay, I understand and forgive you. Call me, okay?"

"Helene, where are you? Please, please call me. This isn't like you to run away. I don't know what you thought you saw, but Chrissy was just helping me pick something up that had fallen on the floor under my desk. You're such a levelheaded, positive person, I know I can help you see that it's better to drop the divorce stuff. Or else . . . Well, never mind that. Just come home, okay?"

Sure, Merrick. It's always me *who's being irrational. Thank god I have your vastly superior brain to help me understand what I saw with my own two eyes.*

And then there's the implicit threat in all his messages. *Or else.*

I roll my eyes. Or else *what?* He's going to send a ninja assassin team after me? Merrick is just a newspaper editor, not president of the United States. He's always had an inflated sense of self.

My phone rings again. I chuck it under the passenger seat. I have more important things to do.

As soon as I step out of my car, though, winter wallops me.

Good god, it's freezing! I zip up my coat (I'm wearing every single piece of long underwear and fleece that I own, all at once) and I button the snaps on the front of my hood until the only visible part of me is my eyes. Was it only a couple of days ago that I called Alaska a magical place with lacy frost woven by a snow maiden? How quickly the luster of newness tarnishes. I'd give anything for a dose of Southern California "winter" right now. I used to think seventy-three degrees was sweater weather.

But I'm here, so I march onward into the dark toward the lights in the harbor to look for Sebastien and the *Alacrity*.

The docks are already wide awake, boats bobbing on the sea while crews shout at one another about whatever it is that fishermen do.

The first boat is the *Crab Monster*, a beast of a ship. It's a towering gray behemoth with shark-sharp teeth painted on the bow. Attempts to talk to the crew are futile, though. They're too busy to be bothered by a random tourist wandering the dock.

The next few boats are equally unhelpful. Finally, I get five seconds of attention from a woman, in between her running from her ship to the dock for supplies.

"Excuse me," I yell over the shouting all around us. "Could you point me toward the *Alacrity*?"

She doesn't even bother with words, just points back toward the parking lot and grunts before she climbs the ladder back up to her crew.

I frown as I turn back in the direction I'd come from. I've checked every single fishing boat along the way. There was *Crab Monster*, *Salt Weapon*, *Filthy Oar*, *Lucifer*, *Chum Bucket*, and *Reel Adrenaline*. There were a few empty berths, too, but I figured those were just unrented slips. Unless . . .

My stomach sinks. What if the *Alacrity* already set off this morning?

But if the boat is gone, why would the woman point me this way?

I walk, and the answer appears beneath one of the harbor lights. A rusty sign announces Offices with a faded red arrow pointing toward the parking lot. There, a set of small trailers sit like afterthoughts to the powerful ships on the sea. The second one down is labeled Alacrity, and the lights are on.

I sigh. There's a chance Sebastien is inside, but I doubt it. He doesn't seem like the behind-a-desk type.

Still, I walk down there and knock on the door.

The office, if you can call it that, is cramped and stuffed to the gills with furniture and stacks of paper. A single floor lamp stands beside a file cabinet, both the kind you get for twenty dollars at Walmart. But there's reggae music playing from a pair of speakers, which lends an unexpectedly cheerful vibe to the trailer. And the man behind the desk is smiling like there's nothing more he wanted this morning than a would-be novelist stumbling into his office. It takes a little of the disappointment out of the very apparent fact that Sebastien isn't here.

"Hi," the man says, rising and offering his hand. "Adam Merculief. Can I help you?"

I wonder how out of place I must look, puffy as the Michelin Man in all of my cold-weather clothing piled on top of one another.

"Helene Janssen," I say, shaking with my glove on. It's probably rude, but my fingers are still frozen, and even from just a first impression, Adam doesn't seem like the type to be offended by something like that. "I'm, um, looking for Sebastien."

An amused grin spreads across Adam's face, and I briefly consider lying, using my original cover as a journalist for the reason I'm here.

But before I can spit out my fib about researching crab fishing, Adam says, "I didn't recognize you at first under that scarf and hood, but you were at The Frosty Otter a couple nights ago, weren't you?"

"What? No." I peel off my glove and fidget with it. "That was probably someone else."

Adam just keeps grinning. "It's a small town during the off-season, Helene. You're the only one in Ryba Harbor right now who doesn't live here year-round." He pushes a pink box of donuts across the desk to me, like atonement for finding me out.

I hesitate to take one. You know I'm in an anxious state of mind when I look at a glazed donut and think, *Is this some sort of trap?* instead of grabbing it immediately. But I'm on Sebastien's turf, and given how our last two encounters turned out, no one can blame me for being a little cautious.

"They're not poisonous," Adam says, laughing. He grabs a donut hole and pops it into his mouth. "Anyway, as I was saying, I remember you from The Frosty Otter. You walked by me, straight to Seabass, I mean, Sebastien. Right before he decided to bolt. What did you do to my usually unflappable captain, Helene?"

My cheeks flush hot, even though my teeth are still chattering from the cold. I don't know what to say; I didn't expect any of the *Alacrity*'s crew to recognize me. And I'm *definitely* not about to explain that I momentarily thought Sebastien was a character I wrote, come to life in the real world.

I take the coward's way out and cram the glazed donut into my mouth.

Adam laughs again, but not meanly, more like a concession of defeat. "All right, whatever's between you two, I'll let you keep it a secret. If you can shake him up like that, I'm all for it. He needs a woman in his life to challenge him."

"Uh-uh." I swallow the mouthful of donut as fast as I can so I can defend myself. "I don't have a thing for Sebastien. You're reading me wrong."

"Am I?" Adam studies me from across the desk.

"Absolutely. A thousand percent."

"Hmm."

"Hmm what?"

Adam looks at me a little longer, then smiles and shakes his head. "It's just that, when Sebastien mentioned you this morning—"

"He mentioned me?" I lean too eagerly over the desk and immediately loathe myself for it. I'm supposed to hate Sebastien. I shouldn't care if he's thinking about me or talking about me or making voodoo dolls of me and hammering pins into them.

My too-fervent interest isn't lost on Adam, though, and he just raises an eyebrow at me, as if to say that my actions are enough proof on their own.

Leave it to Sebastien to have infuriatingly smug friends.

I exhale. Loudly. "Okay, I'm going to go now. Thanks for the donut." I reach for the door.

"Helene, wait. He left these for you. Said you might stop by." Adam digs in the top desk drawer and holds out *The Craft of Novel Writing* to me, as well as the other two books I'd intended to buy.

I frown at them. "H-how did he know I'd come here?"

Adam shrugs. "Like I said, whatever's going on between the two of you, I'll let you keep that secret. All I know is Seabass looked pretty beat up this morning. He might seem tough on the outside, but that's a dog that's been kicked too many times in his life. Makes him skittish. Be gentle with him, okay, Helene?"

"I—"

"And if you want to see him, the *Alacrity* ought to be pulling back up to the docks about now. They went to get bait, but my nephew forgot something in his truck, so they're stopping back here for just a few minutes before they head to sea."

Adam puts the books in my hands and nods encouragement, his previous mirth gone. "Sebastien's a good man. Don't break his heart."

Part of me wants to leave now that I have *The Craft of Novel Writing* back, but part of me is curious about what Adam said. So I head down to the docks again, promising myself I'm just going to peek at Sebastien to prove that Adam's wrong about him being a good guy. Maybe I'll catch him yelling at his crew, being a tyrant of a captain. One quick look, and then I'll be done with him.

The *Alacrity* is in one of the berths that was previously empty. It's a tank of a ship—I suppose it has to be, in order to withstand the winter storms on the ocean—but the hull is painted a tranquil cerulean like the tropical waters of Hawaii. Not what I expected of a crab boat.

I stand in the shadow of a nearby storage shed so the crew can't see me. A lot's going on on the *Alacrity*—rigging and nets moving around, men jogging back and forth to secure the enormous crab traps, other stuff I can't understand.

But then a solitary tenor cuts through the frantic shouting, singing the opening notes of what sounds like a sea shanty. The man to whom the voice belongs comes into view.

It's Sebastien.

His tone is clear and sonorous as he sings the first refrain. It carries in the chill morning air, and just like in The Frosty Otter, his voice rumbles low in my belly. I'm weak in the knees at the sound of it—so cliché, and yet undeniably true—and I have to lean on the storage shed to stay standing.

All around me, though, Sebastien's voice seems to have the opposite effect. Calm descends on the harbor, first as the *Alacrity*'s crew picks up the second verse of the shanty, and then as the men and women of the other crabbing boats join in. Soon the entire port is a swell of sailor song and camaraderie, and I get another weird sense of déjà vu, until I realize that what I think I'm remembering is actually a vignette I wrote a long time ago, a World War II story about a different captain, in a different port—Pearl Harbor.

Jack hums a sea shanty as he admires himself in the mirror in his new lieutenant uniform. He was top of his class at Annapolis and joined the navy as an ensign straight after graduation, and now he's received his second promotion just a couple of years into his service. Sure, it's a little easier to rise in the ranks right now because of the war, but it's not that easy. The United States is still a neutral party, sitting on the sidelines while the rest of the world dukes it out. Promotions have to be earned, and Jack nods proudly at the new bars on the collar of his shirt and the stripes on his jacket.

One of his fellow officers, Darren, knocks on the door and sticks his head in. "Preening like a peacock, Jacky boy?"

Jack laughs, grabs a pillow off his bunk, and hurls it at him. "You're just jealous."

Darren catches the pillow and flings it back. "Jealous that you have more responsibility now? No, thank you, sir. I'm happy as a clam as a low-ranking CO. I'm telling you, it's only a matter of time before we get dragged into this war, and when that happens, I prefer to have fewer men's lives on my conscience."

Jack makes a face. "That's a strange attitude for someone from a navy family."

"It's because of my family's long history in the navy that I have that perspective. It's called wisdom." Darren taps his head solemnly, but he's grinning like a kid who's just set off fireworks on his neighbor's lawn.

Regardless, Jack answers seriously. "Well, I don't intend to let any of my men die."

"That's why we all love you so," Darren says. "It's your earnestness and charming naivete."

Jack is, however, far from naive. He'd already seen too much death before he ever stepped foot in the hallowed halls of the United States Naval Academy, before he reported to duty here at Pearl Harbor. But no one knows that except him. There are some wounds that are too raw and painful for a man to share, so Jack swallows them whole and keeps them buried there.

"Anyway," Darren says, "I came by to let you know that there's a party in town tonight. Live music, stiff drinks, pretty girls . . . whaddya say? Want to get off the base?"

"I don't think so," Jack says. He's broken quite a few Hawaiian hearts in the two years he's been stationed here, and he needs a little break from their crying, which inevitably happens when the girls he kisses want more than he can give.

"Come on, what better plans can you possibly have?"

"I think I'll spend a quiet evening in, reading a book."

Darren shakes his head. "You're wasting the superpower that that uniform—and those fancy new lieutenant stripes—grants you. All you have to do is walk into the bar tonight, and half of Honolulu will swoon for you. Hell, you could take all of them to bed at once if you wanted."

But Jack doesn't want it. One-night stands are the equivalent of vodka shots—you feel good in the moment, but then you're left hungover and feeling hollower than when you started.

"Thanks for the invitation," he says, "but really, I'm staying in tonight."

"You're like an eighty-year-old man in the body of a . . . how old are you anyway?"

Jack shrugs. "What does it matter? I thought you just said I was a comic book hero. Superman's around thirty and immortal at the same time."

Darren chuckles. "You're a curmudgeon, that's what you are. I bet under that fancy uniform you've got on a cardigan, not Superman's cape."

"I'm okay with that." Jack laughs. "Never thought I'd look good in tights anyway."

"Well, if you change your mind about tonight, we'll be at the Tiki Tiki Lounge. See you later, old man." Darren salutes, half in jest, and disappears down the barracks hall.

Jack admires his new lieutenant bars in the mirror one more time, then grabs his hat and heads for the door. If he's going to stay in and read tonight, he better swing by the library before it closes.

He wanders through the three fiction shelves, hoping to find something new. The naval base's library isn't the most impressive of collections, since most of the men prefer drinking to reading in their spare time, but Jack has, on occasion, managed to find a few gems here.

"Excuse me," Jack says to the librarian. Her back is to him, but as far as he can tell, she's the only one in the room.

She turns around, and the instant their eyes meet, a sweet shiver runs through him, and he can't move.

"You'll catch flies with your mouth hanging open like that, Lieutenant." She laughs as she sets down her stack of books. Her name tag reads Rachel Wilcox. She's definitely new; Jack would have noticed her before if she wasn't.

Rachel wears a blue dress patterned with tiny white polka dots, cinched at the waist by a matching belt. There's sass in the swing of her hips, and a teasing condescension in her tone, as if she, too, knows all too well that the men on this base prefer breasts over books. As if she suspects that Jack is just another soldier who got lost in the library on the way to the bus downtown.

Jack pulls himself together and stops gawking. "I, uh, came to return this book," he says, pulling a paperback out of his jacket pocket. "And I was hoping some new novels might have come in, but it looks like the same stuff as last week." He gestures at the fiction shelves.

"Surely there's something there you can read," Rachel says with a teasing glint in her eyes.

"I could," Jack says, "but unfortunately I'm not in the mood to reread anything, and I've already gone through all these books. I am, you may be surprised to find out, actually literate."

Rachel laughs, and the sound is light as a tropical breeze through coconut trees. "Come with me, then. I have a book in the back you'll like. Someone just dropped off a box of donations."

"How do you know I'll like it?"

"Because you seem rather pleased with yourself, and the novel I'm thinking of is all about a very self-congratulatory man and the adventures he goes on."

"Ouch," Jack says, but at the same time, his cheeks and ears grow hot. "I promise I'm not usually this proud. It's just that I was promoted this morning."

She laughs again. "It's okay. Hubris doesn't look good on most men, but it suits you, Lieutenant."

"Please, call me Jack."

"Actually, I think I prefer to call you nothing at all. Calling you boys by name is the first step in getting hooked. And from there, it's simply a reeling in of the line and I'm just another trophy on your wall."

"I don't want to make you into a trophy."

"And I don't want to be one. So there, we're in agreement. Shall we go find your book now?" Rachel smiles, revealing one cute little dimple on her right cheek.

And it turns out that she had it backward, because it's not Jack who reels her in. It's Rachel—and her mischievous dimple—that catches Jack. Hook, line, and sinker.

A LANKY TEENAGER sprints past me, jolting me from my story. He clutches a small, spiral-bound notepad in one hand—I am instantly fond of him, because I know the importance of always having a notebook around—and then he scurries up the ladder onto the *Alacrity*.

Meanwhile, Sebastien's sea shanty comes to an end, and I swear that if an entire harbor could smile, this is what it would feel like. A swell of affection for Sebastien washes over me despite the fact that I'm only here because he stole my books. Maybe I'm feeling this way because of his song. Or maybe I'm projecting the warm fuzzies from Lieutenant Jack's story onto Sebastien. All I know is that, at least for this moment, I'm not mad at him.

Sebastien comes into view at the stern of the ship, a bottle of wine in hand. The rising sun silhouettes him in soft orange light, and even though he's wearing heavy layers, I can still see the strength and confident elegance in the way he moves. I can also see the adoration of his crew as they gather around him, all their attention on their captain.

"To merciful weather, a propitious catch, and the finest crabbers I could have the honor to sail with!" Sebastien says.

"Huzzah!" the men shout.

Sebastien pulls the cork from the bottle and splashes wine on the deck. Then he passes the bottle to the rest of the crew, and each member pours a blessing onto the boat.

Here on the *Alacrity*, Sebastien is entirely different from the man who was so awful to me. Despite my previous determination to hate him, I can't help but see some of my Story Sebastien in this real one.

As if he feels me watching, Sebastien sweeps the dock with his gaze. I try to duck, but his eyes find mine first.

Instantly, sweetness blossoms on my tongue, like nostalgia and love distilled into warm, honeyed wine. I gasp at the taste, which is both familiar and not.

Then I remember. I tasted the same sweetness at The Frosty Otter, but I'd thought it was just a unique signature of the micro-brew Betsy had served me. And I think the same flavor brushed my lips in Shipyard Books, except I'd been too distracted over crashing into Sebastien to notice.

I feel like maybe I've tasted this before Alaska, too.

How?

Sebastien presses his fingers to his mouth and closes his eyes, just for a moment, as if savoring it.

Does he taste the honey wine, too?

I fall a little bit in love with the possibility, and a little bit under the spell of this man who entrances an entire port with his song, who knew before I did that I'd come to the harbor for my books, whom I somehow feel tethered to, even though we just met.

I wish I could climb up the ladder onto the *Alacrity*. I wish I could ask Sebastien what this is all about. Because I suspect he knows a lot more than he's letting on, that maybe that's the reason he's pushing me away.

But when he opens his eyes, all I do is hold up *The Craft of Novel Writing* and mouth, "Thank you."

He gives me the saddest look I think I've ever seen on a man, and nods. Only once.

And then he turns and gives the orders to raise anchor and set sail.

SEBASTIEN

A WEEK LATER, AND I STILL CAN'T STOP THINKING ABOUT HER.

The dark sky is a ghoul's cloak, it's twenty degrees below zero with wind chill, and the *Alacrity* lurches violently across the rough waters. I should be paying better attention to my crew, to the difficulty we're having setting the crab traps, to the fact that we're seven days into this trip and the haul thus far is inversely proportional to the effort we've put out just to survive the stormy sea.

But my thoughts keep coming back to Helene.

"Captain?" Colin hangs in the doorway of the wheelhouse, peering at me like maybe this wasn't the first time he called my name. How long has he been standing there while I stare out the window at the ocean?

"What's up, Merculief?" I say, pretending like everything is fine.

"Piñeros sent me to tell you there's a cot available. He said he can take over steering if you want to get some shut-eye."

I wave off the suggestion. I know I won't be able to sleep, so another member of my crew ought to take advantage of it instead. "I'm good. Let someone else have the cot."

"You sure?" Colin asks. "Because you look like—"

I fix him with a hard stare, and it stops whatever he was going to say like a deer during hunting season. It's not fair of me, but I can't help it. I'm high strung and I need him out of my wheelhouse.

"Right," he says. "Anything I can get you while I'm here?"

"A way to stop the cycle," I mumble.

"Sorry, sir?"

"Nothing," I say. "Actually, I could use some caffeine."

"You got it, Captain." Colin ducks out of the doorway to follow orders.

A few minutes later, he brings a fresh pot of coffee, then leaves me be.

Alone with a tempestuous sea and thoughts just as turbulent.

Juliet

    Juliet

        Juliet . . .

PEARL HARBOR NAVAL BASE, HAWAII – OCTOBER 1941

"Excuse me," I say to the librarian in the blue dress with white polka dots. Her back is to me, but as far as I can tell, she's the only one in the room. "I'm returning this book, and—"

She turns around, and the instant our eyes meet, the familiar shock of honeyed wine brushes my lips.

My jaw drops and I can't move.

It's her.

"You'll catch flies with your mouth hanging open like that, Lieutenant." She laughs as she sets down her stack of books and walks toward me, hips swinging, skirt swishing. I'm hypnotized by the motion. Only when she's right in front of me do I manage to snap my mouth closed.

Her name tag reads Rachel Wilcox.

"You're new," I whisper.

"Started just this morning." She smiles, and the small library suddenly seems warm, bathed full of golden light; the effect of Juliet's smiles on me never wanes.

I tug at my collar, which now feels as if it's starched too stiffly.

"I, er, was hoping some new novels might have come in." I motion at the fiction shelves.

"Surely there's something there you can read," Rachel says.

"I could, but unfortunately I've already gone through all these books. I am, you may be surprised to find out, actually literate."

Rachel laughs again, and the sound is light as a tropical breeze through coconut trees. "Come with me, then. I have a book in the back you'll like. Someone just dropped off a box of donations."

And even though I know it would be better if I could get away, I don't want to. Sure, the curse brings an unhappy ending, but before that, there's always a timeless love, like Paris and Helen. Marc Antony and Cleopatra. Dante and Beatrice.

So when Rachel walks, I follow. She does, indeed, find me a splendid book.

The next week, she lets me take her to dinner. We go off base to a hole-in-the-wall place that serves authentic Hawaiian food: pork lau lau steamed in ti leaves, sour poi that makes Rachel's mouth pucker, and haupia, a rich coconut pudding, for dessert. Later, we stroll down Kapahulu Boulevard and she lets me take her hand.

The week after that, we drive up to the north shore of the island and watch local surfers ride towering waves over forty feet tall. The rise and crash of the water mesmerizes Rachel. And watching her mesmerizes me. When she concentrates, her lips purse, and when she's delighted—like when a surfer catches a particularly monumental wave—she lets out a tiny, smiling breath. The fifth time this happens, I can't resist anymore. I tilt her face toward mine and brush my mouth against hers, as sea spray mists over us and palm fronds rustle overhead.

"I'm sorry, I couldn't stop myself," I whisper.

She answers with that small, smiling exhale. "I don't want you to stop yourself," and she kisses me again.

Two weeks later, we are inseparable whenever I'm off duty. If she's working, I'm in the library, and she spends most evenings with me and the other sailors. I am terrible at billiards, but Rachel is a ringer, which my men—to their dismay—don't discover until after they've bet a night's worth of beers on a game against us. But she's abysmal at poker, so when that's the game of choice, Rachel lets me play while she does her best to bat her eyelashes at the other sailors to distract them from their cards. We always laugh about it afterward, dissecting the evening and whom her performance most affected.

On Saturdays, we rise early to go fishing with her entire family—mom, dad, four brothers, and Grampa Fred. We head out into the ocean on their boat and spend the morning reeling in mahi-mahi, and if we're lucky, a notoriously quick ono or a fatty opakapaka. With several lifetimes of seafaring experience under my belt, I'm usually the one to hook the prized fish. That wins me the immediate respect of Rachel's father and brothers, and Grampa Fred later does me honor by inviting me to help him grill and steam our catch. (On the other hand, Rachel, like all Juliets, can't cook, and is forbidden to come anywhere near the barbecue or kitchen.)

After dinner, her family gathers around the still glowing charcoal to play music. I can never remember chords, but Rachel and her brothers play ukuleles as if they were extensions of their fingers. Rachel can't sing, though—she did for me once, and true to her word, it sounded like dolphins crying—so she leaves the singing to me. Her mother teaches me the lyrics to their family's favorite songs, and I teach her some of my sailors' shanties.

It's blissful to be folded into a family. In my long life, I'm so often alone that I forget what it's like to belong like this. The weeks pass in a joyful fugue, and I almost forget that it's all too paradisical to last.

Until the reality of my existence comes roaring back—into my ears, my arms, my legs, every single cursed cell in my body.

On the morning of December 7, the Japanese blow up Pearl Harbor. Bombs scream down from the sky. Walls of smoke and flame rise like red-hot demons sent to brand us in pain. I am in my barracks one moment, but in the next, I'm swimming in the midst of a shipwreck, pulling men from the sinking hull. I hoist sailors onto my shoulders and drag them through water that seems on fire, setting them on flotsam to be retrieved by the rescue teams, while I swim back into the blazing ruins.

All but two of my command die that day.

When the attack ends, I finally collapse onshore.

After only a moment of respite, though, I summon the last dregs of willpower in me, and I stagger to the library.

I stop short where it ought to be.

For it is no longer a library, but a blackened shell of ash, nearly unidentifiable.

"Rachel?" I croak.

But she wouldn't have been here, would she? So early in the morning. Her shift didn't start till later . . .

Except she'd mentioned coming in before the library opened, to sort through several huge boxes of donations.

Scraps of paper—embers of former books—flutter through the gray air like doleful ticker tape. One scrap lands at my feet, right next to a name tag warped from the heat of a bomb. I can still make out most of the letters.

Rachel Wil—

I cry out and fall to my knees. I clutch the name tag, all that's left of her, and howl until my voice is raw and my throat bleeds, until my lungs are choked with smoke and ashes, and even then, I refuse to leave, refuse to get up from the skeleton of the library, from the final resting place of my love. I try to light myself on fire, to add my corpse to the grim pyre, but the wind blows out each of my matches, and then a drizzle starts to fall, and Pearl Harbor will not take me.

So I lie there until Rear Admiral Kimmel himself appears and pulls me from the smoldering remains of the library. And later, when President Roosevelt awards fifty-one men, including me, the Naval Cross for our extraordinary heroism in battle, I throw my medal into the Pacific.

Because I don't deserve it. I couldn't protect my crew. I couldn't protect Rachel.

The only thing I deserve to keep from Pearl Harbor is another somber reminder of my failures: the melted tag with her name.

SEBASTIEN

SHOUTS STARTLE ME AWAKE IN THE MIDDLE OF THE NIGHT. EXHAUSTION must've caught up with me. I'd fallen asleep at the wheel, and that never happens.

Fists pound at my door. "Man overboard! Man overboard!"

My heart leaps from my chest. I race out into the storm, slipping on the wet deck. Squalls with sleet batter the *Alacrity*, and fifty-foot waves slam into our hull. The crew already has the night lights blazing. I run over as fast as I can to Piñeros, who's at the railing.

"Who?" I shout over the storm.

"Merculief! Crab trap got loose, swung and hit him in the head."

For a nightmarish moment, I remember the accident that took out Adam's leg. The traps weigh eight hundred pounds each. And now a trap might be the reason another Merculief retires from the sea.

Shit. If Colin was hit in the head, he's likely unconscious in the raging ocean. This is much, much worse than Adam's leg.

"Where?" I yell.

Piñeros points some distance into the water. It's black with night and frothing like a rabid sea creature. Colin is nowhere in sight.

I strip off my jacket.

Piñeros's eyes bug in alarm. "What're you doing, Captain?"

"Going after Colin."

"You can't, sir! You'll drown."

"Hell if I'm leaving a man behind," I shout as sleet pummels my face. The memory of Pearl Harbor is still raw on my mind, and the thought of losing another crew member to the sea hollows me out inside. The only cure is action. I yank off my boots and survey the dark violence of the ocean. "Give me as much light as possible."

Piñeros hesitates for a second.

"Go!" I yell. I might be crazy, but my crew follows orders. Piñeros takes off to direct the night lights.

I dive over the railing.

Visibility is almost nil. The ocean churns, water like ice. I'm not invincible, but I know that if I pass out from the subzero temperatures tonight, my body will still somehow float up to the *Alacrity* so the crew can fish me out. The curse always finds a way to intervene, even when I try to die. That is usually a burden, but tonight, I am grateful for it.

Colin, however, will only survive a few minutes in conditions like this, and that's if he hasn't already been sucked under.

I would do anything for my men, but especially Colin. He's just a kid. And I promised Adam I'd keep his nephew safe.

Jones, another of the crew, shouts something through the bullhorn, but I can't understand him through the storm. Piñeros directs the spotlight, though.

There! I see Colin fifty yards away, his body a rag doll, the sea like a kraken tossing its prey back and forth on the savage waves.

I swim as hard as I can. The maw of the ocean attempts to swallow me whole, and I choke on the frigid saltwater that surges into my mouth and up my nose.

But I keep swimming.

The raging sea tries to prevent me from taking away its prize, pounding me again and again with everything it has. Icy water. Colossal waves. Sleet and wind and darkness, despite the *Alacrity*'s lights.

I grit my teeth. *You can't have him!* my mind yells at the ocean. I'm only a few yards away from Colin now.

The sea lashes at me, hurling needles of saltwater into my face. My eyes sting, I can't see. And for a few seconds, I lose my place, forget myself. I am back at Pearl Harbor, flailing, desperately trying to save sailors. Sirens shriek, and the air is thick with smoke. I swim and I swim, yet I am aware that my efforts are futile, that the men will drown, that I can't shield them from the greedy grip of death.

The ocean wallops me across my face, but ironically, it is this watery uppercut that wrests me from my past, back into the present. Perhaps I couldn't save everyone at Pearl Harbor, but today is not that day.

That boy belongs to me, *do you understand?* I snarl at the sea and fight my way closer to Colin.

His head goes under, and he begins to sink.

"No!" I swallow a mouthful, saltwater going up my nose, burning in the back of my throat. I ignore the sting and dive.

I cannot see a thing in the churning, Stygian blackness. All I know is the trajectory in which I dove, and the direction in which he sank. I kick as hard as I can.

And collide with Colin's limp, heavy body.

My arms latch around him immediately, and I propel us upward. As I break the surface and gasp for air, the ocean roars, furious at the theft I'm committing.

I battle through the seething waves, kicking with everything that's left in my legs. Close enough to the *Alacrity,* the crew throws a life preserver, and I lunge for it, nearly missing in my exhaustion.

Jones and the other two members of the crew—Hsu and Grunberg—haul me and Colin up. Just in time, too. My limbs go numb as we tumble onto the slick deck.

Grunberg immediately begins CPR on Colin. In our line of business, we all know the protocol for drowning. Unfortunately.

As I look at Colin, a surge of terror wells up in me, finally hitting now as the adrenaline of the rescue recedes. Colin is pale as a squid. His entire body lies limp as Grunberg forces breaths into him, alternating with pumping his chest. I can't look away, even as I vomit all over the deck.

Piñeros has already set course for the harbor, turning the *Alacrity* around. We'll have to fight the storm the whole way back.

Jones kneels beside me and drapes a heavy blanket around my shoulders. Hsu activates hand and body warmers from the first aid kit and places them on me. But we're all watching Grunberg and Colin.

Please don't die please don't die please don't die.

The chest compressions are sickening to listen to, Grunberg's hands hitting wet flesh, pushing over broken ribs. I convulse with every pump, as if I'm the one under each pounding compression.

I wish it *were* me. Colin is only eighteen. He has so much life left to live. I've already had enough—too much. What I wouldn't do to shave decades off my life to give to him.

Suddenly, Colin coughs, and what seems like a gallon of seawater spews from his lungs.

"Thank fucking god!" Hsu shouts as Grunberg sags next to Colin, checking the pulse on his wrist and confirming that, yes, our greenhorn is still alive.

Tears stream down my face—hell, we're all crying—but every man glances away from the others, giving each a moment to compose himself and pretend it was just sleet in his eyes. Crabbers are a gruff lot who wear their hearts under layers of armor, self-defense when your job involves constant danger and death. I have plenty of experience in locking up my feelings, too.

"Get Merculief warm and into a cot," I yell into the storm.

Hsu and Grunberg pick up Colin gingerly and disappear belowdecks.

Jones is still kneeling next to me. I'd thought he was paralyzed in place like I was, watching whether Colin would live or die, but now I realize Jones was also keeping an eye on me to make sure I was all right.

"We should get you down below, too," he says.

I nod. "Just . . . give me a minute."

"Sure, Captain. But . . . for what it's worth, I think what you did out there was incredible." Then Jones gets up, giving me a little space while staying close enough that he can run to my aid if I need it.

He's wrong about my behavior, though. It wasn't incredible. It was irresponsible.

My head drops into my hands.

I fell asleep at the wheel in the middle of a vicious squall, because I've been too preoccupied with Helene to get the rest I need. And because I wasn't paying attention and navigating the storm, Colin got knocked overboard. It was only luck that allowed me to save him. The sea could just as easily have swallowed him or otherwise left him for dead.

Colin deserves better than that. This whole crew deserves a captain who can focus on them, not on himself. And Helene deserves to live, to write her novel and follow her dreams without getting tangled up with me.

Jones returns. "Come on, Captain. Let's get you belowdecks. There's a hot shower and a cot with your name on it."

I let him help me up. But my legs aren't just unsteady from the effort expended rescuing Colin. They're also shaking because I know what I have to do next.

If I can't get rid of Helene, I have to take myself out of the equation. I have to leave Alaska.

HELENE

"HE DOVE INTO THE OCEAN?" KATY SAYS THROUGH THE PHONE. "IN Alaska? In the middle of winter?" She's as much a California girl as I am, and it's a completely alien idea that anyone would even step foot near the ocean if it's less than eighty degrees outside.

"It's the only thing people here have been able to talk about for the last three days," I say as I flip the sign on the door of Shipyard Books to Closed. "The mayor of Ryba Harbor came into the store today and was telling her friends about the parade she'd wanted to throw in Sebastien's honor, but I guess he turned it down."

Katy snorted. "I'd thought an arrogant asshole like that would *want* everyone fawning all over him."

"I don't know that he *is* an arrogant asshole." As I slip behind the counter to close out the register for the evening, I remember how the whole harbor sang that sea shanty with him. "Everyone here loves Sebastien. And they say he wouldn't leave his crew member's side at the hospital until he knew the kid would be okay. Maybe Sebastien just doesn't get along with me, specifically."

"You *did* come on kinda strong," Katy says. "You tried to jump him your first night there."

"That isn't how it happened."

"Maybe it should've, though." Katy's phone chirps. "Oh hey, Mom just texted. Wanna hop on a video chat with her?"

I smile. I'm lucky that my mom and sister are my best friends. The three of us talk almost every day. "Yeah, sure," I say. "Just give me a few minutes to close up here."

"Okay, call us when you're done." Katy hangs up.

I tidy up the children's play table, lingering for a minute over *Naming Ceremony*, the picture book I read to a group of adorable little girls earlier. They were just beginning to toddle and were still young enough to smell of milk and baby lotion, and their delight in every single thing in the book just lit me up inside.

Being with them made my heart twinge a little, knowing that I might never have a baby of my own. But mostly, their bubbling laughter, the soft clapping of their hands, and the pureness of their curiosity filled me with a peaceful kind of joy. Maybe even after this job is over, I can volunteer to come in and read stories to them.

Once the kids' area is cleaned up, I head into the back room and haul a box of new shipments onto the worktable so I can log the books into the system. Angela comes back from Arizona tomorrow, and I want to make sure everything is organized and in tip-top shape for her return.

I dial Mom and Katy.

"Hi, sweethearts!" My mom, Beth, grins into the camera. In fact, all I can see is her grin.

"Back the iPad up a bit," Katy says. "I'm getting an extreme close-up of your chin hairs."

"I thought you liked my chin hairs," Mom says, adjusting the camera so we can see her face. (Well, two-thirds of it. "I'm chrono-tech challenged," Mom likes to say, which really means "I'm too old to care about getting the perfect framing and lighting, and you are my daughters, so you'll love whatever part of my face you get.")

"You don't even have chin hairs, Mom," I say.

"Yes, but if I did, you'd tell me they looked good, wouldn't you?" She winked. "So, Katy was just catching me up via text on the latest antics of Storybook Hero."

"He's not my storybook hero." I really regret telling them that Sebastien looks like the guy I'd cast in my head for all the vignettes I'd written.

"That's right, he's not Storybook Hero anymore," Katy says to Mom. "Remember? We changed his name to Sebastien McSwoon."

"We did not!" I say.

"Mom and I did."

"Mom!"

She shrugs. "Sebastien McSwoon was better than Prince Bodacious."

I groan. "Why do I even talk to you two?" I grab the pocket knife off the table and slash open the box of new shipments.

"Sorry, sweetheart," Mom says. "Let's talk about something else. How's the novel coming along?"

"Mrph."

"What does 'mrph' mean?"

I sigh and slump into a chair. "I don't know what I'm doing wrong. I've spent the last week and a half on that craft of writing book, and I understand what it's telling me, but it's not helping at all."

"Well you've only just begun," Mom says. "Maybe it takes practice. I know you've written short stories since you were in middle school, but a whole novel is a different beast. Be patient with yourself. Katy and I both know how talented you are. It'll come together."

"That's the problem. It isn't the craft of writing. It's . . . the story itself." I poke at the box in front of me. "You know when you have a sixth sense about something? I feel that way about these vignettes. There's a reason I wrote all of them. Like, there's some way to stitch them together into a single, cohesive story. I just don't know what the answer is."

"They're historical, right?" Mom asks. "How about a time travel novel?"

I shake my head. "I don't think so. You know I love sci-fi, but this doesn't feel like that kind of book to me."

"Oooh!" Katy leans into the camera. "What about an ancient witch's recipe for a love potion that's passed down through the ages? Maybe your vignettes are what happens whenever a couple gets their hands on the witchy elixir."

I make a noncommittal noise. I haven't been an aspiring novelist for long, but I have a feeling this happens a lot: well-meaning friends and family trying to brainstorm for them, but coming up way short of the mark.

"Or perhaps," Mom says, "you're overthinking it. You're isolating yourself to write, but you're not taking advantage of what's around you."

"The arctic weather?" I say sarcastically.

"No, sweetheart. You know I believe that everything happens for a reason. Why did you end up in Alaska? Perhaps your answer is out there"—she points offscreen—"instead of in your head."

"Maybe." But I smile, because even though Mom's and Katy's ideas didn't help, I appreciate them trying.

My three-year-old nephew, Trevor, jogs into view next to Katy. I start waving emphatically at him, because he is my favorite kid ever. He doesn't notice me, though.

"Mama?" he says to Katy. "I bring booger for you." He holds it out like a treasure he's mined just for her.

She doesn't miss a beat. "Wow, thanks, buddy. But you know what? You've given Mama so many boogers already. I think Daddy needs one. You want to go give it to him instead?"

Trevor studies the booger on his finger, as if determining whether the quality of this particular prize would suit his dad.

"You no want it?" he asks Katy, puzzled. "Is a good one."

"Law of diminishing returns, bud. Tell Daddy that's why I'm sending it to him. He's more booger-deprived than I am."

Trevor looks skeptically at her, then wanders off. In the background, we hear him shouting, "Dada? Mama says this boogie for you because law mimishing return."

Mom and I burst into laughter.

Katy smirks. "I love that kid, but I am *really* looking forward to a few weeks in Amsterdam and Cannes with you, Hel. I think I'll pass out from shock when a waiter comes over, serving something other than boogers. So get that novel done, okay? I want to live it up in Europe."

"Yes, ma'am," I say, still laughing over sweet little Trevor. "Anyway, I should probably go. I have to process this box of new books that came in."

"We love you very much," Mom says. "Call us tomorrow?"

"Wouldn't miss it."

We exchange air kisses and hang up. The happy afterglow from talking to Mom and Katy lingers like a rosy cumulus cloud around me, and I tackle the box with vigor.

Processing the new shipment is pretty straightforward. I find the order on Angela's computer and mark it as received, then set the books into two piles: for the shelves or for a specific customer. If it's the latter, I print out the invoice and wrap it around the book with a rubber band, then write the customer's last name along the spine—where the invoice covers it, not on the book itself—in Sharpie in all caps.

I get through the box quickly. It's seven o'clock when I have one book left, perfect timing for the end of my shift.

My stomach flips.

The novel is *The First Fifteen Lives of Harry August*. Ordered by Sebastien.

My hands shake as I wrap the invoice around the book and write his last name along the spine.

M O N T A G U E.

How did I not know his last name before?

It didn't occur to me to ask. I was too wrapped up in my own drama—still focused on him as the many characters I'd invented—instead of seeing Sebastien as a real person with his own identity. But now I stare at the Sharpied spine of the book.

Montague Montague Montague.

I first imagined him as Romeo Montague in eighth grade.

This has to be a coincidence.

Lots of girls obsess over Romeo and Juliet when they're younger, right?

And maybe Montague is a common last name.

Just because I made up an imaginary friend in my head to play Romeo, and just because he looks exactly like Sebastien, and just because both their last names are Montague, and just because he touched his lips at the harbor at the same moment I tasted honey and wine on mine . . . doesn't *have* to mean anything.

But it also could.

Mom says everything happens for a reason. I'm not exactly sure what the universe is trying to tell me, but I know this: I am standing here holding a book that Sebastien ordered, with his address printed on the invoice.

Brave New Helene steps up to the task—I'm going to hand deliver this book to his house.

The drive takes forever, because Sebastien lives in the boonies—which is saying a lot, since Ryba Harbor is already pretty isolated. Plus it's dark, the roads twist and wind, and it's started to snow. I've never driven in the snow before. God help me.

Forty-five minutes into what's supposed to be an hour trip, I glance over at the map on my phone to check that I'm still going in the right direction. The navigation assistant hasn't spoken to me in a while.

The map screen, however, is frozen on the location from fifteen minutes ago. A rainbow wheel graphic spins in the center of the screen, and the bars at the top show there's no signal whatsoever out here.

That explains why I haven't heard any directions recently.

Fantastic.

I must be going the right way, though. There hasn't been a fork in the road in several miles. I look away from my phone and back on the road. It takes a moment for my eyes to readjust to the dim headlights.

A looming shadow suddenly appears up ahead. I yank the wheel to follow the curve of the asphalt and hope it's just a tree—

Fuck! A moose! It charges onto the road, over six feet of muscle and fur and antlers.

I scream and swerve. The tires skid, and I slam on the brakes, which is probably exactly the wrong thing to do. The steering wheel refuses to help, and I spin out, the whole world a blur of winter white.

My car smashes into a snowbank. The air bag smacks into my chest and face.

"Shit," I moan when the airbag deflates. That really fucking hurt. In a daze, I irrationally try to stuff the air bag back into the steering wheel before I realize what I'm doing.

As my brain gets back online, I wrinkle my nose. The air has an electrical burn stink to it, related to the air bag deployment, I guess.

My vision clears, too. Through the windshield, the moose bellows and glares at me.

I lean on the horn. "Yeah, well, screw you, too!"

Pretty sure the moose rolls its eyes at my petulance. It crosses the road and abandons me.

I hate driving in the snow.

When I finally get my breathing under control, I take stock of my body. Other than the rude revelation of impact, I seem to be okay. No bleeding, no sharp pain of broken bones, only a little ache in the left ankle.

My next instinct is to grab my phone and call for help. It's fallen to the floor, and I have to scramble over the gearshift to get to it.

But once I have it, I groan. Right. No cell service.

Somehow I manage to shove open the car door, sending a cascade of snow onto my lap right as I try to step out. The headlights crook at a sixty-degree angle, shining into the trees instead of level on the ground. The hood belches out a hiss of steam.

"Wonderful," I mutter. I can see the headline now: "Promising Novelist Found Frozen in Alaskan Tundra: Bones Picked Clean by Wolves. Moose Laughs at Her Demise."

Buck up, Janssen, I tell myself. *You're not going to die in front of a jeering moose tonight.*

Unfortunately, I'm going to have to walk the rest of the way to Sebastien's.

I thought fate would look prettier than this.

The snow falls faster.

I swear at fate under my breath. Then I grab my purse and Sebastien's book and limp down the road.

SEBASTIEN

SHE SWEEPS IN ON THE COATTAILS OF A SNOW FLURRY, AND THERE'S nothing I can do about it. One moment there's a knocking at my door. The next, I'm gawking at her face. And then all of a sudden, she's in my house, this sanctuary that's supposed to be mine alone but she has now, somehow, breached. My palms turn clammy at her closeness, my breathing running double time with her so unexpectedly near.

"H-Helene," I stutter as we stand just inside the front door. She looks like a snowplow swallowed her, then spat her back out. "What are you doing here?"

"I, um, was working at the bookstore. And the novel you ordered came in." She fumbles in her bag and pulls out *The First Fifteen Lives of Harry August*. "Surprise?"

As if that explains what she's doing at my house. At this hour. After everything that happened on the *Alacrity* and spending the last few days at the hospital with Colin and Adam and their families, the last thing I am capable of dealing with is Helene and the curse.

Seeming to sense my unease, she adds, "Don't worry, I'm not trying to jump you or anything. I get that you're not interested. But I just thought I'd bring you your book, as thanks for returning mine."

The thought of her jumping me—of her body on mine—sends my pulse racing even faster than it already is. This can't be happening. *Shouldn't* be happening. I have to get ahold of my faculties, take back control of this night.

To distract myself, I frown at the book in her hand. The blue jacket is creased at the corners, and the binding is damp. I'm particular about the condition of my books. Even the ones I keep in my coat remain in mint condition; they look better that way on the shelf, after I'm finished reading.

But then I look over at Helene and notice she's putting all her weight on her right leg, while her left foot is cocked up off the tiles. And the beginning of a bruise is forming on her cheek.

Worry overtakes my other emotions. "Are you hurt?"

"I might have crashed my car into a snowbank."

"What? Why didn't you lead with that?" I usher her inside.

I know this is a terrible idea. But what else am I going to do? Turn her out into the night, injured and without a way to get back into town? There are bears and wolves out there, and my house is the only one for three miles in any direction, and Ryba Harbor is an hour away. In *good* weather. From the looks of it out there, a blizzard's coming in.

It'll be all right, I tell myself. I'm leaving Alaska on the first flight out tomorrow morning. I have a ticket and a plan. Piñeros will be a great captain in my place, and my lawyer will take care of transferring my half of the *Alacrity*'s ownership to Adam. A professional moving crew will pack up my belongings here and put them in storage for me. I can handle giving Helene a little first aid, calling a tow truck, and sending her on her way.

I lead her into the living room, self-conscious of how indulgent it appears: exposed wooden beams, a picture window with views of the snow-dusted landscape, a wrought-iron chandelier made to look like antlers. There are overstuffed leather couches, flannel throw blankets, and a stone fireplace at full blaze. But it isn't ego that drove me to build a house like this; it's just that my existence consists mostly of waiting for Juliet to arrive and then losing her again. Having a comfortable home is the small solace I allow myself in a life defined by going without.

But now she's here, in my private retreat, and I don't know how to handle it.

"Whoa," Helene says as she takes in the living room. "This is like a five-star lodge in a glossy travel magazine. I didn't know crab fishermen made that much money." But as soon as the words are out of her mouth, her hand flutters up to cover the faux pas. "Oh god. I didn't mean to say that out loud."

"It's fine," I say, sparing her. Crab fishermen do make good money, but not *this* good. But I don't want to talk about where my money comes from, because that would mean either lying or explaining how someone amasses wealth over centuries. And I definitely don't want to do the latter.

"Sit anywhere you like. I'll get the first aid kit."

Helene looks at me like I'm speaking a foreign language. I do a quick mental check—I *was* speaking English, right? I've been known to accidentally switch from one language to another sometimes, usually when there's a word or concept that's more accurately expressed in another tongue. Like descriptions of snow in the Sami languages of the Nordic. Or the adjective for the chewy, bouncy quality of noodles in Mandarin.

But no, I'm certain I spoke to Helene in English.

"Sorry," she says, "I was just caught off guard with you being nice to me." She's still standing on that one leg, like she doesn't believe I'll actually let her sit down.

It's your own fault, I remind myself.

Nevertheless, I snap at her, because maybe it'll be a little easier to leave Alaska if she detests me. "It's just common courtesy to help someone who shows up at your door after a car wreck. That's all." Then I rush out of the room before I can see the inevitable disgust on her face at the way I'm treating her.

The worst part is, it hurts to be hated by her. I *want* to help Helene, I *want* to throw myself into her path. Every fiber of my being wants it.

Desperately.

No. Patch her up, get her a ride back into town, and be done with it.

It's for her own good. For mine, too.

I go into the bathroom first and grab the first aid kit and a roll of adhesive bandage wrap, in case her ankle is the problem. Then I veer into the kitchen and put on a pot of coffee, because even if I'm trying to get rid of Helene, I can't bear being so cruel as to not offer her something hot to drink after she's been out limping through the snow for who knows how long.

While the coffee's brewing, I use my landline to call the only tow company in Ryba Harbor. I don't own a cellphone, and the signal out here is nonexistent anyway.

"Hello?"

"Hey, Ron, it's Sebastien Montague."

"Sebastien! I'd say I always like hearing from you, but if you're calling this number, it's 'cause you're in some trouble."

"Not me, someone else," I say as I open the liquor cabinet and reach for a bottle of Bailey's. I could use a shot in my coffee, and I suspect Helene could, too. "She crashed into a snowbank near my house and needs a tow and ride back to town. I know it's a trek for you, but I'm happy to pay for the round trip."

"Sorry, man, wish I could help you out," Ron says. "But didn't you see the news? Blizzard's bearing down fast. Wasn't even on the weather report an hour ago. Stupid fuckers over at the Weather Channel don't know shit. Downtown's already blanketed, and the roads out in your direction are being closed as we speak."

"Are you serious?"

"As the dead," Ron says. His analogies, as usual, make little sense. But his knowledge of road conditions is impeccable.

"How long till driving's possible?" Maybe I can take Helene in my truck, and Ron can extract her car from the snowbank later.

"This storm's gonna be a bad one, man. You might be snowed in for two, three days out there in the sticks."

Fantastic. There go my plans for getting Helene out of my house. And for me taking that flight out of Anchorage tomorrow morning, leaving Alaska behind.

I grab a bottle of vodka off the shelf and knock back a slug, even though I'm not ordinarily a fan of plain shots of vodka. Bailey's, however, wouldn't be strong enough.

What am I going to do?

Think, think, think.

All right. My house is big, so that will help. I can put Helene in the guest suite, which has its own kitchenette. We can probably stay out of each other's way for a few days. Then when the roads open, I'll drop Helene off in town and drive straight to the airport to get on whatever flight will take me away from her. The important thing is not allowing her to know me, to connect with me. If I can keep her despising me, maybe the curse will stay at bay. Then Helene can live.

Ron starts talking again. I'd forgotten he was still on the phone, that I still had the handset to my ear.

"I'll give you a ring when the roads open again, okay, man?"

"Yeah, okay. Thanks." I hang up and take another shot of vodka.

When the coffee finishes brewing, I load a tray with the Bailey's, the coffeepot, and mugs, and I tuck the first aid kit under my arm.

Helene is settled on one of the leather couches, under a blanket, her left foot propped up on the armrest. She's cast off her jacket, hat, gloves, boots, and socks on the ledge in front of the fireplace to dry, and she doesn't hear me coming, so I have a moment to study her—the way her hair cascades over the soft lines of her face. The faraway yet intelligent sharpness in her eyes as she thinks about something that isn't here. The subtle curve of her mouth that makes me want to skim my lips against hers.

Stop it.

I clear my throat to break the spell. Helene startles out of her thoughts.

"Drinks," I say as I set the tray down on the coffee table. Short sentences provide less room for error.

She sits up and winces.

"Ankle?" I ask.

"I think so."

Against my better judgment, I sit down on the coffee table across from her. "Put your foot up here. Let me take a look at it."

Helene doesn't move right away. I've definitely flummoxed her by being hot one minute and cold the next. Mostly cold.

But she needs help, and no matter how much I want to push her away, I'm not going to deny her medical attention.

Instead of putting her foot on the coffee table, though, she sets it on my knee.

I recoil involuntarily. Not because I don't want to touch her, but because I *shouldn't*.

Helene misinterprets my reaction. "Oh god, does it stink?" She immediately retracts her leg. "My foot stinks, doesn't it? Argghhh, this is not going well at all."

"You smell fine," I say gruffly. I pick up her leg and set her foot on my knee again; however, I make sure I only touch her jeans, not her skin. It's a compromise, a half touch. "Can you move your ankle around?"

Helene tries to rotate it, but she flinches. "Ooh, not good."

"Is the pain over the ankle bone, or the soft part?"

"The soft part, I guess? Hard to tell."

I squeeze her ankle cautiously.

As soon as my fingertips meet her skin, a surge of heat washes over me. It's what I'd wanted to avoid, but now, touching her, I'm suddenly drunk on the feeling of sunshine, even though it's the middle of the night.

I draw in a sharp breath. But I can't let go of Helene. I don't want to.

I tell myself I'm holding on because someone has to wrap her ankle to give it stability. She won't be able to see a doctor for days, until the roads clear.

My fingers are clumsy, overwhelmed by being so close to her. And when I finally finish with the wrap, I hold on to her for a few seconds longer than necessary. My pulse trips over itself.

I have to put distance between us again. Not only physical, but emotional, too. I set her foot on the coffee table and all but sprint to one of the leather armchairs on the other side of the living room.

"Thank you for wrapping my ankle," she says.

"I only did it because I need you mobile," I say, letting the former iciness settle into my tone again. "I don't want to be your servant while you're stuck here."

Helene cringes at the return of brusqueness. But she recovers quickly and asks, "What do you mean, 'while you're stuck here'?"

"Oh, I forgot to tell you," I say, as if I couldn't care less what she does and doesn't know. "The tow truck isn't running because the roads are closed, due to an incoming blizzard. It might be a few days."

I think she might scowl at me now, or tell me off. She'd be justified.

But instead, Helene pours a hefty slug of Bailey's into her coffee and says, "Perfect. Then you have plenty of time to explain why you're such an asshole to me, when apparently you're a saint to everybody else."

OXFORD, ENGLAND – 1839

For twenty-five years, I work as a naturalist under the name of Charles Montague, traveling the world collecting plant specimens and studying animals. There are people in these far-flung places, of course, but none interest me as much as the flora and fauna. And because of this, I accumulate a bit of a reputation for being an eccentric—as the Royal Society puts it, I am "the only man in known history to prefer the company of flower pistils to human females."

I have a jolly good laugh at that.

My single-minded dedication is noticed not only by my colleagues at the Royal Society, however, but also by Queen Victoria. Her Majesty bestows upon me the order of Knight Commander of the Bath for "great British contributions in the realm of botany," and I gain the title "Sir" in front of my name. It is a singular accomplishment of which I am proud, even for a man such as myself who has tried so many different things in my lifetime.

As the years pass, however, I consider the possibility it's time to hang up my explorer hat. My friend and fellow scientist Richard Banks sits slowly in a leather armchair in front of the fire. Richard's sixty-eight-year-old joints creak—they are the legacy of many decades crouching down into bushes and grass to examine root systems—and the damp in my home in Oxford doesn't help his old bones. He drapes a blanket over his legs.

"You're lucky you still have your youthful looks about you," Richard says, sipping on brandy. "God only knows how you manage to spend all your time outdoors and maintain the spryness of a man two-thirds your years."

"It's the elixir of eternal life," I jest. "Didn't I tell you I discovered it on my last trip to the Qing Empire? Why, the elixir of eternal life is the reason the queen knighted me."

Richard smiles at my joke. "You selfish rotter, you've been keeping this secret all this time? I could have used a dose or two of your elixir."

"Oh no, dear friend. You're much too far gone for it to do you any good."

Richard guffaws. "All the better, I suppose. I wouldn't want to live forever anyway."

"No?" I pour myself another drink from the bar cart. "Not even for the promise of discovering a species that had previously only been a myth?"

"Such as a unicorn?"

"Why not, for these hypothetical purposes. A unicorn, Richard! Would you live forever if you knew you'd discover unicorns and go down in history a legend?"

Richard takes a long pull from his tumbler as he thinks it over. After two more sips, he shakes his head. "Not even for everlasting glory. Can you imagine how much my joints would torture me when I was 550 years old?"

I laugh. "Fair enough."

"I reckon that you, on the other hand," Richard says, shifting the blanket over his legs to better cover them, "still have an adventure or two left in you. Do you seriously mean to retire from your professorship here at Oxford for a life of dull leisure in the countryside?"

"Would it be so bad?"

"You excel at many things, Charles. But being idle is not one of them."

"Funny you should say that," I reply. "I was actually considering a move overseas. To the former colonies."

"My word, that would be fascinating," Richard leans forward in his armchair. "To observe a still-young nation growing from the roots up—"

"Well, I would continue to focus on actual botany," I say, "rather than metaphorical political ones. The northeastern coastal forests, in particular, interest me."

"A fine pursuit. When would you go? Next year? The year following?"

"Actually . . . I've already booked passage on a ship. I leave next month."

Richard nearly drops his glass. "You don't dally about, do you?" He swirls the remains of his drink and examines his swollen knuckles that clutch it. "Well then, Charles, I wish you Godspeed. I shall miss your witty companionship, but perhaps in the Americas, you'll finally find a woman who suits you."

"Doubt it, my friend."

"I'll wager you a unicorn that you're wrong."

"A unicorn?" I smirk at the circle of our conversation. "How so?"

"The loser must send a unicorn to the winner."

"You're mad, old chap."

"Madness is a benefit of age," he quips. "So what do you say? Will you accept the wager?"

"I'm not one to back away from a bet," I say.

"As I suspected." Richard lifts his glass in a salute. "Then cheers to you and your new adventure. And to women, and to unicorns. Do write me, please. I shall live vicariously through you."

A year later, I post a letter from Chautauqua Lake in upstate New York to Oxford. Enclosed in the envelope is a small, carved wooden unicorn.

Dear Richard,

I hate to admit you were right, but you were right. I thought myself immune to the charms of the female species, but that was before I encountered the women of these new United States of America. They have been forged by the spirit of revolution; there is a feisty hardiness to them that differs from our British kinfolk, who have lived in relative stability for generations.

And so, I have fallen headlong in love with Meg Smith. She is a clever twenty-eight-year-old schoolteacher, so beloved by her students that they follow her around as if they were her own brood, even when lessons are done. Because of that, our days are consumed with tiny voices laughing, and I declare it the most wonderful sound in all the world. I hope to soon start a family of our own.

Suffice it to say, I traveled to the United States to discover new plants, but instead, I have discovered a new version of myself. Like the Buddhists of Tibet, I feel as if I have been reincarnated, granted another chance to live, to do it better this time than in the past. Meg is my salvation— please forgive my mingling of religious similes—and I am ever grateful to be in her presence.

But enough about me. How are you, my dear friend? I hope the tincture of Harpagophytum procumbens root that I sent along last month has helped with your aching joints. Please send word when you have a chance. I miss our gin-tinged conversations by the fire.

Ever Yours,
Charles

P.S. One of Meg's students whittled this unicorn for you. Consider it your winnings from our wager.

Not long after, I receive a short letter from Richard, written in a much shakier hand than I'm accustomed to from my old friend.

Dear Charles,

I was quite cheered to hear of your happiness with Meg. I've oft worried that you buried yourself too deeply in the world of fauna, and too rarely in the bright company of women.

It is dreadfully wet here—why does the rain favour England so? I hope the sun shines more generously on you in New York than it does on me in Oxford. Thank you for the Harpagophytum procumbens. It has, indeed, provided relief to my rheumy joints.

All the best to you, Meg, and the little angels who surround you.
    With Fondness,
    Richard

It is a surprisingly short letter from a man well known for his verbosity. But a month later, an explanation arrives via telegram from his sister, informing me that Richard has passed away peacefully in his sleep. He hadn't been well for some time.

I press the telegram to my chest. I never get to keep those I love for long.

As if on cue, Meg contracts tuberculosis the next day. The disease takes her swiftly, painfully. And my only consolation is that she got to live a fulfilling life before I crossed her path and ruined it.

It's hardly any consolation at all.

HELENE

ADAM TOLD ME THAT SEBASTIEN ISN'T AS TOUGH AS HE LOOKS, AND this close, I'm beginning to see the cracks in the facade. On the surface, it seems like Sebastien hopes I'll fall off a very high, very jagged cliff, possibly because I keep turning up at the places he considers his turf—his favorite bar, his local bookstore, his boat. And his *house*.

But he also does these inexplicably gentle things, like leaving my books for me at the *Alacrity* office, and cradling my twisted ankle as if touching my skin is a balm for his broken soul. That's not how you treat someone you suspect as a stalker. Sebastien is inconsistent, and that makes me wonder whether his hostility is an act. But I don't know why he'd do that for a complete stranger.

Unless I'm not a stranger. Unless, like me, he's also nursing an impossibility. Maybe not a decades-long crush on an imaginary friend who suddenly appeared in real life, but something else equally baffling that Sebastien's afraid to say out loud for fear of sounding crazy.

But when I say, "Perfect. Then you have plenty of time to explain why you're such an asshole to me, when apparently you're a saint to everybody else," he just armors up. Drawbridge raised, moat full of serpents, archers at the ready on the castle walls. Sebastien becomes more reticent than he already is, and there's no way to break through that fortress.

He gets up and says, "I'll show you your room," then starts down a long hall without offering to help me further. He walks slowly, but I'm even slower, half hopping, half hobbling.

The house is *immense*. We pass the entryway again (I think "foyer" is a more fitting name, given its size and all the marble), then a library, then an open, museum-like space full of sculptures on pedestals and glass cases of things I can't make out from here. There's a massive floating staircase made of gorgeously polished wood that could be a cover shot for *Architectural Digest,* but we walk by it, staying on the first floor.

Finally, we arrive at a guest suite on the other side of the house.

"Fully functional kitchenette." Sebastien points at a stove, microwave, refrigerator, and round table. "Bedroom and bathroom through that door, clean linens in the closet. I'll go get food for you."

"Wow. This is—"

But he's already gone.

I sigh and sink down onto the mattress; my ankle sends thankful shivers of relief to my brain. The suite has the same rustic but modern lodge feel as the rest of the house—lots of reclaimed wood stained dark, and glass and metal accents, like the reading sconces on either side of the headboard, as well as all the fixtures in the bathroom.

Sebastien returns ten minutes later with coffee beans, milk, bread, eggs, cheese, deli meats, dried pasta, and tomato sauce. He puts two plastic containers into the freezer. "That should be enough food for a few days."

He presses a sticky note to the fridge. "This is the Wi-Fi password, and you can use the landline if you need to." Sebastien points to an honest-to-god phone mounted on the wall, complete with curly cord.

"I didn't know they even made those anymore," I say.

"No cell service out here."

"But you have one, right?" I don't know why I'm asking this, other than I'm curious whether I've just stumbled on the last person in America who relies on a landline.

Sebastien tilts his head and looks at me like my question is nonsensical. "Why would I need a cellphone if there's no signal out here?"

I give him the same you-make-no-sense look back. "But what about when you're driving around and have an emergency or something?"

"Like crashing into a snowbank?" He says it with a smart-aleck curl of his lip.

A flare of loathing for him rises in my chest.

He glances away dismissively at me. "Ryba Harbor is a small enough town that there aren't any emergencies I can't solve myself. And there's a radio on my boat, if anything happens at sea. No need for a cellphone." Then Sebastien turns and starts walking out the door, as if a conversation simply ends when he decides it does.

"Wait, that's it? You're just going to leave me now?" I get up from the bed and limp across the room after him.

Sebastien turns around, brows furrowed as if confused what else I could possibly want. "You should have everything you need here. I'll let you know when the roads clear. And don't wander around the house. There are valuable works of art and other collectibles, and I don't need you damaging any of them."

I scoff. "So you're confining me to this suite? What do you think this is, *Beauty and the Beast* and I'm forbidden to go into the west wing?"

"If referencing a Disney movie is what it takes for your child-like mind to understand, then yes."

I slap him.

Sebastien gapes at me. He touches his face where I hit him.

Instinctively, I cower back a few steps, suddenly aware of how reckless I've acted. I'm stuck in a house in the middle of nowhere with a man I hardly know, and nobody knows that I'm here. My pulse races like a chipmunk who's just noticed she's in a fox's den.

But Sebastien doesn't raise a hand or even his voice. Instead, his broad fisherman's chest seems to cave in, and his shoulders sag as if he's Atlas, carrying the burdens of the world.

"I have to go," Sebastien whispers as he flees.

And even though he's the one who was rude, this iteration of the I-show-up, Sebastien-runs-away routine leaves me feeling guilty, along with a nagging sense that I ought to know why.

HELENE

I HARDLY SLEPT LAST NIGHT, TOSSING AND TURNING AS I THOUGHT about that broken look on Sebastien's face, about slapping him, about showing up unannounced at his door and him taking me in despite the tense unspoken *something* between us.

At six-thirty, I give up trying to fall back asleep. It's still pitch black outside and will be for hours, so I switch on one of the reading sconces next to the bed and chew on my lip while I lie in bed and stare at the wood beams in the ceiling.

Without a doubt, Sebastien is rude and awful. He's nothing like my imaginary soulmate, and maybe it's time to let go of that daydream. With Merrick, I wanted so much to believe in the story I told myself—a perfect marriage—that I purposefully glossed over his actual actions. Part of me wonders if that's what I've done here, wishing too hard that Real Sebastien is the same as Story Sebastien. It's only now truly setting in that the man who owns this house is a nonfictional, honest-to-goodness person, complete with his own flaws and history. Maybe I shouldn't have come out here. I've overstepped, let my imagination run away from me again.

And yet there's an unrelenting niggling at the center of my chest that tells me this is different from what happened with Merrick. Here exists a man who looks exactly like the one I made up in my head, and that, at the very least, deserves some investigation, especially since I'm snowed in at the same house as him for a few days.

You know what? Old Helene would sit around and do nothing. But New Helene takes action. It's time to get to the bottom of this.

Maybe if I lay it all out there, Sebastien will open up. Hell, maybe there's something he knows that can help me stitch together my stories. It's far-fetched, but so is inventing a boy when I was in middle school, having him star in all the vignettes I wrote, and then discovering that this boy is now a real, live man in the tiny fishing village where I chose to write said novel.

Who knows, there might be a logical explanation for this whole situation. Or maybe there isn't but we'll laugh it off and be able to stop being so cagey with each other.

Or Sebastien will genuinely think I'm insane, in which case I'll promise to stay in this guest suite until the roads clear, and then I'll leave him alone forever.

I roll out of bed and land a bit too hard on my bad ankle. After a few seconds of wincing, though, the pain passes, and I pull on my sweater and jeans from yesterday, since I don't have a change of clothes. They're a little dirty from my nighttime adventure in the snow, but whatever. Putting on my dad's watch somehow salvages the outfit.

I pause for a second as I pass through the kitchenette. Sebastien had brought a box of Cinnamon Toast Crunch, which is my favorite cereal ever, and I'm tempted to have a bowl (or two) to strengthen my resolve before I reveal my preposterous secret to him.

But no. My nerves are standing on end and I want to get this talk over with. Anyway, if the conversation goes poorly, I'll be locked up in this guest wing for a few days, so the Cinnamon Toast Crunch and I might have plenty of time together after all.

The hallway through the house is tiled with gray stone and

seems to be heated from underneath. I'm struck again by the luxury of this home and wonder (a) how Sebastien affords it and (b) why he has such a big house if he lives here all alone. Does he have family who visits? Does he entertain a lot?

The smell of bacon frying incentivizes me to walk faster, even though my ankle still hurts and my body aches with the aftershock of the accident.

Unsurprisingly, the kitchen is as magnificent as the other parts of the house I've seen—stainless steel appliances like in an upscale showroom; black marble countertops with veins of gold throughout; copper pots and pans hanging from a gleaming ceiling rack.

"Good morning!" I say cheerfully, because bacon makes me happy despite my nerves.

Sebastien's back is to me, but I both hear and see his sigh. It reminds me of long-suffering Reginald, the refrigerator in my rental cottage.

"I thought I gave you everything you needed in your kitchenette," Sebastien says without turning around.

Oh god. It occurs to me again that I'm being very stalkery. And now I won't leave him alone, even though he's clearly trying to separate us and keep me in the guest suite.

I laugh, trying to sound lighthearted and not at all creepy. "But there's no bacon in the guest kitchen."

"Of course," he mumbles, although it sounds less like annoyance and more like he's realizing an actual oversight on his part.

"I didn't mean to make you feel bad," I say. "I appreciate your hospitality. You've gone above and beyond for someone who didn't expect a houseguest in the middle of a blizzard." I glance out the kitchen window. Only a little moonlight illuminates the sky—par for the course for an Alaskan winter morning—but the storm is definitely raging. Snow flies sideways, and the branches of the pine trees whip in the wind. The insulation and soundproofing in Sebastien's house are excellent, though. I can't hear the weather outside at all.

Sebastien lets out a single, rueful laugh under his breath. "You're one of those people who sees the silver lining in everything, aren't you?" He scoops the finished bacon onto a plate lined with paper towels to drain, then turns and sets the plate on the kitchen island between us.

"I suppose so. I *am* an inveterate optimist." I pick up a piece of bacon but drop it immediately. "Ouch. Still hot."

This time, he laughs for real. "Case in point. So optimistic, you think you're immune to hot bacon grease."

There. That's a glimpse of the Sebastien I know. The one who teases me, the one who has so many laugh lines because he smiles all the time. I lean over the kitchen counter as if magnetically drawn to him.

And suddenly, I don't want to tell Sebastien anything yet. I want to stretch out this tiny moment, if possible, so I can hold on to the version of him that I know.

How do I do that, though? I fiddle with my dad's broken watch, and then it hits me. Pecan pie French toast. Dad invented the dish for me, and he made a heaping plate of it before each of my *Romeo and Juliet* performances (I adore breakfast for dinner). I'm a lousy cook in general, but this is the one recipe I can make.

"Let me cook breakfast," I say.

Sebastien frowns quizzically.

"I'd like to do something to repay your kindness from last night," I explain.

That makes him frown harder. I get it. He wasn't exactly Prince Charming yesterday. But he wrapped my ankle. And he brought me coffee with Bailey's. He couldn't have known I love a good Irish coffee, but still, it was lovely.

And I know that he loves French toast, too. Well, the Sebastien I've made up in my head likes it (maybe because the creation of his character coincided with the play and Dad's French toast dinners).

But anyway, if I ingratiate myself to Sebastien, maybe I can earn a little more openness from him for when I tell him he's been the star of all my stories since forever.

I take the bold step of walking around the kitchen island and planting myself at the stove next to him. Old Helene would never have done this. But I'm New Helene now, even if it takes an extra dose of courage to embody her. "You just sit down and relax and eat bacon. I'm going to whip up my specialty—pecan pie French toast."

His eyes widen for just a fraction of a second. "I do love French toast."

My heart skips a beat at the possibility that Story Sebastien's breakfast tastes align with Real Sebastien's.

But then he shakes his head. "Who doesn't like French toast, though? That doesn't make me special."

I think there's something else Sebastien isn't saying. Or I could be reading too much into it, because I want it to be true, I want him to know something that will render all of this logical.

Regardless, he surrenders the space at the stove and sits on the other side of the kitchen island on one of the barstools. He picks up a piece of bacon and eats it, just like I suggested. I purse my lips to hide my smile.

Then I get to work. It's easy to find what I need—so easy that it's uncanny, as if I already knew this kitchen and where Sebastien would put things. The cooking utensils are in the drawer to the left of the stove. The brown sugar, corn syrup, and pecans are on the highest shelf in the pantry, and the maple syrup is in the fridge behind the milk, between the loaf of bread and eggs.

However, the actual cooking part goes . . . less smoothly. When I crack the eggs, little shell bits end up inside the bowl and I have to pick them out. When I finally get the eggshells out, I pour in a few glugs of milk, but I don't remember how much cinnamon goes into this recipe. (Why can't I remember?)

This is why I usually buy premade meals or order in. Some people notoriously can't keep plants alive; I notoriously can't cook to save my life. But I *have* made this French toast before successfully, and now Sebastien's expression is so dubious as he watches me that I refuse to retreat. Anyway, I figure more cinnamon is better, right? So I add a heap to the eggs and milk. It'll be fine. Dad always said French toast doesn't require exactness.

I steal a glance at Sebastien to see if he noticed about the cinnamon. I can't tell. He's got a poker face on now.

Sliced bread goes into a casserole dish, and I pour the custard mixture all over for it to soak in.

"Now I'm going to make a pecan pie topping," I announce with loads more confidence than I actually feel.

Sebastien's mouth quirks for a second, but then it's back to his poker face. However, I suspect he's onto me and my complete cooking ineptitude. Why did I offer to make breakfast?

Because New Helene is brave, I think. Maybe also a little foolhardy. Or a lot foolhardy.

But what's done is done. I'll just have to make this breakfast so mind-blowingly good it proves Sebastien wrong.

Knowing he's watching me makes me more nervous than usual in the kitchen. I toss the butter into a pot to melt, but I must have turned the stove on too high, because the butter starts to turn brown really fast. And then it smokes.

"Uh, your butter—" Sebastien points.

"Don't worry, I got this! Relax and eat your bacon." I smile at him, then turn as casually as I can back to the burners.

Holy mother of dairy, the butter's burned and now the kitchen reeks. I want to blame the stove—I didn't know how fast it would get hot—but I know it's really just me, an already terrible chef, cracking under the pressure of having an expectant audience. I fumble around, trying to find the switch to turn on the overhead fan.

"It's a dial on the right side of the stove control panel," Sebastien says, even though I don't ask. He's not mean about it, though. If anything, he sounds a little . . . amused.

I turn on the fan and start over with the butter. I don't turn around again until I've got the butter melted and the brown sugar, corn syrup, maple syrup, and pecans stirred in. But, like with the cinnamon, I don't remember the proportions for each ingredient, so I wing it. The result is kind of a thick sludge, instead of rich, gooey goodness. God, I hope it tastes better than it looks.

"Everything all right over there?" Sebastien asks from the other side of the island.

"Yup, going great!" I say. (The truth: We might be eating just bacon for breakfast.)

I fry up the bread, which is now soaked with custard. A more accurate description might be *soggy* with custard.

I am not a cook. I'm a walking disaster who happens to be holding a spatula.

Finally, I plate the French toast and spoon on some pecan pie goop, which, to be honest, has the consistency of brown slime. Not the most aesthetically pleasing breakfast, but I'm still hopeful that it tastes good. How can sugar and syrup and pecans be bad?

When I turn around, though, I block Sebastien's view of the plate next to the stovetop. "Whipped cream?" I ask, because maybe it'd be a good idea to cover up the ugliness of the French toast.

He smiles, forgetting that I'm an unwanted intruder in his home. "Yes, please. But I prefer Cool Whip."

I have to stop myself from squealing. *My* Sebastien loves Cool Whip. It's what Dad always used, so of course my imaginary soulmate grew up with it, too.

It might only be a coincidence, I remind myself. I don't have a monopoly on preferring Cool Whip.

Still, I'm bouncing a little on my feet as I find a container of it in the fridge and spoon a generous dollop onto Sebastien's French toast. Then I push it across the island countertop to him.

He picks up a fork and digs in to my breakfast disaster.

At the first bite, he chuckles quietly. "It's just like I remember," Sebastien says.

And then he freezes.

"What did you say?" I ask, blinking at him.

"Uh, nothing."

"No. I heard you. You said, 'Just like I remember.' What do you mean?"

Sebastien sets his fork down with a loud clatter. "You know, I wouldn't have agreed to breakfast if I'd known it was going to be an interrogation. I just meant the French toast tastes like I thought it would, all right?"

I don't know why, but he's lying again. I'm not going to back down this time, though.

"This is going to sound impossible," I say, "but when I saw you at The Frosty Otter, I recognized you."

He opens his mouth to protest, but I hold up my hand to silence him.

"Hear me out, please. I recognized you not from meeting you in person, but from my imagination." As soon as I say it, I realize it sounds even more absurd and creepy out loud than it did in my head. But I've already started, so I might as well keep going.

"When I was in eighth grade, I made up a friend for myself, and he and I grew up together. I know that makes me sound like a loser, but having that boy—then man—in my life helped me cope whenever reality was too hard to bear."

For a second, Sebastien's face falters. It's just a twitch of his mouth, and then it's gone and his lips are pressed into such a bland, ruler-straight line again I wonder if I imagined that they ever moved at all. Even if he had reacted, though, I don't know whether the twitch was a good sign or a bad one. So I just press onward because I have to get this out in the open.

"I wrote a bunch of short stories over the years, and in my mind's eye, that same guy was always cast as the star character. He was a Swiss clockmaker. Or a Transylvanian count, mistaken for a vampire. In other vignettes, he sailed on Portuguese explorers, led expeditions across the Sahara, or danced on The Bund in Shanghai during the Roaring Twenties.

"But I digress, because the main point is . . . that imaginary friend is you. Or at least, you look exactly like him. I'm sorry if my behavior around you has been bewildering, because the truth is, I *am* bewildered. How can it be that someone I invented actually exists in real life? And what are the chances that our paths crossed? I can't help but think it has to *mean* something."

Sebastien flinches again, and this time there's no mistaking it: He looks like I've zapped him with a taser gun at full force. I wouldn't be surprised if he fell face-first into his Cool Whip.

"Oh god, I'm sorry." I start rambling, because that's what I do when I'm nervous. "I've done it again and come on way too strong, haven't I? First I confront you at The Frosty Otter without warning, then I show up at the same bookstore as you, and at your harbor. Now I've arrived on your doorstep just as a three-day blizzard started and I forced you to take me in, but I promise I'm not a stalker! This is all just nuts and I'm overwhelmed. Shit shit shit, what was I thinking . . ."

I'm about to cry, or at the very least hurl myself out into the blizzard so I can die from mortification alone.

But then Sebastien reaches across the counter and takes my hand in his and says softly, "It's all right." And there's a crease between his brows, one I recognize as the expression on my imagined Sebastien whenever he gives in to me. It's the equivalent of a white flag of surrender, but one borne out of kindness.

"You think I'm crazy," I whisper, voice quivering.

He shakes his head and looks at me, but his eyes are deep blue pools of remorse, not pity.

"I don't think you're crazy," he says with the gentleness of a man who once coaxed a frightened polar bear cub off an iceberg and onto his boat to safety. "In all honesty, you might end up concluding that *I'm* the one who's out of his mind."

I rub my eyes and swipe away the tears that had threatened to fall. "How is that possible?"

Sebastien closes his eyes for a brief moment, then slides off his barstool and walks around the kitchen island, never letting go of my hand.

"Come with me," he says. "There's something I think you'll want to see."

SEBASTIEN

I TOLD JULIET ONLY ONCE WHO SHE WAS—IN THE LIFE IMMEDIATELY after her first—and that didn't go well.

But Helene somehow knows about our past, even if she doesn't realize it's more than stories in her head. And if I don't tell her the truth, she'll blame herself for me pushing her away. She's so earnest. I can see how much she wants our connection to be true, as badly as I want it.

Telling her about our history is either a brilliant idea or a disastrous one.

The self-sacrificing side of me hopes that what I'm about to show Helene will send her running as fast as she can. That the knowledge of what will happen if we fall in love will scare her.

Then maybe she can move on from these vignettes she's written—and from me—and have a life free of the shadow of the curse. Even if letting her go means ripping out another piece of my heart, like it did last time.

The terrified side of me fears that Helene will dig in and want to stay after I reveal our history. That there's nothing I can do against fate, that Avery Drake was an anomaly, and we won't escape from the curse again.

I know I should be rooting for setting Helene free, but if I'm being honest, I want to be hers, and I want her to be mine. Despite everything.

Romeo and Juliet, the way it was supposed to be.

HELENE

SEBASTIEN LEADS ME UP THE STAIRCASE, THE ONE MADE OF GLASS AND thick planks of polished wood arranged so they appear to be floating in the air. The wall next to the stairs is a two-story-high window, which gives the impression that the forest isn't outside, but that the house is actually nestled inside of the woods. As we ascend higher, I get the distinct sensation that I'm levitating among the pine trees. The only difference is I can't feel the wrath of the blizzard on the other side of the windowpane.

It isn't until we travel deeper onto the second floor that my stomach starts to express its misgivings, and it's not just because I didn't feed it any breakfast. Here, the hallways are dark, the only light from dim sconces on the walls that flicker like waning candlelight.

Cautious Old Helene rears her head again. *You could be walking into a serial killer's den.*

I'd texted Mom and Katy last night to let them know where I am, but what can they do from L.A.? Nothing. I'm in this on my own.

But Sebastien just opens an ordinary-looking door and holds it open for me, and the chivalry, I have to admit, is flattering. I know a lot of women these days would find the gesture antifeminist, but for someone like me who hasn't been respected enough in past relationships, it's awfully nice to be treated like I'm worth waiting for.

"Is this . . . your bedroom?" I ask, on guard again. But this doesn't look like how I think a serial killer's room would. Light gray walls, a platform bed with a simple (but likely expensive) wooden headboard and crisp, military-tight white sheets, and a leather bench at the foot of the bed. There are two nightstands that match the headboard, but it's clear that only one of the tables is ever used, because it has a small analog clock and a landline-connected phone on it, whereas the other is completely clean.

Sebastien stands at a distance to avoid hovering while I look around, and he leaves the path to the door clear, so I can sprint for it if I need to. I appreciate him trying to help me relax.

Framed wildlife photographs line the walls. They aren't standard shots of prowling lions and fleeing wildebeests, though. Instead, whoever took them had an eye for quiet moments—one picture is of a pair of gorillas in the jungle, dozing with heads resting against each other. Another is a long exposure of the northern lights, with the one constant being a mother seal and her pups on the ice, a family huddled together watching nature's rainbow unfurl. And the most striking photograph is of a mourning wolf, mid-howl with his paws protectively over the body of his dead mate.

"These are incredible photos," I say. "Who took them?"

Sebastien hesitates before he answers.

"A woman I loved." He pauses. "Her name was Avery."

A pinprick of jealousy stabs at me. Which is stupid, because of course he's allowed to have a history. Of course Sebastien isn't exclusively mine, just because I've daydreamed him before.

He seems to pick up on my discomfort, because he says, "It was like another lifetime ago." But there's a hitch in his voice, and he clears his throat to hide it. "This isn't why I brought you here, though. What you need to see is this way."

Sebastien walks into a closet the size of my bedroom back at the cottage. He pushes aside a bunch of dark jeans—all neatly pressed and hanging like they belong in an expensive store—and there is a locked door. It's metal (maybe fireproof?) and there's a security panel above the handle.

He lifts his hand to type in the code.

My fears about being murdered in a serial killer's den come flooding back. "Wh-where are you taking me?"

"It's better if you see it for yourself."

My heart is in my throat. "Actually, I think I'd rather not." I begin to back toward the hallway.

He sighs, a weighty sound I'm starting to think is a key expression of his. Either that, or I'm particularly exasperating.

My temper flares. "Do you think it's unreasonable of me to distrust a man who's about to take me into a locked room with a reinforced door, hidden inside a closet?"

At that, Sebastien's expression softens.

"The code for the door panel is July tenth," he says. "The date of the Capulets' ball."

My jaw drops. I remember every detail of *Romeo and Juliet,* because those performances are so entwined with my memories of my dad. Juliet's parents threw a party "a fortnight and odd days" before her birthday (*my* birthday, too, coincidentally)—July 31, otherwise known as Lammas Eve. Which does indeed put the Capulets' ball around July 10.

But that doesn't explain why Sebastien thinks the ball would be significant to me, and why he's using the date as a pass code.

I forget worrying he might be a murderer and instead, my brain starts churning out theories, each wilder than the next: Juliet was his childhood literary crush (the equivalent of a celebrity crush, for nerds). Or, Sebastien and I are soulmates brought together by a common love of Shakespeare. Or, because I invented Sebastien while I was in the *Romeo and Juliet* play, that's how he sprang to life—fully formed with *Romeo and Juliet* as his origin story.

Meanwhile, Real Sebastien enters July 10 into the security panel in European fashion, with the day preceding the month: 1-0-0-7.

The lock on the door clicks open.

"See?" he says. "Now you know how to get into the room. And

there's no need for a code to get out because the door just opens from the inside. Does that help you feel safer?"

Being scared is several emotions ago, so I just nod.

"But before you go in," Sebastien says, "I need you to take a deep breath."

"Why, what's inside?"

"Just take a deep breath. Please."

"Okay . . ." I do as he says, keeping eye contact the whole time so he knows when I've satisfied his request.

He also breathes in and lets out a long, possibly too forceful exhale. It seems he needs the meditative pause more than I do.

Then he turns the handle and pushes the heavy door open.

I step inside as he flips on the lights.

It's an art gallery.

And all the paintings are of characters and scenes from the stories I've written.

HELENE

"WH-WHAT IS THIS?"

Trembling, I spin, gaze darting from one painting to another.

The closest one is a medieval portrait of a teenage girl, in the exact same costume I wore for my role of Juliet—a long yellow gown with wide, ribbon-hemmed sleeves, a bonnet-like hood over her hair, and silk slippers. How can that be? Mom made my costume for me, and as far as I know, she didn't do any historical research. Did she come across this painting online and copy it?

On another wall, there's a portrait of a tanned woman with piercing gray eyes and a hawkish nose, riding a camel in the desert. Her features, the way she holds herself proud and upright on the saddle, and her colorful woven headwrap in reds, purples, and oranges match with my character Mary Jo Phoenix, an intrepid explorer, who, along with her husband, Nolan, crossed the Sahara on camelback in search of the mythical Land of Gold. She was the dreamer; he was the logistics man who could make her fantastical quests come true. The bronze plaque on the frame dates this scene to 1711, exactly when my vignette is set.

There's a painting of a stout waitress with a cuckoo clock behind her, showing the time as exactly noon. The plaque says 1561. "Clara in Switzerland," I gasp in recognition.

Then there's eighteenth-century Amélie Laurent with her pretty blond ringlets and parasol, strolling through the gardens of Versailles. And a flapper girl dancing in a nightclub in Shanghai in 1920; she looks just like I described my character Kitri Wagner.

Oh god. My stomach flips frantically, a fish without water. "How is this possible?" I whisper.

I don't recognize all of the paintings, but as I skim them, a few more stand out, corresponding with vignettes I wrote.

I walk up to a painting of a horse race; the plaque puts the scene in New York, 1839. The men wear waistcoats and trousers and top hats. The women show off high-waisted gowns and carry dainty parasols. On the right side of the painting, one couple faces the artist instead of the horses.

The man is Sebastien, but old-timey.

"I know that scene, too." My knees go weak; I have to sit down on one of the leather benches in the middle of the gallery.

"You remember that?" Sebastien says, eyes wide.

"What do you mean, *remember*?" I'm dialed up to full freak-out mode now. I made up that horse race scene during my first year of grad school, when I was renting a room near the Northwestern University equestrian team's stables. I recall how pleased I was about the fancy hat I wrote for my character—blue feathers, lavender roses. The same hat as in the painting in front of me.

"It's another one of my stories," I say, voice quivering. "No one except my mom and sister have ever read them, though. How can these paintings exist?" I turn to stare at Sebastien. "How do *you* exist?"

My nerves are beginning to short-circuit from too much input.

Sebastien sits down on a bench a few yards away, as if making sure to give me space to breathe. "Do you know the story of Romeo and Juliet?"

"Of course." We already established at the locked door that I knew what the tenth of July signified.

"How does their story end?" he asks.

Sebastien's patient, teacher-like tone rubs me the wrong way. This is *not* the time for a literature lesson. "Juliet takes a sleeping potion that fakes her death," I snap. "Romeo hears the news and, distraught, buys poison. He drinks it in the Capulet tomb so he can die next to Juliet's body. But then she wakes up and finds him dead, so she kills herself with his dagger. But how is that relevant?"

"Do you remember that you said you knew me?"

I let out an exasperated huff. "Please stop asking me questions. I can't handle the Socratic method right now. Just tell me what this is all about because I'm about to lose my mind."

"All right." He gets up and crosses the gallery, removes a gilt frame from the wall, and brings it over to me, setting it down on my bench. It's an oil painting of act 5, scene 3—Juliet lying asleep in the Capulets' tomb. Shockingly, she is wearing a white gown nearly indistinguishable from the one I wore for this scene in my middle school play. That's two identical costumes, in paintings I've never seen before. My stomach drops like I'm free-falling on a roller coaster.

"You say you've daydreamed about me for a long time," Sebastien says. "But while you thought you made up all those adventures, I think you were actually remembering past lives. Because the places that you mentioned during breakfast—and in these paintings—are places you and I have been together."

"That makes no sense," I whisper, even though somewhere in the foggy recesses of my mind, it does.

"I agree," Sebastien says. "But it all goes back to Romeo and Juliet, whose story doesn't quite end like you think. Shakespeare got it wrong. I know because I was there—I am Romeo."

VERONA — 1376

I hurl myself down the steps inside the Capulets' mausoleum. I had been banished to Mantua, but upon receiving a letter with news from Friar Lawrence, I broke the terms of my exile and rushed back to Verona under the cloak of the moonless night.

In the good friar's letter, he recounted how Juliet's father had betrothed her to Count Paris, unaware that she was already secretly married to me, her family's enemy. In an effort to thwart the wedding, Juliet took an elixir from Friar Lawrence that feigned her death.

The Capulets mourned her and laid her to rest in their tomb yesterday. But according to the friar, Juliet will wake tonight. I shall be there, holding her hands when she opens her eyes, and then we shall flee to begin our new life.

I stop short on the mausoleum steps, though, when I see her.

Juliet lies on a slab of white marble, hands folded over her gown of white silk and lace, hair arranged in soft curls around her angelic face. She's beautiful, a porcelain goddess, the Psyche to my

Cupid. I know she is only asleep, but she is so still, it's as if she's truly gone, and my heart flounders.

But then I notice the quirk in her lips, a slight smile as if she's committed some final mischief that no one else knows.

And I laugh. Yes, the potion. That's why I'm here. It'll wear off any minute. I run down the last of the steps to her side.

I sit, however, for hours. The torch I brought has burned out, and I've had to light another. As time passes, I grow increasingly anxious and begin pacing around the marble platform where she lies. What if Friar Lawrence's potion didn't work?

No, I tell myself. *Only the estimate of the hour of waking is wrong.* The friar had calculated forty-two hours. It's only been forty-five.

Patience has never been my strong suit. I force myself to sit and wait.

There's a noise behind me. I jump up, smile already stretching across my face to greet Juliet, hands ready to hold her, my lips ready to kiss her.

But she is still.

Instead, footsteps sound down the stairs.

Who comes to Juliet's tomb?

I duck behind the marble slab on which the body of Juliet's cousin, Tybalt, lies. I don't want to be here, for I am the one who killed Tybalt. I hadn't meant to, but the anger between the Montagues and Capulets had boiled over, and Tybalt murdered my dear friend Mercutio . . .

My thoughts are interrupted by the voice of Count Paris at Juliet's tomb. He must have come to pay his respects to the woman he thought was his fiancée.

"Sweet flower," he says, "with flowers thy bridal bed I strew—"

I imagine Paris caressing Juliet's face.

And I cannot stand the idea of him touching her.

I leap up from behind Tybalt's resting place. "Step away from Juliet."

"You." Paris draws his sword from its sheath. "Are you here to defile the Capulets' tomb, Montague?"

"No, I—"

"I apprehend thee as a felon, and I hereby arrest you on behalf of the citizens of Verona!" Paris lunges at me with his sword.

Mine is out in an instant, flashing in the torchlight. Steel clashes against steel.

He swings.

I dodge.

He spins and darts in again. I narrowly avoid being impaled by his blade.

"Paris, please, we dishonor Juliet by fighting," I shout as my sword meets his again.

"Nay, I honor her. She would not want a Montague in her tomb!" Paris swings at my face, and the edge of his blade slices across my brow and glances over my left eye.

I cry out and grab at my face with my free hand. Blood obliterates my vision.

With my defenses down, he strikes my sword out of my hand, and it clatters onto the stone below.

I don't go down easily, though, and I hurl myself at him. The collision knocks the torch from his hand, and blackness swallows the mausoleum whole as we both tumble to the ground. The force of impact breaks my grip on him and we roll apart.

I fumble for the dagger in my belt. I cannot see anything through the blood and the dark, but I know Paris is near.

"Truth be told," he says, "I would be doing all of Verona a vast favor were I to exterminate you tonight."

His condescension burrows under my skin. But now that he has spoken, I can track his voice. He is next to the bier upon which Juliet lies.

I dash at him and jab so deeply the handle hits flesh. He gasps as I yank out the blade, and then there is a flurry of movement, the silk of Juliet's gown rustling as Paris scrambles against her resting place to escape my attack, and I am so enraged that he might be climbing over my beloved's sacred body that I launch myself at Paris again and impale him with my dagger, twisting violently to ensure his end.

But the cry that is uttered is not the voice of a man.

It is Juliet's.

"Oh God, no!" I shout.

Light enters the tomb as someone else opens the heavy mausoleum door. "Romeo!" Friar Lawrence's voice echoes down the stairwell.

Paris is slumped on the ground, bleeding on the stone floor.

And Juliet is sitting upright on the bier, eyes wide in shock as she looks down at the deep crimson unfurling like petals of death on the white lace of her gown.

My dagger is stuck straight in the center of the bloody bloom.

She must've woken during my struggle with Paris, and my second blow was not into his torso, but hers.

"Romeo?" she whispers, confused eyes meeting mine for a fleeting second.

Then she collapses onto the bier, her final breath escaping in a single, sorrowful rush.

"No! What have I done, what have I done?" I throw myself over Juliet's body and try to staunch the flow of blood, as if my embrace can somehow force the life back into her.

But Juliet doesn't move.

Friar Lawrence bursts into the room. He stops short at the sight of me with Juliet, and Paris dead at my feet.

"What in heaven's name has transpired?" the friar whispers.

I cannot answer. All I can do is stroke Juliet's cheek, run my fingers through her hair. Tears fall from my face onto hers.

This is all my fault, my doing. If I hadn't killed Tybalt, if I hadn't rushed Juliet to marry me, if I hadn't been a coward and insisted that we hide our love from our families . . .

Yet none of that matters now. Blood pours out of Juliet, and she is no longer pale, but gray. She was my light in a world driven by bitterness and vengeance. How can I continue to exist when she does not?

I yank the dagger from her side and press the tip of the blade just below my breastbone. A single thrust upward, and it will impale my heart.

"Halt!" Friar Lawrence grabs my wrist. "There has already been too much bloodshed today."

"If Juliet does not live, nor shall I."

"This is not the solution." He twists my wrist until I drop the knife. "You will live, Romeo."

"But how?" A wail escapes from my mouth, and the fight leaves me. I crumple. The friar catches me before I fall.

"You will find a way," Friar Lawrence says, "as all men do to survive. But quick, you must flee Verona now. The noise of your duel with Paris has alerted the night watch, and the Montagues and Capulets are on their way as we speak. Go far, far away, Romeo, change your name, and never return."

I am drowning in grief, and I want to die. And yet there's a traitorous part of me that latches on to the friar's suggestion, a part of me that selfishly wants to live.

Guilt hangs around my neck like a millstone.

In the distance, I hear shouts and the pounding of horses' hooves.

"It is time to go," Friar Lawrence says gently.

"But Juliet—"

"Is truly dead."

The finality knifes through me as if it were a blade itself. I collapse over her body, weeping as I kiss her farewell. "My Juliet, my Juliet, forgive me . . ."

Forgive me for our star-crossed marriage.

Forgive me for the dagger meant for another.

Forgive me for living without you.

SEBASTIEN

HELENE LOOKS AT ME LIKE I'M DELUSIONAL. IT ISN'T A BAD OUTCOME, is it? If Helene doubts me, she'll want to put as much distance between us as she can.

And yet, now that we're in this gallery together, surrounded by the paintings of all her past reincarnations that I've loved, I desperately want her to believe me. I've lived too long without my Juliet, and the pain of missing her is a living, sharp-toothed thing inside me that gnaws at me every day I'm alone. With Helene standing before me, all I want to do is bow down at her feet and beg forgiveness for what will happen if she decides to stay.

But I have to remind myself that Helene doesn't fully understand yet that she's Juliet. So far, I've only explained the part about me.

Helene shakes her head, still processing my story. At least she's not panicking anymore, now that she has a problem to puzzle over. "That's not how Shakespeare told it," she says. "Romeo and Juliet both died in that tomb."

"Shakespeare wrote the story about two centuries after it happened," I say. "He took some artistic license to convey his own literary motifs. But it wasn't fact."

She studies the oil painting beside her, thinking through my version again.

Meanwhile, I think on our past as well. I still remember the rush of calling to my original Juliet from the base of her balcony, and the moment she parted the curtains and answered my call. It was as if everything around her shifted to black and white and she was the only burst of color in its center. Even that early in our love, I knew she was my destiny.

Here in the gallery, it happens once more. The color seems to seep from all the paintings, and Helene is the only thing worth gazing upon. How could I have thought I could bear to be without her in yet another lifetime?

Juliet is the sun, Shakespeare said.

Indeed she is. And now again, I fall for her as if she is gravity itself.

Helene is the one to break the silence.

"If what you're saying is true, then you're . . . what? Claiming to be immortal?" She wrinkles her nose, just a barely perceptible scrunch that I've seen a thousand times across past lives. It is so dear a motion to me, but I have to restrain myself from crossing the gallery and kissing her where her nose wrinkles.

Instead, I ask, "Is immortality any more preposterous than you making up an imaginary friend, only to discover that he's a real person?"

"Yes, it is."

I consider this, then nod in concession. "Probably. But still in the same category of unlikely."

She chews on her lip, thinking again. "Okay, let's assume for a minute that I believe you're the same Montague from Romeo and Juliet's time." Helene fixes me with a firm look, to make sure I understand this is only an assumption for the sake of discussion, not that she truly believes. "It still doesn't explain how *I* know the stories behind some of the paintings or how I'm even a part of all this."

I steeple my fingers, because this is the most far-fetched part of the story. I take several deep breaths, and even then, the truth sticks in my throat. The only other time I told a reincarnated Juliet who she was, it ended disastrously.

But no other Juliets have ever remembered our past, save Helene. She may not remember overtly, but the memories are there.

She knows our love stories.

Why?

Because I tried to cheat the curse by leaving the last version of her alone, I think ruefully. *And now we're paying the price for my arrogance, with a curse renewed in force.*

But that isn't what I tell Helene. What she needs—what she's asking for—is how it began.

"Mercutio cursed us as he died," I say. *"A plague o' both your houses."*

Helene wrinkles her nose again. "That was just an admonishment to the Capulet and Montague families for their feud."

I lift one shoulder in half a shrug. My friend Mercutio's dying words have never stopped haunting me. It was my fault he was killed; he died in a duel, defending my honor. I can't think of any other way the curse could have engendered, and I don't know exactly how it came to power, other than there was a confluence of blood and pain and those final words uttered on his deathbed—all stemming from events I set into motion. I was selfish then, impulsive. I saw Juliet at the Capulets' ball and had to make her mine, regardless of the consequences to my family and friends. And Mercutio died because of it.

His words, too, are apt—for other than Helene, Juliet keeps being reincarnated without any memory of the past, and I am doomed to watch her die over and over again. That seems to me the definition of a plague on both the Capulet and Montague lineages.

"We find each other, fall in love, and then catastrophe strikes," I say. "No children, no growing old together . . . Juliet always dies. What can it be but a curse?"

Helene frowns as she digests what I've said. Then she laughs once—quick and short, the sound of a skeptic. "So you're saying that *I'm* Juliet. That the women in these paintings aren't just my characters, they're *me,* born again. That's why you said the stories I've written are actually memories."

"Yes," I say softly. "You're Juliet."

"That's . . . not possible."

"Yet it is. I've loved you again and again, across lifetimes. Our story defies reason and science and everything we're taught to know about the world, but it *is* possible. And I think, perhaps, you know it, too."

Her breathing quickens, and I can see the jittering panic, the crush of being overwhelmed by this gallery and its possibilities. I want to cross the room and hold her in my arms, tell her that it'll be all right.

But I can't promise that. It has never been all right for us. I've tried breaking the curse before.

And I have always failed.

So I sit helplessly on my bench like a ship adrift, the gallery between us an ocean keeping us apart.

She stands suddenly, fingers fluttering restlessly. "I can't do this here. I need space to think."

"Of course." I rise, too. "I'll walk you back to your room."

"No." Helene holds up a hand, as if physically pushing me back. "I need to not be near you."

I falter and sink back onto the bench. Every time Juliet comes into my life, it knocks the wind out of my lungs, as if she's a prize-fighter and I merely the punching bag with the dubious privilege of receiving her blows. But this time is exponentially worse, because I can feel fate mocking me. And it's also worse because I induced Helene into disliking me, and now I regret that deeply. I can withstand the whole world blaming Romeo—Juliet's death was my fault, and I loathe myself for each and every time she dies—but I can't bear being hated by Juliet herself.

Still, if space is what she wants, I'll give it to her. I'd give her anything.

"Whatever you need," I say quietly, "it's yours."

Helene nods, then pivots abruptly on her good foot and limps hurriedly out of the gallery. I listen to her uneven footsteps echoing down the hallway and the stairwell, until they're too faint to hear anymore.

Then I fall backward on the bench and shut my eyes tight, knowing that I've been in this position before, telling Juliet who she is.

I can only hope Helene reacts better to the revelation than Isabella did.

SICILY — 1395

After fleeing Mantua, I live on the streets as a beggar for many years. Wretched with guilt over Juliet's death, I try to take my life many times. Yet somehow, my wounds are always superficial. If I stab myself, it manifests as only a surface wound. If I try to let the heat of the midday sun dehydrate me, a kind old woman will wander by and offer me a drink, refusing to leave until I imbibe it all. Even drowning fails; my body can no longer sink. I am by no means invincible, but it's as if a curse will not allow me to die.

Grief tries but cannot kill me either, so I drift from year to year in a swamp of sorrow. Some days, I subsist on stale heels of bread and rotting apple cores cast out in the garbage. Other days, I don't eat at all. I have no identity, no purpose, no anything. I am gutter trash, and it's better than I deserve.

Eventually, though, grief tires of being my companion, and without its company, I slowly stitch myself back together. If I can't die, I have to create a semblance of a life.

I make my way to the Kingdom of Sicily in the far south, where

I change my name to Lucciano. There, I apprentice myself to a cobbler in a small shoe store in Palermo. The owner, Gianni, tends the front of the shop, whereas I spend my days in the dimly lit backroom workshop. I have no need to speak to others. Human connection brings only heartache, and I prefer the stoicism of leather and nails.

One sunny July morning, however, Gianni receives an invitation for his niece's wedding in the Duchy of Milan. I suggest closing the store while he's away.

"Nonsense," Gianni says. "It is not so difficult to tend to the customers. You know ladies' shoes better than most women know their own feet. I shall return in a fortnight. I expect my shop to still be standing when I do."

Which is how I come to be in the front of the store when Isabella Caruso strolls in on the tenth of July.

"I wish thee a fair morning," I say without looking up from the counter. I'm working the final touches on a pair of slippers, sewing gold beads onto the red leather, and I don't want to stop my progress.

A delicate laugh fills the small showroom. "Is it still morning in your world, sir? For as I see it, the sun has traveled well past noon."

At the sound of her voice, I drop the shoe to the ground.

"Juliet?" I whisper.

It's been nearly two decades, but she is just as I remember. Light brown hair, green eyes that flash with wit, and perfect, rose-tinted lips. Is it possible that she, too, survived as I did? That she didn't die in the crypt?

The memory of the honeyed wine from the Capulets' ball skims my lips. Today is exactly nineteen years from the night we met as Cupid and Psyche.

I emerge from behind the register and take a tentative step toward her.

"I beg your pardon?" she says. "Who's Juliet?"

"You are," I say, voice barely audible.

She laughs again. "I am quite sure I'm Isabella Caruso. I have been my entire life."

But I can't stop staring. I cross the shop in two long strides, take her hands, and kneel at her feet. "I know not if you are an angel who has come to finally take me away, or if you are my true love, come to rescue me from my suffering. But regardless, you are the most heavenly vision I've ever laid eyes upon, and I beseech you to accept the gift of my love, in this moment and forevermore."

Isabella blushes. "My good sir . . . I am quite lost for words."

"Say nothing but yes. If you'll be mine, I swear to make you happy for all time."

The door behind us chimes. "What is the meaning of this?" A matronly woman—Isabella's chaperone—charges in.

Before the chaperone can tear us apart, Isabella leans in and whispers into my ear. "Yes. On impulse and on intuition, yes."

Then, louder, she says, "The slippers sound perfect. I shall expect you to deliver them to me on Sunday. My companion shall give directions to my residence."

With that, Isabella walks out of the shop. And she takes my scarred but hopeful heart with her.

Two weeks later, we lie naked together in a bed on the island of Pantelleria. We are drunk on moscato and our elopement, and even though we've just woken from a brief nap, I kiss Isabella's thighs where the skin is soft and pale, untouched by the summer sun and known only to me. Although she drowsily bats me away, it's halfhearted, because we're newlyweds, and there is no such thing as enough of each other.

We make love with the fervor of explorers mapping new lands, and when we finish, we do it again only an hour later. Eventually, though, we are spent, and I wrap my arms around Isabella; she rests her head on my chest.

I haven't told her that she was Juliet—I don't understand how this wonder has come to be—but she is unquestionably the very same girl I loved almost two decades ago in Verona. Everything about her is the same, from the rise and fall of her voice to the scent of lavender on her skin, from the velvet of her touch to the way she kisses me urgently, as if we are going to be caught at any moment. The only difference is that Isabella has no clue that she'd ever been a Capulet.

But now that Isabella is my wife, it's time to tell her what I believe.

"My beloved," I say.

"Hmm?" Isabella murmurs.

"Do you believe in miracles?"

"I am Catholic. Of course I believe in miracles." She smiles and kisses me.

"As do I. You, here in my arms, are a miracle."

Isabella laughs. "You are prone to hyperbole, my love."

But my face is serious. "I speak the truth. Nineteen years ago, I lost my first wife, and every day since, I have prayed to be reunited with her."

Isabella sits up in bed, the blankets falling gloriously from her body, her breasts on full display. I stop myself from reaching out to touch her.

Which is for the best, because she scowls and says, "You were previously wed?"

"Yes, but—"

"I believed I was your first and only love."

I reach for her hands. "You are. I'm trying to explain. When you walked into the shoemaker's shop, my prayers were answered. You not only look like Juliet, my first wife. You are her. I don't understand how the Lord has brought you back to me, but I don't question his divine will. I am only humbled by his generosity."

Isabella snatches her hands away. "You think I'm your dead wife? That is why you declared your love to me?" She gathers a blanket around her and scrambles off the bed.

"You don't understand—" I jump off the bed and catch her wrist.

"Unhand me!" She jerks away. Then she pulls on her undergarments and begins to dress hastily.

"Please stop," I say. "I love you."

"No, you are mad. I've been deceived, and I shall not play a part in this sham marriage a moment longer." The buttons on her gown are misaligned, and her ribbons poorly done. But Isabella is already halfway to the door.

I dare not grab her again, so I dart in front of her to block her path. "Where are you going?"

"To the ferry. Back to Sicily, where I shall petition the pope to annul our marriage. You shall send my things and never come near me again."

"Please, don't be rash. Let us be reasonable."

She lets out a scornful laugh. "Reasonable! There's no reason in what you claim—that I'm your dead wife risen from the grave. Now move aside. You've already taken my virginity and ruined me. Do not take my freedom as well."

I step out of her path. But as she opens the door, I whisper, "Juliet. Please. I love you."

She glares at me with the full force of the sun that she is.

"My. Name. Is. Isabella."

I let her go because that is what she wants. But I don't understand that the curse has already sunk its talons into us.

An hour later, I watch from afar as Isabella boards the ferry. I wave sadly as it sails from the harbor.

Then, inexplicably, the ferry capsizes a mile offshore. I jump into the sea and swim, but they are too far and I am too slow, and by the time I reach the ferry, it has sunk, taking Isabella and my happiness with it.

A plague o' both your houses, I recall Mercutio saying.

It is only then that I truly begin to realize what he has done.

HELENE

I AM HYPERVENTILATING ON THE FLOOR OF THE SITTING AREA IN THE guest suite, because this is as far as I got before I fell to pieces. I'd put on a show of strength when I marched out of the Gallery of Me, but all that bravado is gone. Now my head is between my knees, and I'm gulping air like a beached dolphin.

I wanted Sebastien to be my soulmate. But this is insane.

Breathe, I tell myself. *Breathe.*

However, I've always been shitty at meditation. One of my college friends, Monica, was really into it and once recommended a book that taught an "easy" way to meditate. I got through all of three pages before my mind drifted off to other thoughts. That was years ago. I kept meaning to go back and actually read the book, but life has a knack for throwing itself in the way of all your well-intentioned plans.

Still, I remember the most basic concept from those introductory pages, which is just to say hello to each breath and then say goodbye when it leaves. The idea is to be kind to yourself, rather than putting a lot of pressure on doing meditation "right" or perfectly.

I try it now.

Hello, breath, I think as a panicked inhale wheezes through my lungs.

Goodbye, breath. It's like my body can't wait to get rid of everything it contains—carbon dioxide, outdated ideas about imaginary friends, thoughts of being trapped in a remote Alaskan house with a madman.

Hello, breath. Another inhale, short and hurried.

Goodbye, breath. The air rushes out too fast.

But I keep at it. *Hello, goodbye, hello, goodbye,* until it starts to work, almost without me noticing. My breathing begins to resemble that of a normal human, and the fog from light-headedness clears.

My stomach growls, as if recognizing that this is its chance to get attention before I fall down the rabbit hole of what that gallery of paintings and Sebastien's *Romeo and Juliet* claim mean.

Now I remember that I didn't eat any of the French toast at breakfast. I don't function well without food in my system. I force myself to get up, legs weak from everything that's happened in the last hour, and stagger into the kitchenette.

Bread, eggs, cheese . . . it all seems like too much effort. I open the freezer, thinking there might be a microwaveable meal, but all I see are those containers Sebastien stuffed inside. They're labeled Chocolate Hazelnut Cornetti, and I gasp as I pry off one of the lids. The container is packed with crescent-shaped, Nutella-filled pastries made from scratch.

Suddenly, I want to cry. If I were on a desert island and could only eat one thing for the rest of my life, this would be it.

How did Sebastien know?

My pulse hiccups. Is it possible that what he claims about us is true, that we've known each other over lifetimes? That he really is Romeo, and I'm Juliet?

No. Preposterous.

I grab two cornetti and throw them into the microwave. I'm

sure they would taste better if I reheated them in the toaster oven, but I need sugar in my blood, stat. Ninety seconds later, they're steaming hot and I don't even care that they're soggy. I just stuff one after the other into my mouth right there at the counter, scalding my lip on the Nutella filling and showering my shirt and the floor with flaky pastry bits.

What I need is something to hold on to that makes sense.

The Juliet paintings with the costumes! That can't be happenstance. I grab my phone. There's no cellphone reception out here, but Sebastien did leave me a Wi-Fi password. I open a browser and spend well over an hour running search after search, trying to find pictures of those dresses so I can prove that my costumes were just reproductions of something Mom found on the internet.

But there's nothing. As far as the world knows, the Juliet paintings in Sebastien's private gallery don't exist. Somehow, Mom happened to make costumes for me that matched them.

I immediately shove two more cornetti into the microwave.

When those are gone, I make myself a cup of coffee, then sink into one of the chairs at the little round dining table. What am I supposed to do now?

"New Helene can think logically." I say it out loud to ground myself in the here and now, to remind myself that I can be a practical person who doesn't get swept away by daydreams and old Shakespearean love stories. I can analyze the facts.

And writing always makes me feel better, so I grab a notebook from my purse (a good reporter is never without something to write on), and I jot down what I know:

- *I began seeing Sebastien in my head when I was cast as Juliet in the middle school play, and I imagined him as Romeo.*
- *There is a secret, locked art gallery full of paintings of women who look exactly like the characters I've written. The portraits span centuries, with plaques dating back to . . . when? I didn't pay enough attention, because I was too busy freaking out.*
- *Sebastien claims to be Romeo, who is cursed with watching his beloved die over and over, while he himself can never die.*

- *Juliet dies a lot—and it sounds like always tragically, and often young.*
- *Sebastien also claims that Juliet's soul is reincarnated endlessly, although she doesn't realize it.*
- *Until me. Those short stories I wrote correspond with some of the paintings. Supposedly, my made-up adventures are actually memories.*
- *And if I'm Juliet, then am I also doomed to die?*

No, I refuse to even consider that last point. All of this is utter nonsense. From my experience as a journalist, I know there *has* to be a reasonable explanation for what's going on.

Even if that's completely at odds with how I felt when I saw Sebastien in The Frosty Otter.

I drain the entire cup of coffee and brew another. This time, I pour in a shot of Bailey's, which Sebastien must have left for me after wrapping my ankle last night. I sort of resent that he can predict what I'll want before I even know.

But I also kind of love it. And that terrifies me. Never in my life have I been this confused.

I need to talk to Mom and Katy. They'll know what to do.

I message them to convene an emergency family meeting.

Five minutes later, we're on a video call. Trevor is behind Katy, half eating his lunch in his high chair and half painting everything within reach with ketchup. Mom is in the back office of her folk music store. They've both dropped whatever they were doing to hop on this call for me, and I love them for it.

"You okay, Hel?" Katy asks. I messaged them last night to let them know I was snowed in at Sebastien's, but we haven't talked since I got here. (I left out the part about totaling my rental car; Mom would have worried endlessly and called the National Guard to extract me and bring me to a hospital.) So the concern on Katy's face now isn't about the car crash. She glances at Trevor, who's preoccupied with decapitating his dinosaur-shaped chicken nuggets, then leans closer to her screen and says in a low voice, "Are you safe? Is Sebastien . . . ?"

"Oh! Don't worry about that. I have my own room. Actually, I have my own wing of the house. Sebastien's not a creep." As I tell her, I realize I believe it. Despite the gallery being full of paintings of my stories, Sebastien doesn't seem like a stalker. After all, *he* was the one who tried to distance himself from *me* both at The Frosty Otter and outside of Shipyard Books. *I'm* the one who went down to the harbor to try to find him, and I'm the one who showed up at his door in the middle of the night, uninvited. If one of the two of us is a creep, it's definitely me.

"Glad you're safe," Mom says. "So why did you call an emergency family meeting? Is it about Merrick?"

"Why would it be about Merrick?"

Katy belts out a dramatic groan. "Your ex has been calling my cell nonstop, trying to get ahold of you."

I set my coffee down with a clunk, and it sloshes all over the table. "Merrick's been doing *what*?"

"Don't worry, I haven't picked up or anything. He's probably just frustrated because you haven't answered your phone. It's, like, the world's greatest insult to Merrick Sauer if he calls and people don't jump up to do his bidding right away."

"Yeah but he shouldn't be harassing you. I'm so sorry, Katy. Block his number, okay?"

She shrugs and smirks. "I took your lead and changed his name in my phone. Now instead of 'Merrick,' my phone says 'Little Penis calling.'"

Mom grins. "Good thing my grandson can't read yet."

But the brief moment of levity vanishes as I remember why I called this emergency family meeting. "Okay, so the reason I wanted to talk was, you know how I thought Sebastien looked just like the characters I'd written for so many years? Um . . . things just got weirder."

"Things just got weirder!" Trevor exclaims as he rips off another chicken nugget dinosaur head and tries to connect a different dinosaur's tail onto its neck, so that now it essentially has two butts. He laughs maniacally, which to be honest is kind of how I feel at the moment, too.

Katy glances indulgently at Trevor, then quickly turns back to me. "How can it possibly get any more bizarre than it is?"

I'm about to recount my morning, everything from me spilling the beans to Sebastien about my vignettes, to his pass code being the date of the Capulets' ball, to the hidden art gallery of uncannily familiar paintings.

But I stop myself before I say anything. Because I realize how it will sound: Thirty-year-old woman ends marriage abruptly, runs away to Alaska, and suddenly takes up believing in past lives, reincarnation, and a centuries-old curse.

Mom will definitely call the National Guard to rescue me from whatever cult she'll think I've joined. And Katy will send in the FBI to lock up Sebastien as the lead con man. Merrick was the king of gaslighting, and Katy hated that any time I had even a microscopic concern, Merrick would rewrite history and convince me that his version of reality was right, and mine was wrong. Katy wouldn't want me plunging into another potentially messed-up relationship.

And yet, I don't think Sebastien and Merrick are in the same category at all.

Regardless, I can't tell Mom and Katy about Romeo and Juliet and the curse. I'm not even sure if *I* believe Sebastien, and I've seen the paintings. I know how they match up with my own stories.

"Hel?" Katy asks. "You were telling us things got even weirder?"

My skin itches at the strangeness of keeping a secret from them; I'm so used to telling them everything. But this is for the best, at least for now, so I shake my head and smile. "Never mind. I just, um . . . I think I might have figured out the thread that connects all the vignettes I've written."

Mom claps her hands. "That's wonderful, sweetheart! What is it?"

"Wait, don't tell me," Katy says with a smirk. "You wrote Sebastien into existence." She starts laughing, and Mom joins in.

I pretend to laugh, too, although her guess is a little too close to home. When I was looking for a through line for my vignettes, I was expecting something fictional. Not a real, live man with a real, live past.

Trevor bangs on the tray of his high chair, demanding to be released from his meal to watch *Sesame Street*. Katy swipes his hands with wet wipes, then lets him go. He runs off, and a few seconds later, Elmo's voice echoes from their living room.

"Okay," Katy says, turning back to the screen. "Tell us for real, what's the answer to how your stories come together?"

"Nope," I say, aiming for lighthearted as I attempt to steer this conversation away from a topic I no longer want to discuss. "You made fun of me, so now I'm not going to tell you."

"Aww, Hel, come on."

I waggle my eyebrows at her.

"In all seriousness, though, I think I actually want to keep this idea to myself for a little bit. It's so new, and I'm kind of afraid that if I share it, I'll stunt its growth or something."

Mom nods. "It's like when I write a song," she says, picking up one of the many guitars that are always lying around her store. "A new melody is just a baby idea. I have to keep it safe from the outside world for a while, nurture it on my own. You should follow your instincts, Helene. Keep your story thread to yourself until you're ready."

I nod and take a long sip of my Irish coffee. "Oh, but Mom, I had a question for you . . . Do you remember the costumes you made for me for my *Romeo and Juliet* play in middle school?"

"Of course."

"I was wondering . . . Where did you get the designs for them? Did you see them online somewhere?" My hands are shaking as I ask, and coffee splashes on my phone. *Shit shit shit.* I grab a napkin and sop up the mess before it can seep into the phone's innards.

"You don't remember?" Mom says. "You gave me the details for the costumes."

"Me?" I freeze, and the coffee-soaked napkin drips over the phone.

"Yes. Colors, fabrics, everything. You said they came to you in a dream. You really don't recall?"

"Oh, right," I say, lying, but my mind is racing, throwing open the file cabinets of my memory and dumping out all the contents in a desperate attempt to remember. There's only a faint familiarity, like seeing the hazy outline of a tree through thick fog.

"Speaking of costumes," Katy says, "have I told you two about the debacle of the preschool talent show?"

I'm grateful for her change of subject. Katy goes on to regale us with her misadventures in trying to organize Trevor and his friends' skit, which involves dinosaurs (obviously) and three different costume changes as the kids morph from brontosauruses to velociraptors to dragon-like pterodactyls.

Then Mom updates us on the fundraising concert she's organizing with a network of other folk music stores, and the normalcy of the conversation lowers my pulse enough that I can function like a human being and, for example, make sure my phone hasn't been ruined by Irish coffee. It seems, thankfully, to be fine, if a bit sticky and boozy.

By the time we hang up, I feel almost stable. Even though I decided not to tell Mom and Katy about Sebastien yet, I feel better just knowing that they're there.

I do spend a few more hours thinking about the curse, though. It sounds completely absurd. But so does inventing a man in my head and then running into him in a bar. And Sebastien knows my stories. I've never shared them with anyone except Mom and Katy. How could Sebastien know what I'd written—and have really old paintings of them—if he wasn't at least partially telling the truth?

I eat probably half a dozen more Nutella pastries while I'm pondering all this. And then after several hours of going around and around in circles in my head, a possible solution hits me.

What if I don't have to decide what's true or not?

I'm on the brink of creating a new life for myself. What if I just look at this bizarre situation as a gift from the universe for my novel, but don't wade deeper than that into the mystery of my vignettes and Sebastien's paintings? I can pursue my dream of becoming an author—write this plot into my book—and leave the rest as one of the unexplained secrets of life, like an extreme case of déjà vu. I don't have to believe Sebastien or even understand him.

I turn the idea over in my head. Basically, I could keep Story Sebastien if I wanted to. I could preserve my perfect imaginary soulmate in a novel, and I myself can stay in the dream. I don't have to wake up and accept a flawed Real Sebastien with all his baggage. I can leave him behind in Alaska once I'm done drafting my book.

But is it possible? Because the fact is, I fell in love a long time ago with Sebastien, before I even knew he was real. Maybe I can't turn back.

I need to consider this from another angle, but I also need more brain fuel. I pour myself a bowl of Cinnamon Toast Crunch and jot down a chronological list of all the vignettes I've written.

> *1395: Kingdom of Sicily—Lucciano (cobbler) and Isabella (wealthy patron)*
>
> *1456: Mainz, Germany—Albrecht (assistant to Johann Gutenberg) and Brigitta (dairymaid)*
>
> *1498: Lisbon, Portugal—Simão (sailor) and Ines (port-maker's daughter)*
>
> *1559: Bern, Switzerland—Felix (clockmaker) and Clara (waitress at inn)*
>
> *1682: Transylvania—Marius (rumored vampire) and Cosmina (rumored witch)*
>
> *1711: Sahara Desert—Nolan and Mary Jo (husband and wife explorers searching for the Land of Gold)*
>
> *1789: Versailles, France—Matteo (Venetian ambassador) and Amélie (minor nobility)*
>
> *1839: New York, upstate—Charles (British botanist) and Meg (schoolteacher)*
>
> *1920: Shanghai, China—Reynier (translator) and Kitri (daughter of German exporter)*
>
> *1941: Pearl Harbor, Hawaii—Jack (soldier) and Rachel (volunteer librarian)*

When I finish the list, a lead weight sits heavily in my stomach, and it's not just the fault of the cornetti and Cinnamon Toast Crunch. I regret running out of the gallery. Sebastien had more paintings in there than I have vignettes, and I should have paid more attention. I wonder if they fill in the longer gaps in my time-line.

Who am I kidding? I can't just leave the mystery of how we're connected alone, using it only to construct a novel. My journalism training is too ingrained in me, and the old instincts to dig until I find an answer take over.

I need to understand what's real and what's not.

I need to understand the story of us.

I grab my notebook and head back into the rest of Sebastien's house. There are answers out there, and I'm going to find them.

My first stop is the museum-like space we passed by last night. I suspect this is one of the parts of the house Sebastien didn't want me wandering through—"*There are valuable works of art and other collectibles, and I don't need you damaging any of them*"—but since he already showed me the Gallery of Me, I figure this is less off-limits than it was before. Besides, Sebastien's nowhere to be seen.

I gasp as I step inside the white room. No, not room. *Hall.* The ceilings are at least twelve feet high, with attentively placed spotlights overhead, designed to showcase all the statues on pedestals and the displays in glass cases. There's a marble bust from old Rome, a soldier's uniform from medieval Russia, a metal goblet, a blue and white porcelain vase, and more. In the corner, there's a huge wooden sleigh—the kind that horses used to pull through snow—covered in intricate, Scandinavian-looking carvings and faded red and yellow paint.

Never have I known anyone with a private museum of artifacts. Sure, I've written fluff pieces about art collections; there are plenty of wealthy philanthropists in L.A. who love throwing charity galas so they have an excuse to invite journalists to photograph their homes. But Sebastien's Hall of History (my name for it, not his) is different. There are no pretentious, museum-style descriptions mounted next to each piece, and I can't imagine him inviting a ton of people into his home just to show off what he owns.

No, everything in this room is personal. Has Sebastien collected it all himself, mementos of the different lives he's lived?

I laugh under my breath, because immortality is such a ludicrous idea. But I quickly remember that it's because of an impossibility that I'm even here. I wouldn't have talked to Sebastien in The Frosty

Otter if not for those familiar blue eyes, that smile accompanied with a one-shouldered shrug, and the way he spins his cup on the table just like my characters do. And then there was the wisp of sweet wine on my lips, a hint of something I ought to remember, but don't.

If there's a correlation with my vignettes and Sebastien's past, this Hall of History is as good a place to investigate it as the gallery. I flip my notebook open to a fresh page and begin writing down a catalog of what's here, so I have a record to cross-reference with my stories.

For example, the Roman bust could be from Sicily, or if Sebastien's curse is to be believed, from Verona or Mantua. The yellowed book could belong to a printer's apprentice. There's a dented bucket (inexplicable), but next to that is a dress that looks like a cross between a Chinese *qipao* and a 1920s flapper dress. I gasp as I recognize it, the burgundy silk flowers identical to the embroidery on my character Kitri's favorite dress. All I have to do is close my eyes; I know the words of my vignette by heart.

Kitri Wagner is the daughter of an exporter from Germany, and her family has lived in Shanghai—"the Paris of the East, the New York of the West"—for a year. She knows her way around the city, although her favorite part is The Bund, a strip of waterfront that's also home to some of the most exclusive social clubs in Shanghai. Being a young woman, Kitri isn't allowed into most of them, but she loves to people watch, sketching the men in their expensive suits, admiring their beautiful wives with their perfectly bobbed hair and strands of real pearls draped over their colorful dresses. Kitri herself is plain, but she imagines what it would be like to be pretty, to know you would invite attention wherever you go.

"That's a beautiful drawing," a voice says from over her shoulder.

Kitri jumps from the bench she's sitting on and instinctively covers up her sketch pad.

"My apologies," he says. "I didn't mean to startle you. I tried talking to you several times, but I suppose you were too lost in your work."

He looks appropriately abashed, wringing his hat in his hands. He has a handsome face, Romanesque despite the crook in his nose and two silvered scars, one that starts at his left brow and finishes under his eye, the other, a curve like the letter "J" that traces his jawline.

"It's all right," Kitri says. "I just didn't expect anyone to talk to me. I'm not accustomed to being noticed."

"I think it would be impossible not to notice you."

Now it's her turn to be embarrassed.

"Forgive me for being bold," he says, "but I was about to partake in afternoon tea, and I was wondering if you'd like to join me."

Kitri finds her voice again, although she's still not brave enough to look at his hypnotically blue eyes. So she focuses past him, at the quay, when she answers. "Thank you kindly for the invitation, but I'm not in the business of running around with strange men."

He dips his head in acknowledgment. "I'm Reynier. Does that help? Strangers don't have names, but I do; ergo, I'm no longer a stranger.

She laughs, but does not relent. "And yet, for all I know, you'll take me to an opium den, drug me, and I'll never see my family again."

"For the record, I've never been to an opium den," Reynier says. Then he tells Kitri more about himself—he's a translator who works at one of the big trading houses on The Bund. She notices now that he's dressed impeccably— his suit is well tailored, his shoes polished to a shine—and even though she doesn't know him, there's something about him that's familiar, as if he is déjà vu in person form.

He presents his business card, further validation that he is who he claims. Their fingers brush as she takes the card from him, and a honeyed breeze blows past her. Kitri is suddenly overcome with a titillating buzz, the pleasant feeling of drinking a particularly fine glass of champagne.

"If I were to be interested in afternoon tea," she says

coyly, "where would you propose to take me? Lotus Flower Teahouse? The Society of Dragons?" She lists ritzy places she's only heard of, let alone seen.

"No, somewhere even better," Reynier says. "To a street of food carts selling the best Shanghainese cuisine you'll ever taste—*xiao long bao* dumplings, spicy *ma la tang* soup, and crayfish by the bucket."

Kitri's eyes nearly bulge out of her skull. "Crayfish by the bucket?"

Reynier bursts out laughing.

"I wager you've never had a suitor offer you crayfish, have you?" he says.

She gathers herself and crosses her arms. "Oh, are you a suitor now? I thought this was only an afternoon commitment for the sake of dumplings."

He smiles at Kitri, and her knees turn to jelly. She'd like to look at that smile all day.

"Well, are you coming or not?" He offers his arm.

Kitri glances back across the street at the fancy buildings of The Bund and thinks of all the hours she's spent here on these benches, imagining the exciting escapades happening to the beautiful people behind those gilded doors. And then she looks at this handsome man beside her, extending an invitation to have an escapade of her own. It might not be a sumptuous teahouse or club, but it's more exciting than sketching by herself on the quay.

So she rests her hand on Reynier's elbow and says, "You know, I've always wanted to eat a bucket of crustaceans."

I open my eyes and look again at the dented old bucket next to the Chinese flapper dress. Could it really be the same bucket that contained Shanghainese crayfish? I can practically taste them on my tongue now, spicy and briny, just like Reynier's kiss that I imagined afterward . . .

But that was just a story. Something I made up. It couldn't be real.

Could it?

I tear myself away from the display and make my way deeper into the mini museum. The evidence begins to pile up. A ribboned medal bestowing the order of Knight Commander of the Bath matches up with a vignette I wrote about Sir Charles, a renowned botanist of the British Royal Society. A beautiful old monstrance clock could be a set piece in my story about Felix, a Swiss clock-maker, and Clara, the waitress he fell in love with. But my heart palpitates when I come across a velvet display containing a charred and melted bronze tag with Rachel Wil stamped onto it, the rest of her name lost to some fiery disaster.

That isn't how my Pearl Harbor story of Jack and Rachel ended. They just went into the naval base library to find a book . . . So could it be true that my stories were wrong? Or had I just never seen past their beginnings?

Then there are also other artifacts that don't match anything I've written. Bricks of sunbaked clay. An antique sword and a bow with a quiver of arrows, a fox fur cap and rifle, and a string of worn rosary beads.

Of course, Helene. I shake my head at my own ego. If Sebastien really has lived for centuries, his life would have been about a lot of things other than Juliet. Just because the only vignettes I've written are love stories doesn't meant that's all that's ever happened to him.

Still, it's disturbing to think that maybe there's been a version of me—versions, plural—whom Sebastien knows, but I don't. Am I always the same me? Or am I different each time? And if so, which past Helene has Sebastien loved best?

If he's actually immortal. I still don't believe it, although it's getting harder to defend that stance. Logic's hold on my brain is blurring at the edges, and the inexplicable is moving in.

The smell of something delicious cooking also wafts in. I glance at the time on my phone.

How is it already four in the afternoon? But then I remember that I spent a few hours after my call with Mom and Katy thinking over the whole *Romeo and Juliet* thing. And I lost track of time here in the Hall of History, examining every artifact as if it might give me the answers I need.

"You know what?" I say aloud. "That's enough."

Enough being in my own head. Enough hemming and hawing. I didn't set off on this "New Helene" project to play it safe. If I want answers, I'm going to demand them from the source.

And that source, it seems, is in the kitchen.

SEBASTIEN

WHEN I'M TENSE, I COOK.

It was originally a skill I picked up out of necessity, because after fleeing Mantua, there was no one to take care of me. The Montagues had a full staff that'd done everything I needed, from polishing my swords to acquiring books I requested, from attending to any hair out of place on my head to making my meals. But on my own in Sicily—after my period of grieving homelessness— I had to learn not only how to do my own shopping but how to cook the ingredients. A man can't survive on salami and raw zucchini alone.

These days, however, I use cooking to release pressure. I spent too many hours today wallowing in my gallery, reliving all the Juliets who came and died before Helene. If I could have cried, I would have. But the tears have long dried up; I've lived through too much tragedy and exhausted that physical reservoir. The sadness and grief, unfortunately, are as eternal as my life.

Still, I knew I couldn't stay with the paintings—with the past— forever. What if Helene needed me? So I eventually scraped myself off the bench in the gallery and drifted downstairs to cook.

First, I made more dough for Nutella cornetti, because Helene will need them to replace the ones I'd brought to her guest suite earlier. If she's anything like my past Juliets, she'll lean on sugar as fuel as she works through the gargantuan mess of history I've dumped on her today, and that means the supply of pastries in her freezer is going to run low. Besides, the complicated process of making proper cornetti dough takes time and care, and I was glad to have the distraction. I couldn't stop replaying what happened in the gallery and worrying what Helene must be thinking—about me and about herself—but having something to do helped.

After the dough was in the refrigerator to rest, I made a batch of cannoli, also for Helene. If she decides to never speak to me again and to leave after the blizzard clears, then at least her last impression of me will be sweet.

At the thought, I have to brace myself against the counter. I don't want her to go. And yet I know she has to. The curse can try its best to throw us into each other's lives—giving Helene memories of our pasts, catching me off guard by bringing her to me in January, not July—but I won't give in without a fight. I lived without Avery, and so Avery lived. I can do the same for Helene.

Can't I?

I fling myself into making risotto, another complex, single-minded undertaking like cornetti dough that crowds out the warring passions in my head. Every step of cooking risotto is detailed, like coating each grain of rice in butter and heating it until it's slightly translucent. Attentively stirring gives me a task on which to focus and keeps me from being paralyzed by my own desires and fears.

When the rice begins to smell toasty, I pour in a splash of white wine to deglaze the pot. Then I stir some more, carefully scraping up the caramelized bits from the pot.

Stir . . . Stir . . . Stir . . .

Next comes strands of bright red saffron. Then meticulous, small ladles of warm broth. With each addition, I fold the rice until it's absorbed all the liquid before I add more.

When the risotto is finished cooking, I add butter and Parmesan cheese.

And Helene marches into the kitchen as if she's on a mission.

HELENE

I meant to confront Sebastien about the Gallery of Me and the Hall of History. I meant to demand logical explanations for why I've written vignettes about him, about why being around him feels like never-ending static shock where each spark is another flicker of déjà vu. I meant to be angry at him for heaping all this on me, for being horrible to me at The Frosty Otter and the book-store, and even for the ridiculous tall tales the townsfolk tell about him rescuing baby polar bears.

I meant to get to the bottom of it all, I really did.

But when I step into the kitchen and he looks up from the stove, I see how ragged he looks and I know instantaneously that he's spent the morning blaming himself after I left the gallery. I see how stiffly he carries his shoulders, as if it takes all his willpower to stay standing, and how his hand trembles slightly as he clenches the wooden spoon just to hold on to *something*. Never could I have imagined that a burly crab fisherman who wages war against the vicious winter sea could look so . . . vulnerable.

His rawness breaks my resolve. And then suddenly, I don't want to think about the vignettes and the paintings and how Shakespeare got Romeo and Juliet's story wrong. I don't want to think anymore that the world might not work the way I'd always believed it did.

I don't want to think about what it would mean for me if what Sebastien said about all the Juliets is true.

So I decide not to, at least for tonight. Compartmentalizing is something I'm good at; I've had a lot of practice in the past, not thinking about Merrick working late or not thinking about being denied a promotion or not thinking about all those overseas job offers I could have had instead of wasting away on insignificant stories under my husband's thumb.

I know I'm supposed to be letting Old Helene go, but New Helene needs a break. It's exhausting being independent and in-trepid all the time. My brain is tired, my body is tired, and hon-estly, what I need is to just pretend for an evening that these last few days didn't happen.

I wonder if Sebastien will let me.

SEBASTIEN

WHATEVER HELENE WAS ABOUT TO SAY WHEN SHE MARCHED INTO THE kitchen seems to evaporate in the fragrant steam floating from the stove. At first she was coiled with determination, one fist clutching a notebook and the other a pen. But then she blinked, and the steeliness that had been in her eyes gave way to something softer. Her grip on the notebook relaxes, and she sets it with the pen on the counter.

"Wow." Helene approaches and leans over the pot, as if I hadn't traumatized her with knowledge of a centuries-old curse only hours before. "That smells incredible," she says.

I close my eyes as I gather myself. She's so close. I can smell the hint of floral lotion on her skin, feel the shift in the air when her hair swings from side to side. I want to touch her. I want to say so much to her.

But instead, I only say thanks, erring on the side of caution until I have a better grasp on her state of mind. And until I have a solid grasp on mine.

She chews on her lip, like she's considering what to say next. Then she shakes her head, as if pushing off a previous decision, and just smiles and says, "Except for French toast, I'm a terrible cook."

I try not to laugh and manage to say "Oh?" as if I'm surprised. But I'm not. Historically, Juliet has been a lover of food, but not a maker of it. It's peculiar how there are certain characteristics of hers that remain consistent through every reincarnation, while others change. Her core personality is always the same—clever, excitable, optimistic—but details like how she looks and what she's interested in vary from lifetime to lifetime. Nonetheless, she's consistently a miserable cook.

"You won't believe how many times I've ruined frozen pizza." Helene smirks to herself, as if at a memory. "Anyway, I can't cook, but I'll do the dishes for you, if you want. I actually find it meditative."

"Really?" I'm happy to take her up on the offer. I loathe washing dishes.

"So, what're you making?" she asks.

"Risotto. But, Helene, about earlier . . ."

"Shh. Let's not talk about the gallery, okay?" she says.

I have to know, though, where we stand if we're going to be in this house together. I have to know whether I can release the chains around my heart, or whether I should keep everything under lock and key.

"It was a lot to lay on you—" I say.

Her fingers flit through the air like she's casting a magic spell. "I know it's the walrus in the room, but I've decided not to talk about it. Not yet, anyway."

Helene seems to be looking at everything but me as she says this, her gaze flitting from pot of risotto to espresso machine to kitchen towels to tray of cannoli. My heart clenches, because I recognize the nervous energy from previous Juliets. I've seen this before, the stages she goes through when a situation is too big or too frightening to grasp.

First there's a facade of bravery. Then there's panic. Next is the need to do something, to gather as much information as possible. Then there's retreat. That's the stage Helene seems to be at now, the impulse to burrow like a small mouse deep into the ground and forget what's happening outside for a while. Only after that will she emerge rested and ready to face hardship again. And then that's when her optimism and real bravery take charge.

This, however, is the most fragile stage, and every Juliet handles it differently. I have to follow her lead, lest I scare the mouse deeper into her burrow.

"All right," I say. "We don't have to talk about it."

"Exactly!" Helene beams. "I mean, I was thinking: We're both coming at this with a lot of outrageous baggage. But we're forgetting that none of it matters if the basics don't work. So what if someone who looks like you has been my imaginary best friend for years? And so what if you claim you're, like, almost seven hundred years old? If you and I, right now, don't get along, it's all moot anyway."

I wince, because seven hundred years old makes me sound alarmingly decrepit. And I look as if I'm in my thirties, because I've physically aged only about a decade since I was Romeo.

In any case, I'm about to point out that her soul is essentially the same age as mine—seven hundred years—but I stop myself as

I realize it would mean highlighting the worst part of the curse: that Juliet dies again and again.

Now I understand why Helene put her defenses up. It's not just the eternal Romeo part that she can't quite swallow. It's the fact that, if she believes what I've told her, it'll mean accepting her own death sentence.

Even though I've known it for centuries, it doesn't make it any easier. No wonder she wants to hide in her burrow for a while.

"So what I propose," Helene is saying, oblivious to the dread of eternity and inevitability swirling in my thoughts, "is that we set aside what we *think* we know about each other, and actually get to know the other person in the here and now. We're going to be in this house for a while together anyway. And then when this blizzard ends, maybe we'll have figured out if we even like each other as people, because if we don't, any grand ideas of 'destiny' don't matter."

It's difficult to comprehend—because she and I are *all* backstory—but what Helene is asking is completely reasonable. I may know all the Juliets of the past, but I don't know Helene yet. And she may know her made-up version of Sebastien, but she doesn't know *me*.

"No talk of your stories or Romeo and Juliet or curses?" I ask.

"None whatsoever," Helene says. "Just two people hanging out, doing crossword puzzles or playing board games or whatever it is that people do during snowstorms."

I laugh then. "Crosswords and board games? Is that what you think of me?"

She shrugs, but smiles at the same time. "I dunno. That's kind of the point, right? I don't know anything about you. But I'm going to find out."

"Okay, then," I say. "I'll take you up on the offer you made back at Shipyard Books. Let's start from the beginning. Hi, my name is Sebastien. And the first thing you should know about me is, I'm a damn fantastic cook."

HELENE

GOOD GOD, THE MAN WASN'T LYING WHEN HE SAID HE COULD COOK. Once Sebastien got going in the kitchen, there was no stopping him. Besides the promised risotto, he made pasta by hand, with eggplant, tomato, and basil. Then a swordfish dish with olives and capers. There was crusty bread with ridiculously good olive oil, and salad so fresh I would've sworn he grew and harvested the lettuce straight from the garden, except that it's currently thirty degrees below zero outside. And finally, he made a cheese platter to cap it all off. I didn't know that much food and wine could fit in my stomach, but if this is the first impression he's going to make in our get-to-know-each-other phase, I give Chef Sebastien five stars.

"I have espresso and cannoli as well," he says, "but I suggest we bring dessert with us and retire to the library."

"How posh." I laugh.

Sebastien's skin flushes beneath the shadow of evening stubble, and he smiles shyly. He takes my teasing in stride; I like that.

While he brews espresso, I find the tray he used last night for coffee and load it up with cannoli. As full as I am, I can't resist licking off some of the sweet, creamy filling that ends up on my fingers. I catch Sebastien watching me with his lips slightly parted. Not lasciviously, but as if I'm an objet d'art in the vein of Botticelli, worthy of worship.

"Sorry," he says, spinning swiftly back to the espresso machine.

I smile to myself. I don't hate the attention.

Sebastien doesn't make eye contact again until we get to the library, and then it's sheepish, like he's still embarrassed. I want to tell him he shouldn't be, though. It's a nice change of pace to be admired like that. There are women out there who are routinely ogled and hit on at bars, but I'm not one of them. Compliments tend to center on my intelligence, which, don't get me wrong, is wonderful. But it's also electrifying to have someone enraptured by my looks for once. A girl ought to be allowed to feel pretty from time to time.

When I actually notice the details of the library, though, I forget my vanity. Because this room isn't the tiny study I thought it was when we passed it in the hallway last night. That, apparently, was just the entrance.

Like the museum room, the library is palatial—two stories high, with a stained glass dome overhead patterned with spruce trees along the edges and art deco clouds in the middle; it probably lets in incredible light during the summer months, when the sun shines for nineteen hours a day. Beneath the dome are stairs like an ammonite spiral, and the walls on both the first and second floors are lined with hardcover books with pristine, uncreased spines, some leather bound and obviously very old, and others more modern, wrapped in shiny, colorful jackets. Deep, velvety armchairs and sofas fill the space in the center of the library, all on top of plush carpet that muffles the sound of my clunky limp. In the back corner, a gorgeous, antique gold lantern clock stands on display under a spotlight.

"This library looks like it belongs in Hearst Castle or something," I say.

Sebastien smiles. "It's one of my favorite rooms in the house, after—" He breaks off abruptly, but I suspect he was about to mention the gallery.

I'm grateful that he stopped himself. I am too happy on good food and wine right now to spoil the mood with our possibly impossible past and my—*la-la-la,* let's not talk about it—future.

He sets the tray down on a low table in the center of the library and sits on the couch across from it. I could join him, but I'm too enchanted by the shelves to settle down quite yet.

"You're obviously a big reader," I say, running my hands along a shelf of volumes. I can practically smell the centuries on them—there's something very specific about the scent of old paper and the ink that was used before mass manufacturing became a thing.

"I am," Sebastien says. "One of life's greatest pleasures is living the experiences of others through poetry and prose."

The way he says "pleasure" sends a quiver through my belly. Maybe it's the alcohol or maybe it's the fact that Merrick never looked at me like Sebastien did several times over dinner tonight, but has anyone ever been able to make reading sound so, uh . . . I have to lean against the bookshelf for a second.

When I've recovered, I climb up the spiral staircase to the second floor, while he stays downstairs, sipping his espresso. As I explore the shelves up here, I quickly realize that Sebastien isn't just a voracious reader and book collector. He's a hardcore nerd.

"Your books are organized by the Dewey decimal system!" The wooden shelves are elegantly engraved to indicate the range of numbers that belong there. But the books themselves aren't labeled with Dewey decimal numbers like in a normal library. "Oh my god," I say, leaning over the banister to look down at him on the sofa below. "Do you have the filing system memorized so that you don't even have to look it up to know where a book belongs?"

Sebastien laughs, and the sound is deep and resonant as it echoes through the library. It's probably the most relaxed I've seen him since we met.

"Guilty as charged," he says.

"That's really impressive," I say. "I mean, I've spent most of my adult life in the company of journalists and other word nerds, but organizing your personal library like this might take the cake."

He raises his espresso cup up toward me on the second-story landing, as if modestly accepting an award I've given him.

"What's the best book you've ever read?" I ask.

"That's like asking someone to choose their favorite child."

"Fair enough. Then tell me about a bunch that you've loved."

He begins with The Mistborn Saga, a series about gentlemen thieves who use magic to pull off an epic heist. It's a series that I also adore, and I'm surprisingly pleased that Sebastien likes fantasy. After hearing him mention José Saramago at Shipyard Books, I'd pegged Sebastien as the smug kind of reader who only read Nobel Prize winners and looked down their nose at everyone else. Instead, it turns out that he just reads *everything*. Even in this short time of getting to know him, he seems to have two feet on the ground. *Romeo and Juliet* curse theory notwithstanding.

I continue talking to Sebastien about his favorite books, peppering him with questions while I stay upstairs, winding my way through the labyrinth of bookcases. I pause for a moment as my fingers brush against the spines of the British literature section, freezing over a worn copy of *Romeo and Juliet*. But then I shake out my hand and turn the corner to browse another section of shelves.

It's a dead end with a couple of library carts in it, the kind with wheels, used for reshelving books. The carts are half full with what look like relatively new purchases that Sebastien hasn't put away yet.

Because I'm a nosy journalist, I walk over to thumb through what he's bought recently.

That's when I see that this dead end isn't just for carts. Behind them is a small black bookcase, made of metal instead of wood like the floor-to-ceiling shelves that populate the library. The bookcase has a glass door with a handle on it—almost like a wine fridge— and it's full of slim leather journals.

Being a lover of notebooks myself, I slide the glass door open, curious. Cool air gusts out.

Temperature controlled. Interesting. Maybe rare first editions?

"Helene?" Sebastien calls from downstairs. "I'm going to the kitchen to brew more coffee. Do you want anything?"

"No, I'm good, thanks."

While he's gone, I reach into the strange bookcase and pull out one of the volumes at random. It's old leather, beat up on the edges. I turn to the first page.

It's written in neat, slanting Italian, and I'm grateful that Dad made that offhand suggestion years ago that I learn Juliet's native language.

The private journal of Reynier Montague

I gasp.

My vignette about Kitri and Reynier in Shanghai.

I almost shove the journal back onto the shelf, because I didn't want to deal with the intersections of my stories and Sebastien's tonight.

But then I think maybe Reynier is just a popular name. Maybe it's just a coincidence.

I flip open the journal. The first entry is dated July 10, 1920, and it's about meeting Kitri Wagner on The Bund. My hands tremble. The story is almost identical to the vignette I wrote. Kitri on a bench on the quay, sketching the pretty ladies coming and going from the society clubs. Reynier strolling behind her, sneaking a peek at her work, then inviting her for afternoon tea of dumplings and crayfish.

Did it really happen?

And if so, how did it end? My vignette wrapped up after Kitri said yes to tea. But if this journal is what it seems—the diary of a Romeo past—then that means Kitri was Juliet. And Sebastien said things always end badly for them.

I should put the journal back. I should give myself this night off, protect my fatigued mind. And I shouldn't pry like this if it's really a diary.

But now that I've read the first part, I can't stop. I can hardly breathe as I skim the rest of Reynier's journal, flying through pages of their courtship, of happier times. There are months of entries, painstakingly recorded as if the writer couldn't bear to part with a single detail—the charcoal pencil smudged beneath Kitri's fingernails on a particular Monday morning; a seagull with one leg that she stopped to feed on their way to a speakeasy-style nightclub; and how she always insisted on eating dessert before her meal, because she preferred to fill her stomach with sweets first, and vegetables only if there was any space remaining afterward.

There is dancing and flapper dresses, Big Band jazz and elegant cocktails. But what I desperately want to know is what ultimately happened to Kitri and Reynier. I keep turning pages, thinking there will never be an end to their Roaring Twenties romance, when suddenly it comes to an abrupt halt, a little over half a year after it started.

DECEMBER 25, 1920

I knocked on the Wagners' front door. It was quite early to visit—the sun had not yet risen—but it was Christmas morning, and after her father gave me his blessing last night after supper, I was too eager to surprise Kitri with the best Christmas gift of all—a ring.

But no one answered the door.

Dread crept up my throat, bitter with the taste of the past. A portent I was all too familiar with.

You're jumping to conclusions, I tried to convince myself. They're simply still asleep.

Even if the Wagners hadn't risen, though, where was Gerald, the butler? Or Helga, Kitri's stern German nursemaid who'd become their housekeeper?

I knocked louder. Again, no answer.

Now I could taste the dread on my tongue.

Then I heard a wail from within the house, like the keening of a broken animal.

No . . . please say I'm wrong. Please say I haven't tainted her with my misery once again!

I broke one of the windows that flanked the front door and hurled myself through, glass tearing through my clothes and into my skin. I tore through the house, a bloodied madman, and up the stairs, following the howling.

Gerald, Helga, and the rest of the household staff stood pale and motionless in the hall. The door to Kitri's room stood open. The keening sliced through the air again, coming from inside.

"Oh, Herr Montague . . ." Helga said through a sob. "Miss Wagner suffered a sudden brain hemorrhage in the night. The doctor said no one could have known it would happen, there was nothing we could have done . . ." She burst into more sobbing.

I pushed past Helga, into Kitri's room. Frau Wagner—the source of the keening—wailed on the mattress, next to her daughter's lifeless, gray body. Herr Wagner sat in a limp heap in the rosewood chair in the corner.

"How could this be?" Herr Wagner entreated me, his eyes red where he had exhausted his tears. "How could there have been no signs? Kitri looked the peak of health . . ."

He was not truly asking me, though. He hardly saw me.

But I knew the answer all too well. It had happened out of thin air because of me.

I collapsed onto my knees at the side of Kitri's bed.

"Not yet, my love, not yet," I pleaded, even though it was pointless. "We weren't finished yet." My hands fumbled inside my coat for the velvet box. "I—I was going to . . ."

I couldn't say it. Not in the past tense. Trembling, I held her hand in mine. Cold. So cold, so unlike the sweet warmth of my Kitri, my Juliet. I took the emerald ring from the velvet box and tried to slip it onto her finger.

The ring wouldn't slide on. Her fingers were too stiff. Too strangely swollen.

But I couldn't let it be true, I couldn't stop. "Kitri, marry me." I kept pushing the ring.

"Marry me." I shoved harder on the ring. It wouldn't budge.

"Marry me, marry me, marry me!" I shouted, desperation cracking my voice.

Strong arms came up behind me and pulled me gently away. "Herr Montague," Helga said. "Come away."

"But I love her!"

"She's gone."

"We weren't done . . ."

Helga simply held me for a moment. Only when I'd stopped flailing did she let me go.

"I'm sorry," I whispered to Kitri, and left the ring on her bed. "A thousand times over, I'm sorry."

Staggering to her father, I said, "Bury her with the ring. Please?"

He closed his eyes, pained, and managed only a small nod.

Then I let Helga lead me away. There was nothing in the house anymore for me.

It was not only a ring, however, that I left on Kitri's bed, but also another shard of my long-shattered heart.

I wonder how many lives it will take before I have no heart at all.

* * *

Oh god. I press Reynier's journal to my chest. Oh god oh god oh god.

This really happened, didn't it?

My vignette was wrong, concluding with two strangers skipping off to tea, as if a happy first meeting is the prophecy of a happy ending. My version of the story was too chirpy, too trim, too conveniently happy.

But this . . . oh god, this. Something unlocks in the deep recesses of my brain, like a creaky old vault door, and the truth of this story rushes out, stale and dusty but sincere.

No. It's too much. I want to slam the vault in my head shut.

And yet, I can't resist . . .

I pull other journals from the shelf. Like in the Gallery of Me and the Hall of History, some of them match with characters I've written—Lucciano, Albrecht, Simão, Felix, Marius, Nolan, Matteo, Sir Charles, Jack . . . The only difference is, all their last names are Montague; I hadn't made that connection in my vignettes. I'd given all my characters different surnames, although now that I think about it, none of them had ever felt right.

"I brought some chocolate back with me," Sebastien calls from below when he returns from the kitchen.

I'm still reeling from the fact that there are very old, very genuine diaries up here that match my own stories.

"Helene? Did you get lost up there?"

Did I get lost up here?

Maybe.

I wasn't supposed to think about Romeo and Juliet, about the curse, about Sebastien and me. Tonight was supposed to be about taking a break, about drinking espresso and eating cannoli.

But life rarely does what you want it to.

Now I'm faced with a very real possibility: Maybe I don't have power over destiny anyway.

And, for me, destiny could very well spell doom.

SEBASTIEN

SOMETHING'S CHANGED. HELENE LOOKS FAR AWAY WHEN SHE COMES down the stairs. Physically, she's here, but mentally, she's elsewhere.

What happened during those ten minutes I was gone? Did she find my old journals in the corner up there?

If she didn't, I don't want to bring them up. But even if she did, I can't say anything. I promised not to mention our histories. I promised to treat Helene as herself, in the present, and not mire her in the Juliets of the past.

So what should I do?

She clutches the curved railing to keep herself steady on her injured ankle, but perhaps also to keep herself steady for other reasons. I get up from the couch and wait at the bottom of the stairs, where I offer my arm for support.

Helene's body is warm, the soft curves beneath her sweater pressing against me. As I hold on to her, I sigh, content for that brief instant to be reunited with her, like the right combination has been spun on a lock.

It's fleeting—just the span of a few steps—and then we're apart again as we sit on opposite sofas with the table of espresso and cannoli and whatever she discovered upstairs between us.

I want that closeness back. I crave the ease that I usually have with Juliet. But at the same time, I want to respect that Helene is her own person entirely. It's always tricky to perform this feat—knowing your soulmate's entire past yet accepting that you know nothing at all. I suppose, in a way, that's how it is with all relationships. You fall in love with one person, and then they keep changing, because that's what people do. If you love them enough, though, you try to keep up.

"Do you want a cannoli?" I ask, picking up the plate. "Or chocolate?" I hold up the small basket of confections I have shipped from Switzerland and Belgium every month. I may be American now, but I'll always prefer European chocolate.

Helene shakes her head. That's how I know something is really off. No matter how different my Juliets are, every single one of them has a sweet tooth.

I make it my mission to rescue the evening. It started out so well, and I don't want us to lose the little ground we've won. Between the two of us, Helene is the more talkative—as a general matter, I prefer to listen and let others speak—but I'll have to pick up the conversational mantle tonight. I can't talk about my journals or our pasts, but I can honor Helene's request to focus on who we are now.

Tonight, I think, is a bit like a first date. We're starting over from a blank slate, and we're sitting awkwardly around cups of coffee, not sure what to say. Because of that, I launch into first-date conversation.

Rather than "What's your favorite color?" though, I say, "What do you think is the best book title you've ever heard?"

"Huh?" Helene blinks at me, like she's confused why I'm trying to chat about inconsequential things.

I press on anyway, gently steering her from whatever's preoccupying her. "Best book title ever. I'll go first—*Cloudy with a Chance of Meatballs.*"

A snort of a laugh escapes her, catching her by surprise, and she can't resist responding. "*Cloudy with a Chance of Meatballs?* Really? And here I thought you were a Very Serious Fisherman."

I shrug. "Only on weekdays."

That gets a genuine smile out of her. But then I see her mind retreating again, so I pounce. "Your turn. Let's see if your favorite title is any less juvenile than mine."

Helene bites her bottom lip as she thinks. "Oh, I know," she says. "*The Seven Husbands of Evelyn Hugo.*"

"Never heard of it."

"But it's so good, right? You can't hear that title and *not* be curious how or why a woman would be married seven times. Is she a flake? A murderess? A serial widow?"

I flinch at the last question, because, well, that's one way to sum me up: a serial widower. But I quickly paste a smile back on my face, so as not to lose the momentum we're building, moving away from brooding and toward cheerful instead.

"You're right. That *is* a great title," I say. "Okay, what about the most iconic book cover of all time?"

"Oh, that's easy," Helene says, scooting to the edge of her sofa. *"Twilight."*

"Please, no." I cringe. "The most iconic book cover would have to be *The Godfather,* or maybe *A Clockwork Orange."*

"Ew," she says. "Those are both so . . . I dunno. Simple?"

"But *The Godfather*'s cover was so striking it also became the movie poster. How often does that happen? Almost never."

"I see your point, but I still don't like that cover. Okay, my turn to ask you something. Who was your first book crush?" Helene picks up a cannoli and takes a big bite as she waits for my answer. I interpret that as a sign that she's starting to relax. Good.

"Book crush?" I sip some of my espresso. "What's that?"

"The first time you fell in love with a character."

I make a face. "People do that?"

"Sure, all the time. My sister Katy's first book crush was Holden Caulfield."

"Holden Caulfield?"

Helene grins. "Katy's a strange one. So come on, tell me. Who was your first book crush?"

I suppose I could say that I fell in love with a woman who later became a character, written about by everyone from Bandello to Shakespeare to Baz Luhrmann. But that's breaking the rules of engagement—avoiding the topic of Romeo and Juliet—so I skirt the issue. "I don't think men have book crushes."

"Book lusts, then?" Helene asks, teasing.

I choke on my coffee, and I'm sure my face has flushed crimson all the way to the tips of my ears. All I can manage is a cracked "Pass," as if I'm a teenage boy again.

She laughs.

When I stop coughing up the espresso, I turn the question back on her. "Who was your first book crush or book lust, then?"

Her laughter falls away suddenly, and I get the sinking feeling that I've pushed the joke too far. "I'm sorry," I say. "Let's skip the question."

"No," Helene says as she sets her cannoli back onto the plate.

"I posed the question, so it's only fair that I answer. But I didn't think it through before I asked. Because the thing is . . . the first character I fell in love with was you."

Joy and fear ripple simultaneously through me. I knew she'd made up a character who looked like me for her stories, but I hadn't realized the extent of her feelings for me. If I'd only been an imaginary friend, that alone would've been enough for Helene to be flummoxed by my appearance in real life. But if she loved my character, then perhaps it's only a few more inches before she falls for the actual me.

Only . . . there will be consequences to that. The curse was why I tried to conceal myself from Helene, to hide away in a frozen town on the edge of the world. And still she found me, because I tried to evade the curse last time, but it's inescapable. Maybe the curse let Avery Drake go, but Helene's knowledge of our bygone relationships makes it that much harder for me to break our bond.

Neither of us knows what to say after Helene's confession. We're not supposed to talk about our backstories, and yet they're there, no matter how hard we try to bury them. Does free will exist at all? Or are our futures dictated by the pasts that came before them?

"You know what?" Helene says. "I think maybe we should turn in for the night. It's been . . . a big day."

It's not even late, but I know what she means.

"Do you need help getting back to your room?" I rise from the sofa and offer my arm, in case her ankle's bothering her.

"I'll be okay," Helene says, but it's unclear whether she's talking about her ankle or our truncated conversation. "Do you need help with—?" she gestures at the coffee, cannoli, and chocolate.

"No, thank you. You go ahead to bed."

"Okay. Um, good night, then." She gives me a diffident smile.

We walk out of the library together, and she turns toward the guest suite, in the opposite direction of the kitchen.

I watch her for several more beats and sigh.

Good night, my love.

HELENE

I WAIT FOR HALF AN HOUR AFTER I HEAR SEBASTIEN GO UPSTAIRS before I sneak back into the library. It's too early to go to bed, and even if it weren't, there's no way I'm going to be able to sleep, knowing his journals are there.

Am I snooping? Am I invading his privacy? Yes and yes. But my brain is already two steps ahead of me, rationalizing that (a) those shelves aren't locked, (b) Sebastien let me go upstairs and didn't put any limits on what I could explore, and (c) *if* those journals really do contain true stories about us, then it's a shared history that belongs to both of us. Which means I have as much right to read them as he does.

Yes, I am the worst, and I know it.

But here I am anyway, at the foot of the library staircase. I'm using my phone as a flashlight, because I don't want to turn on any of the lamps and broadcast what I'm up to.

My original plan was to go up, grab the journals, then bring them back to the sofas downstairs. But my ankle throbs—it turns out that tiptoeing is *not* good for a twisted ankle—and I can also picture myself trying to carry the tall stack of notebooks and tumbling down the stairs, not only making a ruckus but ruining all those carefully preserved diaries. Some of them are supposedly hundreds of years old and really ought to be in a museum, not manhandled by the likes of me.

So instead I grab a couple of the throw blankets on the couches, as well as an armful of pillows. I'll make myself a cozy reading nest among the shelves, and that way I won't have to transport the journals anywhere. I'm also less likely to get caught, since the sitting area downstairs is visible from the main corridor, but upstairs, I'll be safely tucked away.

When I reach the second-floor landing, though, I freeze. Were those footsteps I just heard down the hall? I breathe as quietly as I can and try not to move. My elbow itches. Dammit. *Don't scratch it, don't scratch it, don't scratch it.* If I try to scratch it, I'll drop all the blankets and pillows.

I keep listening, and there's nothing. Probably just my nerves conjuring up footsteps where there are none. I continue deeper into the library.

Sebastien's journals are exactly where I left them, the temperature-control fan inside humming softly. I arrange my blankets and pillows, then open the glass door and take out all of the notebooks, stacking them neatly and carefully on the carpet. The leather is buttery soft, the edges of the oldest journals worn and well loved.

Once I'm settled in my reading nest, though, I just stare at the notebooks. I *think* I want to know what's inside them . . . but do I really? This is the precipice either where I retreat and keep my perfect Story Sebastien safe in my head, or where I take a leap after Real Sebastien, without regard to whether I fall or fly.

But my world has already been turned upside down and shaken in all directions, hasn't it? I'm no longer a minor reporter at a newspaper, the job I've held for so many years. I don't have a marriage anymore. And I've already seen my invented character walk and talk in real life, and my private stories rendered in antique oil paintings. There's no stepping back from that; I'm already over the precipice, even if I'm clinging to a lone, scraggly branch hanging over the cliff's edge.

I take a deep breath and open the closest notebook: The private journal of Felix Montague.

Bern, Switzerland—July 10, 1559

I am a clockmaker now. Not a master, nor an apprentice. Rather, I keep myself staunchly in between; I like it that way. I come into the shop every morning at quarter past seven and greet Johann Miller, the old, revered artisan who oversees the four clockmakers here. After that, I gather my tools and walk over to my project for the day. It's usually a complicated, gold-plated monstrance clock or sometimes an heirloom display piece; I enjoy being entrusted with my clients' most valuable treasures.

At nine o'clock, I pause for *znüni,* a midmorning break for a small bite to eat. I always have a pastry of my own invention, one I bake at home and bring to work wrapped neatly in paper. The pastry is filled with chocolate hazelnut cream and scents the workshop with a near-magical aroma of butter, heady yeast, and featherlight sugar like snowfall. It is my Juliet's favorite—consistent through every lifetime— and I have a cornetto every morning to keep her with me, especially in the long years that I'm alone. It's these small indulgences that get me through an eternity mostly spent waiting.

When the clock strikes noon, the shop closes for an hour for lunch. Most others in town flock to the cafés with views of the Alps or Bern's landmark clock tower. But today I felt the urge to try something different. A customer yesterday had mentioned Café Hier, a quaint, homey restaurant tucked into the Nuessle Inn. I took a left at the fork in the cobblestone streets while the other clockmakers took a right.

There were a handful of other diners at Café Hier, but the space was small enough that it required only one waitress. There were no windows, and the beams of the ceiling were so low I felt a touch claustrophobic and began to second-guess my decision to eat there, rather than in the wide-open outdoor cafés of the main square.

But then the waitress came to greet me, and everything around me fell away because I tasted honeyed wine on my lips.

Juliet.

I forgot all about the low ceiling. I could've been in an underground cavern for all I cared, because this waitress— Juliet—was the only view I needed. She was, as ever, brighter than the sun, and more dazzling than any clock tower or Swiss mountain range could ever be.

There were so many things I wanted to tell her. *I've missed you! I thought of you only this morning when I had my cornetto! I am sorry about Lisbon, Mainz, Sicily, everything. Do you remember who I am this time, what we are?*

But I said nothing while she led me to a table, because I was capable only of awe in that moment, not speech. Instead, she chattered away, the consummate hostess. Her family owned the Nuessle Inn. Her name was Clara. The special today was schnitzel.

Clara. I tried the name on my tongue.

She smiled at me, and I realized it was the first word I'd uttered aloud in her presence. *Clara.*

I think I shall dine at Café Hier every noon from now on.

That's the end of Felix's first entry, and it's almost identical to a vignette I wrote. But what I didn't have was a specific date for when Felix and Clara's story began. This journal, though, begins on the tenth of July, the same date as the Capulets' ball when Romeo first met Juliet. Just like the other journal I read earlier tonight, the one about Kitri and Reynier.

Do we always meet on the same day? Is that why that date is the security code to Sebastien's gallery?

The other thing I didn't have in my own vignette about Felix and Clara was any story past their first encounter. I'm starting to see how I had a Disney fairy tale approach to my stories, setting up love at first sight and then presuming the happily ever after.

Both intrigued and scared by how this story I thought I invented might develop, I delve into more entries. They're detailed accounts of every single encounter between Felix and Clara, the minutiae carefully preserved: What he ordered for lunch. How she wore her hair. Whether he said hello first that day, or if she was the first to speak.

To anyone else, the details might seem boring, even tedious. But I'm beginning to understand that these are the habits of a man who is used to losing what he loves. It reminds me of when my dad got the diagnosis for his brain tumor and the pronouncement that it was aggressive and incurable. Like magpies, Mom, Katy, and I began to obsessively collect every second with Dad. I'd write down everything he said, especially the end-of-life advice he wanted to impart. Katy shot videos of him every day. Mom saved a clipping of his hair when it began to fall out, dried a flower from every get-well-soon bouquet, and even kept every hospital wristband as if it were a ticket stub from their first date, or, rather, their last one.

Because we never really knew when the last of anything would come.

I wipe away a tear as I think about Dad in the audience of *Romeo and Juliet,* watching me in a role that, it turns out, was astoundingly prescient.

"What would you say about all this, Daddy?" I ask.

I can almost hear him chuckling. *Life is like a mechanical bull,* he'd say. *You never know what's going to happen, but you can hold on tight and enjoy the ride.*

Or something like that. Dad was never one to shy away from adventure.

Me, though?

Well, New Helene is trying.

I turn my attention back to Felix's journal. I'm about a year in, and it's another entry similar to the others before it, a lovingly documented snapshot of their growing relationship.

BERN, SWITZERLAND—APRIL 22, 1560

"I'm sorry I'm late," I said as I hurried into Café Hier. "The monstrance clock I was working on is caked with dirt on the inside."

"You're not late," Clara said as she approached me. She wore her hair in a crown of braids, and I thought her more beautiful than the baroness in nearby Bâtie-Champion.

"How do you know I'm not late?" I said, teasing. "You don't even have a clock in the restaurant."

She shrugged mirthfully. "Papa doesn't like our customers to feel rushed. As for me, I don't much like counting minutes. I enjoy simply existing, in this very moment. Does that make sense?"

I smiled but shook my head. "I'm a clockmaker. I live by the ticks of the minute hand. So no, it does not make sense to me, but I love that you think that way."

The apples of her cheeks grew a touch rosy. Then Clara remembered we were still standing and she was supposed to take me to a table.

Once seated, she tried to tell me what the cook was making this afternoon so that I could choose.

"I would prefer whatever you recommend," I said, as I do each day.

She pretended to study me. This is the little game we play every lunch hour.

"Hmm," Clara said. "I think today you would benefit from *zürcher geschnetzeltes.*"

"So hearty a dish?" I nodded sagely, feigning serious consideration over the veal and mushroom stew. "Well, I suppose I am feeling a bit tired. The monstrance clock I worked on this morning was rather heavy. All right, then, zürcher geschnetzeltes it is."

Clara beamed, pleased that I'd agreed with her choice, even though it wasn't a surprise, because I always agree. I would do anything Clara asks.

We are deeply in love with each other, but I've rushed the previous reincarnations of Juliet. I want to try a slower approach with Clara. Perhaps that is what will break the curse. Perhaps, if the relationship is done right, it will last.

She tended to her other customers for a while, giving them all the attention they deserved, even though we both knew she'd prefer to spend the entire lunch hour with me. She takes care of the diners not only because it's her job but because it's in her nature to be generous, just like Juliet the first time I saw her, when she descended the Capulets' staircase and acknowledged everyone from the musicians to the servants cleaning up empty goblets.

When Clara returned with my lunch, that fetching blush again colored her cheeks. "I hope you enjoy your meal."

I gazed at her and smiled. "I assure you, I already am."

★ ★ ★

I press my fingers to this last line, and a twinge of envy vibrates through me like a plucked violin string. Am I jealous of Felix and Clara, and the way Felix clearly adores her? Even in my early days with Merrick, he never looked at me like that. I think we liked the idea of each other more than the reality of each other. We were seduced by the potential that people would look at us and think, *Wow, what an impressive journalistic duo! Number one and number two in their graduating class. How can one couple possibly have so much talent?*

But Romeo and Juliet were the opposite; they didn't give a damn what other people thought. Sure, their impetuousness was a flaw, but it was also love in its purest form, untainted by outside opinions. So yes, I'm a little jealous of Felix and Clara—their certainty, their quiet and deep history. This journal is thick, the pages weighted from nearly two years of ink and emotion.

And yet, it still ends. There is no volume two of Felix and Clara.

Bern, Switzerland—June 13, 1561

After lunch, I returned to the clockmaker's shop. The ticking of the timepieces welcomed me back to work, their steady rhythm assuring me that all was in order with my life. Clara would come by in a few hours. She wanted to see the lantern clock I've been building for her. It was to be a wedding gift and would sit in the entryway of our future home. It was almost finished.

Tick.

Tick.

Tick.

At forty-three minutes past four, the lantern clock malfunctioned and began to chime as if it were midnight, and it would not stop.

At forty-four minutes past four, a runaway carriage flew through the streets outside the shop.

At forty-five minutes past four, the lantern clock finally ceased its chiming, but the sound was replaced by screaming in the streets.

At forty-six minutes past four, I found Clara's body trampled on the cobblestones.

There's a bunch of writing that's been scratched out angrily, tears bleeding the script until it's just a mess of illegible smeared ink and heartbreak.

And then, lower on the page:

I have done it wrong again.

I thought patience was the key, but . . .

I'm sorry, my love.

I DO NOT KNOW HOW TO SAVE YOU.

The paper is partially torn at the word "how"; it was written with so much force and grief the pen went through the page.

Downstairs, the lantern clock on the first floor of Sebastien's library chimes.

I start to cry.

After a while, I get ahold of myself again, and I pick up another journal. But unlike the others, this journal is written in what looks like an old Slavic language, and I can't read it.

I don't know the story either, because I've never written one set in Eastern Europe.

But there are only two entries in the notebook, and I can understand the dates because they're just numbers: *10-7-1604* and *11-7-1604*.

July 10 and 11, 1604.

No . . .

The sum total of this relationship is contained in two mere pages. The rest of the journal is entirely empty.

I choke back a sob, but it only comes back with the next breath, and I start crying again, but harder. Two days? That's all they had together?

Two days?

How does Sebastien bear it?

I squeeze my eyes and fists tight, as if that will push back the surge of sadness. I remember how grief feels, how after my dad died, life was an absolute vacuum of nothingness combined with a shrieking banshee ripping my soul apart. It's an agonizing, lonely torment. And Sebastien has to go through it over and over.

Of course, then there's the other part of the curse, that Juliet never lives for long once she and Romeo find each other again.

And if I really am Juliet, that means I could die soon, too.

But I don't want to think about that right now. I *can't.* I have survived this day because I haven't let my mind go down that line of inquiry.

I shove those thoughts into a dusty corner of my mind for now. I want to keep reading the journals, even though it's gut-wrenching to wade through Sebastien's pain. Other than the one notebook in Cyrillic, the others all seem to be written in Italian, which I'll be able to read. Maybe the two-day life was so traumatic that Romeo never wrote in another language again.

I reach for what looks like the oldest journal. It belongs to Lucciano the shoemaker and Isabella, who he thought was literally the same Juliet. It's penned in an antiquated Italian that I ought to have trouble with, yet the words click as easily in my mind as if they were modern Italian. I absolutely do *not* want to think about why that might be. Instead, I throw myself headlong into Lucciano and Isabella's love story and cry as she rejects him, then drowns, all during their honeymoon.

The next journal I read belongs to Albrecht Montague, who worked with Gutenberg on the printing press, and his wife Brigitta, a dairymaid. I know the beginning of their story, because I wrote a similar vignette, but I didn't know Albrecht and Brigitta had only a year together. Then I remember that a year is probably good, compared to two days (or even five, for the original Romeo and Juliet), and with that realization, I'm submerged in melancholy again for them. I read all of Albrecht's detailed notes about how much they want a child and how Brigitta grows smaller and smaller each day as she blames herself for their failure to conceive. In the end, she died of despair.

Simão the sailor married Ines, the port-maker's daughter, but she was crushed in the winery when several racks of barrels collapsed.

Marius leaped into a bonfire to try to save Cosmina, who was burned at the stake because the townspeople thought she was a witch.

There's a trek across the Sahara in search of a mystical land of gold. It ends with the expedition lost in a terrible, violent sandstorm. For months afterward, Nolan Montague, the sole survivor, lay in the sand with his beloved, Mary Jo Phoenix, until she was only bone, and he a shell of a man.

And there is more. Sadness upon sadness, death after death after death.

My body quivers as I keep reading, tears splashing onto old pages too fragile to take them. I thought I knew these stories; I'd written many of them in my own notebooks. But I *don't* know the stories, not the true span and depth of these histories.

Our histories. If the curse is real.

Hours later, it suddenly becomes too much. There's too much suffering, too much loss and pain.

I curl up in my soggy nest of blankets, weeping, the journals strewn all around me.

I am nothing but deep, jagged sorrow.

SEBASTIEN

WHEN I RETREAT TO MY BEDROOM, I DO WHAT I SHOULD HAVE DONE ages ago: I look up what happened to the Juliet before Helene.

Of course, I'd inadvertently caught snippets of Avery Drake's success now and then, on magazine covers and whatnot. But other than that, I'd willfully made myself blind to her existence, in order for her to *have* an existence. I didn't even keep a journal to record our single meeting. I thought if I could pretend she wasn't there, the curse would leave her be. I didn't buy any of Avery's photographs until after she'd passed.

In fact, I didn't know she'd died until I came across Helene at Pomona College a decade ago. For all I knew before that moment, Avery Drake was still alive and well into her seventies. When I saw Helene, though, some quick backward math proved that Helene must have been born in the early 1990s, which means Avery lived a little past age fifty. Still quite a lifespan for a Juliet, who generally got only two or three decades on earth.

Even after Avery's death, though, I never looked into how she'd lived. It was as if that were something sacred to her, something I could give to Juliet to have for her own, because I had tarnished all her other lives.

But now, with Helene here, I think it might be important to know what Avery's life was like. Was it happy without me, as I hoped? Because if so, I will do whatever it takes to make that happen for Helene. Even if the curse is bent on revenge for my evasion last time.

My computer screen casts an eerie glow in my otherwise dark bedroom. Thousands upon thousands of results come up for a search about Avery Drake. There are interviews and features in *The New York Times, China Daily, National Geographic,* and every other prominent news source in the world; endless catalogs of her wildlife prints for sale; a nonprofit foundation for nature conservation named after her; and more.

"Good for you, Avery," I smile at the search results. "The only thing you don't seem to have are children's books about you, holding you up as a role model."

But when I click on a posthumous story about her in *Rolling Stone,* I suddenly understand why.

Avery Drake was a drug addict who bounced from one abusive relationship to the next. She went through dark periods of crippling depression and frequently cut herself, which is why she wore long sleeves in all of her photos. And although she died of natural causes, she'd harbored dreams of suicide many times.

"Despite all my achievements," she'd said in one of her last interviews, "I'm haunted by a hollowness, as if there's a ghost by my side—or maybe more accurately, *not* a ghost by my side, just . . . nothing. There's always an empty space next to me, like something or someone is supposed to be there but isn't. I've tried my whole life to fill it—with awards or with cocaine or even razors and pain—but nothing ever feels right." The interviewer noted how she laughed nervously, then said, "Maybe this is where I'm supposed to say I'm glad my life turned out the way it did, huh? Because if I'd been happy, I wouldn't have poured myself into my work. Maybe misery is what drove me to success."

"Oh, Avery," I whisper, my fingers touching the screen as if I can soothe the image of the sad woman there.

In the hours that follow, I read dozens more stories on her. And while most stay positive and focus on her talent and boldness in getting shots that other wildlife photographers wouldn't dare, the ones that delve into Avery as a person have a universal theme: Her internal life was tortured by suffering.

I thought I had spared her the curse, but it had found her anyway.

Found *us*. Because I also suffered in that lifetime without my Juliet, knowing she was out there but that I couldn't have her.

I had actually made Juliet's—Avery's—life worse by taking myself out of the equation.

Damn this wretched, godforsaken curse!

I shut down the computer and fall into bed. But I can't get comfortable, can't stop thinking that I had condemned Avery when I'd meant to set her free.

If I hadn't run away when I met her in that café in Kenya, would it have been better? A brief but intense period of happiness in exchange for a longer life of external success but personal anguish?

And what does that mean for me and Helene? If I take the next flight out of Alaska and leave her, maybe she'll be miserable, doomed to spend her time haunted by the sense that something is missing, just like Avery did.

At least when the other Juliets and I have fallen for each other, we've been blissfully happy for however much time we had.

Perhaps a life well lived isn't measured in months or years, but in love. In kisses and gentle twining of hands, in fiery embraces and soft, whispered affections.

After centuries with the curse, I still can't predict how it will punish me. But after reading about Avery—after dispelling my delusions that I'd helped her—I think that giving in to fate's desire for Helene and me to be together might not be the worst thing.

Doleful whimpering rouses me from thoughts. It reverberates through the corridors and up the stairs, the pained hiccupping of someone trying to muffle their sobs but failing miserably.

Helene!

I jump out of bed. Did her ankle give out? I imagine her lying crumpled on the wood floor somewhere, and I swear at myself for building this house with so many hard surfaces. I careen through the hallways, following the sounds of her crying.

It's loudest in the library. I should have known. She's on the second floor, and I fly up the curved staircase and to the back corner where she's huddled in a fort of pillows and blankets, my journals splayed open all around her.

"Hey . . ." I gather her into my arms. "Shh . . . it's going to be okay. They're stories. Just stories."

That's a lie—there's nothing *just* about them—but I don't know what else to say. All I want is for Helene not to be upset or frightened. I only want her happy and safe.

It's all I've ever wanted.

"How long have you been here?" I ask, stroking her hair. She's still crying, but silently now, each convulsion rattling through me as if her distress were my own.

Helene looks up at me, her eyes puffy and red. That's answer enough for me. It looks as if she's been in tears off and on for hours.

"But they're not just stories, are they?" she asks, her voice strangled between ragged gulps for air.

I let out a long exhale. "No, they're not. But you still shouldn't read them all at once. You'll overdose on heartbreak and go mad."

She squeezes her eyes closed and buries her face against my chest. "How do you do it?" she asks.

"Do what?"

"Go on."

I shake my head, although she can't see it. The honest answer is, I don't know. I go on because I have no choice.

Does it help that Juliet always comes back? Some, but not much. Her return never takes away the pain of losing her previous incarnation. I live with festering wounds that never heal, because the half-life of grief is forever.

However, that's not important tonight. What matters is Helene and how she's dealing with the revelations of our past. I've carried the knowledge of the curse for a long, long time. She's known about it for less than twenty-four hours.

"Are you okay?" I ask, even though I know there's no way anyone could be.

She murmurs something, but it gets lost against my shirt.

"I'm sorry, I didn't hear you."

"Two days," Helene whispers. "Sometimes I die in *two days*."

Zlata. Poor, innocent Zlata.

"Or two years," I counter, as if that's much better. In 1682, I fell for a self-proclaimed sorceress, Cosmina, when she showed up at my castle door. Cosmina lived for two whole years afterward, the longest of my loves.

But still the time is never enough.

"Do you think we might be different?" Helene asks. It comes out meek, like a hope that's crushed before it's even conceived.

"Because you remembered our pasts, via the stories you wrote? Maybe," I say. I don't tell her that I doubt it means we're free of the curse, that this is just another way for it to torture us, to make us suffer.

"And all the journals . . ." she says. "We always meet on July tenth. But I came to Alaska in January. That's different, too."

I hesitate. "Actually . . . I saw you before. On the tenth of July, ten years ago. In Claremont, California."

She jerks upright. "At Pomona College?"

I nod.

"Where was I on campus? Specifically." Her eyes are wide, and I wonder if she might remember that day, too.

"On a picnic blanket on the grass," I say. "You were with friends, and you were wearing—"

"A honey-colored sundress," Helene finishes for me. "It was new, the first time I'd worn it, and I remember the strangest thing happened to me that afternoon. I was just lounging on the lawn when suddenly I thought I tasted honey on my tongue. I laughed because it matched the color of the dress. And every time I wore it afterward, I waited to see if it would happen again, like some kind of sweet magic, but it never did. But now I realize, it wasn't the dress. It was you, wasn't it?"

"Yes," I say softly. "It was me. *Us.*"

"Ten years. That's a lot longer than two—something else that's different from the other Romeos and Juliets. Why didn't you come introduce yourself then?"

My chest tightens and I feel a little ill, knowing now what I know about Avery and what happens when I leave Juliet alone. "I didn't introduce myself because you looked happy, and I couldn't bring myself to steal that from you. I had . . . a theory. That perhaps the curse only starts the clock when we fall in love with each other. I'd left the previous version of Juliet alone, and she went on to live a significant life. So when I saw you . . . I walked away."

"That's the reason why you were horrible to me when we met at The Frosty Otter, wasn't it?" Helene asks. "You wanted to make me leave."

I wince but the accusation is fair. "Yes."

"And now . . ." Helene says. "We haven't fallen for each other yet. We could still go our separate ways. Is that what you want?"

"No." It slips out before I can think better of it, before I can remind myself that this should be her choice, not mine.

But yearning swells in my chest like a dam about to burst. I should let her go, but I'm beginning to think there's no such thing as free will, at least not when it concerns me and her. Perhaps soulmates are inevitable. Perhaps we can't outmaneuver fate.

I lean down and kiss her. Only a soft graze, but the jolt of honeyed wine on our mouths is so potent it sends fire through every vein in my body. Helene gasps as the shockwave of our first kiss in this lifetime roils through her.

"Oh god," she whispers. "Does that happen every time?"

I nod. "Every time."

No matter where we are, no matter who she is, when she kisses me, it's always like this.

HELENE

I KISS SEBASTIEN AGAIN, AND THE ELECTRICITY BETWEEN US IS A coiled live wire, ready to spring. But, as if by unspoken pact, we force restraint, and everything moves in languorous slow motion.

Velvet mouths.

Sweet wine on the tongue.

Silken hair against flushed cheeks.

If I could bottle up time, this would be a moment to keep.

But then the thoughts I'd shoved away in the back of my mind burst out of their captivity in a rush, and I'm suddenly drowning in the implications of what it means if I'm really Juliet.

I jerk back from Sebastien. "I—I can't do this."

"Helene, please . . ."

Tears prickle my eyes again, and when I see the wounded expression on his face, I start to cry in earnest.

"If we try—" he says.

But I cut him off by shaking my head violently. "No. You have to understand, I *do* want what Romeo and Juliet had. And Simão and Ines, Felix and Clara, Nolan and Mary Jo. Ever since I was in middle school and invented my imaginary Romeo, all I've wanted is to be loved for being me. But I . . ."

The tears come faster now, not sad, but scared.

"Sebastien," I choke out. "I don't want to . . . d-die."

He closes his eyes for a long, pained moment, his whole body shuddering as if he's trying to hold all his emotion in. When he finally opens his eyes again, the blueness looks as if it's faded to gray.

He doesn't say anything.

He doesn't try to change my mind.

He simply takes my hand and says quietly, "Okay."

HELENE

I AM SO WORN, AND I DON'T THINK MY ANKLE WILL SUPPORT THE weight of my emotional and physical fatigue, so Sebastien carries me to the guest suite. He draws down the covers, sets me gently on the bed, and tucks me in.

"I'm sorry," I say.

But he just shakes his head and gives me a brave smile. "Rest. I'll see you when you wake up, if you want. But for now, just rest."

He leaves without another sound, miraculous for a man his size to walk so featherlight.

My brain, which has been sprinting like a hamster on a battery-powered wheel, finally loses its battle with exhaustion. The proverbial hamster falls off the wheel, my thoughts dissipate, and I immediately pass out and sleep until noon.

When I wake, my eyes are pink and swollen. It looks like I punched myself in the face last night. Which I kind of did, metaphorically speaking. Spending hours wading through centuries of Romeo's grief while also freaking out that I might be Juliet and condemned to die is pretty close to punching myself in the face about a thousand times.

My entire body aches—from the car accident, from sitting huddled on the library floor half the night, from . . . life.

Maybe a shower would help.

As soon as the hot water hits my body, my muscles begin to unclench a little. I spend an entire half hour in the shower, partially to relax and partially to procrastinate, to avoid having to think about what comes next. When I finally make myself get out, I ignore my pile of wrinkled, tear- and snot-stained clothes on the floor and just put on my dad's watch and wrap myself in the robe hanging on the hook on the bathroom door.

Then I eat three bowls of Cinnamon Toast Crunch as my lunch.

Outside, the blizzard has calmed to a mere flurry, but from the looks of the snow piled up six feet high outside my window, I'm not going anywhere soon. It'll take the plows a couple of days to get out here.

Which means I'm stuck in a house with a man who might be my soulmate, who tastes like memories and honey when I kiss him, but who could very well be the reason I die.

No longer willing to procrastinate, my mind begins to flip through the list of past Juliets' horrific deaths like a morbid Rolodex: knife wound, drowning, crushed by wine barrels, stampede of horses, political revolution and war (more than once), burned at the stake, dehydration in the desert, illnesses like tuberculosis and brain hemorrhage . . . A fresh sob wracks my body, and it takes all my energy to keep it from devolving into tears.

Don't cry, I try to tell myself firmly. *You chose to stop kissing Sebastien last night. You're not going to be the next victim of the curse. You're not going to die.*

The face of my dad's watch glints in the kitchenette's light, and for a moment I feel like such a wimp. He got sick young, and he didn't get hysterical about it. He was so brave, always pointing out what a great life he'd had, always with a ready smile for Katy and me, a long hug and tender kiss for Mom.

But was he that brave at the outset, right when he got his diagnosis? a voice in the back of my head asks.

I don't know, because I was just a kid then. But maybe he wasn't brave. Maybe he collapsed and cried behind closed doors. Maybe it took him a while to become brave.

I look down at Dad's watch and stroke its broken face. I bet he'd wished he could stop time then, to stay with Mom and Katy and me a little longer.

Then again, his last words to us were, *I sure am lucky that I crammed a whole lotta life into thirty-eight years. I wouldn't want it any other way.*

"But you're still with me, aren't you, Daddy?" I whisper as I clutch the watch against my wrist. I can feel him watching over me right now, giving me permission to be scared. Telling me that being strong doesn't mean not being overwhelmed or terrified. It means letting yourself feel those things, and then getting up and carrying on anyway.

All right, then. Here's the bare truth: I don't know if I believe that I'm Juliet. But there's an awful lot of evidence in Sebastien's library, and what if I really am? I'm nowhere near ready to die. I wasted too many years on Merrick and I let him suffocate my dreams of a career and a family. Now it's just become *my* turn, and I want to use it. To think about that all fading to black when I'm only getting started . . .

A chill shivers through me, and I wrap the robe around myself tighter.

"I have no intention of dying," I say out loud, as if that will fend off the possibility.

And maybe it's in my control. Even if I give in to the belief that I'm Juliet, Sebastien said he left the previous version of me alone, right? And she lived "a significant life." If I can find out about her, then maybe I can feel better about my own prospects when I walk away from him.

So who was she?

My reporter training kicks in. I think back to the journals in the library, and because this is now for the sake of research, it doesn't make me shaky to remember them.

The last notebook was from 1941. That leaves a stretch of more than eighty years between Rachel Wilcox at Pearl Harbor and me. And based on the dates of all the other journals, it seems like Juliet's spirit reincarnates immediately after she dies.

So if the attack on Pearl Harbor was in December 1941, that means the Juliet before me would have been born in 1942. And she would have been an adult in the sixties, so Sebastien could have met her anytime from then onward.

But how do I find a single woman in all of the 1960s through the early '90s, when I was born?

Do I know anything else about her?

Think, Helene, think.

Oh!

The photographs on Sebastien's bedroom walls. When I'd asked who took them, he'd said it was a woman he loved. I can't remember if he told me her name, but the photos were high enough quality that they *must* be from the last Juliet. Especially because before World War II, I was Kitri in 1920s Shanghai . . .

I catch the fact that I used "I" in that thought. *I* was Kitri.

I think I believe I'm Juliet more than I'd admitted to myself.

But I shove that aside for now, because I'm on a roll. The previous Juliet *had* to have been the wildlife photographer, because color film like in Sebastien's framed pictures wasn't around before 1901, when Kitri Wagner was born.

I run out of the kitchenette into the bedroom and grab my phone.

A quick image search for "female wildlife photographer 1980s" (I figure that would put her in her forties, which would allow for more time to build a career) yields a promising list of names. Then I cross-reference those with another search for "seal family watching Northern Lights," and—

"Gotcha!"

Avery Drake.

Time to learn everything I can about her.

SEBASTIEN

HELENE DOESN'T LEAVE THE GUEST SUITE FOR TWO DAYS. I DON'T want to bother her—she should have all the space she wants, even if it's forever and it nearly kills me—but I also desperately want to know if she's all right. I keep walking down that hallway, hovering and trying not to eavesdrop, yet at the same time, trying to hear sounds of crying or any other sign she might need me.

I do knock, once, to let her know that I made a fresh batch of Nutella cornetti for her and left the containers outside her door. And that I also brought her a set of my flannel pajamas—too big but at least clean—and if she wanted me to wash her clothes since she'd been stuck in them for a few days, she could leave them in the pajamas' place.

The next time I go to that part of the house, the containers and pj's are gone, although there's no dirty laundry for me to take. At least I know she's doing okay enough to want to eat the pastries. But I'm disappointed there's nothing more for me to do. If there were, I could put my attention on consoling Helene.

Instead, I have to face the excruciating fact that the only love of my long, lonely life is here . . .

And I cannot have her.

HELENE

I BURY MY FACE IN THE PILLOWS. I HAVE READ EVERYTHING ON THE internet about Avery Drake. I wish I hadn't.

Because here are the choices before me:

- *I am Juliet, I fall in love with Sebastien, and I die soon.*
- *I am Juliet, I walk away from Sebastien, and if Avery's life is evidence of what happens when Juliet is separated from Romeo, I live for twice as long but it is full of its own ghastly horrors, so much so that I will court death and wish I'd died earlier.*

- *I am not Juliet, and my vignettes and Sebastien's paintings, artifacts, and journals are all a massive, extremely detailed coincidence. There is no such thing as the curse, no eternal Romeo, no
doomed reincarnations of Juliet. Which means I can do whatever
I want.*

I want the last bullet point to be true. But laying it out like that
only emphasizes that it's almost as unlikely as the other two.

And if, somehow, point three *is* true? Then I am still left with
less than I began with when I came to Alaska (which, frankly,
wasn't much), because I couldn't go forward with writing a book
based on the vignettes. There's too much reality attached to them
now. If I want to reject that there's a reason my stories and Sebastien's are all connected, then I can't think about those vignettes
ever again.

My dad's watch is cool against my cheek, and I raise my head
from the pillow to look at it.

"How do I be brave enough to move forward?" I ask.

The watch doesn't respond. But when I shut my eyes, I remember a conversation I heard through the walls of our house late
one night when Mom and Dad thought Katy and I were asleep. It
was early on after his diagnosis, and Mom was crying. Up till now,
I think I'd blocked this memory from my mind.

"What am I going to do, Mike? I can't survive without you. I
can't raise the girls on my own. I can't—"

"You can, Beth. I have faith in you."

"I can't. I don't even know how I can get through the days right
now. How can you be so . . . steady?"

"Because I'm not dead yet."

That made her bawl harder.

He comforted her, and when her sobbing quieted to hiccups,
he said, "There are infinite things that could happen, Bethie. Infinite things we could worry about. I had to let them go. Otherwise,
the life I still have would be governed by fear. That's all I meant
when I said I wasn't dead yet. Every second of life is worth too
much to waste on the infinite what-ifs."

I press Dad's watch harder against my cheek, trying not to cry for the loss of him, and for what might be on the threshold for me.

But I know he was right, too. Maybe I'd saved this memory for now when I truly needed it. It's as if Dad is here, showing me the path through from terror to bravery, and how to be happy even in the face of uncertainty.

And truth be told, uncertainty is all I've got. I might be Juliet. I might not be. Even if I'm just Helene, I might die any day. That car crash in the snowbank could have killed me, or the glaring moose right afterward. I could be diagnosed with the same kind of brain tumor Dad had. Or maybe I'll live till 103.

Nobody knows the future. But I know *today*. And hard or not, good or bad, every day is a gift, and I don't want to waste it.

"Thanks, Dad," I say, and gently kiss the watch.

As if he's listening, a sunbeam finds its way through the melting snow outside the windows and lights up the room.

A minute later, Sebastien knocks on my door.

"Helene?" he asks. "The plow has finally come through, and the roads are cleared. Do you think you're ready to venture out?"

I relish the sunbeam and my dad's memory for a moment more. And then I nod and get up out of bed.

"Yes," I say quietly to myself. And then, more loudly, "Yes, I am."

HELENE

THE SILENCE IN SEBASTIEN'S TRUCK IS AS AWKWARD AS IT GETS. WE pull out of his just shoveled driveway as if in slow motion, not only the speed at which he drives on the ice, but also how long every minute of nonconversation feels. What do you say to someone after your worlds have collided in the most improbable way? And what do you say when you're on the brink of goodbye to those possibilities?

"Uh, thanks for letting me stay at your house."

"Of course." He doesn't take his eyes off the steering wheel.

I wait for something more, but there's nothing forthcoming. A minute later, we're on the road, which has been cleared just wide enough for two cars. I almost don't see my rental car when we pass it, because the blizzard dumped so much snow over the last few days. Only part of its rear fender sticks out, dented a little from where the plow probably hit it, not knowing there was an abandoned car in the snowbank.

A grim shadow suddenly passes across Sebastien's face. "I'm glad you weren't hurt worse than your ankle."

"I'm tough. Don't worry about me."

But I suspect he's thinking of the supposed curse, and how that accident could have killed me. And I can't tell him it isn't true, because the crash really could have, regardless of a curse.

Yet that's the peace I've made with myself, Juliet or not. Like Dad said, there's an infinite number of things that I could worry about. Alternatively, I could choose to focus on good possibilities. Statistically speaking, the most impossible positive things are just as likely as the most impossible negative things. So I choose the good.

It feels right to be Optimistic Helene again, even though she's a little out of practice after the walloping of the last few days at Sebastien's.

"I'll call the rental car company when I get back to my cottage," I say.

"I already talked to Ron, the tow truck guy," Sebastien says. "He'll extract your car later today and take it back to the airport."

"You didn't have to do that. I got insurance on the rental."

"The car company would've sent him anyway. He's the only tow truck in Ryba Harbor."

"Oh, well, thanks then."

Sebastien makes a small noise of assent but doesn't say anything else.

I turn to look out the window. It's a beautiful day—the sun is shining, and the blizzard has left a soft white blanket over the forest like I'm living in a snow globe. Despite the clumsy silence in the truck, a smile spreads over my face, and it stays there as I watch the landscape go by.

After a while, Sebastien asks if it's okay to turn on some music.

He has terrible taste. An eighties hair-metal band screams from the speakers, and I can't read the name off the radio, because Sebastien's truck is possibly even older than the band.

"Is this all right?" he asks.

"It's not what I would have expected . . ."

"Which was?"

"A station playing sea shanties?"

He laughs, and thank god it breaks the tension between us. We compromise (I prefer Top 40, but he doesn't like pop) and settle on a throwback station playing bands from the '90s and 2000s. There's still no conversation between us, but at least there's music to fill the drive.

Eventually, we arrive at the edge of town. I start to give Sebastien instructions to my street, but he waves me off, because Ryba Harbor is tiny and everyone knows where I'm staying (since I'm the only wacky tourist to come to a remote Alaskan town in the middle of winter).

But when we pull up in front of the house, there's someone sitting in the beat-up rocking chair on my porch. As we park, he stands up.

"Oh god."

"Who is that?" Sebastien asks, already alert and on guard because of the tone of my voice.

"That," I say, "is my ex, Merrick."

HELENE

SEBASTIEN STARTS TO UNBUCKLE HIS SEATBELT, AS IF HE'S COMING with me.

"It's okay," I tell him.

"I can come and—"

"No. Please. Stay in the truck. Actually, you can just drop me off."

"Helene, I'm not leaving you alone."

I look from Merrick to Sebastien to Merrick again. Merrick's standing on the porch, arms crossed over his Prada wool coat. I never liked his penchant for too expensive labels, but he looks dapper, and I hate that he still looks so handsome despite what he's put me through.

"Merrick won't hurt me," I say. Not in a physical way, anyway. I'm not in any danger like that.

"Nothing good ever comes out of an ex showing up unannounced," Sebastien says. "I'll stay in the truck, but if you need me, just give me any kind of signal, and I'll be there."

I have to admit I'm relieved Sebastien is staying.

As soon as I'm out of the truck, Merrick spits, "You're shacking up with *him* now?"

I guess that Prada suaveness isn't going to extend to our actual conversation. While Merrick was charming when we first met, he's long since dropped that facade with me. (He is, however, still slayingly charming with the interns, as well as with anyone he needs to butter up to further his career.)

"No, I'm not shacking up with anyone," I say through gritted teeth as I stomp up the icy path. "I have my own place, which you clearly know because you're standing on my porch. Not that what I do is any of your business."

"You're my wife, Helene. It's all my business," he says like a possessive vulture.

"We're not married anymore, Merrick."

"Au contraire. We are until the divorce papers are signed and a judge makes it final. And I refuse to sign."

I scowl as I climb up the front steps. Face-to-face, he's less intimidating. He's only a few inches taller than me, and unlike Sebastien, Merrick's not a muscular guy. The heaviest lifting he does is keeping that massive ego from wobbling on top of his neck.

"Merrick, you do realize that California law doesn't require both parties to agree to divorce, right? I filed the papers. Our marriage will be over whether you acquiesce or not. How did you find me anyway?"

"Credit card bills," he says. "You changed the email address they'd be sent to, but that doesn't mean I can't still log in to the credit card website to see what you've been buying. Once I realized that, it wasn't hard to figure out where you'd gone."

"You had no right to pry like that."

"Come home, Hel," Merrick says, suddenly softer, as if he can still sweet-talk me into doing what he wants. "You and I are great partners."

"Are we?"

"Of course we are. Our life together is seamless. We work and live together but don't get in each other's way, our house is set up exactly the way we both like it, and—"

"A relationship should be more than two people being really good roommates but living separate lives, Merrick. You only think everything's great because you do whatever you want, and I never challenged you about it. But I'm sick of it. I don't want to be nice and quiet and 'seamless' anymore. I don't want to be a sideshow to your life, I don't want a career that's going nowhere, and I don't want to pretend that you're not fucking your interns."

"Helene, I told you that's not what happened. And you have no proof."

"Oh, so walking into your office and seeing Chrissy on her knees in front of you isn't enough proof?"

Despite the composure of his tone, Merrick's face is purple. But he takes several deep breaths, then deploys one of his trademark tactics: pivoting the conversation so he doesn't have to address the topic of his own mistakes. Because Merrick hates making mistakes, even if the mistake was just getting caught.

"Look, Helene," he says with a false veneer of reasonableness. "You've had time to blow off steam, and I've been patient. But this has gone on long enough, and it's time for you to come home. I canceled the rest of your rental on this cottage and packed your things. Our flight leaves for LAX tonight."

"You did what?" I shout.

The volume is alarming enough that Sebastien jumps out of his truck. I turn to look at him and shake my head. I can handle this.

Sebastien stays back, but he doesn't get back into the truck.

Merrick keeps talking as if he were simply dealing with a logistical matter at the newspaper. "I temporarily shut off your access to our joint bank account and credit cards, too, since it's obvious you can't be trusted to think rationally right now. Oh, and I canceled your plane tickets to Europe. I tried to call Katy to give her a heads-up, because I know she'd lined up childcare for Trevor, but she didn't answer her phone."

"You are a piece of work, Merrick." I want to rip his head off. Literally tear it off, like in one of those old arcade games like Mortal Kombat where the winner stands victorious with the loser's skull and spine dangling from their fist. Where does Merrick get off acting like I'm an irresponsible child, and he's only doing what's best for me? And then to make it seem like he was *extra* magnanimous for giving Katy "a heads-up"?

At the same time, I curse myself for not withdrawing half the contents of the joint bank account and opening up my own. It seems obvious now that I should have, but when your life is crumbling faster than you can catch the pieces, you don't think about small details you've always taken for granted, like the money that's rightfully yours being available to you. And then I was out of state, with no access to our regional California bank other than ATM machines.

I curse myself for not being smarter, for rushing out of the house without a fat envelope of cash, for underestimating the wrath of my ex-husband.

But then I recognize that I'm doing the Old Helene thing again, where I blame myself for the shitstorm that Merrick's caused.

"I have a right to that money, Merrick. I own 50 percent of it."

"I'm sorry it had to come to this, but you've been gone for several weeks. I've tried to approach this civilly but you don't answer my calls. Therefore, the only way I can get through to you is by cutting off the funding to your Alaskan revenge vacation."

"This is *not* a revenge vacation."

Merrick glances at Sebastien, who's moved from the street to the sidewalk.

"Can we go inside to discuss this?" Merrick asks.

"I think the porch is the perfect place to discuss this," I say. "It's unremorsefully frigid, like your heart."

Merrick pretends he doesn't hear that last part and sits down on the creaky rocking chair. I wonder how long he'd been here before I arrived; obviously long enough that he'd cleaned the snow off the chair. He rubs his temples. "Hel . . . I didn't want to do any of this, but you left me no choice. Do you know how bad it looks that my wife ran off?"

"I'm not a damn puppy you tied too loosely to a pole."

He exhales in that "why do you have to be so emotional" way. "You know what I mean. I graduated top in our class at Northwestern." (He conveniently forgets that I graduated number two, right behind him.) "I'm the youngest ever bureau chief for *The Wall Street Journal.* I'm going places. I need my wife beside me."

I roll my eyes. What he means is he needs his wife beside him for photo ops and articles about how amazing he is. He wants me for optics. Not for who I actually am.

"Well maybe you should have thought of that before you cheated on me," I say. "Before *every* time you cheated."

"I told you, Chrissy was just picking up a paper clip from the floor!"

"You are unbelievable, do you know that?" I'm seething now. I'm surprised my anger isn't hot enough to melt the snow on the porch roof and the front walkway, and hell, all of Ryba Harbor. I swear the snow on the banister starts to steam a little, though. "We're done here, Merrick."

"No, Helene. I booked the first flight up here as soon as the airport reopened, and I drove a shitty-ass tin can of a rental car to this godforsaken town in order to retrieve you, so I will *not* leave until you get your suitcases and get in that car!"

Out of the corner of my eye, I see Sebastien, still respectfully keeping his distance. I nod at him, and he approaches at the same time I say, "Merrick, you can boss your writers around and you can convince your interns that your dick is worth sucking, but I neither work for you nor am I susceptible to your charm or your manipulations anymore. So when I say that we're done here, it means we're done. You need to go."

"Make me," Merrick says, glaring at me while settling deeper into the rocking chair.

"Is that a challenge?" Sebastien says, taking all four front steps in one stride.

I cross my arms and look at Merrick. "Sebastien can lift you *and* that chair into the back of his truck and dump you at the curb at the airport if that's what you want. Although you'll probably get charged overage if you don't return your rental car, and I hear the fees are pretty hefty."

Merrick and Sebastien stare each other down for a minute. But while Merrick has plenty of swagger, he's not stupid, and he knows when he's outmatched.

Still, he has to get the last word as he rises from the rocking chair and retreats down the walkway. "I tried to be nice, Helene, but if you want war, I'll give you war. I've got the top Beverly Hills divorce lawyer on retainer, and that's only the beginning. You'll rue the day you met me."

"I already rue the day I met you," I mutter.

"Your plane ticket home is on the rocking chair. Nonrefundable, so don't think about trying to cancel it to get money out of it. That ticket's your last chance before I destroy you."

He gets into his car and slams the door. The rental labors to start, and for a moment, I'm horrified that we'll have to give him a ride. But then the engine turns over, and Merrick skids out of the driveway, tearing out of Ryba Harbor like he's a race car driver with a serious Napoleon complex.

"Hey," Sebastien says softly. "You okay?"

"Yes. And no."

He opens his arms to me, and even though I'd resisted him before, I need a place to be safe now, and I collapse into his embrace. Because I don't know what I'm going to do with no money, no credit cards, and no place to stay.

I can pretend that the next thing I do is walk calmly and quietly into my kitchen, plate some leftover cake, and rationally think through what just happened.

What really happens, though, is I lose my shit as soon as I step inside the cottage. "How can he do this to me?" I yell as I yank open poor Reginald the Refrigerator's door.

"I'm sorry, Helene," Sebastien says, hanging back a few feet so he doesn't get caught in the crossfire of me with half a chocolate cake in one hand and a knife in the other.

"How could I have been married to that asshole for so long? How did I not realize what he was?"

"It's not your fault," Sebastien says as he carefully takes the knife and cake from me. "People change. Merrick probably wasn't like this when you first met him."

"Still! How could anyone be that evil?" I flop down onto a bar-stool and stuff my hands into my hair.

I keep swearing and banging my fist on the counter. Sebastien puts the knife away, finds a fork, and slides the cake to me without taking any for himself. He knows intuitively that what I need right now is an entire half of a chocolate cake and space to bash out my fury. Or maybe it's not intuition, but lifetimes of collected knowledge. Either way, I'm grateful.

When the cake is demolished—partly eaten, partly jabbed at until it's a mess of crumbs—I'm finally pacified enough to speak again. "I should call the bank and see what's going on with my account."

"Good idea. I'll clean up while you're doing that." Sebastien starts wiping up my cake massacre.

I go into the bedroom and dial Sunnyside Bank of Southern California. After several minutes getting lost in their call menu and then a while on hold, I'm connected to a service rep. I quickly explain my situation.

"Okay, let me look into that for you," Linnea, the bank rep, says.

I can hear her clucking her tongue on the other end of the line. It doesn't give me much confidence.

"All right, Ms. Janssen. What I see here is that a freeze has been put on this checking account by the other joint holder, Mr. Sauer."

"Yes, I know. I'd like to lift the freeze."

"Unfortunately, I can't do that over the phone," Linnea says. "For security reasons, you'll need to come into a branch in person with two forms of ID and proof of current address."

"But my name's on the account! I don't understand. I literally own half that money. Why can't I do what I want with it?" I drop myself angrily onto the bed.

"I understand this is frustrating, and I sympathize," Linnea says in that infuriating customer service voice that gets used to "manage" difficult clients. "I wish I could help you, I truly do, but it's corporate policy. However, it'll only take a few minutes once you're in the branch—"

"I can't come into a branch! I'm in Alaska!" Goddamn Merrick. He planned this. Our bank is a small regional one, and while I can access a network of partner banks' ATMs nationwide, the only physical branches are in Southern California. Merrick knew that ATMs would be useless to me without a functional debit card, and in order to get that card working again, I would have to come home to L.A.

"I understand your problem, Ms. Janssen," Linnea says, still placid. "Maybe you could speak with Mr. Sauer, and he can come into a branch in person to unfreeze the account?"

"No!" I pick up a pillow and hurl it across the room. "I'm trying to divorce him, and I own half the money in that account, but he's locked me out of it."

"Oh." Linnea is lost for words. I hear her clicking through the customer service script that's probably on the computer screen in front of her, trying to find the right thing to say in this situation.

"Is there a manager I can speak to?"

"Of course," Linnea says. "Please hold while I connect you. And I am sorry for your troubles, Ms. Janssen. I really am."

That last bit was definitely off script. I sag on my bed. "Thanks, Linnea."

A minute later, the manager comes on the line. "Hello, Ms. Janssen. This is Richard Hinkle. I understand you have some questions. How can I help you?"

"I don't have questions. I have a major, major problem."

"Tell me about it," Richard says, again in that sedate "this is how you handle a troublesome client" tone.

I have to go through all the details I'd told Linnea.

"I see," Richard says when I'm finished. "I'm sorry you're in such a pickle, Ms. Janssen. Unfortunately, the bank can't side with one party or the other when divorce proceedings are involved, so actually, you'll need to have a certified court order to unfreeze these accounts."

"What? Linnea said it was just two forms of ID!"

"I understand this is frustrating, and I sympathize," he says, repeating the script. "However, in my experience, the lawyers are able to get this resolved fairly quickly with the court, and then you just have to come into any branch—"

"I'm in Alaska!" I scream before I throw the phone at the pillow that I'd already flung across the room. I crumple facedown onto the bed.

"Hello? Hello?" Richard's muffled voice says. When he gets no response, he says, "If we can help you with anything else, Ms. Janssen, please call us again anytime from 9 A.M. to 5 P.M. Pacific. Thank you for choosing Sunnyside Bank of Southern California!" With that peppy sign-off, he hangs up.

Sebastien knocks softly on the door. "Didn't go well?"

"Mrrrph," I mutter into the mattress.

I feel the weight of him as he sits down next to me. He lets me stew for a few minutes, and then I roll over to face him. "What am I going to do, Sebastien? I can't go home. But I can't stay here either. Even if I could convince the landlady to reinstate the rental, I don't have any way to make money." Other than the fortuitous stint at Shipyard Books because Angela wanted to visit her granddaughter, Ryba Harbor isn't exactly job central during the tourist off-season.

"Well, I know it's not much, but you have this." Sebastien waves the plane ticket Merrick left on the rocking chair.

I glare. "I am *not* going back to L.A.!"

"That's not what I meant." Sebastien raises both arms in surrender. "I was just trying to say that you could exchange this ticket for cash."

"No, I can't. Merrick said it's nonrefundable, remember? He thought through everything."

"Not everything," Sebastien says. "I, uh, actually made a couple calls while you were talking to the bank. I hope you don't mind. The money for this plane ticket will be waiting for you at the airline's main office in Anchorage, if you want it."

I scramble up to sitting. "Wait, what? How?" I'd just been through the "what you want is against corporate policy" rigamarole with Sunnyside Bank, which is supposed to be known for its personal customer service. I have zero faith that a giant airline would be any better.

"Dana's cousin's husband works in the main office," Sebastien says. "He pulled a few strings. I know it's not much, but at least it's a few hundred dollars."

"You called your friend, who called her cousin, who called her husband, who did a favor for *me*?" I blink at Sebastien. "That worked?"

He shrugs. "Alaskans protect their own and those they love."

Love. I don't think he meant to let it slip, but now that it's out there, I can feel what it would be like to have someone by your side all the time. I'd imagined it with Story Sebastien, but now I sense how powerfully love emanates from Real Sebastien. And that's with him restraining his feelings.

Is that how you know you've found the right person? Merrick always assumed I could take care of myself, and because I could, he let me. It's a strange but wonderful luxury to have Sebastien fighting my fight *with* me.

I'm overwhelmed by the sudden desire to kiss him.

I put my hands on either side of his face and press my lips to his. For a brief moment, honey-tinted sparks light up where my lips touch his.

Then Sebastien jumps back and nearly falls off the bed. "I thought—"

"I know. I said I didn't want us to get involved." I shake my head. "But what if I was wrong?"

"What if you were right?"

I stare down at the plaid comforter and trace the lines.

"I know about Avery," I say.

Sebastien freezes.

"She was really successful," I say. "But she was also really un-happy. Do you think what happened to her is what would happen to all Juliets—to me—if we didn't end up together?" I look at Sebastien.

He swallows hard, his Adam's apple bouncing. "I don't know," he answers carefully. "I don't think one case sets a rule."

"And you're willing to risk it again? Leave me and see what happens?"

"I . . . I was trying to save you," he says quietly.

"You don't have to save me," I say. "I already saved myself." Because I have. I extracted myself from that toxic relationship with Merrick, I severed the ties keeping me in L.A., and I made my way here, to the middle of nowhere in Alaska. I gave myself permission to start over.

"Right, of course," Sebastien says sheepishly. "You don't need me riding in to rescue you. I just meant . . . What if we do this, and it ends badly? Again?"

"If you hadn't left Avery, if you had stayed and given the relationship a chance, do you think you two would have been happy together?"

"Without a doubt," he says, not even a beat of hesitation.

"That's what I thought."

Sebastien looks at me as if he's afraid I'll disappear right before his eyes. "So what does this mean?" he asks, barely audible.

"It means this." I rise from the bed, take his hands in mine, and kiss him again.

This time, he stays and lets the sweet warmth of our mouths thaw what had been wedged between us.

I think I was aiming at the wrong target when I left Merrick. Maybe this new life I'm trying to build isn't only about writing a novel or going to Europe with Katy. Maybe the purpose of all those crazy stories that have been struggling to get out for nearly two decades was to show me what it's like to be loved. Both someone loving me, and me accepting and loving myself.

And that also means focusing not on "what if I die," but on the more positive "what if I don't give myself this chance?" Perhaps the unknown comes to an end within two years, but what if it also holds the sort of love I've always longed for, the kind I wrote about in story after story?

Sebastien pulls away from our kiss. "But the curse—"

"There's no love worth having if it doesn't break your heart when it's over," I say. "Besides, some of those journals . . . there were full lives in there."

"A year or two doesn't constitute a full life."

"A life is what you make of it." So I tell him about my dad. In high school, he did an exchange program to Mongolia because he wanted to study golden eagles. On the first day of college, he fell in love with Mom, who at that time was still just "Beth who lived across the hall," and told her right there on the spot that he was going to marry her. He learned to play the didgeridoo for the hell of it, and the same with whittling soapstone and playing badminton. And he died unexpectedly at thirty-eight.

The truth is, no one ever knows how much time they have on this planet, so you'd better make however long or short it is good. And my dad, despite the brief time he was with us—and the gulf he left in his wake—made all our lives richer and brighter.

"Amélie and Matteo lived it up at Versailles," I say. "Clara and Felix got to savor falling slowly in love. And Cosmina and Marius had a wickedly good time experimenting with all her witchy potions and spells, even if they didn't work."

"Yes, but none of them—"

"Ended well? I know . . . Still, a sad ending doesn't undo all the happiness that came before it, right?"

Sebastien runs his hand through his hair as he considers this. He shakes his head.

But then he sighs heavily and does the thing where he creases the space between his brows when he's about to give in to me.

"I'd rather have seven hours with you than seven hundred years without," he says. "But it doesn't mean I stop wanting more. Or that I have the right to make that choice for you."

I touch his arm. "Maybe we'll have more this time. Just because two years has been the limit before doesn't mean it will be the limit again. And things *are* different this time."

He gives me a small smile, tinged with sad skepticism. "Juliet's always been the optimist of the pair."

"Romeo was optimistic, too. He thought they could run away from their families and elope."

"Romeo *was* optimistic. Until time wore him down."

There again is that weight on Sebastien's shoulders, the burden of centuries lived and countless Juliets come, then cruelly gone.

I stroke Sebastien's face. "I guess I'll have to be optimistic enough for both of us, then."

"Helene—"

"It's my choice. My decision." And right now, I don't want to wallow in the shadows of our supposed curse. I press my mouth to his.

After a moment's hesitation, Sebastien gives in, and the sense of inevitability rushes out in a torrent. Our tongues meet, hot and hungry. My lips scrape against the slight stubble on his skin, but I don't care if it hurts, I want to be closer, and closer still. His mouth tastes like honeyed wine again, and I am drunk on this man who has possibly loved me his entire, eternal life, and who, through my vignettes, I've loved for almost all of mine.

"Helene—"

"Shh."

"I only wanted to say—"

"Don't."

So he doesn't. Instead, Sebastien lays me down on the bed. He kisses me, and our clothes come off and our bodies find each other, slowly at first, like the night meeting dawn. And then tempestuously, like fire meeting water, years of fantasized encounters finally freed from the constraints of imagination into reality.

And then we are a detonation of pent-up desire, and time itself ruptures and all the stars in the galaxy burst free. I am Helene and he is Sebastien. But I am also all the names that came before—I am Isabella on a beach, consummating my marriage to Lucciano in the sand. I am Meg in a greenhouse, making love to Charles among rows of crimson zinnias and purple verbena. I am Brigitta, Ines, Mary Jo, and Amélie. He is Albrecht, Simão, Nolan, and Matteo.

And in that single, fiery moment of detonated stars when time ceases to exist, I know for certain:

He is Romeo, and I am Juliet.

SEBASTIEN

Afterward, I do not stop looking at her.

I do not think about the sorrow that will come.

Instead, all I do is hold her in my arms, feel her slowly melt into sleep, her body soft and warm on mine, her breath like dragonflies' wings on my skin.

I kiss the top of her head, gently, and she murmurs something that sounds like a smile.

She is here again. Finally.

And she is mine, she is mine, she is mine.

HELENE

I DRIFT OFF TO SLEEP FOR A LITTLE BIT, AND WHEN I WAKE, GONE IS the bottomless pit of despair from the confrontation with Merrick. Instead, it's replaced with the kind of drowsy, deep-seated contentment of finding what you've spent your life looking for. Story Sebastien is the same as the Sebastien spooned against me in the tangle of plaid comforter. I didn't make him up; he was here, waiting for me all along. I sink into him.

In response, Sebastien holds me tighter, as if he, too, needs to keep me close, in case all this vanishes like a dream. But then I'm reminded that he's had no delusions about us from the start. Sebastien's known since I walked into The Frosty Otter who we are and what we've meant to each other, even if he tried to keep our paths from colliding.

I nestle into him as I think about what he calls his "curse." It's still incomprehensible how it could be true, and yet, when he made love to me, I felt our history coded into every cell of my body.

I am Juliet, I think. *I live for a while, then die, then forget everything and come back to do it all over again.* Impossible. And at the same time, utterly real, and tragic and romantic at the same time. Instinctively, I clasp Dad's watch in my hand as I contemplate it all.

Sebastien shifts behind me and kisses my hair. "I could fix that for you, you know."

Right. Because he was a clockmaker, once upon a time.

Maybe someday in the future, I'll want the watch to work again. But for now, I don't want it tinkered with. As Mom likes to say, things happen for a reason. And I think the watch is broken in order to serve as a reminder to me to live unapologetically, like

Dad did. I suspect he left it to me, rather than Katy, because he knew I'd need the reminder more.

"It's okay," I say to Sebastien. "I need the watch this way, for now."

But he must hear the slight quaver in how I say the word "need," because his next question is, "Are you all right?"

I don't answer right away. I'm still contemplating our complicated past, and our fate. The part about me dying lingers like smoke after a fire. I can have this mad, all-encompassing love, but at the cost of my life.

Sensing my tension, Sebastien kisses the nape of my neck. He brushes his fingertips along the backs of my arms, which sends tremors through my body and leaves me breathless. He murmurs my name across my skin, leaving behind a hot trail of wanting in its wake. A history of knowing.

Am I scared of dying?

Utterly terrified.

But—as irrational as it is—if this is our curse, I still covet it.

"Yes," I say, finally answering Sebastien's question. "I'm all right. More than all right."

"Are you sure?"

I answer by kissing the white scar over Sebastien's eyelid. I kiss a faded nick on his chest, left behind by an arrow shaft. There's a ghost of a stab wound under his ribs, burns from when he dove into the flames to save Cosmina from the stake, and countless other scars, a constellation over his body. Skirting death for centuries leaves marks behind.

I know a few of the stories.

But I want to know them all.

HELENE

AFTER LINGERING IN BED AWHILE LONGER, REALITY DEMANDS TO BE dealt with.

"What are you going to do about this place?" Sebastien says as he brushes a lock of hair from my face.

"I don't know. Maybe I could talk to the landlady and promise I'll pay her rent as soon as my lawyers can sort things out with the court and the bank. But I'm worried about what Merrick will do if I don't show up at the Anchorage airport later today. When someone makes an enemy of him, he crushes them."

I think about what happened to those poor editors at our grad school newspaper, when they kicked Merrick and his friend Aaron Gonchar off the staff. Merrick and Aaron dug up every piece of dirt on those editors and waged a massive smear campaign by anonymously sending the so-called "dirt dossiers" to every media company the editors were applying to for jobs.

Not a single one of them landed anywhere good postgraduation, even with prestigious Northwestern journalism degrees in hand. Meanwhile, Merrick and Aaron emerged with nary a scratch on them—Merrick on the fast track at *The Wall Street Journal*'s West Coast bureau, and Aaron with a well-paid gig at TMZ, finding and airing celebrities' dirty laundry.

Sebastien props himself up on a pillow. "About Merrick . . . I have resources who can help."

The way he says it is an odd combination of bashful plus spy-novel mysterious. I tilt my head and ask, "What do you mean, *resources*?"

He blushes, and it's adorable on a man as big as he is. "You've heard of Swiss banks? Well, Julius A. Weiskopf Group in Geneva is kind of like my Swiss army knife. When you've been around as long as I have, you need a few people you can trust. They're my financial advisers, lawyers, procurers of false identification papers . . . anything I need. I could ask them to take over your divorce case, if you'd like. They'd get your bank account unlocked, for starters, but also be able to handle anything Merrick and his attorneys try to throw at you."

I just stare at Sebastien, because I'm still stuck on the first thing he said. "You have a Swiss bank account? That's only for, like, mega millionaires. In movies."

He shifts his weight on the bed, embarrassed at my gawking. "I met Julius, the president, when he brought an antique monstrance clock to me in Bern to restore. We became friends."

As if that explains how Sebastien has a supersecret, private bank account. I'm still getting used to the truth that he's lived for centuries.

But I do appreciate Sebastien's modesty about how he got the account. I wouldn't have fallen for him if he were a flashy big spender, if he'd strolled into The Frosty Otter that first night all blinged out.

"Wait a second," I say, suddenly recalling his journals. "You were a clockmaker in Switzerland in the 1500s. You've been with the Weiskopf Group for five hundred years, and they've never been like, 'Hey, that's kinda weird, someone should take a closer look at this account'?"

Sebastien shrugs with one shoulder. "Something like that. They're very discreet; they've never asked me about myself, and

I've never offered. Like I said, it's good to have a few people you can trust. They could handle Merrick, if you want."

I'm about to tell Sebastien it's okay, he doesn't have to bring in his team, but then I think about how great it's been to have him here today—as backup on the porch with Merrick, to bring me cake when I needed it, to put in a call to his friend at the airline. I don't have to do everything on my own.

"That would give me some peace of mind, thanks. I'm not sure my bargain basement suburban divorce lawyer is up to fighting Merrick's Beverly Hills bulldogs."

"Consider it done. I'll give Sandrine Weiskopf—the current president—a call in a minute. As for what to do about this rental cottage, I was thinking . . ." Sebastien wraps his arms around me. "What if you came and stayed with me instead?"

"You've already done so much—"

"Hear me out," he murmurs into my ear.

With his voice all low and rumbly like that, Sebastien could sell me snake oil. I'd buy a gallon of it.

"My house is big enough that you'll have as much peace and quiet as you need to work on your novel," he says. "Not sure if you noticed, but I'm not a particularly garrulous guy."

I laugh. "No, you're not."

"Also," Sebastien says, "my journals are in my library. If you were at my house, it would be easier for you to access them, if you need them for your story."

I pick at the comforter. "I'm sorry I read through them before, without asking."

Sebastien cups my cheek and kisses me. "It's your past, too."

I shake my head. Not because I don't believe, but because I'm still trying to understand it.

I'm thinking about this when it occurs to me. "Are you inviting me to stay with you so you can keep watch over me? Because of the curse?"

He hesitates.

So there's some truth to what I've said.

But then Sebastien looks me in the eye. "Helene, I would never . . . The point of me moving to Alaska was to try to let you live your life. If you told me that you wanted to keep working on your novel in Ryba Harbor but I had to leave, I would. I'd get on the first plane out of Anchorage to wherever it would take me, just to do as you wished. So I promise, I would never, ever invite you to stay with me in order to keep you in a gilded cage. This is *your* life, and you get to decide if you want me in it or not."

Sebastien flinches at the final sentence, but no matter how hard it would be for him to leave me, I believe it when he says he would. He's already tried to hide from me in the remoteness of Alaska. Then when I showed up anyway and insisted on chasing him down, he attempted to make me hate him. Plus, Sebastien rarely says this many words all at once, which proves to me how much this means to him. I'm guessing it takes a lot to get him to hold forth like that.

I hug him and rest my head in the crook of his neck. "Are you always this good to me, Romeo?"

"I try," he whispers.

"Thank you for letting me stay with you. I'll pitch in around the house however I can—cleaning, cooking . . . Well, maybe not cooking."

"No, please don't cook," Sebastien says. "I don't want my kitchen to burn down."

We both laugh.

"Okay," I say. "I accept the terms of your offer. No cooking, I swear."

HELENE

Sebastien has to run a few errands in town before we head back to his place, so I take the opportunity to tidy up the cottage before I leave it for the last time. There isn't much to do, though, since I haven't been here for days, and Merrick has so generously already packed my things.

So I sit down at the kitchen counter and pull out one of my notebooks. I've been thinking more about Romeo and Juliet, and particularly Avery Drake and Cameron (that's what Sebastien said his name was when he was a cartographer in the 1960s and '70s). And here's the thing:

I think there's a chance the curse is breaking. Or maybe it's already broken.

I start another list, because I do some of my best thinking with bulleted lists.

★ ★ ★

Reasons the Curse Might Be Broken (or Almost Broken)

- *Reincarnated Juliets only reappear in Sebastien's life on the tenth of July. It's been consistent for hundreds of years, and yet this time, I showed up in January.*
- *(Okay, subpoint: Sebastien <u>did</u> see me on July 10 when I was in college. But that was ten years ago. And no Juliets have ever lived longer than two years after she falls for Romeo, so in a way, this is further evidence that things are not what they used to be.)*
- *Avery Drake survived the curse.*
- *Unlike past Juliets, I have some memory of our past. Well, a <u>lot</u> of memory. I just didn't know what it was.*
- *Maybe it takes both of us to break the curse. Other Juliets haven't known who they were, but <u>I</u> do. Maybe if Sebastien and I work together, we can end the torturous cycle.*

I sit back and look at my list. The reasons are tenuous, at best. But then again, Sebastien said the cycle has always been the same (other than with Avery), and it's undeniable there are differences this time from all the Romeos and Juliets before.

Plus, Sebastien admitted that he doesn't know exactly how the curse came into being. He only has a theory that it was Mercutio's dying words, so we're really going on conjecture here. I mean, for all we know, it was because, in the Capulets' mausoleum, Friar Lawrence told Romeo, "You will live," and coming from a man of God, that became, like, a holy command.

Or maybe the origins don't really matter. I don't know.

If the curse isn't already broken, though, I think it's worth trying to break it. With all the variances from our past lives—plus Sebastien's sacrifice in his last lifetime, with Avery—maybe there's one more difference this time around: Maybe we finally have the chance to change it.

Still, most important, I get to be part of the most epic love story of all time. The one we all grow up swooning over. Who wouldn't take the chance if they had it?

Maybe extraordinary things *can* happen to ordinary people.

SEBASTIEN

I FIND HELENE'S BULLETED LIST ON THE KITCHEN COUNTER. SHE WAS in the shower after I returned from my errands, and I can't help but read what she's written.

I wince at her optimism about breaking the curse. Should I have told her that it can't be done? That I've tried, again and again, and failed?

Over centuries, I've drunk innumerable potions and paid a king's ransom for spells. I've traveled the world to consult with gurus in remote Indian villages, medicine women on snowcapped mountains, and shamans in Africa where they still practice the old ways. I ran away when I met Avery; the curse simply adapted and came back with renewed fervor—a wretched, relentless boomerang of ill fate.

But I think Helene needs to believe there's a solution to the curse. Her nature is so primed toward optimism, she craves the light at the end of the tunnel; that's how she's survived a life that hasn't always been the easiest. It might break her to know for certain that there's no recourse for us, no sanguine goal to work toward.

I touch the last bullet point on her list: *Maybe it takes both of us to break the curse.*

I close my eyes. If only that were true. But I've tried that approach, too. When Cosmina came into my life, I thought we finally had a chance. I didn't tell her who she was, but I *did* tell her that I was cursed, and that anyone who fell in love with me was doomed.

Cosmina didn't care. That's another thing consistent about my Juliet—she does what she wants, and I love her for it.

I only wish the thing she desired most in every life didn't lead to losing hers.

THE MOUNTAINS OF TRANSYLVANIA – 1682

In the superstitious age of witches and vampires, I, an eternally young recluse in a castle on the cliff, ought to be the target of stake-wielding mobs led by priests carrying holy water.

And yet the townsfolk don't bother me. Perhaps it's because no babes have gone missing from their cradles. Or that women don't wander out of their thatched-roof homes in the dead of night, only to return with twigs in their hair and bite marks on their necks, like in other parts of the country where vampires supposedly roam.

Or perhaps it's simply because I've been generous with my wealth. I make sure the nearby villages always have enough food, and I've given them paved cobblestone streets and sturdy stone bridges, whereas most in Transylvania still drag their wagons through muddy roads and cross rivers on frayed ropes. Here, there are even extra funds to host celebrations every spring, summer, harvest season, and winter. My money buys goodwill and a blind eye.

Over the decades, my legend has grown. They say I am a benevolent vampire, that I've shunned the ways of my kind and instead spend my days in repentance, in the hopes that God will one day see fit to forgive me the sin of my existence and release me from my immortality. It isn't far from the truth, other than the vampire part.

Thirty-one years into my residence in that isolated castle, though, a woman climbs the long, winding road up the cliff. She has blue-black hair like a raven's and wears a cloak nearly as dark. The moon is high in the cloudy sky by the time she knocks on my door.

When I answer, she cocks her head and studies me for a moment. Then she smiles. "I hear a vampire resides here."

I am speechless. Not because of what she said, but because of who she obviously is. The taste of honeyed wine skims my lips, and I would recognize those bright eyes and the soul they contain anywhere.

She frowns, though, unimpressed with me. She clears her throat. "Perhaps you did not hear me the first time. I understand a vampire lives here. Would you please let him know he has a visitor?"

"A visitor?" I shake myself out of my daze. "I am afraid that your sources have deceived you, Miss . . . What did you say your name was?"

"I didn't."

"Ah. Well . . . if a vampire did indeed reside here, a lady like you ought to avoid him, I think."

She scowls. "I am far from a 'lady.' I have followed rumors and traveled hundreds of leagues to be here, because no ordinary man can satisfy my needs—intellectual or otherwise. A vampire, however, may suffice."

I laugh, both awed by her fearlessness and titillated by her innuendo. "But what, pray tell, would a mortal woman have to offer a vampire other than a vein on which to feast?"

"Spells," she says, lifting her cloak to reveal a satchel full of vials, as well as a thick leather grimoire strapped to her waist. "I am a sorceress. I can help the vampire obtain anything he desires—power, fame, and more."

I hear time stop in this moment.

"Anything?" I whisper.

"Anything."

"Can you lift a curse?"

"If there's anyone you will ever meet who can lift a curse, it is I." She arches a brow. "But I should prefer to continue this conversation with the vampire, rather than his butler."

Time begins to march forward again. "I am Count Marius Montague. I am no vampire, but I have lived hundreds of years and I cannot die."

The sorceress moves closer and traces a long fingernail across my lips. Heat flares through my body.

"I am called Cosmina. Let me inside, and I shall help you the best I know how."

For two years, we practice Cosmina's lustful magic—a combination of incantations, elixirs, and carnality. I may be the one with the reputation as a wild creature of the night, but in truth, Cosmina is the wilder of us, although she doesn't limit her thirst to moonlight hours.

In the early morning, she will crawl under the bedcovers to wake me with her mouth, her lips lined with a balm of elderberry juice and herbs that are said to end curses. If I'm reading in the library, she climbs into my lap and makes love to me as she chants a hex-breaking spell. There are more conventional attempts at breaking the curse, too, if sorcery can be called conventional. Necklaces of dove feathers. Ancient protection spells. Runes carved into stone under a new moon.

Yet nothing cures me. An accident chopping wood results only in a scar on my hand the next morning. Cosmina's experiment of piercing my neck and sucking out my blood—to draw the curse from my body—does not work in the slightest. Even falling into river rapids only renders me unconscious; I cannot drown.

The servants in the castle whisper about Cosmina, in the way that all staff do when they feel a mistress is not deserving of their master. Eventually, the servants' tales reach the villages at the base of the cliff. Some stories merely accuse Cosmina of attempting to poison me in order to inherit my riches. Other allegations are more wicked, full of black magic and conspiracies with the devil.

Ever loyal to their altruistic lord in the castle, the villagers decide I have been bewitched, unable to see the evil under my own roof. Hence, they take matters into their own hands.

One afternoon, while Cosmina forages in the woods for mushrooms and other ingredients for her latest brew, four men abduct her. They gag her and bind her in iron chains, and hurry on horseback to deliver her to the waiting pyre at the base of the mountain.

By the time I notice she's been gone for too long, and by the time I run out to the parapet and see the plume of thick, black smoke curling from below, it is far, far too late.

With a cry of anguish, I mount a horse and charge down the mountain into town, hurling myself into the bonfire to untie my love from the stake, to save her from the ravenous flames.

But it matters not.

Cosmina is dead, mere ashes.

And as ever, I live on.

HELENE

ON THE DRIVE BACK TO SEBASTIEN'S, I'M SO HAPPY I SING ALONG TO the radio. He doesn't say anything, but when there's a break in the music and the DJ comes on, I see Sebastien smirking to himself.

"What?" I ask.

"Nothing."

"No really, what?"

He glances over at me. "You've always been, uh, *creative* in your interpretation of 'in tune.'"

I can't help laughing. I know it's true. Katy banned me from karaoke a long time ago. We always wondered how a musician mother could birth one daughter with perfect pitch and another with the voice of a squealing cat.

"Well, nobody's perfect," I say.

Sebastien smiles. "You are."

It's the corniest thing. But the way he looks at me is so damn tender and sentimental I melt anyway. And let's be honest—I've always wanted someone to say nauseatingly sweet things to me. We only pretend comments like that in movies are sickening because we never think we deserve them ourselves.

But I'm telling myself right now: *I deserve this.*

His gaze lingers, as if he'll never tire of looking at me, and I smile back before poking him. "Eyes on the road, please. I don't want to reenact my accident in the snowbank."

Sebastien cringes, and I'm sorry I reminded him of what he considers a near brush with death. I lean over the gearshift and kiss him on the cheek instead.

He sighs, and there it is again, that heaviness he carries. It's patently unfair that Sebastien has to shoulder all the burdens of our past. Even a fender bender sends his mind racing toward my demise.

From his journals, I can tell that Sebastien thinks the curse is his fault, that he inflicts the tragedy on me in every lifetime. But dying is the easy part; it's the people left behind who suffer most.

I trace the face of Dad's broken watch. In his last days, he wasn't afraid of death. Mom, Katy, and I were, though. We were terrified of the emptiness of life without him. Terrified we lacked the strength to carry on without him to support us. Terrified of missing him so badly it would eat into us, afraid of making memories without him, afraid of the guilt of eventually moving on.

If the curse inflicts death on Juliet, it inflicts something equally bad—or worse—on Romeo.

But the thing is, Mom, Katy, and I survived. And we have great memories of Dad to hold on to, because he made sure that our family never missed a moment to enjoy each other, to throw ourselves into school plays (me) and swim meets (Katy) and folk music jams (Mom), to live the heck out of whatever life had to offer.

Admittedly, I lost a lot of that instinct when I grew up, but that's part of what being New Helene is about. I'm reclaiming it.

And maybe that's how I can help Sebastien, too. For as much as he's endured, he ought to be rewarded with less suffering, not more.

I slide my hand onto Sebastien's thigh and leave it there for comfort. "It's going to be okay," I say.

"How?"

"Destiny brought me here because it wanted me to be happy, and I *am* happy. And I'm going to make *you* happy. We're going to enjoy the hell out of everything."

Sebastien lets out a reluctant laugh despite himself. "I suppose that if I have to be trapped in a never-ending curse, there's no one I'd rather be stuck with than you."

"Aw, that's the most romantic thing anyone's ever said to me."

He laughs for real now. "And that's why I don't talk that much. I'm better with actions than words."

"Oh yeah? What kind of actions?"

He lowers his voice into that rumbling growl that renders me senseless. "When we get back to the house, I'll show you."

SEBASTIEN

WE DON'T GET ANYTHING DONE THE FIRST FEW DAYS HELENE IS AT MY place, not because she has much to unpack, but because we can't keep our hands off each other. I wake up in the mornings to her kissing the scar along my jaw, then kissing my neck, my chest, trailing down across my abdomen and disappearing under the sheets. When she showers, I can't resist her naked silhouette, and I join her under the hot water, lifting her up against the tiles and taking her until her cries echo through the bathroom. Even going downstairs is interrupted by making love on the staircase, Helene's hands braced against the towering wall of glass—wild Alaskan forest on one side, and us, untamed, on the other.

But eventually, our focus shifts, because Merrick makes good on his promise to put up a fight. He sues Helene for slander, claiming that she's spreading lies about him committing adultery. His lawsuit puts a damper on our euphoria.

"Don't worry," I tell Helene. "He doesn't have a case. The lawyers at the Weiskopf Group will take care this. They're excellent. They'll get this thrown out, easily."

She nods, but I can tell she's anxious. Still, every minute Helene spends dwelling on Merrick is time wasted; I'm aware of each second of her life as if I were watching the grains of sand slip through the funnel of an hourglass. I want Helene to spend her life happy—however much time there is left of it. And I have learned over the centuries to savor the moments we have together, even if they'll be fewer than I wish for. It's the way it has to be.

"I promised you peace and quiet to work on your novel," I say. "Let me give that to you. I'll tell you if there are any big developments on the Merrick front. And that way, you can let it go and focus on your writing. What do you think?"

Helene closes her eyes and leans into me. "You promise you'll tell me if there's anything I need to know about what Merrick's up to?"

"I do."

She holds out her little finger and links it with mine. "Pinkie-swear."

"I pinkie-swear that I will tell you if there's anything you need to know about what Merrick's up to."

Helene heaves a huge sigh of relief, and I can actually feel the stress leaving her, just by the way her pinkie relaxes against mine.

A few days later, while Helene's hard at work, I meet up with Adam at Dana's restaurant. The Smokehouse is all country music, neon beer signs, and rustic Western ranch atmosphere complete with recycled wood picnic tables and tin wall paneling. It smells of wood smoke and meat—two of the best smells in the world—and a huge, punny sign above the kitchen door reads This Is Grill Life. I always smile at how much of Dana's personality comes through in that single sign.

About a third of the seats are full for lunch, but Adam's at the bar in back, shooting the breeze with the bartender and pretty much everyone who walks by on their way to the barbecue sauce station—Dana makes fifteen different kinds from scratch.

"Hey, Seabass!" Adam hollers as I approach. He gets up and gives me a hug, not the typical one-armed, pat-on-the-back kind that most men do, but a full vise grip, because, well, Adam is Adam, and he genuinely loves everybody that damn much.

"Thanks for meeting me," I say.

He snickers. "So formal. Come on, man, sit down, have a beer with me."

"What're you drinking?"

"Pineapple Jalapeño Gose."

"Sounds revolting."

"Nah, it's surprisingly good. Local brew." Adam turns to the bartender, who's in his midtwenties and, like everyone else who works here, wears a horseshoe pin with his name, Daniel, engraved on it. "Can you get Seabass one of these?"

I settle onto the barstool next to Adam. "How's Colin doing? I'm going to stop by his family's place later this afternoon to see him."

"Our greenhorn's nearly recovered."

"Thank god."

"He's real eager to get back on the boat."

"So soon?"

"You know how Colin is. He's wanted to be a crabber since he was a kid."

I nod. I still remember back when Adam and I were greenhorns ourselves. Colin was eight then, and obsessed with king crab boats. His mom—Adam's sister-in-law—brought Colin to the harbor to greet us after our first trip out to sea. He ran to Adam, shouting "Uncle, Uncle! Did you bring me a crab? Did you wrestle an orca? Tell me everything!"

Daniel sets my drink in front of me. I take a sip while Adam waits for my assessment of the peculiar combination of pineapple and jalapeño in a beer.

"It's got a nice kick to it. A little sour, with a sweet finish."

"See? Not bad, right?"

"Not bad at all."

I should probably get to business, which is why I'm here. None of what I felt after Colin's near death has changed; I still believe I should step down as captain of the *Alacrity* and pass that on to Piñeros. Initially, I'd planned to just leave Alaska and have my lawyers take care of all the legal transfer of title, et cetera. And then I'd meant to broach the subject with Adam a few days ago, after I dropped Helene back at the cottage, but Merrick showed up, and all my plans were once again cast aside.

"You're doing that thing," Adam says, "where you spin your glass in that obsessive pattern of yours. What's on your mind?"

I look down at my hands, and I am, indeed, spinning the beer on the bar. Clockwise twice, counterclockwise once. I've been doing that for so many centuries I don't even register the movement anymore. I stop and take a long drink instead.

"All right," I say. "You know how much I've enjoyed being in business with you, and god knows I love the *Alacrity* and our crew, but . . . I'd like to retire."

Adam just stares at me, expression inscrutable.

So I continue. "I know the boat could go out once or twice more before the crabbing season ends, but I'll cover the pay for the crew for the rest of the season. And Piñeros will make a great captain—"

"I don't understand," Adam says. "You want to quit? Right now? Is this because you feel guilty about Colin? 'Cuz it's not your fault, Seabass. That shit happens on the water all the time. It's a fact of the biz, and you can't let it hound you." He jostles his maimed leg to make his point.

"It's a little bit about Colin, but it's also . . ." How do I explain to him that my soulmate—whom I only see once every few decades—has come back to me? And that I know my time with her is short, so I can't spend another second on the ocean without her?

But Adam and I have been friends for too long, and he already has an inkling. "Oh, I see how it is," he says, grinning. "It's about a girl."

"It's complicated."

"That's what you told me the night she walked into The Frosty Otter. I heard through the gossip mill that she's living with you now."

I sigh. Small town talk is so . . . well, like this.

"Is she that special?" Adam asks. "You just met her. She seems nice, but still. You're going to give up your entire life's work because of her?"

He doesn't know that Helene—Juliet—*is* my entire life. All the years in between her reincarnations are just treading water. I'm not truly alive except when she's with me.

Dana comes out of the kitchen with a basket of barbecue for Adam.

"Thanks, babe." He pecks her on the cheek.

"Didn't know you were here, Seb," Dana says. "I'll get you some food, too."

"But first," Adam says, "can you help me talk some sense into him? Seabass is trying to retire from the *Alacrity* because of a woman."

Dana puts her hands on her hips and surveys both me and Adam.

"Adam, honey, any bad decision Sebastien makes due to a woman is probably your fault. As I recall, the *last* conversation we all had about his dating life involved you telling him to sleep with only tourists because then they leave town and he doesn't have to make any commitments."

"Ouch," Adam says, laughing. He turns to me and says, "More advice: Get yourself a stupid woman. These smart ones push back and cause trouble way too often."

Dana grabs a spatula out of her apron pocket and whacks him with it. "Focus on what you're good at: Eat your chicken and stop doling out relationship advice."

Adam smirks.

She turns to me. "In all seriousness, though. What's this talk about retiring?"

"I'm tired," I say. "And captains without an appetite for the job make mistakes."

"Like Colin falling overboard?" she asks gently.

I flinch, my remorse stinging like alcohol in a wound. "Yes, like Colin falling overboard."

"Seabass is offering to cover the crew's pay for crabbing trips we'll miss," Adam says. "But I object. We're running a business here. You can't just quit in the middle of the season."

"The season's almost over," I say.

"We're close to our quota, but not there yet. The *Alacrity* could go out a couple more times. There would be lost catches, and Piñeros can't do it with a crew short one man. And it's too late in the season to find a good replacement."

I nod. "Okay. No problem. I can pay for the lost catches, too."

Far from appeasing Adam, though, my offer only incenses him. "You have a trust fund somewhere I don't know about?"

I didn't mean to come across like an obnoxious railroad baron, swooping in to buy him off. Yes, I have a substantial investment account. But I earned every penny over hundreds of years of work—which were also hundreds of years of suffering through a curse. I can't tell him any of that, though.

"I, uh, made some lucky investment decisions in the past," I say.

Adam snorts. "That would explain how you paid for that enormous house of yours. And why you think it's fine to cut and run on me like this."

"I don't want to leave you," I protest. But unless I offer a better explanation, the evidence is against me.

"No, Mr. Moneybags," Adam says. "I refuse to let you out of the business just because you got bored and want to spend your time sleeping with some woman from the Lower 48."

"What did you say?" I leap up from my barstool, livid.

But it's not because of the insult that I'm mad. Not really. It's everything unsaid beneath it, everything that Adam can't even comprehend. I'm furious because it must be nice when your only problem is what engagement ring to buy your girlfriend, that when you think of "the rest of our lives," you get to think in terms of *decades*. Not days or months or—only if I'm lucky—a measly couple of years.

"Simmer down, boys," Dana says, a note of warning in her tone.

That brings me back to myself. To what this is really about, from Adam's point of view. He doesn't know what's going on with me, why I have to do this. He only sees me abandoning him.

It's not his fault. It's mine, like it always is.

I sigh and try to lower the temperature. "I just . . . I can't do it anymore, Adam. You don't know what it was like, watching the ocean throw Colin around."

"You think I don't know what fear of the ocean is like?" Adam kicks at the bar with his bad leg. "That boat took something from me, too. What I wouldn't give to be able to sail again—and you're just taking it for granted. You need to get your shit together."

"Adam . . . I don't know what to say."

He scoffs. "So that's it? You come in here, tell me you're abandoning our business with zero notice, and expect me to be happy about it? We built this company, you and me, from nothing. I thought that meant something. But apparently not. So fuck you, Sebastien."

Adam never calls me by my actual name.

Dana tries to step in. "Why don't you both take a breather, and then I'm sure we can have a levelheaded discussion. If you guys—"

"No, babe. Sebastien made it clear—he's done with me and the boys and the *Alacrity*. So I'm done with him." He turns to his basket of chicken and begins attacking it.

"Adam," I say. "I didn't want it to be this way—"

"Get out."

Dana frowns. "Hey, this is my restaurant, and I say who stays or—"

Adam ignores her and fixes his stare on me. "Get. Out. And don't you dare stop by Colin's if you're not going to be his captain anymore. He looked up to you, and you don't deserve his admiration."

I glance at Dana. She shakes her head sadly. I can tell she wants to help us get through this, but at the same time, she has to stand by Adam. And I'm clearly the asshole here anyway.

I push my barstool under the counter and lay some cash on the counter for the beer.

"I'm sorry," I say to both Adam and Dana. And then, just to Adam, "I'll transfer the costs for the crew's wages and the lost catches into the company's account this afternoon."

He doesn't even acknowledge me, just crams more chicken into his mouth. He's furious, and he has every right to be.

"Take care of yourself, Merculief."

I trudge out of the Smokehouse less a crew, a job, and a friend. The curse always comes with steep costs.

HELENE

I DON'T KNOW WHAT HAPPENED BETWEEN SEBASTIEN AND ADAM, BUT I know something upsetting went down, because for the next couple of months, Sebastien doesn't need to go to the harbor. Instead, while I'm writing, he buries himself in the kitchen, cooking as if he's in that novel *Like Water for Chocolate*, where the protagonist's emotions flavor the food. I can taste the angst in Sebastien's Bolognese, the guilt in the beef bourguignonne, and even the melancholy in his fish-and-chips.

My middle gets noticeably pudgier. I tell myself I'm eating everything he makes because it's my way of showing support for whatever he's going through, but let's be honest—I'm eating because I love food, and I've never lived with a gourmet chef before. (Sebastien, I discover, worked in the royal kitchens of Monaco in the late 1800s.)

When I try to talk to him about Adam, though, Sebastien clams up.

"What can I do to make you happier?" I ask.

"Write your novel," he says. "That's all I want. If you're happy, I'll be happy. Go. Write."

I don't believe him, but since it's the only thing he'll tell me, I do as he wants. I throw myself into the story, and finally, in the quiet solitude of Sebastien's house, I begin to make progress. The manuscript is a messy, ugly thing full of plot holes and purple prose, but at least it's taking shape. Besides, *The Craft of Novel Writing* says that the rough draft is supposed to be clumsy and illogical and meandering, because it's really the author telling herself the story. Only after I've gotten to know the characters and wandered through many wrong turns of the plot will I know what the novel wants to be.

With the help of all of Sebastien's journals, I am piecing together our story.

My time in the library isn't all joyful discovery, though. While my vignettes were happily ever afters, all of Sebastien's were tragedies. Some days, I'm able to pretend that the couples in his journals were other people, not us, and then I can focus on using the material for the purpose of writing my book. But other days, the weight of our past is too real and too much.

If the curse still holds, how much time do I have? I could die tomorrow. Or anytime in the next two years. That's the longest any past reincarnation of me has had. It's unsettling, to say the least.

I try to push the thought away. But it flits in and out of my mind, like a fly in the house. You think the fly's gone—maybe it escaped out the door that one time you opened it—but all of a sudden, it's buzzing around in your kitchen while you're eating breakfast or in your bedroom when you're trying to fall asleep.

The one solution I've found that works to shoo the thought of the curse away, though, is touching Dad's broken watch. Because whenever I hold on to it and look at it, I remember what he said: If you live with one eye fixed on the end, you've already lost.

I won't lose. And I refuse to accept that Sebastien and I are done for.

SEBASTIEN

I TRY TO DELIVER HELENE WHAT I PROMISED—LETTING HER LIVE HER life. I show her how to shovel snow, how to build a snowman, how to spot white foxes and white rabbits in the winter landscape. She plays the guitar by the fireplace, teaches me the lyrics to folk songs her mom has written and laughs at her own inability to stay in key, and points out constellations in the sky, telling me all the legends and myths behind them. And I don't bring up the curse anymore, because I don't want her to feel the scythe poised over her head.

I can never forget, though. Sometimes, I'll be watching her do something pedestrian, like washing the dishes, and I'll suddenly find myself on the verge of breaking down because I can already imagine her gone, my kitchen empty. Or I'll be brushing my teeth and see two toothbrushes on the counter, and the knowledge that soon there will be only one will kick me in the chest and knock me backward onto the tiled floor. I miss her when she's still present, and then I have to stop and yell at myself—*She. Is. Still. Here.*

There ought to be some comfort in knowing that Juliet will

eventually return to me. But what comfort there is, it's far outweighed by the grim nature of the curse. Juliet will suffer and die each time. It makes it no better for her that her soul had previously inhabited another body; every version of Juliet is a real and separate person who has to endure the agony of disease or a brutal, sudden death, and all the terror that comes with it. And I have to watch it happen. I have to *know* it will happen.

And afterward, there is always the chance that Juliet won't come back again. That that reincarnation was the last one. Because the fact is, I don't understand what the curse is, how it works, or if it's forever. I only have a theory about Mercutio and evidence from centuries of repetition. Death makes no guarantees, however.

Which is why I can't waste this precious time. This moment, right now, is Helene's.

And so I put in the effort every day of shoving aside my storm clouds. Some days it's easier than others. But I try.

Today, however, is a harder day. I am sitting outside on the cold bench on the porch, fancy envelope opened on my lap. It's March but still winter—spring comes late to Alaska—and I shiver as I hold the pearlescent card to read again.

> *Dana and Adam are getting married!*
> *Come celebrate our happiness*
> *(and Dana's giant honking ring)*
> *The Smokehouse*
> *March 29*
> *7 p.m. until the BBQ and the booze run out*

Jealousy rears its fanged head, the same as when I watched the elderly couple at Shipyard Books holding hands and celebrating their anniversary. Helene and I will never have what everyone else can. I crumple the invitation in my fist.

Obviously, Adam had nothing to do with mailing it. In the two months that have passed since we argued over my retirement, I've tried calling him so many times that I lost track, but he refuses to answer. I drove out to Ryba Harbor to the *Alacrity*'s office, but Adam peeked out the trailer window and saw me coming up the ramp, and locked the door before I could get there.

Now Helene sticks her head through the doorway and steps onto the frozen porch. "Hey . . . I've been looking all over. What're you doing out here?"

My hands fly over the card and envelope in a pathetic attempt to hide them.

She wrinkles her nose skeptically. "The junk mail is so compelling that you decided to read it in the cold?"

I sigh and hand over the crumpled invitation.

Helene skims it, then says, "You could go to the party."

"I'm not going to show up and ruin their celebration."

"But if Dana sent it to you, maybe she thinks there's a chance you and Adam could make up."

"Maybe. Or maybe she's trying to fix us, when he's not ready for the fix yet. If ever."

"I'm sorry." Helene moves the invitation onto the pile of mail next to me and climbs onto my lap. "Can I share some good news to cheer you up?"

"Please." I wrap my arms around her; she's not dressed warmly enough to be out here. But as soon as I hold her, I know that I need her close to me more than the other way around. Because her nearness is an antidote to any darkness I ever feel; her touch alone could save me from the brink of extinction.

Helene leans in and whispers into my ear. "I finished my manuscript."

"What?" I pull back so I can look at her, and any remaining thoughts of Adam evaporate. "You finished? Congratulations!"

She grins, so happy that she's bouncing in my lap. Which has another not unwelcome effect.

"Well, it's only a zero draft," Helene says.

"What's a zero draft?"

"It's muddled chaos, masquerading as a loosely coherent story."

"But it's enough pages to be a book?"

Helene squeals and nods.

I pick her up and spin her on the porch. "You wrote a book! A whole damn book! Do you know how many people dream of doing that, but never get to where you are?"

She laughs as we get dizzy together and fall back down onto the bench. "I have to admit," she says, "I'm pretty proud of myself right now."

I lean down and kiss her. "Let's open up some champagne. I'll cook something special for you tonight—whatever you want. We'll also plan a proper celebration."

This is what all the wealth I've accumulated over the centuries is for. Not for me, but for Juliet. To spoil her, because my time with her is short, and I want as much of it as possible to be everything she could ever want.

Helene grins. "And what does a proper celebration entail?"

"Surprises."

Her eyes gleam, even brighter than the sunlight reflecting off the snow. "Surprises, plural?"

"At least one surprise," I say. "But maybe plural, if you're lucky."

HELENE

A WEEK LATER, WE WALK IN THROUGH THE HEAVY WOODEN DOOR OF Axes and S'more.

"Oh my god," I say. "I already adore this place." Half the interior is axe-throwing cages (like a shooting range for target practice, but with hatchets), and the other half is a restaurant with table-top fire pits in the center of each table. It feels so quintessentially Alaskan—or at least how a tourist like me imagines "Alaskan-ness" would be distilled.

"Thought you'd like it," Sebastien says, kissing the top of my head.

"Welcome to Axes and S'more," the hostess says. She's appropriately clad in flannel and a faux fur hat, and she has a twangy Alaskan accent. "Are you here to throw or roast or both?"

"Both," Sebastien says. "But we've already got a table, thank you."

I look up at him, confused. "We do?"

"Surprises, remember?" He winks, pulls a handkerchief out of his pocket, and blindfolds me.

I jump up and down. I've always loved surprises. Even as a little girl, I never tried to find where my parents hid the birthday gifts, and I never shook the presents under the tree; for me, the anticipation is part of the thrill.

Sebastien leads me past the hostess stand and into the restaurant. Miraculously, I don't bump into any furniture or waiters on the way, which is testament to Sebastien's careful steering.

"Okay, ready?" he asks when we've stopped.

"Ready."

He takes off the blindfold. I blink at the tables and chairs in front of me, but I don't see what the surprise is. I don't know any of the people here. Am I supposed to be looking at the huge wolf mural on the wall? Like, is there a clue in the painting?

Sebastien puts his hands on my shoulders and turns me one hundred and eighty degrees toward the corner of the restaurant.

Mom and Katy jump up from the booth. "Surprise!"

I scream, and all those people at the tables behind us probably glare at me. But I don't care, because I'm suddenly enveloped in bear hugs from my two favorite people. "What are you doing here?"

"Sebastien flew us up to celebrate your finishing the draft of your book," Katy says.

Still wrapped in my mom's and sister's arms, I turn to look at him. "You did?"

He just smiles, and I love this man who doesn't always say much, but shows it instead.

Katy and Mom and I hug some more, and I don't even need to introduce them to Sebastien, because they already "met" on the phone when they were planning this surprise party. Finally, we settle into the booth. There's a small fire pit in the center of the table, presumably for s'mores. Sebastien grabs a stack of laminated menus from behind the napkin holder.

"Oooh," Katy says as she checks out the options. "I could go for venison steak."

"You're going to eat Rudolph?" I say, teasing.

She shakes her head. "Blitzen."

Mom arches a brow. "Now we know where Trevor gets his penchant for gnawing on dinosaur heads."

"Who eats dinosaurs?" Sebastien looks at me for help deciphering the conversation.

"My grandson," Mom explains. "Katy's boy. He has chicken nuggets shaped like dinosaurs, and he likes ripping off their heads and dipping them in blood . . . well, ketchup."

Sebastien laughs.

"But seriously," Katy says, "is the venison good?"

"Kit Kat," I say. "I think you're missing the point of this place." I reach across the table and flip her menu over from the dinner options to the side titled "Alaskan Stars," presumably named after the state flag.

She gapes at the menu. "Are these all—?"

"Yes, indeed," Sebastien says.

I join Katy and Mom in gawking at the two dozen different s'mores platters available.

- *The S'moreo: Oreo cookies instead of graham crackers.*
- *Cheesecake: blackberry jam, whipped cream cheese, marshmallow, and milk chocolate.*
- *Mexican hot cocoa: spiced chocolate, dulce de leche, marshmallow, and cinnamon graham crackers.*

And on and on.

Who knew it was possible to improve something as perfect as s'mores? And yet, here's proof, because I want to order and eat every single one of them.

"I think I'm going to move in here," I say.

Mom nods. "Me, too."

Sebastien squeezes my knee. "As long as I'm still allowed to visit."

The waiter comes over. He's wearing the same Axes and S'more uniform as the hostess, complete with fur hat and a flannel shirt embroidered with his name, Jim, and a happy cartoon marshmallow wielding an axe. Jim is a burly guy—he looks like he's been throwing axes since he was a toddler—and the cutesy logo is incongruous on him.

"What's up, man?" Jim exchanges fist bumps with Sebastien. Of course they know each other. Small town and all. "Long time no see."

"Hey, Jim. This is my girlfriend, Helene, and her mom, Beth, and sister, Katy. They're visiting Alaska for the first time."

"Sebastien brought you to the right place, best s'mores in the whole country. What can I get started for you?"

Mom orders the piña colada s'mores. Katy gets a venison steak *and* the peanut butter and bacon Elvis Presley s'mores—Janssen girls like to eat—and Sebastien orders something called the Traditional. I go for the Nutty Chocoholic. The name seems apt for me.

"Excellent," Jim says. "I suggest a round of axe throwing while you wait. The kitchen's a little backed up tonight, so it might take half an hour to get your food out."

"What do you think?" Sebastien asks me. "Are you up for throwing some axes?"

"Sign me up," Mom says, already climbing out of the booth.

We head over to a walled-in cage with a big wooden target on the wall. A chain-link fence separates us from the next lane, which is occupied by a foursome of scrawny, bespectacled guys. But their scoreboard has an impressive number of tally marks, and every time one of the skinny guys throws, the axe hits bull's-eye or close. A crowd has gathered and erupts in cheers for each hit.

The cage on the other side of us contains several drunk girls who probably shouldn't be wielding axes. A couple of them make googly eyes at Sebastien, but Katy steps right up to the chain-link fence and glares at them. The girls beat a hasty retreat to the other side of their cage.

Mom suggests we forgo keeping score and just have fun, which I'm all for. She hefts an axe and throws it, hitting the outer ring.

"Pretty good," Katy says. "But let me show you how it's done."

She hurls her axe and hits the third ring from the outside, one better than Mom's.

"Ringer," Mom says. "Have you done this before?"

"Maaaybe," Katy says, adopting her I'm-so-innocent face she used to use when she was caught tiptoeing in late at night from parties.

"Your turn," Sebastien says to me.

"Can you show me, I don't know, the proper form or whatever?"

"No fair," Katy says. "We didn't get lessons. You have to throw using just your natural instinct."

"Or your previous, undisclosed experience," Mom quips.

Katy smiles smugly.

"You heard what they said, Helene." Sebastien steps back and crosses his arms, but relaxed, as if he thinks I'll magically know what to do.

Okay, well, you get what you pay for. I step up to the line marked on the cement, wind up my arm like the skinny guys in the next cage, and get ready to throw. But right before I do, something shifts inside me, like muscle memory, and I adjust my arm just so.

Then I let loose, and the axe flies through the air.

It hits the bull's-eye.

"Hot damn, Hel!" Katy gives me an approving nod.

Sebastien looks at me proudly, but also like he suspected all along that I'd ace it. I wonder which of our past lives was the one where we threw axes to the point that I'm this good at it.

By the time we get back to the table, I'm ravenous. Thankfully, Jim arrives with the food at the same time. Another waiter accompanies him, because there's so much to bring over.

Each order of s'mores is the size of a baking sheet. Mine alone has two ramekins of Nutella, giant cubes of house-made chocolate marshmallows, and chocolate chip cookies baked flat for optimal s'more smashing, artfully arranged on the sheet pan.

Jim flicks on a switch under the table that gets the fire in the center going. "All right, gimme a holler if you need anything else." He leaves four long-handled skewers around the little fire.

I stare at my Nutty Chocoholic platter and can't imagine needing anything else, ever.

Katy picks up a skewer and stabs one of Mom's coconut marshmallows.

She swats at Katy's hand. "Eat your own first."

Katy sticks out her tongue and pops the coconut marshmallow into her mouth anyway.

"Incorrigible," Mom says.

I smile at them, and notice that Sebastien does, too.

"Thank you," I say to him. "This is the most perfect celebration I could imagine."

"It is?" he says. "Then I suppose I don't need to give you your second surprise if this is already perfect."

I set down the cookie I was about to smear with Nutella. "There's another surprise?"

"You requested plural surprises. Close your eyes and hold out your hands."

I obey. Sebastien sets what feels like a brochure in them.

"Now open."

It's not a brochure, but a paperboard sleeve. I open it, and my jaw drops. "Plane tickets? To *Europe*?"

I'd thought my dreams of gallivanting through the Netherlands and France were over when Merrick canceled my flights.

"And accommodations, for two," Sebastien says. "You can take Katy to celebrate finishing your manuscript, just like you originally planned."

"Nuh-uh," Katy says. "We already talked about this, Sebastien, and you're supposed to be a man of your word." She turns to me. "Sebastien called me, offering an all-expenses-paid trip for you and me. But Mom and I have never seen you this happy, Hel. You're glowing, for god's sake. So I want you and Sebastien to go together. He and I discussed it and I negotiated a compromise; that's how we came to the solution of him flying me and Mom up to Alaska for a week. Then you two will be off to Europe soon after that."

"But—" Sebastien says.

"Don't even try to renege," Katy says. "A deal's a deal."

He hesitates, but when he sees how intent she is, he dips his head in concession.

I stare at Katy, Mom, and Sebastien. "You three did all this for me?"

"We're so proud of you, sweetheart," Mom says. "These past few months have been some of your hardest, but some of your bravest, too." (She tactfully leaves out mention of Merrick.)

"Wow . . . I don't know what to say."

Sebastien presses his hands on top of mine, the plane tickets sandwiched between them. "Say yes."

I look down at the plane tickets. And at the strong, weathered hands holding on to mine, as if they have always belonged together.

"Yes." I nod so hard my head almost falls into the pots of Nutella. "Yes yes yes."

And in this moment, I don't believe in the curse. Because the cursed don't get to be this happy.

SEBASTIEN

A COUPLE OF DAYS LATER, WHILE HELENE TAKES BETH AND KATY ON a tour of the wild horses on a nearby island, Merrick's next move in the escalating divorce battle arrives in the form of a manila envelope. There's actually no return address, but when I open it, I know exactly who it's from.

"You unbelievable asshole."

There are photos of Helene taken by a long-range camera, the kind that private investigators and paparazzi use. None of the pictures are scandalous, but there are a few photos of us inside my house, and the threat is implicit.

My heart slams against my ribs so violently it might shatter them. How dare Merrick violate Helene's life like this? She thought he wasn't a danger, but this goes far beyond the normal rancor of a divorce.

I snatch the phone off the wall and dial the Julius A. Weiskopf Group in Geneva. I'm immediately transferred to the president of the firm.

"Sebastien, *Es ist eine Freude von Ihnen zu hören*," Sandrine says. What a pleasure to hear from you.

I slip into German as well. "Thank you for taking my call."

"You know I would drop anything for you," she says. "How can I help you today?"

This is why I have the Weiskopf Group on retainer: They don't know my past, but they also don't question my name changes or when I need new identification papers or why my account has been open for as long as it has. They work with the most successful and private businesspeople in the world—as well as top celebrities—and their job is simply to help their clients with whatever they're asked to do, and to do it very well.

"Another issue with Merrick Sauer has come up." I pace through the halls of my house and tell Sandrine about the photos I just received in the mail.

Ever professional, she doesn't give a hint of any reaction to the news.

Instead, she dives into action, listing off what her lawyers will take care of, including filing a temporary restraining order and a countersuit for trespassing, invasion of privacy, and everything else their aggressive, brilliant legal minds can think of. If Merrick wants war, we'll give him war.

Knowing Sandrine is on it, I can finally sit down. I sink into a chair in my study.

"Do you need us to hire security services for your property?" Sandrine asks. This is de rigueur for her more famous clients.

I consider it for a minute. I know I promised Helene I'd tell her if there was anything she needed to know about Merrick, but there's also a part of me that wants to shield her from this. Not only because I want to protect her from the feeling of utter violation from being spied on, but also because there's a sword's edge to Merrick's anger that worries me. Like he'll play an unintentional part in the curse. And I've sworn to myself not to mention the curse, to give Helene as much freedom from it as I can negotiate for her.

I decide to keep the knowledge of this envelope of photos to myself. I hope I don't regret it.

"Send security," I tell Sandrine. "But only for a couple of weeks, because we're leaving for Europe then. Keep them in the woods around my house, unseen. I don't want any former Mossad assassinating whatever amateur private eye Merrick has sent over."

"Understood, just a deterrent, very discreet. Do you require security services while in Europe?"

"No . . . for now." I am hopeful that Merrick won't have the resources to follow us there. He has a grudge, but not unlimited funds.

"Let me know if you change your mind," Sandrine says.

I nod, even though she can't see. But she'll infer it.

"There's another thing I need," I say as I pick up Dana and Adam's engagement announcement from my desk. "I want to transfer my half of ownership of the *Alacrity* and the related business."

"Is this a sale of the company or a gift?" Sandrine asks, already running through the tax implications of both.

I trace my fingers along a scaled model of the boat, between a lamp and a stone paperweight. I've spent a lot of time in my life on ships, but the *Alacrity* was the first that was mine; I'm going to miss her. I already do.

"It's a gift to Dana Wong," I say. "For her engagement to Adam, owner of the other half of the business."

"Very good," Sandrine says, and I'm again grateful for her discretion. Anyone else would want to know why I'm not giving the business to Adam. The answer, of course, is that Adam would refuse it, and that would cause more legal headaches and paperwork. Dana, however, will get that I need to do this as a peace offering, and that Adam will one day understand. Hopefully.

"What else can I take care of for you, Sebastien?"

Helene's passport lies slightly open on my desk. I run my finger across her photo, her birthdate, and the date the passport expires—nine years from now.

My stomach sours. She won't live long enough to apply for another one.

I smash the passport shut and thump a paperweight onto it.

"Sebastien?" Sandrine asks. "Anything else I can take care of for you?"

Can you break the curse? Can you save Helene from dying?

But I only say, "That's all for now, Sandrine, thank you."

"Always a pleasure. I'll be in touch soon." She hangs up without a lingering goodbye, another hallmark of the Julius A. Weiskopf Group. They are not my friends; they're my advocates and, when I need them to be, my attack dogs.

I close my eyes and rest my head against the tufted leather of my chair. Life, ceaseless as it is, can be exhausting. I think if people knew what I knew—what I've seen and lived through—they would stop chasing immortality. No more fad diets or biohacks for longevity. No more research to prevent aging.

Immortality isn't all it's cracked up to be, I'd tell them.

I pour myself two fingers of Scotch and sit in my study, staring out into the woods, watching. And thinking, for a very long time.

HELENE

THE FIRST CITY ON KATY'S AND MY ORIGINAL ITINERARY—AND NOW on Sebastien's and mine—is Amsterdam. I've always wanted to visit the Netherlands, because it's where Dad grew up before his family immigrated to the States when he was a teenager. Sebastien and I arrive just in time for Koningsdag, the celebration of the Dutch king's birthday.

When we land at Schiphol Airport, a chauffeur is waiting for us in the arrivals terminal with a bouquet of tulips and holding up a sign that reads Helene Janssen.

"You're too good to me," I say to Sebastien.

"There's no such thing," he says with a kiss. He'd seemed stressed recently, but the moment we stepped foot in the Netherlands, his mood seemed to warm by several degrees. It probably feels like a relief to get away from Alaska. (I still don't know the details of what happened between him and Adam; Sebastien has been characteristically closed as a vault on that topic.)

"*Goedendag, Mevrouw* Janssen, *Meneer* Janssen," the chauffeur, Lars, says. "*Het is leuk u te ontmoeten.*"

I assume it's a greeting and I smile. Then I realize he thinks I'm Dutch, seeing as my last name is. I'm about to explain that I only speak English when Sebastien replies to him, and they have a full-on conversation in Dutch.

Sebastien smiles shyly when he sees me staring. "Did I not mention I speak Dutch?"

"Good day, Ms. Janssen," Lars says to me in English now. It's perfect, with only the barest hint of an accent, just like my dad's. I touch my watch at the reminder of him.

"It's nice to meet you," Lars says. "Mr. Montague explains you have not been to our beautiful city of Amsterdam before. I will take the scenic route to your accommodations."

Soon after we drive out of the airport, the landscape turns vibrant, brightly hued fields of tulips as far as I can see. This is the Netherlands as I envisioned, and it's hard to believe I'm finally here.

"You are here at a very exciting time," Lars says. "Koningsdag begins soon. The streets fill with revelers, and all of Amsterdam celebrates day and night. Do you have some orange clothes? It is the color of the Netherlands, and we have a bit of *oranjegekte*—orange madness—during Koningsdag."

I've read up on how everyone spills into the streets and canals, wearing orange. "No, but I thought Sebastien and I could do some shopping for Koningsdag wear."

"A brilliant idea," Lars says. "I will write down the address of my wife's favorite boutique for you."

As we drive, I gawk at the city. It's even more beautiful than I've seen in pictures. Tall, narrow houses press against one another, blue skies overhead, serene canals at their doorsteps. Houseboats float in the water, and young couples stroll hand in hand over old stone bridges.

Bicycles zip by in orderly fashion, some with large, open-air wooden boxes in front of them containing smiling children who wave to us. Being in a car, we're far outnumbered by the bicycles; it's a fascinating thing to watch. After all, I'm from Los Angeles, where you can't even run errands without a car.

Too soon, our driving tour ends. Lars parks, opens our doors, and begins to unload our baggage from the trunk. I step onto the sidewalk but turn around confused. There's no hotel anywhere.

Sebastien points me toward the canal instead.

It takes a moment for me to understand.

"You mean . . ."

"Yes."

In front of us is a gorgeous, modern houseboat with matte aluminum sides, large windows overlooking the water, and a deck that wraps all along the outside.

I squeal, even though it sounds ridiculous. "In college, my friend Monica and I talked about running away to Amsterdam and living on a houseboat for a while."

But instead of mirroring my delight, Sebastien looks pained for a moment, looking through me and through the boat, as if there's a window into something in the past. He does this sometimes; I know our history haunts him, even though he tries not to let it show. But sometimes when we're sleeping, he wakes up in a panic, and it's only when he realizes I'm still there beside him that he calms down, falling back asleep wrapped in my arms.

He never cries, though. In all the time we've spent talking about past Romeos and Juliets, and all the time I've cried over the journals, Sebastien has never shed a single tear. I wonder if he's lived through so much loss that he has no tears left.

"Hey." I touch his shoulder so as not to startle him. "You okay? Come back to me."

Sebastien blinks. "Oh. Sorry."

"Past Me wanted to live on a houseboat, didn't she?" I say gently. "What was my name then?"

"It was Kitri," he whispers. "She loved sketching the ships in the quay and dreamed of a boat of her own someday."

"We'll do it for her, then," I say, taking Sebastien's hand and leading him slowly down the dock.

But he shakes his head. "Kitri had her time," he says. "Now you're Helene, and we'll make new memories." He kisses me, then smiles, only a tint of sadness lingering.

I love this man and the gargantuan effort he makes, despite his own suffering, to make me happy.

★　★　★

It's impossible not to be cheerful among the tree-lined streets and tranquil waterways, and all traces of Sebastien's earlier melancholy vanish like clouds in the clear blue sky as we spend the afternoon exploring. Colorful awnings and wooden signs grace many of the narrow lanes, and tulips seem to bloom off every balcony. Everywhere we go, bicycle bells ping merrily as people pedal by, and little birds chirp as if providing a quaint European soundtrack for our adventure.

Sebastien and I buy *poffertjes*—little puffy pancakes sprinkled in powdered sugar—from a street vendor, and stroll along the canals and bridges. At the boutique Lars recommended, we pick out orange shirts for Koningsdag, and I also get a beautiful handwoven basket that will be useful for the springtime farmers markets. While Katy and I had originally planned to spend only two weeks in Europe, Sebastien and I don't have any reason to rush back to the States. I can revise my manuscript from anywhere, and crab season is over. So I can already imagine myself spending mornings meandering through stalls full of freshly cut flowers, displays of bright red cherries and blushing apricots, and green mountains of asparagus and artichokes, piling whatever I want into my new basket. Everything about being here feels lighter and brighter than Old Helene's life before.

"How about we have a picnic on the deck of our boat tonight?" Sebastien asks.

"Oooh, Gouda and bread and wine? Yes, please."

The sun is moving lower in the sky, and as the workday ends, the streets around us again fill with bicycles, commuters heading home after work.

We take our time returning to the houseboat. Unlike at home, specialty shops are still common here, and I'm captivated by it. Buying Gouda is a conversation with the cheesemonger, not a chilly grab-and-go in a sterile megamarket refrigerator case. Wine is a long discussion about the terroir of different vineyards. While Sebastien talks to each purveyor, I take pictures to send to Mom and Katy—giant wheels of cheese, racks of artisan bread displayed in baskets, walls of wine lovingly curated by sommeliers.

Back outside, we walk past a coffee shop. Suddenly a wave of nausea roils through me. Oh god, what is that smell? I clutch my stomach and sprint past the storefront, not stopping until the next street corner, where I double over, dry heaving.

Sebastien runs after me, slower because he'd insisted on carrying all our shopping bags.

"Helene! What's wrong?"

I brace myself against the brick wall. I'm pretty sure the bicyclist commuters in the intersection are all staring at me, because it's gotten so quiet; unlike Americans, they're too polite to gossip about the woman gagging on the sidewalk.

I realize now what the smell was. "Th-that coffee shop . . ." I gasp. "It reeked of pot."

Despite my circumstances, Sebastien starts laughing. I mean, full-belly, echoing-through-the-canals kind of laughter. "That was a cannabis dispensary," he says.

"The sign on the window said Coffee Shop." I'm still bent over, but the dry heaving is receding.

"That's what they call dispensaries here. A place that serves coffee is called *koffiehuis*."

"That's . . . confusing."

"I know." He rubs my back.

I take a few deep breaths. The nausea subsides, and I unfold myself slowly, although I still lean against the bricks for support. When I finally feel like myself again, I say, "I've never had a problem with pot before. In grad school, the people who lived below us smoked all the time."

"Dutch cannabis is stronger than American," Sebastien says.

"Maybe that's it," I say. But I still think it's weird that it affected me so much.

We walk even slower the rest of the way back to the houseboat. The fresh air does wonders, and I'm as good as new by the time we arrive.

That is, until we step foot onto the boat. With the waves moving us up and down, nausea lurches through me again. I run to the railing and throw up into the canal.

Sebastien drops everything and rushes to me.

"We should get you to a doctor."

"No, I'm fine," I say, wiping vomit from my chin.

"I'm worried." The gray storm clouds return over his brow, and I realize Sebastien's not just concerned that I have a stomach bug; he's afraid this is the curse, that I'm about to die.

But I'm not. I know it. I feel so alive here in Europe with him. I've *never* been more alive than this.

"Shh," I say, trying to calm him down. "This isn't the curse. I'll be okay. It's probably just the aftereffects of the pot."

"You only breathed it for a millisecond."

"I promise you. This'll pass soon."

Still, I sink down onto the deck, where I can pull my knees tightly into my chest.

Sebastien rubs his eyes with the heels of his palms, then starts pacing. "It's my fault. I've worked on a boat for so long with crews who all have their sea legs, I just assumed—"

"Don't worry," I say. "I just need a few minutes. But please stop pacing, because it's making the boat rock even more."

"Helene . . ."

To reassure him, I give him my brightest smile, like I'm *not* fighting the urge to throw up again. "Just sit with me. I swear, I'll be fine."

Sebastien lowers himself to the deck and puts an arm around me protectively, as if he can keep me safe by holding me close. Just the two of us, forever and ever.

My stomach heaves again.

Just the two of us, forever and ever, I repeat to myself like a mantra to convince myself I'm going to be okay.

The poffertjes from earlier churn inside me.

Just the two of us, forever and ever . . .

My gut twists so hard I wince. Do I have food poisoning? What the hell is going on? I wrap my arms around my middle—my squishy, too-much-Nutella, rapidly expanding belly.

Oh my god.

What if it's not Sebastien's cooking that's been making me fatter? What if it's not "just the two of us"?

What if it's *three*?

I swallow the poffertjes threatening to come back up.

Nausea plus weight gain . . .

I think I might be pregnant.

I spend most of the night awake. Not because I'm worried, but because I'm . . . excited. I've wanted a child forever. And I also have an idea about this baby and how it might be a sign that the curse is broken, but I haven't told Sebastien. Not even that I suspect I'm pregnant.

I don't want him to get his hopes up yet.

Before he wakes, I leave him a note that I've gone to the market. Then I slip out of the houseboat to look for a pharmacy. Luckily, even though I can't read or speak Dutch, they're easy to find, since most have bright green crosses in their shop windows. I see one a few blocks away and duck inside.

There are multiple tests on the shelf. Do I need to buy one of the expensive ones? They're usually more sensitive. But if I've been pregnant awhile, there'll be more hormones in my system, and the cheaper tests will work just fine.

For most women, it would be easy enough to count backward to a missed period. But I'm on one of those birth control pills that has the side benefit of skipping periods (although in the upheaval of my life the past few months, I have definitely forgotten to take my pills a few times). Still, I haven't bled in years, and I've always considered it a modern-day luxury. It never occurred to me that actually getting a monthly period would be helpful. I spring for one of the more expensive tests.

As I'm paying, I ask, "Is there by any chance a toilet I can use here?"

"Sorry, employees only," the clerk says. "But you can go to the café across the street. Buy a piece of cake, and they'll let you use the WC."

★ ★ ★

The aroma of coffee and pastries is usually enough to soothe my nerves, but today I'm still jittery as I wait in line to place my order. For once, I can't concentrate on a menu, so when I get up to the counter, I just ask for a cookie, which I stuff hastily into my purse.

My hands shake badly as I lock myself in the WC. (The water closet. Europeans don't call these "bathrooms" like Americans do. Which makes sense, since no one is taking a bath in the back of a restaurant.) When I'm finished with the pregnancy test, I set it on the back of the toilet to wait for the results.

Three minutes until I know.

I wash my hands, then pace the tiny room, five steps this way, five steps the other. I understand why Sebastien was pacing last night when I was sick. Anxiety requires movement.

This is a different type of nerves, though. I've always wanted to have kids. Merrick didn't. Maybe this is yet again the universe showing me that things happen for a reason. Maybe I was meant to wait for my soulmate before I could have a baby—one with Sebastien's pale blue eyes or my wavy brown hair.

And then there's the matter of the curse, and how being pregnant might help us.

It's such a fragile idea, though, I don't want to think about it yet. Not until I know if the test is positive.

I glance at Dad's watch before I remember that it doesn't work. The clock on my phone, though, says it's only been two minutes. The test is supposed to take three. But my pulse rattles in my veins like gunfire, rapid and relentless. I can't wait any longer.

I open the stall door. The pregnancy test is where I left it, perched on the back of the toilet.

The bright blue "plus" sign is undeniable in any language.

Yes!

Take that, curse! I dance around with the pregnancy test and let out a whoop of victory that I'm sure has the rest of the koffiehuis patrons wondering what the hell the crazy American woman is cheering about in the WC.

SEBASTIEN

I WAKE TO FIND HELENE GONE. SHE LEFT A NOTE, BUT DISMAY descends upon me anyway—she didn't say "I love you" before she left. I try not to demand much of her, but this is one small thing that's incredibly important to me. Because every time one of us leaves—to shovel the driveway, to get the mail, to run an errand—it might be the last time we see each other. She could slip and fall on ice and die, or be hit by a truck, or any number of horrible scenarios.

Am I paranoid? Yes. History has conditioned me so. But saying "I love you" before leaving at least ensures that, if the curse strikes while we're apart, those will be our last words to each other. Not, "Do you want me to pick up some bread at the store?" or, "Remember to move the clothes from the washer to the dryer."

But Helene forgot.

Dread, however, quickly replaces dismay. How long has she been gone? *Did* something happen to her?

I'm throwing on my clothes as fast as I can to go out searching for her when Helene flies onto the houseboat, into the bedroom, with a smile that could light up the entire continent.

I rush to her and sweep her into my arms. "Thank god you're all right."

"Oh no," she says, "I didn't want you to worry. I left you a note."

"I know. I'm sorry I panicked," I say, holding her tighter and kissing the top of her head. I memorize the feel of her cradled against me, the way she shifts to fit even closer against me. The smell of her almond shampoo. The sound of her breath, still coming quickly like a little bird's because she'd been running. The fear from earlier still clings to me, and I hoard these details of Helene, just in case.

"Shh," she says softly. "I'm here with you."

For now, I can't help but think.

She lets us stand together like this for a minute, knowing that I need it. I'm so grateful for these small kindnesses.

Finally, when I'm grounded in reality again, I release her, giving her one more kiss.

"It looks like you're feeling better today," I say. "No more seasickness?"

"No more seasickness. And I have something exciting to tell you." She grins. "But you should sit down."

"Er, okay." I sit as directed.

She clasps her hands in front of her face as she bounces in place. Her skin glows, her eyes sparkle, and even her hair seems fuller and silkier in the morning sunlight. I wait on the edge of the bed.

After a minute, though, Helene still hasn't said anything.

I laugh, buoyed by her mood. "Are you planning to actually tell me, or are you just going to spend the rest of the morning like a pogo stick?"

Blushing, she stops bouncing, although the energy simply transfers to her fingertips fluttering.

"Okay, remember how I felt sick yesterday?" she asks.

"Yes, we were just talking about that . . ."

"Oh, right. Well, also, you know how I've been getting fatter?"

"I like soft curves."

Helene waves away what I'm saying, like it's beside the point. "Anyway, it's a fact that I've gained weight. But I guess I'm glad you like it, because I'm going to gain even more."

I shake my head, not following.

"We're going to have a baby!" She throws her arms in the air like we've just won the jackpot on a game show.

I stare at her. "What do you mean?"

Helene smiles, like she's amused at how slow men can be sometimes. She sits in my lap and puts my hand on her stomach. "I'm pregnant, Sebastien. My nausea was morning—or afternoon—sickness."

"No," I say.

"Yes." Helene misinterprets what I mean, so she's still using a patient tone to explain the basics to me. "I didn't actually go to the market this morning. I went to a pharmacy and bought a test. It was positive. But I'm not only excited about the baby," she says, smiling as brightly as she did when she returned to our houseboat. "I'm also excited because I think this is evidence that the curse is broken!"

I try to swallow the lump that's formed in my throat, but it doesn't budge.

"How?" I manage to whisper.

"Back in Alaska, you told me that we've never had kids before, that our reincarnations got stuck at the *Romeo and Juliet* phase but never progressed. But *this* is progress!"

"How?"

"Well, I mean, *one* difference, like me living perfectly well for ten years after our paths crossed, might be random chance. *Two* differences, like me remembering our pasts, could be coincidence. But *three* . . ."

I muster a small smile for her. She snuggles into me, and I hold her—and our baby—tight.

I want to believe Helene's theory. I want to believe so desperately I begin to feel ill.

But we've been close to this situation before. Not pregnant, but close enough.

And every time we start dreaming of a family, it's the beginning of the end.

MAINZ, GERMANY—1456

All Brigitta Schultz wants is a baby. Now that she's married the love of her life, the last missing piece of the puzzle is a child.

As her husband, I am more than happy to oblige. Every evening when I come home from my job with Herr Gutenberg, I take Brigitta to bed. I smell of ink and vellum paper, and she smells of fresh fields and the dairy farm she still helps her family with. I make love to her as if she's as sacred as the Bibles I print.

But despite our diligence, Brigitta and I cannot conceive a child. Unfortunately, in these times, the blame rests solely on the wife. Her barren womb is viewed as such a grave defect that the world judges her useless.

Not me, though. "I love you," I whisper to Brigitta every night after we're spent from our efforts. "It matters not if we cannot have a child. If that be God's will, I love you still."

Then I tumble headlong into sleep. But Brigitta does not rest. The desire for a baby gnaws at her from the inside out.

Thirteen months after we begin trying, Brigitta dies—from lack of sleep, lack of child, lack of dreams fulfilled.

And I mourn the loss of my beautiful wife, and the loss of a child who never was.

LISBON, PORTUGAL – 1498

When my ship docks after several years exploring the New World, the first thing I see on Lisbon's shore is Senhor Lourenço Pereira and his wagon full of casks of port, ready to take advantage of sailors who missed the drink of their homeland or, frankly, are simply looking for an excuse to get drunk.

The second thing I see is Ines Pereira, the port-maker's daughter, who stands self-assured in a fine dress among the chaos of the returning ships. The sun shines in a halo around her, as if protecting such pureness from the flea-ridden louts milling around the harbor.

She is so alluring any man would have dropped to one knee and proposed on the spot. But for me, it is more than that, for the instant I see Ines, I recognize my Juliet. Dark-haired this time, instead of blond; strong-shouldered from helping in the winery, rather than fine-boned as the last Juliet had been. I love Ines instantly, as with all her incarnations, and I elbow aside the other disembarking sailors so I can be the first one to shore.

When I reach Lourenço Pereira, I offer to buy the entire wagonload of port as proof of my devotion to his daughter.

Ines and I are married three weeks later.

This, however, is when I commit a fatal mistake. Wanting to give Ines what I could not give to Brigitta, I immediately declare my desire for a child. It is not about demanding that my wife produce an heir, but about wanting to create something together through our union.

Because of this sweetness, Ines's sole ambition from the moment we're married is to conceive a child. But failure again and again wears down even the strongest of women, until what she carries in her womb is not a life, but yearnings for death.

After eight months of fruitlessness, Ines drinks herself into a stupor. Her father finds her body the next day, in the wine cellar, buried and crushed under a collapsed rack of barrels.

I never drink port again.

TRANSYLVANIA — *1682*

It's a blessing that Cosmina did not want a child, for even though she lived for only two years after she met me, we made love nearly a thousand times.

Some might have said she couldn't bear children because God would never allow someone with such a wicked, lustful appetite to become a mother.

But I know the real reason—it's our curse, which always brings us together, yet holds us at arm's length. Like the original Romeo and Juliet, we were never permitted to advance beyond nascent potential. Instead, we were frozen in time, doomed to start and fail, start and fail.

When Cosmina dies with nothing in her womb, I am not surprised.

I am numb. Because I have learned to stop dreaming.

HELENE

"You're having a baby!" Katy shrieks over video.

"I'm having a baby!" We do the ridiculous victory routine that we invented when she was six and I was eight, involving jazz hands, twirls, and full-body shimmies. In the background, Trevor joins in, giggling at his mama's dancing, and that just encourages us to do it some more.

Mom looks on fondly. "I'm going to be a nana again. And how fitting that you found out in Dad's city."

I stop my victory shimmy for a second and nod vigorously at the screen, happy tears in my eyes. "I know. I can feel him smiling down on me."

"I feel it, too."

We all look up at the sky and smile back at him. I rest his watch against the tiny bulge of my belly and say, "You're gonna be a grandpa again, Daddy."

But then Trevor shouts, "Don't stop dancing!" and the sentimentality breaks. Katy and I laugh. And then we oblige, starting up our victory jazz hands once more.

* * *

Maybe it's the joy of knowing that I'm finally going to be a mom after all these years, but Koningsdag is even more spectacular than I thought it would be. All of Amsterdam pours out into the streets and canals to celebrate King's Day. Bridges overflow with people clad in orange, tossing orange confetti at the boats full of more orange. Children wear crowns fashioned from orange balloons. Adults run around wearing orange wigs, hats with flashing orange lights, and even orange traffic cones. And everywhere, people have set up folding tables on the sidewalks, selling random knickknacks from their homes—Koningsdag is not only the celebration of the king, it's also, oddly enough, the biggest Dutch flea market of the year.

"Ooh, how about this one?" I say to Sebastien, picking up an adorable porcelain figurine of a little boy wearing clogs. "It could be the first gift I buy for our baby."

"I think we should see the doctor before we start outfitting a nursery." Sebastien plucks the figurine from my fingers and sets it back down on the card table without meeting my eyes. "Come on, if you want to catch the king giving his birthday speech, we'd better get going."

I give the porcelain figure a final glance but leave it behind. I know Sebastien is terrified that this pregnancy is going to kill me. Wanting a baby has killed Juliets before, and I understand why he doesn't want me getting too attached to this one either. For all we know, the baby is only a few weeks old and I could easily miscarry. But because of the Koningsdag holiday, the earliest doctor's appointment we could get is tomorrow.

And yet, I feel with my whole heart that this is how the curse ends. Maybe it's the pregnancy hormones that have me so bullish, or maybe it's just my underlying optimism, generally. But also, knowing there's a little life growing in my belly is a triumph I can't suppress. I'm already in love with this baby and the idea that it represents a new beginning, whether that's a rational sentiment or not.

"Hold on to my hand tightly," I say to Sebastien. If we get split up, we won't be able to find each other in this crowd. When we first landed at the airport, I'd suggested he rent a cellphone, but he'd shrugged it off. He's gotten by just fine for close to seven hundred years without one and doesn't see a reason to start now. I have to admit I'm a little envious; sometimes I feel like I don't know how to survive anymore without an electronic device attached to my fingers.

We weave through the canal-side celebrations. Music blasts from old-fashioned boom boxes as well as high-tech portable speakers, changing from block to block: hip-hop, classical, jazz, the Dutch national anthem. Every single person, young and old, is celebrating with us today.

We pass by a carnival with a Ferris wheel, Tilt-A-Whirl, and other rides. A group of shirtless, orange spray-painted frat boys jog down the middle of the street, whooping and shouting "*Lang leve de koning! Hoera, hoera, hoera!*" Long live the king! Hurrah, hurrah, hurrah! I shoot videos of them for Katy and Mom.

Sebastien and I find our way to the square where the king is going to make his birthday speech. Sebastien asks a couple on a bench if I can sit. Upon hearing that I'm pregnant, they jump up to offer me their seats and clasp Sebastien's hands, congratulating us profusely. For a brief moment, he looks happy. But it's fleeting, and wariness over the pregnancy sets back in as soon as the couple is gone.

Later, the streets and canals grow rowdier as the celebrations continue. I want to stay out and experience it all, but a curtain of fatigue falls over me.

"Would it be wimpy to go back to the houseboat this early?" I ask. Earlier, Sebastien had picked up some ginger candies from the pharmacy for seasickness when the water rocks the boat.

"Not at all," he says. "It'd probably be more fun, given that we're just going to get jostled around out here as the crowds get drunker."

So we retreat, except I think of it less as retreat than a new vantage point, and I spend the rest of Koningsdag blissfully sitting on our deck, watching the floating parties sail by.

SEBASTIEN

"Congratulations, both Mom and the fetus look very healthy," Dr. De Vries says as she runs an ultrasound wand over Helene's stomach. I, however, am not as ecstatic. I stare at the three-dimensional ultrasound on the staticky screen, not sure how the doctor can draw that conclusion from such a small picture.

Shouldn't there be more tests? More time, more opinions, more certainty? I've had centuries of experience watching Juliet and many, many others die, and I know there are myriad ways it can happen.

Helene, on the other hand, coos at the ultrasound. "Oh, it's beautiful! Can we find out the baby's sex?"

I interrupt and speak in Dutch to Dr. De Vries. Helene rightfully makes a face at me for leaving her out of the conversation.

"Sorry," I say in English. "I just . . . I don't want to know that about the baby."

"You want it to be a surprise," Dr. De Vries says, smiling and nodding in approval.

I neither confirm nor deny. Better to let the doctor think what she wants.

Helene, however, knows what's going on in my head, and she frowns.

Dr. De Vries doesn't notice, because she's too busy swirling the ultrasound wand around to get at different angles of the fetus. "It's difficult to tell the baby's sex anyway," she says. "I would estimate that you're about fourteen weeks along, plus or minus a couple weeks. The baby's genitals will be more clearly visible in about a month."

She shifts the discussion to the prenatal vitamins she wants Helene to take. Meanwhile, I mentally tabulate when this baby is due—the middle of October.

Every muscle in my body tenses. That's nearly six months from now.

Six months of hoping the baby will live.

Six months of praying the pregnancy won't kill Helene.

Six months of warring with myself, wanting to protect the woman I've loved for eternity, while also wanting us to finally have a child. I can't imagine anything more extraordinary than creating a new life with the woman who is my everything.

When I tune back into their conversation, Helene and Dr. De Vries are talking about the timeline for checkups.

"We'll be in Amsterdam for two more weeks," Helene says. "Then we're off to Cannes for the film festival after this."

"How lovely!" Dr. De Vries says. "Well, I will write down the name of a medical school colleague of mine who runs a gynecology clinic in the south of France. I recommend you see him next month while you're there."

My alarm bells go off. In Dutch, I ask, "Why? Is there something wrong with the baby?" I hold my breath as I wait for her answer.

In English, Dr. De Vries says, "Nothing to worry about, simply part of routine prenatal care."

I glance at Helene in apology. I don't mean to keep switching into Dutch. Perhaps it's a psychological instinct to spare her if there's any bad news. Or maybe my nerves have shaken up my brain so it can't stick to a single language anymore.

"It's going to be okay, Sebastien," Helene says. "No, actually, it's going to be amazing." She reaches over from the exam table and takes my hand. God bless this woman for her patience with me. For her, I'll attempt to act like a normal human being.

"Thank you, Dr. De Vries," I say, still only half believing that both Helene and the baby are healthy. "We'll be sure to see your friend when we're in Cannes."

HELENE

After Amsterdam, the French Riviera has always been the place in Europe that holds my fascination most. It's the seaside playground of the rich, the site of the Hollywood star–studded Cannes Film Festival, an exciting and glamorous world that most of us have only read about or seen on TV.

We pull up to the Villa Garbo in Cannes, a small, charming white building with pretty details on its facade, and wrought-iron balconies outside each large window. It looks more like a graceful mansion than a hotel.

A man in a crisp uniform appears and opens my door. "*Bonjour, mademoiselle.* Welcome to Villa Garbo." Behind him, a bellhop appears and takes our bags before I'm out of the car.

Sebastien rushes over to take my arm, overprotective about me stumbling. I pat his hand and tease him. "Being pregnant doesn't mean I'm suddenly going to lose my ability to balance."

He flushes and withdraws his arm. "Sorry."

I kiss his cheek. "It's sweet. But you don't need to worry about every tiny thing." (I know he will anyway, but at least I can give him permission to relax.)

The man in the uniform—Jean-Phillipe—leads us toward the elevator, without stopping at Reception.

"Don't we need to check in?" I ask Sebastien.

A hint of mirth touches the corner of his mouth. "I think Jean-Phillipe is afraid you might trip on the two stairs that lead up to the reception desk, seeing as you're dangerously pregnant. So he's leading us straight to the room to minimize risk."

"Ha-ha, very funny, Mr. Comedian." I shove Sebastien gently, but I'm glad he can laugh at himself. He's been through a lot with past Juliets trying to have children, so this isn't easy for him.

"Actually," Sebastien says as we cross the lobby, "the hotel knows who we are because our driver called when we landed at the airport to let the hotel staff know we were on our way."

"Too bad. And here I thought we were getting celebrity treatment because we really were VIPs."

We take the elevator to the top floor. When Jean-Phillipe reaches our door, he unlocks it and opens it wide. "This will be your apartment. I hope you find it to your standards."

Apartment?

I gasp as I step inside, because I was obviously wrong about not having VIP status. The apartment is how I imagine a chic French home looks, multiplied by ten. Sunlight beams in through floor-to-ceiling windows framed by gray silk curtains, the bottom halves of the drapes folded back like origami to reveal an elegant crimson underside. Velvet furniture clusters around a fireplace intricately carved from white marble. Sconces mounted on curlicue wrought iron adorn the walls.

Beyond the living room, there's a dining room, complete with fresh orchids in a crystal vase in the center of the long table. A mirrored drink cart waits next to it, stocked with what look like bottles of champagne but turn out to be nonalcoholic sparking grape juice made in the vineyards of Burgundy. (Sebastien obviously had a hand in requesting specialty drinks for the pregnant lady.)

There's a kitchenette, two bedrooms, and the coup de grâce: a private rooftop terrace with panoramic views of Cannes, all the way to the sea.

"Oh, Sebastien," I say as I toss open the patio doors and breathe in the warm, salty air. "It's absolute perfection."

Jean-Phillipe takes his leave, and Sebastien and I wander out onto the rooftop. There are chaise longues out here, and umbrellas to shade us from the summer sun. The view of Cannes and the Mediterranean extends for miles and miles.

Sebastien wraps his arms around me, pulling me into the shelter of his embrace.

"A euro for your thoughts," I say.

"It only costs a penny for thoughts," he says.

I shrug. "Inflation. Or maybe your thoughts are just more valuable to me."

He laughs softly. But he doesn't answer my question.

Instead, Sebastien bends down and kisses me, long and deep. Then he gets down on his knees, dips his head under the hem of my dress, and liberates me of my panties.

"*Bienvenue en France,*" he says.

SEBASTIEN

Afterward, Helene drowses in the sun. She's more beautiful than ever, her belly starting to round just a little with the life within. As much as I'm afraid of the curse, the evidence of our baby thriving is one of the greatest sights I've ever seen.

I rest my cheek against Helene's stomach. She reaches down and strokes my hair. "Tell our baby girl a story about us," she says, her voice languid.

"Since when have you decided we're having a girl?"

"It's just a feeling," Helene says. "Mother's instinct, I guess."

I can't see her face from where I'm lying, but I can sense her smile in the way she says it. *Mother's instinct.*

"Tell her a story about us," Helene repeats. "But give it a happy ending."

I tense at this request. Romeo and Juliet don't have happy endings. The weight of all our tragedies casts its yoke around my shoulders again.

Helene seems to realize this, because she pushes up on her elbows and looks at me. The sea breeze ripples through her hair. "Hey," she says gently. "Have faith."

"It's hard."

"I know. But think of the story as encouragement for our daughter. She's going to change our destinies. And she'll also grow up knowing her mom and dad's incredible history."

I close my eyes for a moment. Tacking on a happily ever after would be disingenuous. For Helene's sake, I'm trying to believe the baby will break the cycle of the curse, but I won't pretend the past didn't happen.

At the same time, what kind of monster tells horror stories to their unborn child?

I decide to compromise.

"*Bonjour, ma petite chou,*" I say, pressing my cheek again to Helene's stomach. "Your *maman* wants you to know all about me and her. But *I* want you to know all about how impressive she is. So I'm going to tell you a story about *her.*"

"Thank you," Helene whispers as she lies back down on the chaise.

"Once upon a time—in 1764—there was a French woman named Florence Gagné. In an era when women were meant only to become wives, she wrote and directed plays. As a child, she'd grown up in Theatre Gagné, her father's playhouse in Lyon, raised on a steady education of theatrical works. As a teenager, she helped her father with bookkeeping during the day and began penning her own plays by candlelight.

"Florence was ahead of her time. In the decades following her, other female playwrights would make names for themselves, although usually under pseudonyms. But Florence—aided by a father who cared as little for social mores as she did—wrote under her own name, and instead of getting married when she turned eighteen, she published her first play.

"At twenty-seven, she made her directorial debut, scandalously wearing a man's coat and breeches on opening night. She made the front page of every newspaper from Nice to Paris to Calais. That's when Pierre Montague saw her photograph in the *Mercure de France,* and he fell instantly in love with the remarkable woman.

"From that moment, Pierre made it his singular goal to work in Theatre Gagné. Without even packing his bags, he hopped on the next train to Lyon and, when he arrived, went straight from the station to the playhouse and applied for a job as a stagehand.

"Every day, Pierre was the first one on set, and he would anonymously set a chocolate hazelnut cornetto on Florence's director's chair. Every morning, from the catwalk above the stage, he watched her face light up when she saw the pastry, and she would look around to see if there was any indication who'd left it.

"Finally, there came a day—two months later—when he did *not* leave her a pastry. That morning, when Florence arrived at her empty director's chair, she let out an audible murmur of disappointment. It was then that Pierre climbed down from the catwalk and approached her, with a cornetto in hand. And that's how a lowly stagehand won the heart of one of the most awe-inspiring women in history."

I leave out the ending, the part about the gunman who killed Florence. He, like many of that time, believed that allowing women outside the home—and allowing them a voice—would lead to the collapse of civilized society.

"That was a lovely story," Helene says, almost asleep now.

I nod against her skin and curl up against her, stroking her belly and feeling both her and the baby close. For a brief moment, joy swells in my chest.

But the knowledge that this is all ephemeral is a constant undercurrent, and I hate that I can't have pure happiness, that Helene and I can't love each other with abandon. And so I press myself closer until we have no space between us, as if I can somehow smash our souls together and keep us this way forever.

Soon, she drifts asleep, and I feel the rise and fall of Helene's chest against me. Its rhythm melds with the sound of the ocean in the distance, shushing against the French Riviera's shore. I imagine our baby's heartbeat keeps the same pace, too, and I try to match the cadence with my own breath.

Perhaps it's better this way. Perhaps the best course is living in the present, while collecting each moment to save like seashells that I can look back upon when the present is gone.

And they lived happily ever after, I say to myself, trying it on for size.

But no matter how many times I repeat it, it still feels like a lie.

HELENE

The more money there is, the wilder the parties, and Cannes is extravagant beyond anything I've ever seen. One night, the hottest DJ in France works turntables on the sand. Another night, ten blocks' worth of roads are closed off, and Michelin-starred chefs set up stands and cook the world's tastiest street food.

During daylight hours, we watch movies at the film festival (Sebastien somehow got us passes, even though we don't have press credentials), watch buskers on the streets more talented than many professionals, and acquire some new friends. Sebastien bonds with Irikefe Oluwa, a restaurant mogul in town for the film festival; he and Irikefe share a common gastronomic language. I get to know a group of tourists from Australia, teachers from a performing arts school in Japan, and a rugby team from Wales that came for the topless beaches by sunlight and the nonstop parties by moonlight.

Tonight, Irikefe has invited us to a fete in his "*petit café*," which is actually located within sprawling gardens and currently the hardest table to book in all of France. Rumor has it some of the actors and actresses in town are going to ditch their own events to attend Irikefe's.

"How do I look?" I ask Sebastien as I twirl in front of the mirror in our hotel room. The floor-length sequined gown glimmers as I move, and the little crystal flowers woven through my hair twinkle, too.

He fastens his tuxedo jacket as he admires me. "You look like a queen."

"An elegant fairy queen? Or a disco queen?"

Sebastien laughs. "Definitely the former."

"Good. And you," I say, coming over to adjust the blue silk square in his jacket pocket, "look like James Bond."

When we arrive at the restaurant, a European pop band is performing among a menagerie of topiaries, and several dozen people dance under strings of lights. Caterers circulate with silver trays of hors d'oeuvres, and roulette and poker tables have been set up on the far side of the courtyard.

Irikefe weaves through the crowd and makes a beeline for us. He's wearing an impeccably tailored purple suit. "Sebastien! Who knew a fisherman could clean up so well?" Then he turns to me and says, "Helene, I ought to kick you out of my café. You're so beautiful you'll steal the spotlight from me."

"You're too smooth for your own good, Irikefe." I air-kiss him on each cheek, as I've learned to do since arriving in Cannes.

Irikefe leads us to the bar and gets us nonalcoholic cocktails. A couple of minutes later, though, he sees another new arrival. "Ah, excuse me, I must go say hello to Penélope and Javier."

"As in, Penélope Cruz and Javier Bardem?" My head whips around so fast it's a wonder my neck doesn't snap. And indeed, it *is* the famous Spanish actors.

"Who?" Sebastien asks.

"You don't know Penélope Cruz and Javier Bardem?"

Sebastien shrugs.

The band ends the song and starts on another, this one slower but still with an underlying pop beat. Sebastien's attention shifts from the movie stars in front of us to the clear night sky in the distance. Nostalgia clouds his expression.

I put my hand on his shoulder. "Do we know this song?"

He nods and gives me one of those smiles that's both wistful and a little sad. " 'Cheek to Cheek' by Irving Berlin. We danced to it in Honolulu once. But this is a different version," he says as electric bass reverberates through the courtyard.

"Regardless," I say, linking my arm through his, "let's dance to it again."

Sebastien doesn't budge, though. "I don't know if—"

"That was a different lifetime," I say soothingly.

He stands still for a few more beats, lost in that amorphous in-between of lifetimes.

"Be here," I say as I stroke his face. "With *me*."

The spot between his brows creases.

And then he comes back to the present with a pained smile and says, "Sorry, you're right. Let's dance."

We thread our way through the crowd, which has grown bigger, to the dance floor. I wrap my arms around Sebastien's neck, and his arms circle my waist.

However, the band's cover of the song isn't exactly the kind you sway slowly to. It's . . . bouncier. Like romance on Adderall. So Sebastien and I kind of sway-bop to the melody, and the ridiculousness of it begins to seep into him. At first he tries to resist a real smile, but then I sway-bop more emphatically, and he can't help it; he actually laughs.

I plant a fat kiss on his mouth. I love how he looks when he's relaxed, when the past temporarily relinquishes its hold on him. The mirthful lines around his eyes crinkle, the tense planes of his jaw soften, and even his steps grow lighter. I want to be *this* for him, the reason he can unwind. I know it's not possible all the time, but I will do what I can to make it often enough.

The song ends, and the lead singer leans into the mic. "This next one is called 'Candy Taco Protest,'" he says in beautifully accented English. "It is, perhaps, profound. Or perhaps simply silly. You decide." He grins at the crowd, then turns to the band. "*Un, deux . . . un, deux, trois!*"

Electric keyboard and drums blast through the speakers, and the guitarist and bassist hammer their instruments. The entire restaurant comes alive with the fierce pulse of the song, the floor vibrating, the wineglasses clinking, even the walls of the courtyard seeming to shudder a little under the beat.

"You were cherry to my lemon, I was sour to your sweet," the singer shouts.

"Like oil and water, we were not meant to be.

You were sugar and gumdrops, I was potatoes and meat.

They do not go together, like boats in the street."

Sebastien arches a brow at the lyrics. I laugh, pressing up against his chest. No, not profound. But the beat is good, addictive even. I can feel the intense rhythm of the drums and keyboards in my core, and every guitar riff like the rat-tat-tat of rain on my skin. All around us, arms fly, and hips swing. Sebastien nods along to the beat, despite his amusement at the lyrics. I close my eyes and let the song move me.

The singer shouts about bad love, about mixing chemicals into explosive combinations. The bassist joins in about the consequences of letting sweetness taint danger, of rust dulling a blade.

And then the chorus rides in on an irrepressible electronica wave.

"I hereby declare

Your sugar cube reign

Overthrown by the fellowship of tacos!"

"Everyone with me," the singer yells, and the audience dances and sings back.

"I hereby declare

Your sugar cube reign

Overthrown by the fellowship of tacos!"

In the crowd's frenzy, Sebastien and I get separated. His face flickers in alarm.

I shake my head, trying to convey that it's okay, that a Cannes garden party is not the curse, and dancing to a song about candy and tacos isn't going to kill me.

"I love you!" I mouth as I get swept up against the stage, still dancing, and he disappears into the throng.

The chorus comes up again, and I throw myself into the bad lyrics. I haven't had this kind of fun since clubbing during my college days. I sing even louder to match the ratcheted-up fervor of the band.

Suddenly, though, I find myself looking at a bald man who seems familiar, but I can't place him.

He isn't dancing, just milling around on the edge of the crowd, partly obscured by the shadow of the speakers and the *Jaws* shark topiary looming above him. Goosebumps prickle my arms.

Then I recognize him—Aaron Gonchar from Northwestern's journalism program, with a lot less hair than when we were students. He was the guy who got kicked off the grad school paper with Merrick.

My heart pounds in a frenzy, my palms sweat. Is Aaron here on Merrick's behalf?

But then I laugh at myself.

Merrick hasn't tried anything since he left Alaska and filed that suit against me for slander, which the Weiskopf Group attorneys did indeed get tossed out of court. And Sebastien hasn't mentioned anything else since then.

Relax, I tell my overactive imagination. I never liked Aaron, but that doesn't mean I need to be creeped out by him being here. Besides, after grad school, Aaron got a job at celebrity gossip media outlet TMZ. I'm sure he's in Cannes reporting on the film festival and all the movie stars. It's just a funny twist of serendipity that we're at the same party.

"There you are," Sebastien says, swooping in through the dancing crowd. He pulls me in close and kisses me.

"I'm fine, you know," I say, teasing.

"I do now," he says, kissing me again.

"And are *you* okay?"

"As long as I'm with you," Sebastien says.

"Good." I squeeze his hand. "Then let's dance."

It might be because the speakers are right behind us, or maybe the band hurls itself even harder at the music, but the song gets faster and louder. I hold on to Sebastien and we wave our arms in the air with everyone else, sing-shouting,

"I hereby declare

Your sugar cube reign

Overthrown by the fellowship of tacos!"

The wild, carefree energy is infectious, and maybe there really is something a little profound about the song, although not, I think, what the singer intended. But there's a magic to music, an ability to carry you away into another realm that gives you permission to get lost, if only for a little while.

Impossibly, the music gets even faster, and we dance furiously to match its volume and rhythm. We're caught up in the frenetic joy of the crowd, enjoying the Candy Land frivolity, and by the time the song is over, I've forgotten all about Aaron Gonchar.

HELENE

Sebastien and I spend June in Spain, beginning in the Basque region up north with lazy seaside days, hopping from charming café to café for *pintxos*, appetizer-sized slices of bread topped with all sorts of delectable things—spicy peppers, mushrooms fried with garlic, and my favorite, *txangurro a la Donostiarra*, spider crab meat and tomatoes, sprinkled with toasted breadcrumbs. My pregnancy-sized appetite is very happy to be in Spain.

Being here also makes me think of Hemingway and his writer friends, and my manuscript starts calling to me. It's been "resting" for a couple of months now, while I've been resting, too. It's probably time to dust off my computer soon and get back to work.

Maybe after Barcelona.

There, Sebastien books a private tour of La Sagrada Família before it opens to the public in the early morning. It's an astonishing feat of architecture, as if someone built a Gothic church out of bleached coral, and I feel utterly relaxed, weaving through the labyrinth of the cathedral without the crush of crowds. (Sebastien, worried about the baby, wanted me to have space so I wouldn't be pressed up against throngs of germy tourists, with me breathing in all their exhalations and touching the same turnstiles and rails. Sebastien is over the top, but I understand why. Still, I dubbed him Mama Hen Montague because of his fussing. He laughed and accepted the compromise.)

Later in the week, as we stroll through Park Güell—a whimsical, Dr. Seuss–like wonderland sprung from fantasy—a bald head gleams in the sun among all the rainbow-colored mosaics. I shade my eyes to get a better look, and I swear it's Aaron Gonchar. My stomach flips, and the baby starts punching me, reacting to my sudden panic.

When I blink and look again, though, nobody's there—not Aaron, not a different bald guy, not anyone at all. Just the squiggly, snakelike benches and wacky-shaped buildings that dot the entire park.

Weird.

"Can we go up to the top?" I point to stairs that lead up a hill to a platform. I want to get a better vantage point of the park to see if the Aaron lookalike is lurking somewhere, or if I'm just seeing things in the heat haze of the Spanish summer.

"Sure," Sebastien says. "I was just about to suggest that. The view is fantastic from up there."

We walk toward the bottom of the grand staircase, flanked by colorful, ten-foot-tall animal statues. Flowering trees burst out of checkered planters, and a labyrinth of shady caves provide respite from the sun. When we arrive at the top of the hill, Sebastien tries to point out all the gingerbread house–like buildings that fill the plaza below.

"Uh-huh," I mumble, distracted, looking for that shiny head again.

I do find a few bald men, but none I could have mistaken for Aaron.

"Hey, are you all right?" Sebastien asks, coming up next to me.

"Yeah, sorry. I thought . . . Never mind. Pregnancy hormones are making me loopy."

He laughs. "I think Park Güell just has that effect on people, too."

After Barcelona, we go on to Madrid, Seville, and Granada. But instead of enjoying the sights, I keep checking to see if Aaron Gonchar will reappear.

He doesn't, and eventually I start to relax again. I even try to work on my manuscript a little in the afternoons, when the heat is too much and everyone retires for siestas.

Mostly, though, I nap during that time. I'm five months into the pregnancy now, my breasts swollen like small cantaloupes, sweating in the relentless Spanish sun. I wear loose dresses when I can, but on laundry days I have to wear my shorts unbuttoned with a waistband extender. I am an accordion permanently expanded.

One particularly hot and sticky day, after falling asleep on my laptop, I wake to find Sebastien smiling at me from the sofa.

"What do you say we get out of this infernal heat? We can rent a small boat and go island hopping in Greece. There will be open horizon. Cool ocean breezes. The sound of the wind in the sails."

"Oh god, that sounds like heaven," I say as I wipe a slick of sweat off my cheek. There's a damp, face-shaped imprint on my keyboard, too. "When can we go?"

"How about today?"

I jump up and start throwing clothes into my suitcase.

SEBASTIEN

SUMMER IS PEAK TOURIST SEASON IN THE GREEK ISLANDS, AND THE usually picturesque towns—whitewashed buildings against a backdrop of sparkling blue ocean—are overrun by sightseers, swarming like ants up and down the narrow staircases that meander through the seaside cliffs. But the boat I rent allows us to spend the days exploring coves and fishing for our own lunch. We only dock in the evenings, when the day-tripping cruise ships have departed and left the towns more tranquil.

We spend a couple of weeks like this, absolutely free of all constraints and responsibilities. I am glad to be on the water again, and even more so to be at sea with Helene, who looks like an ocean goddess with the salty wind in her hair, her loose white dress billowing against the beautiful round belly where our baby continues to thrive.

I immerse myself in this time. Most people have regrets when they lose someone they love. They wish they'd done more together, asked them their life stories, kissed them every moment of every day. But I don't have those regrets. I have plenty of others, but not those; it's a strange side effect of knowing your soulmate is going to die sooner rather than later. I touch Helene every time I pass her. I give her my full attention whenever she speaks. Because I'm always aware that this could be the last. The last time I make love to her, the last time we laugh together, the last time we sit beside each other, saying nothing but understanding it all. If our destiny is sealed, then at least we'll earn the happiness of being together for these fleeting moments that we have.

And I have had Helene for six months. I can almost convince myself now that it's enough. I don't always get Juliet for that long, and six months is a line where I could, if I had to, say to people, "I had her for six wonderful months," and that would sound substantial—more substantial than two days or two weeks. It would possibly even sound sufficient.

Of course, the truth is, it's never enough. But the point is, I can tell myself that if I have to.

I hope I don't.

HELENE

"I don't ever want this to end," I say, smiling at Sebastien's hand clasped in mine across the white tablecloth. We're having dinner at a cliffside restaurant in Imerovígli, overlooking the blue waters of Santorini's caldera. The sun sets over the ocean in a soft sherbet sky of pinks and oranges, and a violinist plays a love song in the background. I'd seen pictures of the Greek islands on posters and in movies before, but I never thought the real thing could live up to them. I was wrong, so very wrong, and I'm happy about it.

"We could live here if you want," Sebastien says, and I know he actually means it. This man would do anything for me.

"I'd miss Mom and Katy too much. But it's tempting." I squeeze his hand.

I continue to ride the wave of bliss through the meal. The bread and fava bean dip are flawless. The moussaka is also incredible, as are the pork skewers and the dolmades. When we get to dessert, I'm technically too full for it, but the baby demands baklava, so I eat three pieces, and no surprise, that is absolute perfection as well.

The waitress comes by and asks if we'd like a digestif. Sebastien turns her down, because he hasn't had a drop of alcohol since we found out I'm pregnant; he didn't want me to feel left out.

"Are you sure?" the waitress asks. "Because we have *mournoraki* tonight."

Sebastien's eyes widen.

"What's mournoraki?" I ask.

"A very rare spirit from Crete," Sebastien explains. "It's astonishingly difficult to make, so the few producers who distill it usually keep it for themselves."

"Then you should have some."

"No, because you can't—"

"Enjoy it *for* me," I say. Framing it as a benefit to me is the only way to convince Sebastien to give himself permission to drink. I turn to the waitress. "A glass, please."

She hurries off before Sebastien changes the order.

When the mournoraki arrives, he savors it, looking out onto the dark ocean and taking small sips, sighing rapturously after each one. I'm glad I made him do it. Sometimes I think Sebastien's spent so much of his life worrying over everyone else—especially me—that he's lost sight of taking care of himself.

"I'll be right back," I say when he orders a second glass. "I just need to use the ladies' room."

As in much of Santorini, the restaurant is carved into the cliffside, with whitewashed staircase alleys twined in and out of the buildings. Our table is on the restaurant's second story—which is basically a rooftop—and I have to go down the steep exterior stair-case to get to the bathroom on the first floor. I make sure to hold the banister; I have no intention of tumbling into the sea.

When I finish in the WC, I head toward the white steps to go back up to our table. But at the base of the staircase is a familiar face, although his bald head is now covered by a Greek fisher-man's cap.

"Aaron," I gasp.

He tips the brim of his hat. "Helene. Did you have a nice din-ner?"

"Wh-what are you doing here?"

"Just traveling on business," he says, leaning in to give me a kiss on the cheek as if we're old friends. "Will you go for a walk with me?"

"So I did see you in Cannes and in Barcelona. You've been fol-lowing me."

Aaron shakes his head. "Not you. Your boyfriend."

I frowned. "What? Why Sebastien?"

Aaron glances at the diners behind me and lowers his voice, which makes him sound more menacing. "After Sebastien got that restraining order slapped on Merrick, Merrick was pretty pissed, so he hired me to dig up some dirt."

"What restraining order?"

"You don't know?" Aaron lets out a grating laugh. "Your boy-friend sure does keep his secrets close." Aaron tells me about the "goons" Sebastien had patrolling the woods around his house and the private eye they booted off the property, and about my legal team's countersuit and temporary restraining order against Mer-rick.

I recall now that the Julius A. Weiskopf Group isn't just a privacy-respecting bank and law firm that Sebastien's worked with for centuries. They're a full-service tactical firm, arranging every-thing from fake IDs to bodyguards to—I'm guessing—everything in between and beyond.

Why didn't Sebastien tell me about the photos? I am *not* happy that he kept that from me. But that takes a back seat right now to how I feel about Merrick spying and trying to blackmail me.

"Obviously the restraining order hasn't stopped Merrick," I say, "because he just found a workaround, huh? Instead of him or that private eye being here, he hired you. You always were a slimeball, Aaron."

Aaron shrugs. "I prefer to call myself morally flexible. Besides, how do you think I knew, even in grad school, that I'd be good in tabloids? My specialty is uncovering the skeletons that people like celebs and politicians work so hard to keep in their closets. And guess what I found? Your Sebastien has quite a fascinating history. But that part you already know, don't you?"

The baby starts kicking, as if I need her to warn me that this is a conversation we absolutely cannot have within hearing range of the diners behind me. "Okay," I say, linking my arm through Aaron's. "Let's go for a walk. A *short* one. But you better say what you have to say quickly, because Sebastien's going to start wondering where I've gone."

We wind our way to another pedestrian alley between some souvenir shops that are closed for the evening and climb up the steps. It's isolated enough for us to talk, but only a shout away for help if I need it. I don't think I need to worry about that; Aaron is a sleazy tabloid gossip hunter and Merrick is an image-obsessed egomaniac, but they're not mobsters.

Still, I make sure I'm on a stair above Aaron, to be safe.

"Just cut to the chase," I say, crossing my arms. "What does Merrick want?"

"You know he has aspirations beyond bureau chief, Helene. To rise up to something like editor-in-chief of *The Wall Street Journal* or the *Los Angeles Times,* though, Merrick needs connections. And to get into the exclusive old boys' clubs where those connections can be forged, he needs his supportive, smiling wife by his side. He has to look the part before he can get it."

I scoff. "And what about this?" I point at my belly. "How does me carrying another man's baby help with Merrick's precious image?"

Aaron shrugs. "You'll say it's Merrick's child. Celebrities do it all the time. Their PR reps manage their relationships." He puts the word "relationships" in air quotes.

My jaw drops. How can anyone deprive their child of knowing who their father is? And for a publicity stunt!

Obviously Aaron and Merrick have no qualms about asking me to do so.

"Fuck you," I say. "I'd never do that."

Aaron leans against the stairway wall and smiles, oozing with condescension. "You don't seem to get it, Helene. Merrick isn't asking. He already tried doing that when he flew to Alaska, and you turned him down. So he's not giving you a choice this time." Aaron reaches into his coat and pulls out a fat manila envelope. "See, what I've got here is a dossier on Sebastien. Or is his name Cameron? Or Jack, Reynier, or Oliver?"

"No . . ." I sink onto the steps. I remember the "dirt dossiers" that Merrick and Aaron compiled in grad school as revenge for the editors kicking them off the newspaper. But as bad as those were, a dossier on Sebastien would be much, much worse.

Aaron delights in flipping through the file in front of me. "It's too bad technology advanced so rapidly since Sebastien took on this identity, isn't it? Before then, it was easy to shift from one name to another and disappear into a new identity. But nowadays . . . Technology can be so inconvenient. Well, inconvenient to men who've somehow lived for at least two hundred years. But convenient for people like me, who know how to mine data to get what I need. You know, Sebastien never seems to age. I found photographs all the way back into the mid–nineteenth century—as well as a painted portrait from 1827 of a botanist, Sir Charles Montague—that look an awful lot like a certain crab fisherman we know today."

I can't stop shaking. All that information, at the fingertips of two journalists who could publish it in a second and ruin Sebastien's life. The U.S. government—hell, *every* government, as well as unscrupulous private companies—would want to lock him up and run experiments to try to extract the secrets of immortality.

How does a man avoid death? Can his genes be harvested to create super soldiers? Or to make commercial products for people who want to live forever? The temptation is too great for anyone to leave Sebastien alone.

And then, suddenly, another realization hits me like a cargo ship plowing into a tiny fishing boat: It's not only Sebastien who's at risk. It's our baby, too. They'd want to know if a child could inherit the ability to live forever.

Oh my fucking god.

I curl around my belly, holding it tight, as if somehow I can burrow us away and keep her safe.

But that would still leave Sebastien.

"What do I have to do?" I whisper, unable to even look Aaron in the eye.

"You already know. Leave Sebastien. Go home. Be a good little wife."

I want to shove Aaron down the stairs. But I can't muster the will, because I've already been beaten.

"How do I know you won't publish the information about Sebastien, even if I go back to Merrick?" That kind of exposé would make Aaron's career. He and Merrick would probably win Pulitzers, get million-dollar book deals.

"You don't," Aaron says matter-of-factly. "But you do know that if you *don't* return to Merrick, then we will."

For the first time in months, I feel sick. My stomach lurches, and I throw up all my dinner on the stairs. A nasty splash of it lands on Aaron's too-shiny shoes.

Not shiny anymore.

"Ugh!" he jumps back, stumbles down a few steps, slams into the wall to stop his momentum. "Motherfucker."

I swipe vomit off my face and glare at him, a small victory in the midst of a losing battle.

"Tell Merrick I need time to think about it."

"No. No more time. Merrick has been patient enough."

Ha! Patient. Merrick only took his time over the past few months so he could gather enough evidence about Sebastien's past, not out of any kindness to me.

"I have plane tickets with your name on them, departing soon. Merrick won't be so lenient this time. You and I are going to the airport right now."

"What? No! I can't just leave Sebastien."

Aaron rolls his eyes. "You think I'm going to let you walk back to the restaurant and tell him everything that's happened, so he can intervene? No way. In fact, give me your phone, right now."

I hold my purse against my chest.

He waves Sebastien's dossier at me.

I don't have a choice. Even if I could snatch that file and throw it into the ocean, I'm sure Aaron and Merrick have backups online.

He takes my phone, destroys the SIM card, and pockets the pieces. He doesn't even give me the useless shell of the phone back.

"Car's this way," Aaron says, pointing up the stairs. "Start walking."

A few minutes later, we're out of the maze of Elysian white staircases of Imerovígli and into the hell of a rental car with no air-conditioning, speeding to the airport.

Aaron escorts me all the way to the gate—he has a ticket for himself to Athens to allow him to get this far into the airport—but he doesn't get in line when they call for boarding.

"You're not coming?" I ask. "I thought you'd handcuff yourself to me and personally escort me all the way to your master, I mean, Merrick."

Aaron doesn't rise to the bait. He doesn't have to. He's already won. "I'm going to watch your plane take off, and then I'm staying here on Santorini to stake out Sebastien and make sure you don't try to come back. I leave only once Merrick calls to confirm he's picked you up from the airport in L.A."

I squeeze my eyes tight.

The PA announces the final call for boarding for my flight.

"Time to go, Helene," Aaron says. "Don't piss off me or Merrick, or else—"

I open my eyes and glare.

"Believe me, I get it. If I don't do what you want, you hit 'publish' on everything you know about Sebastien."

SEBASTIEN

AFTER HELENE'S BEEN GONE FOR FIFTEEN MINUTES, I START TO worry. But I don't want to be overbearing; pregnancy does "undignified things" to a woman's body, as she says, so I try to sit still and enjoy the view of night settling over Santorini's caldera, the waves darkening from blue to near black, the lights from the town of Oia visible on the cliffs a little farther up the coast.

When twenty minutes have passed, though, my second mournoraki is long gone and I spin the empty glass on the table.

I flag down the waitress.

"Another mournoraki?" she asks.

"No, actually. My girlfriend has been in the WC for a while, and I'm worried she might have slipped and fallen, or that she's feeling ill. Would it be possible to send someone in there and check on her?"

"No problem. I was heading downstairs to grab more silverware from the kitchen anyway."

"Thank you."

The waitress comes back a few minutes later, shaking her head. "The WC is empty, sir. Are you sure that's where she went?"

"Empty?"

"Yes, I double-checked the stalls. Maybe she went for a walk?"

"No . . . she wouldn't do that without telling me . . ." My stomach plummets. Something's happened. I don't know what, but I feel it in the marrow of my bones.

"Can I have the check, please?" I ask weakly. "And may I borrow your phone to call the police?" I swear silently at myself for not renting a cellphone at the airport, like Helene suggested.

The waitress yelps. "The police? No, no, sir, this is probably nothing. There's no need to make the police come to our restaurant." She's thinking of the scene it'll cause, the disturbance to the diners, her lost tips. "I'm sure your girlfriend just wanted some fresh air—pregnancy can be stifling sometimes. She'll be back soon—"

I bang the mournoraki glass on the table. "Bring me a phone!"

She jumps, then runs off. The other diners gape at my rudeness.

But all I can do is spin my glass forcefully, my thoughts spiraling with it. This is the curse, I know it. I've been waiting for it to appear, feeling its closeness . . . What Helene and I had—and her belief that the curse could be broken—was too good to be true.

My mind begins to race through scenarios of what's happened.

If Helene did inexplicably go for a post-dinner walk without me, she could have lost her footing and slipped off the edge of the cliff.

Or perhaps she was mugged and she's lying injured in an alley.

Or a car careened out of control and hit her on the sidewalk.

Or, or, or . . .

There are infinite ways to die.

I grip the tablecloth and scan the cliffside sidewalk below me frantically. Then the dark rock face and the ocean, as if I could see an unconscious body in the sparse moonlight. She could be anywhere—anywhere except here with me, where she's supposed to be.

The waitress returns without the phone, but with her manager.

"Sir, if you would kindly come with me to settle your bill over there . . ." He isn't happy with me, but he diplomatically gestures to the silverware alcove, away from the guests I've been disturbing.

I apologize and pay in cash, leaving triple the tip the waitress would usually earn. After that, the manager lets me use the restaurant's phone.

Helene's cell doesn't ring. Instead, I get a message in Greek: The number you are trying to reach is unavailable.

Panic spikes in my chest.

I call the police.

"I understand you are worried, sir," the woman on duty at the desk says after I explain what's happened. "But from our experience, if there is no sign of a crime, then your girlfriend has probably gone for an evening stroll."

"Is that the only reason anyone here can come up with?" I am trying not to yell, but I'm yelling.

"Sir, I cannot tell you how many tourists have been entranced by the beauty of Santorini and wandered off to enjoy it, only to return a few hours later, boasting of a stunning secret beach they stumbled upon or a Greek wedding where they were invited to join in the drinking and plate smashing."

"I promise you," I say, "Helene isn't a drunk wedding crasher. For one thing, she's six months pregnant . . ."

"We will start to look for her," the woman says. "But try not to worry too much. I'm sure your girlfriend is okay."

Try not to worry? Helene is the target of an age-old curse that kills her every time. There's no such thing as worrying *enough*.

After I hang up, I call the sole hospital on the island, because I'm not going to rely only on the police.

But no one has been admitted who fits Helene's description. There hasn't even been a single pregnant woman in the hospital all day.

Please be safe somewhere, I think. *Please let there be a reasonable explanation.*

The iron shackles of the curse tighten around my heart. It's harder to breathe, my pulse racing but struggling, as if being squeezed through every artery and vein.

I climb Imerovígli's warren of white staircases. Check every alcove, every pathway. Is Helene here in this alley, slumped over? There in that shadowed corner, mugged and beaten? Or perhaps around the bend, in the lightless niche, hurt or . . .

Stop. I can't let the last thought in. Already, I can feel the whirlpool of defeat churning, reaching out to suck me in.

Every second passes in agonizing slow motion, my chest tight in the grip of fear, my heart ready to explode in grief with every turn I make in the maze of steps and alleys.

Nothing.

Hours later, I collapse on a bench at one of the island's many scenic lookout points. The winding walkway along the dark cliff is mostly empty now. The shops and restaurants have been closed for a while, and the tourists are all back at their hotels.

I have found no evidence of Helene. The curse drapes itself over my shoulders like a boa constrictor, heavy, slippery, cunning.

Where did you go, Helene? It's not like you to just disappear.

Other than that one morning in Amsterdam when she snuck out to get a pregnancy test.

And how she left her ex-husband, filing for divorce and leaving him the same day.

The night sky seems to close in around me.

What if she left me?

I rack my brain for anything I did wrong lately. I *have* been a little stifling in protecting her and the baby. For instance, I asked the waitress tonight four times if there was anything raw or unpasteurized in our meal. But Helene has tolerated my attentiveness with her usual kindness, understanding that I need to feel like I have some control, some way to keep her safe, if I'm to stay sane. The closest she comes to pushing back on my protectiveness is when she teases me, like when she nicknamed me Mama Hen Montague for all my fussing.

And there really hasn't been anything else. Helene and I are complements to each other. She can't cook, but she enjoys washing dishes, which I loathe. She needs absolute quiet when she's writing; I am taciturn and utterly comfortable in silence. The centuries have worn me down into a fatalist, whereas Helene balances me out by being an unrelenting optimist. We have always been like this, Juliet and I. Yin and yang.

My bones ache again with the knowledge that something's wrong. That tonight didn't turn out the way Helene intended.

I kneel in the dirt at the cliff's edge, squeeze my eyes closed, and begin to pray for her and the baby's safety, and for our reunion. I pray to Hera, goddess of women, family, and childbirth. To Aphrodite, goddess of love. To Hygeia for health, Soteria for safety, and to every other Greek god and goddess I can recall.

These are not my gods. But desperate times have a way of making even the most rational people falter.

And so I pray, focusing especially on the most important prayer: Please don't let this be the curse.

HELENE

THE FLIGHT FROM SANTORINI TO ATHENS PASSED IN A BLINK AS I fretted over what had happened. Now, in Athens for a layover, I continue to stew in my own thoughts. The airport is crowded in that way where people don't make eye contact, in an attempt to carve out mental space for themselves where physical space doesn't exist. I'm grateful because it means no one looks at the sad pregnant woman huddled in a pleather seat by herself, sweating through the pretty sundress she wore to a dinner from which she was forced to go AWOL.

How did I end up here? I found the courage to leave Merrick, and then fate led me to Alaska, to the soulmate I've dreamed of since I was in eighth grade.

And then fate lets Merrick drag me back to where I started? I bury my face in my hands.

The woman next to me vacates her seat, and a man in a grimy tank top drops into it, immediately stretching out his legs and bumping into both me and the child on his left. He reeks of stale cigarette smoke and who knows how long without a shower, which is gross in and of itself but made worse in the middle of summer. I try to bear it, because I don't want to give up my seat. But then he unwraps an oily fish sandwich and I can't stay anymore. I flee before I throw up for the second time in a matter of hours.

I want to borrow someone's cell and call Sebastien. But leave it to me to fall for the only man in the modern world without a cellphone. There's no phone on the boat either, and no one at the harbor office at this hour of night. I have no way to reach him. Sebastien must be out of his mind by now, too, worrying about what happened to me.

Without a place to sit, I pace along the corridor. The flight from Santorini to Athens was a short puddle jumper, but now I have a little time before my red-eye from Athens to Los Angeles leaves.

As I walk past the gates, a departures board flashes with the flights that are leaving soon. With nothing else to do, I read it, as if somehow I could get on a different plane that would take all my problems away.

Lisbon: departing in fifty-five minutes.

Morocco: departing in forty minutes.

Beijing: boarding to begin soon.

Geneva: now boarding.

My hand flies to my mouth. *Geneva.* That's where the Julius A. Weiskopf Group is based. Maybe they could help us. If they had the resources to dispatch a patrol to Sebastien's house all the way in the Alaskan boonies, and if he's trusted them for so long, they might be able to stop Merrick and Aaron.

But would they listen to me? I'm not technically a client, even though they've been helping with my divorce case. They're doing that for Sebastien.

Still, I have to try. I can't just give up and let Merrick destroy Sebastien and ruin this new life I've worked so hard to build. I have time . . . Merrick won't know anything's gone wrong until I don't show up in L.A.

The flight to Geneva departs in thirty minutes. I sprint to the customer service booth and jitter impatiently while the two people in line in front of me are taken care of.

Finally, with fifteen minutes left before departure and the plane's door probably closing any moment now, it's my turn. I practically slam into the counter.

"Hi how are you I need to get onto that flight to Geneva please can I switch my Los Angeles ticket," I say in a run-on sentence rush while pushing my Los Angeles boarding pass to the agent.

The man is a bit taken aback, but then he gathers himself and smiles, like he's used to seeing impulsive Americans all the time. Maybe he is.

"Let me see . . ." He types into his keyboard by hunting and pecking with two index fingers.

My own fingers drum on the countertop, as if they could type faster for him. He pauses and raises his eyebrows at what I'm doing, and I ball my hands into fists. I realize I seem rude, but I don't mean to be.

He continues to hunt and peck at the speed of a lazy chicken.

All of a sudden the stress is too much, and my pregnancy hormones burst through the dam. I start bawling.

He looks up in alarm.

"I'm s-sorry . . . I just . . . I"—*gasp*—"I just n-need to . . . get to . . . Geneva." I am now composed entirely of snot and sobs.

The agent suddenly finds the ability to type with two fingers at speeds I didn't think possible. "Don't cry, miss. I'll help you."

But of course the ticket Aaron gave me—which Merrick paid for—is nonrefundable and nontransferable. Sebastien isn't here to pull strings for me either.

Old Helene would crumble. She would just accept the answer as no and go back to the gate for Los Angeles, suffer silently next to the smelly fish sandwich man, then get on the plane to L.A.

But New Helene isn't going to let Merrick crush her that easily.

Thankfully, I have access to my money again. When the Weiskopf Group attorneys liberated my checking account from Merrick's freeze, I drained out my half and stashed it in a separate account, at a different bank. I also opened up a new credit card that was solely mine.

"I'd like to buy a separate ticket, then," I say, handing over my credit card at the same time an announcement blares, "*Final boarding call for Geneva. Doors are closing.*"

The man springs into action, grabbing the phone to call the Geneva gate while madly hunting and pecking on the keyboard and swiping my credit card. "I have one more passenger on her way. Hold the door," he instructs the gate agent.

A minute later, boarding pass for Geneva in hand, I sprint for Gate 33. I'm sure I look like a deranged duck fleeing the foie gras farm, waddle-running as fast as my pregnant belly will allow me.

"I'm here! I'm here!" I pant.

I barely make it to my middle seat and snap on the seatbelt before the plane starts to back up. A kind elderly woman in the window seat pats my leg. "You made it, dear. Now you can relax."

Relax. Ha. All I can think about is wringing Merrick's neck, and hoping that the Julius A. Weiskopf Group can help me do it.

SEBASTIEN

AFTER FRUITLESS HOURS OF SEARCHING—AND NO LUCK ON THE police's end either—I hike up the winding cliffside path to one of the many hotels in Imerovígli. I could go back to my boat, but I need access to a phone. Ironically, the one hotel I stumble into is a wellness resort and spa. As if I didn't already know I could use some rest and rejuvenation.

The place is completely booked except for the most expensive two-bedroom villa. I don't care. I hand over my card, ask them for coffee, and stagger to the room. There's a private infinity pool overlooking the ocean, calming music playing over the speakers, and room service immediately sends a full spread of Greek snacks along with the coffee. But the only thing I see is the phone on the desk.

I dial Sandrine's cellphone. The firm gives the president's number to only a select handful of clients, and I make sure not to use it unless I absolutely have to.

She picks up on the first ring. "Sandrine Weiskopf."

"It's Sebastien Montague. Apologies for waking you."

"Not at all." Professional as ever, she's already swiped away any hint of grogginess from her voice. "What can I do for you, Sebastien?"

I take a deep breath. Then I explain to her that Helene has gone missing, and neither I nor the police here on Santorini have found any sign of her.

"I'll dispatch a team from Athens immediately," Sandrine says. "They can be on Santorini in a couple of hours. Meanwhile, I'll have my team here start work to see if we can get access to CCTV security camera footage, passenger manifests on ferries and trains, digital trails, etcetera."

I exhale for what seems like the first time since Helene disappeared. I'm still incredibly on edge, but at least I won't be alone in worrying about her now.

"Thank you, Sandrine. Call me at this number as soon as you have any information. I don't plan to leave the room."

"Will do. We'll find her. Get some rest, Sebastien." Sandrine ends the call.

Of course I don't rest. I'm dog-tired, but I pour myself a cup of coffee from the room service tray and wait.

HELENE

I'VE BEEN SITTING—SHIVERING—OUTSIDE THE OFFICES OF THE JULIUS A. Weiskopf Group since I arrived in Geneva several hours ago. The kind lady next to me on the plane had looked up their address for me on her phone, and when I landed at the airport, I jumped into a cab and asked to be brought here. I hadn't been thinking how early in the morning it was.

The taxi driver had looked a bit uncertain about dropping off a pregnant woman when it was still dark out, but I asked if it was a safe neighborhood, and he said yes. But he was worried I'd be cold, so he opened the trunk and gave me a jacket another customer had left behind. Thank god for the driver's foresight, because otherwise I'd have hypothermia in my sundress by now.

As the sun rises higher in the sky, the business district begins bustling to life. The fountain in the plaza turns on, sprinkling the black avant-garde sculpture at its center as if with morning dew. Early birds start to trickle into the buildings to get a crack on their workday.

A woman in a smart gray suit and carrying an expensive-looking briefcase marches to the entrance of the Julius A. Weiskopf Group. I jump up from the stone bench I'd been sitting on and hurry after her.

"Excuse me!" I shout.

She doesn't turn around, just scans her badge and slips through the black glass door. It clicks behind her, and when I get there and pull on the handle, it's locked.

I pound on the door. "Hello? Excuse me?" I can barely see inside through the dark glass, but the woman is still in the reception area, making her way to the elevator. She can definitely hear me, but she's choosing to ignore me.

"I'm a client," I yell through the door, even though it's untrue. But it's the only way to let this woman know I'm not some random weirdo from the street trying to get into their building. Even if I am wearing a lost-and-found coat from the trunk of a taxi.

The elevator doors open and illuminate the woman's silhouette. She's about to step inside. I could wait for someone else to come, but it'll be a while before the workday officially starts, and I need to talk to someone ASAP. It's only a matter of hours before the plane I'm supposed to be on lands in L.A. and Merrick realizes I'm not on it. And I'm cold, so, so cold.

The elevator doors are closing, with the woman in it.

"My name is Helene Janssen, and your client Sebastien Montague is in danger," I shout through the doors. "Please. I need your help. *He* needs your help."

The elevator doors close.

No.

I press my forehead to the black glass and close my eyes.

It's okay, I tell myself. She's not the only person who works here. Someone else will come. Be patient.

Except I can feel the bomb ticking. It will take only a second for Merrick and Aaron to hit "publish" on everything they know about Sebastien. If I'm going to stop them, it needs to be soon.

The glass door pushes against my face gently. My eyes fly open.

The woman! She came back down the elevator!

I step back and let her open the door.

"Helene Janssen, you said?"

I nod furiously.

"My name is Sandrine Weiskopf, and I'm the president of the firm. Sebastien's been searching for you. Come in out of the cold and we'll give him a call."

SEBASTIEN

I am attempting to shower away the grime of despair from last night, but it clings to me like cheap frying grease.

Where are you, my love?

How's our baby?

Are you happier without me?

The last question is a blow to the gut, a reminder that perhaps Helene left me by choice. A remote possibility, but still a possibility. Because at 3 A.M., Sandrine had called to tell me her team had discovered a purchase on Helene's credit card in the Athens airport for a plane ticket. Unfortunately, due to Europe's strict privacy laws, they hadn't yet been able to get information on where.

Or why.

The phone rings again as I'm rinsing the shampoo out of my hair. I scramble out of the shower and lunge for the counter, where I left the phone. It's the Julius A. Weiskopf office number; Sandrine must have gone in early.

"Sandrine! Did you find her? Is she all right? Is she . . . ?" I don't want to finish the question, because there are too many terrible ways it could end. *She is leaving you. She is hurt. She is . . . dead.*

"Sebastien, it's me."

I nearly drop the phone into the sink. "Helene? Why are you calling from Sandrine's—?" *No, that's not important.* I slide to the marble floor. *Please, tell me the curse is nowhere to be found. Let everything be okay.* "Are you all right? Are you safe?"

"Yes, but you're not. Sebastien, last night, I'm sorry—"

"Whatever happened, it doesn't matter. As long as you and the baby are all right."

"No, you don't understand," Helene says. "I came to Geneva because Merrick knows about your past and we have to stop him from—"

"What do you mean, he knows about my past?" Suds drip down my face and arm, threatening to get to the phone. I throw on a robe and grab a towel to sop up the water. I can't afford for the connection to short-circuit.

"He, um . . ."

There's a shuffling of papers, then Sandrine says, "I can leave to give you some privacy."

My chest constricts. *Merrick knows about my past.* And Helene can't say anything more explicit because Sandrine is there in a conference room with her.

I've never told the Weiskopf Group about my immortality because I haven't had to. They are in the business of carrying out their clients' wishes, no questions asked. But I'm sure they've wondered why my account has been open as long as it has, and why they have to provide new identification papers every couple decades.

I rub the heel of my hand into my eyes. "No, Sandrine. Stay in the room. It's time you knew my full story. Helene, go on. We can trust her."

Once Helene starts talking, she can't stop. She's had this overwhelming fear bottled up inside her since last night, and I am apoplectic that people she knew—and once trusted—did this to her. And that I wasn't there when she needed me.

Yet Helene is worried about my secret being revealed.

I'm incandescent with rage that Merrick blackmailed and kidnapped her.

"I'm coming to Geneva right now," I say, seething.

"No! You can't," Helene says. "Aaron's watching you. If he sees you leave Santorini, he'll know we're up to something."

I punch the wall. It leaves a fist-sized indentation that will cost me.

I don't care.

"Sandrine," I say, "I want you to ruin Merrick and Aaron. Scorched earth. Whatever resources you have, use them."

"But wait," Helene says. "The most important thing is getting those files they have on Sebastien."

A door opens and closes. Someone else has just come into the conference room at the Weiskopf Group offices.

"I've asked Calvin Hasan, my chief of cybersecurity, to join us," Sandrine says. She must have texted him while Helene was explaining what happened last night.

"Good morning, everyone," Calvin says while tapping on what I'm guessing is his laptop.

Sandrine gets him up to speed.

My stomach twists as I listen to her lay everything out, and I bury my face in my hands. I'm a fool. If I had told the firm the truth about myself years ago, we might not be in this situation. Their team would have had time to scour the internet for evidence of my past identities and wipe much of it clean. Perhaps not all of it, but the evidence that scum like Merrick and his celebrity-dirt-sniffing bloodhound, Aaron, are able to find.

But I'm a relic of a bygone era and didn't think of that. It used to be fairly simple to obtain a new passport, shed a past identity, and merge into a new one. The last time I changed my name was before the turn of the millennium. Internet connections were still dial-up modems then, and websites were made of blocky text that took an hour to buffer. Technology posed no danger to me.

I didn't consider how much it's changed since then, and how it jeopardizes my safety now—and Helene and our baby. My very existence is a threat to them.

Mea culpa. It is always my fault.

"Okay," Helene says after Sandrine's finished. "So we've got rogue files we need to recover, plus we need to figure out where their sources were so we can nuke those, too. But how are we going to do that? We don't know what the files are called or where they're stored. Merrick and Aaron probably have multiple copies backed up on the cloud in different places. And god only knows where Aaron dug up the information."

"Leave it to me," Calvin says. "First place to start is any digital info you've got on Merrick: personal and work email addresses, phone number, and Social Security number, that kind of stuff."

"Why?" I ask, reminding them that I'm still here on the phone.

"If I can find a way into Merrick's emails," Calvin says, "I'll be able to trace all activity between him and Aaron in the last few months. How much time do I have?"

"Eight hours until Merrick realizes I'm not on the plane I'm supposed to be on," Helene says.

Calvin whistles. "Eight hours. That's . . . not a lot of time. But okay, okay, cool."

I can't tell if his rapid-fire speech is because he's nervous or because he's excited. But I am definitely the former. Not only am

I worried for Helene and the baby, but I'm terrified for myself as well. If I'm revealed, I will be held captive forever. Without being able to die, I'll be a guinea pig for all time.

And even if I *could* escape, there would be literally nowhere to hide. The whole world would hunt me.

Sandrine steps in with her calming tone. "If anyone can get this done, it's Calvin and his team. They're the hackers the NSA, CIA, MI-6, Mossad, and every other top agency in the world wish they could have, but can't afford."

It's not a guarantee, but I hear Helene exhale, placated for now.

I, however, am still furious that we have to be doing this. I'm angry at myself, but mostly, I'm incensed at Merrick and Aaron. "That's all fine and good for damage control, but what are we going to do to punish these two for what they did? Lines have been crossed. Helene was blackmailed and kidnapped. And they're threatening my life, too." I stomp out of my bathroom and into the sitting area, which looks out onto the infinity pool. I would like to hold Merrick's and Aaron's heads under the water. *After* I've beaten them both to a bloody pulp.

"I want those two discredited and publicly shamed," I growl into the phone. "Strip them of their reputations and careers. Take away what matters most to them."

Because that's what they've tried to do to me.

But it's Helene who steps in. "Sebastien," she says softly. "I don't think you really want that."

"I do."

"No, you don't. You're angry and you want to protect me and the baby. But you're not a vindictive person. I know you. You don't want this."

"Merrick tried to take our life away from us."

"I know."

"He deserves to be robbed of his."

"I agree. But just because we can, doesn't mean we have to. We're better than he is, Sebastien. If Calvin can find and wipe clean everything Merrick and Aaron have, then let's walk away. Let's leave them behind and be happy—you, me, and our baby."

Be happy. As if that were ever truly a possibility with the curse.

I sag onto the couch. How I wish I could be in that conference room with them right now, rather than here in Santorini by myself.

But I also see that perhaps it's better that I'm here. The deep-seated part of me that is still Romeo has always been too impulsive.

"Letting Merrick and Aaron walk away . . . Is that what you really want?" I ask, trying to exercise restraint.

"It is," she says.

I'm quiet as I think about it.

"But if it makes you feel better," Helene says, "maybe I can get us a guarantee."

"What do you mean?" I ask.

"I can help compile a dossier on Merrick. He may have thought I was a pliable, subservient wife, but even though I never spoke out against him while we were married, I was a journalist, too, and I had eyes and ears. I have dirt on him that could undermine his credibility and reduce his career to ashes; if Calvin's team can get into Merrick's accounts, I can tell them what to look for."

"And what about Aaron?" I ask.

Sandrine speaks up. "I'm sure we can dig up some compromising information about him." Her scalpel-sharp tone makes me more than glad she works *for* me, not against me.

"What do you think?" Helene asks me. "Merrick and Aaron aren't the only ones who can play this game. The only caveat is, I don't want to use the info unless we need to. But we can let them know what we have."

I furrow my brow, because I want to demolish them. Helene is the better person, though, and she's right. "Okay," I say. "We'll only use it against them if we have to."

With the plan agreed upon, Helene scribbles down the information Calvin needs on Merrick, and Calvin dashes off to get his team working.

Eight hours.

Sandrine speaks up. "Helene, why don't we get you set up at the hotel around the corner so you can rest. You've had a long night."

"I can stay," she says.

But I can hear her fatigue over the phone. "I'll be here if they need me," I reassure her, because I am trapped on Santorini while Aaron is surveilling me. "I'll keep the phone by my side, and I'll call you with any major developments. But you should get some sleep, my love."

"You didn't tell me the last time something happened," Helene says, "when Merrick sent a private investigator to Alaska and took photos of us."

I sigh. "I know, and I was wrong not to tell you. I'm sorry for that. I should have trusted that you could handle it, instead of trying to shield you from it. So this time . . . What if we agree that *Sandrine* will call you if there are any developments?"

I can imagine Helene wrinkling her nose, deciding whether she believes we'll keep her in the loop or not.

Finally, she says, "Okay. But call and wake me as soon as Calvin gets into Merrick's accounts."

"Sandrine?" I ask.

"I will make sure of it," Sandrine says.

HELENE

THE WEISKOPF GROUP BOOKS ME A ROOM AT THE BUSINESS HOTEL just around the corner, which gives me comfort that I can run back over to the office as soon as there's news. They also give me a new cell phone, just in case the hotel line isn't enough connectivity for me. My new phone even has the same number as my old one.

I don't think I'll be able to sleep, but apparently the baby has other ideas for me, and I pass out as soon as my head hits the pillow.

Four hours later, I wake to my phone ringing.

"Calvin is in," Sandrine says.

"Oh thank god," I say. Then I realize I have no idea what "in" means.

Sandrine launches into a brief explanation. In short, Calvin couldn't get into Merrick's Gmail account, because Google has some of the tightest cybersecurity in the world, but Calvin *was* able to hack into Merrick's *Wall Street Journal* account. From there, he got Aaron's email address from Merrick's sent box. Then he hacked into Aaron's email, found a cellphone bill, and gleaned Aaron's phone number from there.

"That sounds good," I say. "But still far from finding the files on Sebastien, and all the sources on the internet where they got the information in the first place." I recall that fat file Aaron flashed at me, stuffed full of papers and copies of old photographs. If the Weiskopf Group can't eviscerate all traces of that, the future for Sebastien, me, and our baby is an Area 51–like government lab, prisoners for the sake of science. No longer people, but specimens.

"Don't worry, Calvin and his team are on it," Sandrine says. "Do you want something to eat? Feel free to order whatever you want from room service, on us. I've sent over a change of clothes for you as well. The bellhop didn't want to wake you, so I had him leave the box outside your door."

I glance at the clock on the nightstand. The plane from Athens to L.A. lands in three hours and forty-six minutes. I definitely won't be able to eat.

"If it's okay with you," I say, "I'm going to shower and change, then head back over to your office. I'd feel better being closer to mission control."

"Of course," Sandrine says. "I'll see you soon."

There are three hours to go when I arrive at the office.

"Thank you for the clothes," I tell Sandrine as she meets me in the glass-walled conference room we were in earlier. She—or her assistant, probably—had sent over a soft cashmere T-shirt, maternity jeans, and a light spring jacket that fits a lot better than the hand-me-down coat from the taxi driver.

"Glad to see we got the right size." She sets her computer on the table but doesn't open it. Instead, she chats with me amiably, as if we're new friends meeting for coffee, rather than two strangers in the middle of a tense technological war. But I know she's trying to keep me distracted, and I appreciate the effort. She asks about my family, my work, what my favorite spot in Europe has been. It's hard to focus, and I keep glancing up whenever someone walks by the glass walls of the conference room, but Sandrine gently steers me back to our conversation each time. Somehow, another hour passes.

With two hours left before the plane lands, Calvin comes into the room. His hair is noticeably more disheveled than it was earlier, there are fresh coffee stains on his now-untucked shirt, and he flicks around a miniature Rubik's Cube in his hands, solving it every thirty seconds before mixing it up again, all while giving us a report on where they stand. I wonder how much caffeine he's had.

"We got their files and deleted them," Calvin says.

"You did?" My mouth drops. But I quickly remember that's only the second step in a whole series of things they need to do. There are who knows how many copies of the files out there in the cloud. And then there are all the original sources where Aaron found the information and old photographs of Sebastien. "What about all the rest?"

Calvin solves and resolves the Rubik's Cube again. "We're working on tracking down copies. One of the girls is scouring all their emails to look for cloud accounts. We've already found and wiped a handful of them."

"Good," Sandrine says. "But how's progress on finding out where those materials originally came from?"

"Got half the team hunting all that down. And the rest are looking for information for our dirty dossiers on Merrick and Aaron, including the stuff Helene told us about."

"All right," Sandrine says. "There's still a lot of ground to cover, and not much time. Get back to it."

Calvin salutes with his Rubik's Cube and jogs back to the elevator to rejoin his team in their basement command center.

Sandrine and I call Sebastien to let him know how it's going. Sandrine's assistant brings us lunch, but I'm not the least bit hungry.

With one hour left to go, a woman in her twenties with a pink pixie cut darts into the conference room. "We got some nasty dirt on those bastards." She waves a sheaf of papers around.

I don't want to know the details of what they found on Merrick. Of course, I know what I told them to look for on the destroy-his-career front. But I'm sure there's a whole lot more out there that's less . . . savory. Involving interns with names like Chrissy, for example.

Before I can ask her not to tell me, though, she starts blabbing like this is just some fun game they're playing. "These guys are treasure troves of turpitude! I have lewd photos of both of them that they *definitely* don't want public, like there's this one where—"

I curl into my chair, already imagining Merrick and his parade of sluts, all laughing behind my back while they fuck him.

"That's enough, Aimee," Sandrine says.

The pink-haired hacker stands there blinking, unsure what she did wrong. The sheaf of papers goes limp in her hands. Then her eyes widen as she realizes who I am, in relation to the men she's been babbling gleefully about. "Oh. I'm sorry."

I try to smile and wave it off. "I already knew Merrick was a disappointment of a human being. This just proves it even more."

"True," Sandrine says, "but unfortunately, a handful of compromising photos still might not be enough to stop these guys. What about the leads Helene gave you? Tell Calvin he needs to dig deeper, find more. You've got fifty-four minutes and counting."

I hate to think that dirty pictures won't stop Merrick and Aaron. But I know she's right. That's an embarrassment they could get over. When Merrick is out for blood, nothing will stop him short of his own life being torpedoed.

I start pacing. I must be driving Sandrine crazy, because at forty minutes to go, she suggests I go for a walk.

"Five times around the block," she says. "Fresh air will be good for you."

I speed walk like no pregnant woman has ever speed walked before, and return to the office in record time.

Twenty-eight minutes to go.

I ask Sandrine to double-check the flight schedule online.

She frowns at her computer screen.

My heart is in my throat. "What is it?"

"The plane is landing early."

"Shit! How much time?"

"Seven minutes."

No . . . we were supposed to have close to thirty.

Sandrine's cellphone rings. "Hello, Sebastien," she says. "Yes, we just saw the updated arrival time. Helene and I are headed over to the cybersecurity department now."

He stays on the line with us as we run to the elevator, take it to the basement, and tear into the windowless room. It's a vast space of metal and concrete, all gray but for the glowing lights of all the screens, various hacking devices, and power strips.

Calvin is hunched over his computer. Most of his team, a dozen hackers including pink-haired Aimee, are hammering at their laptops, too.

"Six minutes," Sandrine says.

"I thought we had half an hour," Calvin says, not tearing his eyes from the screen.

From the phone, Sebastien says, "Atmospheric wind speed today is not on our side."

One of the hackers pulls up the airline's flight status page on his computer and projects it on the wall so we can all see the countdown.

"I'll do what I can do," Calvin says. "Where's my dirty dossier?" he yells at his team.

"Coming!" Aimee shouts back from the other side of the room.

"Report what we've got!"

"We found what Helene told us to look for!" Aimee says. "Instant message transcripts from Merrick to his reporters, encouraging them to 'embellish' their stories or make up sources. He's paid to plant stories, too. And for Aaron, we found evidence of him bribing cops to get access to celebrity mug shots and confidential police reports. Emails, bank wires, everything."

Sandrine nods curtly. I dare to take a breath.

This is why I told Calvin to look for this. It's better than the dirty pictures. Because who's going to believe a story about Sebastien being immortal if it's peddled by two guys who fabricate stuff? Plus, Merrick's and Aaron's careers are *everything* to them. You can't win a Pulitzer if there's evidence that you've instructed your reporters to lie. Hell, you can't even be a journalist anymore.

And Aaron would go to prison if it was revealed that he's been bribing cops.

"Upload that file now!" Calvin yells. His fingers fly so fast over his keyboard I swear they almost blur. My pulse races at the same blistering pace.

Four minutes until the plane lands in L.A.

"Final sweep of Montague files complete," Calvin announces. "All copies in the cloud accounts have been nuked."

Three minutes.

"Replacing the Montague files with our dossiers now," Aimee says. "If—when—Merrick or Aaron go to open the evidence they had on Sebastien, they'll be greeted with a data dump of their own trash instead." She looks over at me with a nod of approval, like we're both members of a secret sisterhood of badasses.

I have to admit the plan is genius. And I came up with it.

The uploading bar seems to take forever.

Sixty seconds left.

Upload complete!

Calvin smirks, thinking of one more thing. His hands type even faster than before.

As the flight status on the wall shifts from "estimated arrival time" to "arrived," Calvin pounds on one more button, then throws his arms up in triumph. "Done! Locked those bastards out of all their accounts and changed all their passwords. That'll keep them busy for a while before they even discover that we've swapped out their files."

Sebastien speaks from the phone. "And you deleted all their sources where they got the original material?"

"Pillaged and torched," Calvin says, propping his feet up on his desk and twirling his Rubik's Cube victoriously. "As far as the internet knows, you never existed, other than as Sebastien Montague. And we'll be here to help you, technology-wise, going forward." He makes it sound like no big deal that his client is immortal, and I am so, so grateful at this moment for the Weiskopf Group.

I sink into an empty office chair. The whole room seems to exhale in relief, even the concrete walls.

"Thank you," I say to Calvin, Aimee, the entire team, and Sandrine. "You literally just saved Sebastien's and our baby's lives."

"You were the general," Sandrine says with a rare smile. "We were only the foot soldiers who carried out your stratagem."

I consider calling Merrick to gloat. But then I think, *No, I'm better than that. And I'm done with him.*

Let him wander around LAX for a while, looking for me. Then he can call Aaron, frantic and angry. Afterward, Merrick will get online, full of self-righteous indignation that I dared defy him, ready to publish Sebastien's dossier. But first he'll have to spend hours with IT and customer service trying to get back into his accounts. And when he finally does, Merrick will open up the files on Sebastien . . .

Only to find his own filthy laundry, ready to be hung out to dry for the world to see if he ever tries anything on me again.

SEBASTIEN

WHEN ALL THE CHEERING DIES DOWN, I FINALLY GET HELENE ON THE phone by herself.

"Congratulations."

"Thank you," she says. "And thanks for agreeing not to demolish Merrick's and Aaron's lives, even though they deserve it."

"You've always had a soft heart. It's one of the reasons I love you," I say. "But are you all right? Truly?" I'm still wracked with guilt that I wasn't there for her, that she had to go through all this alone.

"Truly," Helene says. "The baby's fine, too. She started doing cartwheels just now when she heard your voice."

"Hi, sweetheart," I whisper to our child.

"Ooh! There's a kick. She misses you." With all the Merrick mess behind us, Helene's voice has shifted back to her usual buoyant melody. The soundtrack of my life.

"I miss you both, too. Let me come to you. Stay in Geneva, and I'll be on the first flight I can."

"Actually," she says, "I have a better idea."

"And what is that?"

"Let's go home, Sebastien, where it all began. Will you meet me in Verona?"

HELENE

W<small>HEN MY FLIGHT LANDS IN</small> V<small>ERONA</small>, <small>THERE'S A VOICEMAIL FROM</small> Merrick waiting for me.

"You win, Helene. I'm out. You can have it your way."

There's no snark to his voice, just resignation. In all the years I've known him, I've never heard Merrick so beaten, and it thrills me that I was the one to vanquish him.

The next voicemail is from Sandrine, confirming receipt of his signature on the divorce settlement papers.

I start to laugh, and I can't stop. I am free of Merrick, once and for all, and I feel so light I could fly.

With a bakery box in hand, I walk down Verona's cobblestone streets toward the hotel address Sebastien gave me over the phone. He arrived here before me, and my heart thumps in anticipation of being with him again.

I've seen pictures of Verona before, of course. What girl who plays Juliet in a school play hasn't dreamed of visiting? But the town is even more charming in person than online and in movies. The streets are narrow, and the colorful buildings on either side are so close the neighbors can chat with one another across the way. Flowers fill window boxes, and the winged lion that represents the former Venetian Republic appears atop columns, gazing down from archways, and even stamped into the sides of weathered brick buildings.

Outdoor cafés line every street and alley, and the tables and chairs are full of patrons having an afternoon espresso and pastry. I couldn't resist and stopped into a bakery, too, to buy a box of chocolate hazelnut-filled cornetti. I haven't had one since we left Alaska, and being in Italy now, it seems fitting. I hope Sebastien has coffee in his room.

I turn onto a small side street, and the hotel comes into view. Leave it to Sebastien to book rooms in what looks like a former manor. The three-story building is made of old, gray stone. Four grand arches support the building; the keystone in each archway features a marble bust of a man who must have been a notable past citizen of Verona. Princes or wealthy lords, maybe? The second story of the building is lined with French doors and columned balconies. The top floor boasts more windows, with a family crest etched into the stone above.

I walk right in front of the building to get a better look at the crest—it's a wolf and two swords.

"Oh," I gasp, because I recognize it from the descriptions in Sebastien's journals. I haven't seen it in this lifetime, but somewhere in the memory of my soul, I just know.

"The Montague crest," I say to myself.

This isn't a hotel. This is Sebastien's house.

Across the street at the café behind me, a steel chair scrapes against the cobblestones. I turn, and an elderly gentleman sips his espresso, watching me.

He raises his cup and toasts me. "You found secret," he says in broken English.

"I'm sorry?"

He gestures at Sebastien's house. "Tourists go to so-called

'Romeo's house' on Via Arche Scaligere. But they no know where Montague family move after big tragedy." Again, he points at the manor in front of me.

I take it in with even more interest than before.

"Does anyone live there now?" I ask. I wonder if this man is actually aware of who Sebastien is.

But the man shakes his head. "Airbnb. Very sad. Italy's history . . . poof!" He makes a fist and bursts it open to illustrate his point. Then he picks up his newspaper and begins to read. Apparently, his disapproval of modern capitalist greed is the final tidbit he has to contribute to our conversation.

I smile to myself, though. I know more of the secret of this manor than he does.

One of the sets of French doors on the second story opens. A handsome, blue-eyed man with a mess of dark hair steps out onto the balcony, wrapped in a plush robe. A jolt of electricity vibrates thrillingly through my bones.

Suddenly, though, I remember the date. Today is the tenth of July.

For a second, I don't breathe.

But this doesn't count, does it? Sebastien and I have already met in this lifetime.

And it doesn't feel like a day for a curse to strike. It feels like a day for sunny beginnings and clean breaks from the past.

I believe the curse is broken, I remind myself.

Then I take a deep breath, and everything starts to feel like it's in the right place again. Including me.

Sebastien hasn't seen me yet. I shake off thoughts of today's date, smile, and call out, "O Romeo, Romeo! Wherefore art thou, Romeo?"

At the sound of my voice, Sebastien turns to the street below. His eyes brighten with joy, like glaciers basking in a never-ending summer. "But, soft! What light through yonder window breaks? It is the east, and Juliet is the sun."

Behind me, the elderly gentleman snorts, all prior respect for me evaporating. Living in Verona, he's probably heard *Romeo and Juliet* renditions beneath balconies a thousand times.

Not from the originals, though.

I laugh. God, it feels good to be back, to banter with Sebastien again. This is where I belong.

"You know," he says, leaning over the balcony railing, "we have the order of Shakespeare's lines backward. Romeo is supposed to speak first, *then* Juliet."

"We also got the blocking of the scene backward," I say. "I'm pretty sure *I'm* the one who's supposed to be in the balcony, and you're supposed to be down here."

"Fair point," he says. "Does that mean you're going to scale the building now, to be with me?"

I look down at my six-month-pregnant belly, then up at him again. "Odds don't look good. Besides, then I'd have to sacrifice the cornetti." I hold up the bakery box.

"Why didn't you say so?" Sebastien reaches into the pocket of his robe, retrieves a key, and drops it over the railing. It lands squarely on top of the bakery box. "Use that and come in through the front door properly. But walk slowly. Whatever you do, you must protect the cornetti."

I laugh again. And then I run inside.

SEBASTIEN

As Helene steps inside the manor, I hurtle down the marble staircase. I had thought her beautiful before, but now she's truly luminous in the foyer of the Montague manor, the spark in her eyes and the gaiety radiating from her like a ring of light. I think I was wrong about Romeo and Juliet, because this looks a lot like happily ever after.

I begin to scoop her up, but the bakery box almost falls from Helene's hands.

She lets out a small yelp. "Careful! The cornetti!"

"Forget the cornetti." I take the box and set it on top of the banister.

Helene smirks. "You said to protect it at all costs."

"I changed my mind. Some costs—such as this box physically

separating you and me—are too high." I sweep her up into my arms, and she holds on around my neck.

This close, Helene's skin is warm with a subtle sweetness, probably dusted with sugar from the pastry box. But when I kiss her, it's not cornetti I taste but honeyed wine, the hallmark that is always her and me, no matter where or when. I kiss her more deeply, trying to pull us together until we merge into one.

And then I lead her upstairs, because I want to make love to her, slowly, gently. For hours and hours, until the memory of us being apart is completely replaced by the memory of us together between tangled sheets.

HELENE

SEBASTIEN'S BEDROOM IS MUTED ELEGANCE FROM ANOTHER ERA. The bed is made of heavy, dark wood, contrasted by soft, cream-colored linens. An armoire, chest of drawers, and mirror opposite the bed match it, and there's a sitting area with a pale gray velvet settee. Soft, golden sunlight filters in through sheer curtains that billow in the open balcony doors. Regal bronze wallpaper covers the walls.

He lays me down on the bed and insists on undressing me without assistance. Sebastien peels off my jacket, my jeans, then proceeds to kiss from my ankle, up my calf to the back of my knee, and along my inner thigh.

His fingers inch up to the bottom of my shirt, lifting the edge, sending goosebumps rising over my skin. He kisses the swell of my belly, pausing for a moment with eyes closed, as if paying respects to the life we've created inside.

Sebastien brings himself face-to-face with me, and for a brief moment, his mouth meets mine and our tongues dance together again. But then his lips trail down to my neck. My collarbone. His touch is as gentle as a zephyr, but with a searing heat beneath it. I ache with wanting.

"I love you, Helene," he whispers.

"I love you, too."

My hands find the sash of his robe and untie it. His skin meets mine. We dissolve into each other.

Sebastien doesn't just make love to me. He worships me.

And here is a truth I now know: Every woman deserves to be wooed like Juliet, cherished like a queen, revered like a goddess.

As for me, I'm not just one of those to Sebastien.

As fate would have it, I am all three.

SEBASTIEN

FOR THREE BLISSFUL MONTHS, WE HAVE CORNETTI AND COFFEE EVERY morning in sidewalk cafés. In the afternoons, Helene works on her manuscript, and then we make love and drowse together in bed afterward. Every evening, we stroll the streets of Verona arm in arm. We feel the heat of summer shift into the crisp calm of autumn.

Then, in early October, I'm cooking dinner when a glass shatters in the dining room and Helene gasps. I drop my wooden spoon into the pot of tomato sauce and run into the room, all of the fear of the past roaring in my ears. "What is it? Are you all right?"

But she starts laughing. She keeps looking down at the tiled floor, grinning and giggling, but when I follow her gaze beneath the table, I see nothing amusing, only broken glass and a puddle of water.

"What's so funny?"

Helene, still laughing, meets my eyes. "Not funny. Wonderful. Glorious. *Incredible*. Sebastien . . . my water just broke."

"The baby," I whisper, finally catching up. I am terrified, but I've also waited for this moment for centuries. A smile dares to cross my lips.

She beams back at me. "Yes. Our baby's coming."

HELENE

Everyone in the hospital speaks Italian, and the lyrical music of the language tints the evening with a beatific glow. I feel the contractions, sharp and insistent, but even though they hurt, I welcome them because it's our baby announcing her arrival. She wants to make us a family.

All of my focus is on this single fact. The logistics of the maternity ward fall into a blur in the background—a nurse helps me into a gown, inserts an IV into my hand. The anesthesiologist gives me an epidural. Another nurse checks my dilation, times the pauses between contractions.

I only begin to pay more attention to the happenings in the hospital room when the doctor arrives, her hair back in a grandmotherly bun. Instead of coming to me first, she sees something in the expression on Sebastien's face and goes to him. "Everything is *molto buono,* very good," she says, patting him soothingly on the shoulder. "Do not worry."

"It's true," I say, beckoning Sebastien to my side. I take his hand, which is quivering. "You're going to be a daddy soon."

But I know he's scared, that he thinks death might be hiding in a shadow in this room, waiting to snatch me. Sebastien kneels beside the bed, closes his eyes, and bows his head as if in prayer.

"I love you," he says, nearly inaudible. And then he says it over and over again, in every language we've ever known together.

T'amu.
Ich liebe dich.
Eu te amo.
Jag älskar dig.
Ti amo.

Σε αγαπώ.
我愛你
Je t'aime.
And more.

A tear runs down my cheek for all the loss he's suffered, for all the Juliets he's had to say goodbye to, for all the loves he wasn't ready to let go.

I squeeze Sebastien's hand. "I would love you through a hundred lives, and more."

He chokes down an anguished sob.

"But I'm not gone yet," I say gently. "I plan to be around for a long time. All right?"

"All right," he whispers.

"All right," I say again, as if cementing the deal. And then a contraction ripples through me, the strongest one yet.

SEBASTIEN

I NEVER THOUGHT I COULD BE A FATHER, NEVER THOUGHT IT WOULD be possible. But our little girl greets the bright lights of the hospital with a delighted yelp, arms stretched wide as if ready to embrace the entire universe, already optimistic about her future from her very first breath. A nurse whisks her to the side of the room to be cleaned up, and I automatically follow. The sound of my daughter's first cry is a tropical storm, a warm wave of a new kind of love that envelops me, and I want to chase after her, hold her close, defend her from needles and cold, monsters and curses, confusion and fear and all the bad things in the world.

She has Helene's pert nose and pink rosebud lips, and a cotton candy–like layer of hair the color of butterscotch. She has ten fingers and toes, a perfect weight, a perfect length. She is the most beautiful child ever known.

The nurse passes the baby to me, and I cradle my little girl to my chest.

"Hi, sweetheart," I whisper.

She lets out a long, happy coo and melts into me, as if contentment is being in my arms.

It is, I think. Contentment is this tiny being whom so many Juliets past and I have wished for. And now she's here. Finally.

"Can I see her, too?" Helene asks from behind me, voice teasing, but tired from labor. It's only then that I realize I've forgotten to be afraid of the curse, that holding our baby erased all my fear for a precious moment.

But Helene is fine. More than fine. As I bring our baby to her, Helene is rosy and beaming with love and pride for this tiny life we've made.

"*Congratulazioni,*" the doctor says, patting me on the shoulders in the way of an Italian grandmother, as if to say, *See? I told you all would be well.*

"*La ringrazio tanto,*" I say, although there aren't actually enough words in any language to express how grateful I am to her. Helene and our daughter are still with me. Safe.

The doctors and nurses finish the checkups they need to do. Then they leave our little family so we can have some time together.

I stand by the bed, simply gazing at the two most important girls of my long, hard-fought life. I feel nothing but peace, and it's almost uncomfortable in its unfamiliarity.

"Come here," Helene says, making room on the bed for me.

I climb in. There isn't much space, but it's better this way, Helene's body and mine pressed against each other, and our daughter nestled on our chests, breathing sleepily.

"She's an angel," I say, stroking the baby's downy hair. "A blessing."

"Like us," Helene says.

I look at her quizzically.

"These last ten months have been the happiest of my life," Helene says. "Most people never experience love like this. But for us, we get to have it, again and again."

I shake my head. I don't want to have this conversation right now. I don't want this pristine moment shattered by reality.

But Helene twines her fingers through mine, gently resting our hands together on our daughter's curled body. "I don't think we were ever cursed, Sebastien. We were blessed. Getting to spend an eternity with your soulmate is heaven."

I cast my eyes downward. "But all the terrible endings I caused." I can't help but notice that Helene is wrapped up in a white sheet, reminiscent of her white gown in the Capulet tomb, and I am here again beside her. "It all began with Romeo's knife."

"That was an accident. You never meant to hurt Juliet. Accidents happen."

"And each life after that? Isabella drowning, Cosmina burning, Amélie at the hands of a revolutionary mob . . ."

"Not your fault," Helene says softly, but with conviction. "That's just the way of life, no matter how full it is. Joy always holds hands with sorrow. But the important thing is not to zoom in only on the tragedy of the ending. Because as I read through your journals and pieced together our past for my book, I realized something, Sebastien—the through line of our story isn't perpetual sadness. It's indestructible love."

Is she right? I lie quietly beside her. I've believed in the curse for so long, believed that Mercutio's dying words damned us. My primary impulses for centuries have been to either die or endure the suffering.

But what if Mercutio *didn't* curse us? What if it was me—my guilt—that locked me into a never-ending cycle of grief, so focused on Juliet dying that it was the only thing I saw, no matter how many chances I had to change? And what if I was too scared of losing her for good, of not seeing her again, so I never let her go? Could that explain why she always returned?

I think back on every time I've loved her. The original Juliet was a tragedy, but Helene's right: It was an accident. I was young and hotheaded, and the strict codes of honor of that era sent Count Paris and me into a duel in the middle of the Capulet tomb. Killing Juliet was not destiny. It was a circumstance of chance.

Broken, I fled to Sicily, and almost two decades later, Isabella appeared, like a carbon copy of Juliet. But after her ferry capsized during our honeymoon, my self-pity settled back in, and that time, it decided to stay.

After that, I loved . . . but I loved with fear. Whether it was Clara, Florence, Meg, or Kitri, there was always a part of me stuck in the past, like a fly caught in a long-dead spider's web. I blamed myself for all that ever went wrong. And so the pattern continued, perpetuated by my own misery and remorse.

But what if the curse doesn't exist separate from me? What if I can *choose* to end it?

Our daughter's eyes flutter open. They're pale blue, like mine. But there's also a glimmer of sunlight in them, inherited from Helene. I know newborns aren't able to smile yet, but still . . . she does for me. And she reaches out and touches my face with her impossibly tiny fingers.

For the first time in several centuries, I begin to cry.

Because *this* is what I want.

To walk on the sunny side of the street with my beautiful wife and daughter. To see the blooming roses, not the wilting ones. Instead of pointing out storm clouds, I want to trace their silver—no, *gold*—linings.

I want to go back to Alaska and make things right with Adam. I want to watch my daughter grow up, teach her to drive, set her out into the uncertain world to pave a path of her own. I want to give my entire soul to Helene, to embrace the unpredictable, to map our happinesses and our miseries and everything in between with a lifetime of laughter, tears, and wrinkles.

I want to be unafraid.

And I want to stop blaming myself.

Change is never easy. But I want to try.

"Hope," I say quietly.

Helene tilts her head at me, confused. Perhaps what I said doesn't quite track with the last part of our conversation. But the past is no longer my focus. The only things that matter are this moment and the three hearts beating together in this hospital bed. There may still be tragedy, because no one can predict perfect happiness forever and we're not past the two-year mark yet, but we can choose to move forward anyway.

I kiss our little girl's cherub cheek.

"Her name," I say. "I think we should name her Hope."

A smile blossoms across Helene's face.

She squeezes my hand.

And the broken watch on her wrist wakes and begins to keep time.

AUTHOR'S NOTE

I AM IN LOVE WITH A MAN WHO COULD DIE ANY DAY.

Tom and I got married in 2018, but only ten months later, we discovered he had a terminal disease: idiopathic pulmonary fibrosis. It was a gutting diagnosis, come too soon in our young marriage, but one that brought me face-to-face with the question, how do you love someone when you know your time is short?

My own story became the inspiration for Sebastien and Helene's. Life is never a guarantee, but it is harder—much harder—when fate inks that fact like a tattoo to your soulmate's chest. How do you love when grief might be around the corner? Do you put up walls, run away, decide to feel nothing rather than feel it all? Or can you find a way to stay despite knowing the inevitable?

Six months after the diagnosis, Tom's lungs failed completely. He was rushed to the hospital and put on ECMO, an advanced life-support system that siphoned the blood from his body and oxygenated it before pumping it back into his veins, because his lungs were no longer capable of the job. As the days turned to weeks, he grew sicker and sicker. He was near death when we received a second chance: a double lung transplant.

It was a gift of another life.

And yet, lung transplants are incredibly fragile, because the lungs are exposed to the outside world with every breath. Organ rejection or other infections are a constant threat. Sometimes we'll go months where Tom is healthy and all seems perfectly normal. Then other times, we'll suddenly find ourselves back at the hospital. I am in love with a man who has, in a way, been reincarnated, but he could still die any day.

But like Sebastien and Helene, Tom and I choose love, no matter what the cost. We stay, we feel, we treasure every day, every month, every year.

And I comfort myself knowing that when the end comes, it's not really the end.

Because we will find each other again, some way, somehow.

I promise.

ACKNOWLEDGMENTS

THIS BOOK IS MY ENTIRE SOUL, AND IT'S IMPOSSIBLE TO ADEQUATELY thank those who made it possible, but I'll do my best to try.

To my brilliant editor, Anne Groell. You knew what this story could be and you helped to coax it, ever so gently, from my vulnerable heart. Thank you for your vision for the novel, for your kind and generous guidance, and for having hopes and dreams for Helene and Sebastien as big as mine.

To the entire team at Del Rey and Penguin Random House. The outpouring of love, enthusiasm, creativity, and general genius for this book has been overwhelming. Scott Shannon, Keith Clayton, Tricia Narwani, Alex Larned, Bree Gary, Regina Flath, Jocelyn Kiker, David Moench, Jordan Pace, Adaobi Maduka, Ashleigh Heaton, Tori Henson, Sabrina Shen, Lisa Keller, Megan Tripp, Maya Fenter, Matt Schwartz, Catherine Bucaria, Abby Oladipo, Molly Lo Re, Rob Guzman, Ellen Folan, Brittanie Black, and Elizabeth Fabian—I could not have put together a better team for *The Hundred Loves of Juliet* if I had invented you all from whole cloth. What a privilege it is to work with you.

To my agent, Thao Le. There are not enough ways to thank you for your unflinching belief in me and my work, for your wise counsel, and for your talent in always finding the right homes for my stories.

To Andrea Cavallaro and all my foreign publishers and translators. It brings me so much joy to be able to share my stories both near and far. Thank you for bringing my words across the world. And to Jody Hotchkiss for giving *The Hundred Loves of Juliet* a ticket to Hollywood.

To Dana Elmendorf and Joanna Phoenix for reading my early drafts and for your keen and thoughtful insights, and to Karen Grunberg for your sharp proofreading skills. To Tom Stripling, Juan David Piñeros Jiménez, and Elizabeth Fama for your help with foreign languages. All translation mistakes in this novel are mine.

To Elizabeth Fama, Angela Mann, Betsy Franco, Aimee Lucido, Joanna Phoenix, Karen Grunberg, and Seina Wedlick. Our *salons de thé* are always so enlightening and inspiring (and delicious). I am truly blessed to have you in my life.

To all my readers and the incredible community of booksellers, librarians, and social media book lovers. Some of you have been with me since my very first novel years ago and some of you are joining the journey now. Thank you for allowing me the privilege of weaving stories for you. It is the greatest honor of my life to do so.

To the life-saving, life-changing lung transplant team at Stanford Hospital. Thank you, thank you, thank you for your brilliance, your kindness, your tirelessness, your everything. This book about reincarnation, hope, and love was inspired by the second chance you gave to Tom and me.

Our doctors: Dr. Dhillon, Dr. Mooney, Dr. Chhatwani, Dr. Ahmad, Dr. Anson Lee, Dr. Suzuki, Dr. Raj, Dr. Albert Lin, Dr. McArthur, Dr. Sher, Dr. Maldonado, Dr. Britton, Dr. Zein, Dr. Reza, and Dr. Wheeler.

Our indefatigable nurse coordinator: Ellen Arce; Jenny, Fifi, Leeann, and the rest of the PA and NP team.

Our CVICU nurses: Corinne, Lesha, Samantha (Sam), Judy, Dorothy, Meagan, Romeo, Jason, Raina, Michael, Xenia, Eva, Yelena, and Alily.
Our perfusionists: Ari, Barry, and Allan.
Our MICU nurses: Michael E., DeAndre, and Joseph.
Our D2 and M6 nurses: Brittany, Claire, Mack, Erin, Heather, Rena, Gianna, Lauren, Kathryn, Keely, Laura, Ryan, Mary, Kelly, Annika, Whitney, Harry, Chanti, Melissa, Amy, Brian, and Gladys.
Our respiratory therapists: Kepha, Taylor, John, and Cathy.
Our occupational, physical, and speech therapists: Ben, Carolina, Greta, and Nicole.

Thank you for every extra minute you took to take care of Tom or to offer me and the rest of our family comforting words during our most frightening hours, days, weeks, and months. You are appreciated every moment of our lives.

To Tom's organ donor and their family. It is not possible to thank you enough for the gift of life as you were facing your own tragedy. I am infinitely sorry for your loss, and I am infinitely grateful for your act of selflessness. We treasure Tom's new lungs every day and promise to live in a way worthy of your compassion.

To Mom and Dad. You were my first fans and you always told me I could do anything I set my mind to. Thank you for raising me to believe in myself and to believe that anything was possible.

And finally, to Reese and Tom. I am crying as I write this because you two are my entire universe. Thank you for loving me as fiercely as you do, in spite of (and because of) all my Squeaky idiosyncrasies. I love you, I love you, I love you.

ABOUT THE AUTHOR

EVELYN SKYE IS THE *NEW YORK TIMES* BESTSELLING AUTHOR OF EIGHT novels, including *The Crown's Game*. A graduate of Stanford University and Harvard Law School, Skye lives in the San Francisco Bay Area with her husband and daughter.

evelynskye.com

ABOUT THE TYPE

THIS BOOK WAS SET IN PLANTIN, A CLASSIC ROMAN TYPEFACE NAMED after the famous sixteenth-century printer Christophe Plantin (c. 1520–89). Plantin was designed in 1913 by the Monotype Corporation, based on some sixteenth-century type designs of Robert Granjon (1513–89). Plantin's even strokes and lack of contrast make it a highly legible face. It was, later, the typeface from which Times New Roman was modeled.